Bird

LINDSAY WOODWARD

For Mark, thanks for your support and understanding.

ONE

For the first time in her adult life, Beth had woken up that morning filled to the brim with excitement. The Monday morning routine had been typically average, but this morning was far from average for Beth. It was the start of a new life.

She flicked a little make-up on her naturally pretty face and then stood back to admire the reflection of her heeled five foot eleven self.

Her green eyes sparkled with delight as she examined her new business look. It was light years away from anything she'd ever had to wear to work before and she felt her new life had well and truly begun. The days of waiting on people in the coffee shop were gone: she was now a business woman.

She grabbed her light brown jacket and headed out of her tiny studio flat, down the chilly staircase and towards the daylight that poured through the glass of the main door below. She opened it up to find a glorious day awaiting her. The sky was spotless and she felt the sun instantly warming; a new welcomed presence in this early spring day. She breathed in the thick city air and felt free for the first time in her life.

Her new office was located just under a mile away and she marched on. Her feet were already a little sore but the wonderful presence of heels definitely compensated for the blisters that she was sure to find later that day.

Her surroundings grew busier and busier as Beth walked westwards from the more residential end where she lived to the commercial heart of the borough of Heaningford.

As she passed her fellow commuters, she considered her new life and a smile spread naturally across her face. When she'd dreamt of her move to the city, she'd seen herself more living in the centre of London and working for a major, well-known corporation, but she couldn't deny this massive leap forward in reaching her ultimate goal. She now lived in a zone. An actual London zone! Albeit zone 4.

Heaningford lay to the west of London. It didn't have its own Underground Station, another downside, but it was just a short bus ride to a choice of stations and London was effectively just minutes away then.

For the first time in her life Beth was away from the countryside, from the demands of her family, from the commitments that had been forced upon her and from the low expectations that had held her back for so long. She was making her own choices now and it was thrilling.

Her practice run yesterday to the office had done her proud, and she arrived effortlessly at her new workday home. In the midst of other commercial buildings stood the ten storey office block where her desk awaited. Beth hesitated at the end of the concrete pathway that led to the grand entrance and breathed in the essence of a busy working life.

As she admired her new weekday residence, she noticed how, despite it being a bright sunny day, the large glass windows seemed so gloomy, and the building emanated a blackness. A prickly chill swept across her as she observed how the scarlet letters of the company name,

"Bird Consultants", seemed to stand out like the beating, blood drenched heart of the darkness before her.

Shivering a little, she brushed off the eerie sensation, convincing herself that it was just the fear of her new venture playing with her mind. Then she suddenly became aware that she was nervous, a feeling she hadn't even considered up until this moment. Taking a deep breath, she stepped confidently forward and made her way to the glass doors that stood dominantly ahead of her.

She walked in to find the cold, metallic reception area just as she remembered from her interview. She recalled how her heels clanged against the stone floor, and, like last time, she felt compelled to walk on her toes to the reception desk.

Beth's nerves were eased at the sight of the friendly receptionist, Margaret, a lady in her fifties who wore her blonde hair loosely up in a bun.

'Good morning, dear,' Margaret beamed, clearly remembering Beth from her interview, 'welcome officially to Bird Consultants.'

'Thank you. I have first day nerves like you wouldn't believe!' Beth giggled, her usual confident self shining through.

'Why on earth are you nervous?' Margaret soothed. 'Let me get you on your way.' Margaret picked up the telephone and dialled a number. 'Miss Lance has arrived for you,' she stated in a formal yet soft voice. She nodded to the other person, as if they could see her, and put down the phone. 'Please go to the ninth floor, Miss Clock will meet you there.'

'Thank you, Margaret. Wish me luck!' Chuckling to herself, Beth headed to the right of the reception and pressed the button for the lift. The doors immediately pinged open.

As she slowly passed each floor her doubts began to dominate. This was so far away from what she'd been accustomed to at home. She felt a little sick, afraid they would catch her out, afraid that they'd know she wasn't a real business person, but was in fact a country bumpkin whose only real talent was to make a great omelette. The lift finally chimed at the ninth floor and, as the doors opened, Beth took a deep breath and she let her determined spirit once again take charge. She'd had her flaky moment, but deep inside she knew this was exactly where she belonged. She would not be letting her doubts surface like that again, she'd make sure.

She stepped out into a small white corridor. The only way to go was to the left and she headed for the glass doors that were brandished with the company name. Just before she opened them she spied a kitchen through the door to her left. She suddenly felt very much like a nice, soothing cup of tea.

Through the heavy glass doors, she entered the open plan space where roughly forty people, mainly women, sat on pods of desks. The noise of phones ringing, computers whirring, and chatting and giggling overwhelmed the plainly decorated room.

'Bethany! Lovely to have you here!' Beth was pulled from her thoughts by a lady who was grabbing her hand and shaking it loosely. She remembered this untidy woman, with hair like noodles and an ill-fitting suit, from her interview. This was Trisha Clock, her new manager.

Beth shook her hand back as professionally as she could. This was the Administration Manager, the woman directly above Beth in the company hierarchy, and Beth's first port of call for a promotion. Beth had her sights set high, and she was eager to progress as quickly as possible. This lady before her was her first opportunity at that progression and she knew she needed to not only impress this lady but also learn as much as she could from her, soaking up everything to put her in good stead for the future.

Trisha led Beth into her small office and gestured with her rather large nose for Beth to sit down on one of the chairs adjacent to her desk.

Beth's first hurdle was the pile of files on the chair, and, picking them up, she looked for help as to where to put them. She glanced around the office aghast. It was a tip. There were paperwork and files everywhere. The shelves and cabinets were untidily heaped with folders and books, and her drawers were half left open in a haphazard fashion. It didn't look like organised chaos, it was more like a random explosion of laziness. Beth's heart dipped as she placed the documents on another pile of files and took her seat.

Trisha snorted awkwardly, 'You can take your coat off, I won't bite. You're going to be here all day.'

'Oh right, sorry. How silly of me!' Beth shuffled to take her jacket off and laid it on her lap, not really sure where else to put it in the mess. She then waited eagerly for her next task.

'We've got to go over some paperwork, make you legal and all that, and then I'll show you around. Then we'll get you doing some work. Is that all right?

'Sounds fab! Throw me right into it, that's what I'm here for!' Beth replied, a little too enthusiastically.

The paperwork seemed to take forever to complete, and Beth's hands had started to sweat. Still awkwardly holding her jacket on her lap, she was feeling increasingly uncomfortable in her new surroundings. The last dotted line was signed and Trisha collected everything together and stood up. 'Come on then, Bethany, let's get you meeting your new workmates. We can drop this off in HR on the way round.'

Trisha led them both out of her office and then, much to Beth's surprise, she turned round to lock the door before they continued. Saying nothing, Trisha then carried on towards the main heart of the floor.

'This is where all you Admin Assistants sit, along with a couple of PAs to the directors at the back there and a few of the accounts team,' Trisha said nodding around the office as she made her way to the first pod of four desks they came across. 'And this will be your desk,' she finished, pointing to the only unoccupied seat in the whole room. It was on the pod closest to Trisha's office with the chair facing away from the main entrance to the floor.

Opposite it sat a lively lady, roughly in her forties, with dark blonde hair and bright blue eyes, who suddenly jumped up to introduce herself.

'You must be Bethany!' she sang in a cockney accent as she brought her hand out to shake Beth's.

'Lovely to meet you,' Beth chirped.

'I'm Gayle,' the lady smiled, finishing the strong handshake. 'This is Michelle,' she then said, pointing to the young, slim girl next to her. Michelle stood up from the desk across from Beth's, sporting a huge smile on her small but cheeky face, and waved.

'And this is Diane,' Gayle gestured, pointing to the lady to Beth's left who must have been around Gayle's age, but was far thinner with very straight, long, brown hair.

'Bethany,' Diane greeted in a firm yet not unfriendly voice, 'nice to have you on board.'

'Come on, Bethany,' Trisha ordered, 'you can meet the others later, we've got a lot to see.'

By the time lunchtime arrived, Beth felt exhausted. They had visited nine out of the ten floors in the office, although Trisha had actually introduced her to very few people. Beth had now been instructed to sit at her desk and eat her lunch and then she would be allowed to watch the official company induction video in the afternoon.

She finally sat down and rested her now very painful feet, but not before at last releasing her jacket and putting it on the back of her chair.

'How's it going then, Bethany?' Gayle asked joyfully, rolling her chair around the side of the pod so she was sitting closer to Beth.

'Please call me Beth, all my friends do,' Beth responded, opening up her small Tupperware tub to find her homemade cheese and pickle sandwiches inside.

'Of course, love, will do.'

'We've been everywhere! This place is massive. Well, except for the top floor. What's up there? I asked but got a bit of a stony stare back at me and that was that.'

Gayle waved her hand to brush off Beth's question. 'You don't need to go up there. That's where the directors sit.'

'Why couldn't I go and meet them?'

'It's what's known as the Executive Floor, not for our kind. I've only been up there a handful of times to take paperwork and stuff and I've been here for seven years.'

'Not for our kind?' Beth retorted, not liking the idea that she was so segregated from the senior management in the company.

'You won't see much of the directors. They only come down to make a cuppa or to see Trisha or one of the other managers.'

Getting her bearings, Beth looked around and saw four lockable offices like Trisha's in each corner of the room.

'Do they always lock their office doors?' Beth asked.

'You'll get used to the secrets. Don't worry about it. You'll know enough to do your job and the pay's fantastic. What else matters? We know our place.'

Ignoring Gayle's last comment, again not pleased with the fact that she was seemingly of such little concern to the all-important commanders of the company, Beth instead focussed on the intense pang of curiosity that had now hit her. 'Secrets?! Who has secrets?'

'Don't worry, love, take the job for what it is. You don't want to get involved in all that.' With that, Gayle rolled herself back round to her desk and carried on with her typing.

As promised, that afternoon Beth was placed in a meeting room on the first floor. She was joined by Brenda, a stubby lady from HR. Brenda turned on the TV that was attached to the wall at the end of the room and then she sat down opposite Beth with the remote in her hand.

'All employees of Bird Consultants have to watch this video, Bethany. It will tell you everything you need to know about what we do here and how you can be of help. Okay?'

'Yes, that sounds great! I've been dying to know more.' Beth's eagerness to know more had begun when she first looked at the company's website. It gave away so little information with just a few pages generically talking about the importance of teamwork. Then she'd been asked nothing about her knowledge of the company in her interview, despite all the preparation she'd been warned she'd have to do. This was finally when she was going to learn more!

Brenda pressed play and a man appeared on the screen. He was very attractive and his modelled smile and perfect teeth gave him away as an actor immediately.

'Welcome to Bird Consultants! We're thrilled to have you on board! Here's a quick look at what exciting times lie ahead,' the actor gushed. Then the video spent about ten minutes showing Beth all the different floors of the building in great detail, exactly what she'd spent the whole morning seeing. Finally the man reappeared on screen, standing at the entrance of the building.

'The unique factor about Bird Consultants,' he continued with a glittering smile, 'is that we really do help our clients, we don't just talk about it. We take businesses that have hit a bump in the road and we work with them to find the best solution to help them move on. All of our clients, with no exception, have seen excellent results, and our top ten customers have managed to quadruple their turnover in just one year thanks to the magic of Bird Consultants. Your journey with us starts today, and although you may often feel like there are many unanswered questions, please have faith that every little bit you do contributes to the success of the company and we wouldn't be able to achieve our great accomplishments without people like you. We look forward to the road ahead.'

That was it. The screen went blank and Beth felt an eerie sense of déjà vu as she realised the words he'd uttered were virtually the same as those on the company's vague website.

'Your contribution is invaluable to us,' Brenda began, 'but some of our clients work in sensitive fields, therefore we ask at all times that you respect their privacy and ask no more questions than what your job requires. It's only through us working together in this way that we can really meet the needs of our customers. Does that make sense?' Brenda rattled off this statement as if it was imprinted on her brain.

'What sort of customers do we have? Is it illegal?' Beth's eyes widened with fascination.

Brenda cracked a smile. 'Don't be silly, Bethany. Of course not. Everything is utterly above board and legal, but not everyone wants their dirty laundry banded around town, do they? Therefore we promise all our customers that we will keep their business just that – their business.'

'Hence the locked offices,' Beth mumbled, more to herself, slotting in another piece of the puzzle in her mind.

'Most people just accept it,' Brenda stated quite harshly. 'The salary is competitive, what more do you want?'

'What if I want to progress through the company? There will be a time when I have to know, won't there?'

Brenda paused before she responded, not a flinch to her face. 'Should you ever find yourself moving up the ranks in the company then your level of knowledge would be amended accordingly.'

Beth was at first satisfied with this answer, then it niggled her as it all seemed such flimflam. But before she could ask any more questions she was being hurried out the door. 'Get on your way now, look at the time,' Brenda declared, gesturing for Beth to leave. 'Trisha will be eager to get you earning those precious pounds. I mustn't keep you any longer.'

The afternoon sailed by as Beth finally got stuck into her work. She was a little surprised that she'd not spent any more time with Trisha since her half-hearted tour that morning, and it was in fact Gayle that was now showing her what to do. But, Beth surmised, Trisha must be a very busy lady.

The day ended sharply at five o'clock with none of her team hanging around. She slowly hobbled home, her feet throbbing, but she felt an exhilaration she'd never experienced before. The only thing hampering her excitement was the niggling unanswered questions that echoed through her mind.

TWO

By Wednesday morning, Beth was really getting to grips with her new job. She felt insanely proud of her work, giving every task her absolute attention. She wished that her family could see her as she knew they'd come to understand her reason for leaving if they could see how she was thriving in this working environment.

As well as her job, she'd also gotten to know her colleagues a lot better. She'd found out that Michelle was a bit of a rebel. Apparently covered with surreptitious tattoos and piercings, the twenty-one year old was quite the party animal at weekends, maximising her single life.

Diane, on the other hand, was terribly set in her ways. She was nice enough but Beth wasn't so keen on her dark, pessimistic streak.

Gayle was Beth's favourite by far. She was forty-nine with three grown up children and her 'mumsy' character was well balanced with her fun loving side, being very much a regular down her local pub at weekends. Gayle was as good as Beth's line manager, giving Beth all her tasks, with Trisha having been a non-existent entity in Beth's life ever since Monday morning.

On this day, along with letters to type and reports to

file, Beth had been given a pile of orders to process. The orders, though, were all quite strange and incredibly vague. One order had been for two million pounds, yet it just said "resolve staffing issue." Another was for nearly one million pounds and it was for "new entrant resolution". She wasn't even sure what that meant.

She quickly typed the details of her last order in the bespoke accounts system and neatly placed the paperwork on top of her hefty done pile.

'I've finished all that now,' she announced to Gayle, poking her head over the partition between them.

'Already?' Gayle chimed back, standing up.

'You want to slow down a bit, you'll have us all out of a job,' Diane warned. Beth chuckled, not quite sure how serious Diane was.

'I don't know what to give you next. I thought that lot would take you all day,' Gayle mused, looking through the work on her own desk for inspiration. 'Do you know how to mail merge?'

'Yes, but I've only ever done it messing around on Word. I've never done it for real.'

'Why don't you give it a go?' Gayle suggested, walking round the pod to show Beth what to do. Her movement was cut short, though, when Michelle came rushing into the office blurting out some sort of nonsense about sharing a lift with someone.

'He's here!' she bellowed, running to Gayle's side as the whole office stopped what they were doing and stared at her. The atmosphere changed and for the first time Beth felt tension. Hushed whispers rattled through the room and people starting tidying their desks and moving around paperwork.

'Who's here?' Beth asked.

'Mr Bird,' Michelle answered, a little excited yet a little petrified at the same time.

'As in Bird Consultants, that Mr Bird?' Beth checked.

'As in the CEO of this very company. That Mr Bird,'

Diane confirmed.

'He runs a tight ship doesn't he!' Beth chuckled, surprised by the impact he clearly had.

'You don't understand,' Gayle explained, lowering her tone as if someone could be listening. 'Mr Bird is a very powerful man, but he doesn't like people.'

'What do you mean he doesn't like people? He's a consultant!' Beth argued.

'He's exceptional at his job, so we're told,' Diane added.

'But he's killed a man!' Michelle finished, practically whispering.

'What?' Beth coughed.

'We don't know for sure, but apparently someone made him furious once and he took the man's life in a rage of anger. That's all we know. Basically, if he doesn't like you, you're a goner,' Diane stated.

'What else do I need to know?' Beth asked, stunned.

'He spends most of his time in the New York office with his uncle, who owns the business, but as he's CEO of the UK branch he has to come back every couple of months to sort things out,' Diane revealed. 'He's normally here for a few weeks and then he's gone again. But when he's here he causes a severe stir; everything changes. Our workload massively increases and no one talks. You watch, at lunchtime this place empties. It's like a ghost town, no one can relax. He's sacked so many people.'

'Like who? You can't just sack people just like that!' Beth stated, feeling increasingly angered by this overly intimidating man that she was yet to meet.

'I don't know the details. It's just what we know,' Diane explained. 'No one likes him very much, obviously, but everyone respects him. You'll catch no one speaking ill of him around any of the management team; despite the fact that we're all terrified. And be scared, Beth, it's good to be scared.'

Beth found it hard to believe what she was being told.

Could a person really be that scary? The only thing she'd ever felt afraid of in her whole life was not reaching her dream of living in London and making it big time. She was well on her way to doing that, so what else in life was there to fear?

The general ambience had calmed down somewhat half an hour later but there was still a strange anxiety compared to how it had been before. Beth had managed to master her mail merge and she was now happily stuffing envelopes.

Then suddenly everything instantly tensed and the whole place fell eerily silent.

Beth sensed a presence in the distance behind her. It brought with it the most glorious aura. She felt a warmth embrace the whole room, thickening the air around her. It reminded her of being on holiday, when, stepping off the plane, the glow of the sunny climate brings forth its humid wrap.

She heard strong, steady footsteps approach from behind. As a man walked past, she marvelled at his incredible presence and delighted in the heavenly musk that swirled around in his wake. She watched as the well-built man, not much older than thirty, walked purposefully down to an office at the end of the floor and entered it.

She looked around the room and noticed how she was the only one not staring hard at their desk or computer screen. Despite the new warmth, her colleagues looked chilly and Gayle wrapped her woolly cardigan closely around her. Not even his pleasant glow was strong enough to thaw the cold tension.

Subtly, Beth watched the powerful man interact with his colleague in the office. The man in the office was Gus, Trisha's manager, but that's all Beth knew about him. They talked for a few minutes and then, much to Beth's excitement, the powerful man turned round to leave.

Beth's heart was pounding with anticipation as the

mystery man headed back across the floor towards her. He was now facing her direction and her breathing quickened as she desperately desired to look him in the eye. She glanced up to see him fixated on the door ahead of him. He was beautiful.

A wave of passion crashed through her as she glimpsed his dark brown eyes, his dark brown hair and his flawless pale skin. His square face was perfectly formed, but it couldn't hide a faint air of sadness. His haunted eyes made Beth feel such a tenderness towards him.

As he passed her once more, she physically felt his strong, warm essence blow around her, and an overwhelming sense of euphoria surged through her body. She closed her eyes for a second and let his magnificence take hold. Then the warmth quickly vanished and a cold vacuum ensued. She knew he'd gone.

The energy in the room quickly seemed to calm and chit chat once again flourished.

'In case you didn't know, that was Mr Bird,' Michelle piped up, standing to her feet to see Beth's reaction.

'Wow!' Beth exclaimed, not knowing what else to say.

'I know! It's such a shame, he's so gorgeous,' Michelle sighed.

'He has quite an aura about him,' Beth stated, a little dazed by the extraordinary few minutes that had just past.

'It's the fear that he incites in people, it's tangible. I find it quite freaky myself,' Diane declared.

'It's incredible!' Beth smirked.

'Well I'd do him if he wasn't, like, the most terrifying man on the planet,' Michelle chuckled.

Beth just nodded, still a little bewildered. She hoped he'd be down again soon.

By late morning Beth could feel her team were at a lull so she decided it was her turn to make a round of drinks. The marketing department at Bird Consultants insisted that all items in the office be branded. The day before,

Beth had been supplied with her own pen, pad, coaster, mouse mat, sticky notes and a mug, all sporting the scarlet Bird Consultants logo.

To tell the difference between the mugs, Gayle had suggested that they all add their initials in nail varnish to their individual mugs. Having never painted her nails before, Beth only owned a set of three nail varnishes that had been given to her by her friend as a going away present. In the pack was a suitable scarlet sheen and she'd decided to add her initials on to her mug the night before. And, whilst doing so, in the spirit of her new beginning, for the first time ever, she'd decided to paint all her nails too.

As she collected the mugs from her friends, she admired her red fingertips and felt more feminine than ever. She decided that she liked the new person she was turning into.

Carrying the four mugs on a scarlet tray, Beth made her way to the kitchen.

She entered the unoccupied room and headed straight to the sink at the back. The kitchen was clinically white, with the only colour coming from the metal tables and chairs in the middle.

Beth placed her hand on the tap ready to swill out the mugs, but the sound of the door behind her brought her to an instantaneous stop. A familiar warmth overwhelmed the room and Beth knew exactly who had joined her.

She looked round to find Mr Bird, who seemed oblivious to his company, reaching up to take a mug out of the stark white cupboard. Up close now, she could see how his hair was precisely flicked with gel, just enough so it lay perfectly on his head. His crisp white shirt flexed around his toned arm as he brought the mug down to the kitchen worktop; then, as he laid it on the surface, Beth scanned the rest of his body, noting in particular his long, strong legs.

Despite the air of brilliance that surrounded him and all

the warnings that she'd been given, Beth felt utterly compelled to speak to him. She had to get to know this staggeringly handsome man, the silence was aching her.

He went to reach for the tea bags in the glass jar labelled so and she couldn't stop the words leaping out of her mouth. 'You shouldn't be making tea. You must be far too busy for that.'

She put down the mug that she'd started to wash and reached for the mug that Mr Bird had found. He stood back silently and watched her.

'How do you take it?' she asked.

His velvety chocolate eyes stared hard at her, unflinching.

Trying not to lose her composure at the power of his gaze, she continued. 'Milk and sugar? No, I'm guessing you're far too sweet for sugar. Just milk?'

For a moment he remained stock still, then a ghost of a smile dashed across his lips and he nodded, just once.

'I knew it! You take your tea just like me. I guess the best people do!' she beamed, then she took a tea bag out of the jar and filled the mug up with water from the urn in front of them. She then grabbed a carton of semi-skimmed milk from the fridge and, with a throbbing heart, she had to steady her hand a little as she carefully splashed the milk in.

'How strong do you have it?' she asked. 'You look like a strong one to me, I'm guessing you like a cuppa to match?' She couldn't wipe the grin from her face as she desperately desired to control her yapping, but her mouth was now in charge.

Mr Bird had barely moved all this time, but his stare had visibly softened and she could tell he was now engaging with her. Then his lips parted.

'Strong, white, no sugar. Perfect.' That was all he said but the words dissolved her. They were like satin stroking her skin; his deep, silky voice a delight on her whole body. She paused for a second, holding the tea bag delicately above the mug, trying to regain some equanimity. Then she continued her bounce as she knocked the tea bag into the bin next to them.

'You're all done then!' she smiled. She picked up the mug carefully and handed it out to him. He did nothing for a few moments, he just stood still, staring into her emerald eyes, taking her in. He was mesmerising. She felt inebriated from his essence and it was one of the most wonderful moments of her life.

He reached forward to take the mug; his strong hand reaching out from his six foot body. As he placed his hand around the ceramic, his fingers brushed lightly against hers and she felt a bolt of passion shoot through her, for the first time lust taking over.

'Thank you,' he said genuinely, but also a little cautiously.

'It's my absolute pleasure.'

'What's your name?'

Stunned that he was taking such an interest, she replied, 'Beth. Beth Lance.'

'My name's Simon.' He then turned and walked away. As the door closed behind him so did his immense presence, leaving behind the sensation of a huge gaping hole in the centre of the room.

Beth didn't move. It took a few seconds before she snapped back to reality, the amazing sensations still reeling through her. She turned back to the sink, unable to wipe the broad grin from her face, and she made the tea she'd promised for her friends.

'Where the hell have you been?' Gayle asked when she returned to the pod. 'We were going to send out a search party!'

Beth opened her mouth to tell her friends of the incredible event, then she stopped. Words could never explain what had happened, and she knew they would never understand. She decided to keep it to herself. It would be her exciting secret. It wasn't a lie, it was a small gift to herself; it would only be ruined if she shared it with anyone else.

'Needed the loo too, sorry,' she explained, just a drop of guilt at the deceit niggling her, and then she handed out the drinks.

THREE

Simon Bird sat in his silver Aston Martin Rapide S at the back of the office in his reserved space and sighed heavily. What had just happened? No one ever acknowledged him, not across the general office staff. And no one had spoken to him about anything other than work in such a long time. He couldn't remember the last time he'd had a joyful conversation with anyone other than his uncle.

He'd always thought he'd been so content with the fear that seemed to project around him; it meant he didn't have to bother with people unnecessarily. But now that had changed. And he liked it. Who was this Beth Lance? She was fascinating.

Feelings he'd either forgotten he could have or he'd just never felt before rumbled within him and it was a welcome tickle of excitement; like a new lease of life. He couldn't resist the smile that enraptured his lips, it was relaxing to his face. How he'd missed it.

Sadly, it wasn't long before all that was forgotten, though, as Simon drove to his meeting with a client in Surrey. An all too familiar dread was weighing him down. The job was getting tedious. He used to enjoy the problem solving, always dealing with a mass of issues, no two days ever being the same, but over a decade on, he now dreaded every meeting. Whether it was with a new customer or dealing with an ongoing issue, it didn't matter, he hated it.

As he approached the office complex that belonged to "MB Solutions Ltd" he wished he was back in New York. He much preferred his life there. He never had to deal with customers face to face, he just emailed people, supported his staff with phone calls and then, mostly, relaxed, letting the people he paid very generously deal with the crap. His heart sank every time he was told he needed to go back to England as something had been elevated to his attention. He hated facing the reality of his life; New York was his escape, his hideaway. How he longed to be back there.

He pulled up right outside the front of the main entrance, grabbed his black bag from the passenger seat, and walked up to the revolving glass door.

The gloriously white building was well lit inside, the high ceilings letting the warmth of the sunlight project throughout the reception. As Simon walked in, a uniformed security guard came dashing towards him.

'Good afternoon, Mr Bird, it's a pleasure to welcome you again. Please take a seat and I'll get reception to tell Mr Peterson you're here.'

Simon just nodded before sitting on a sofa in the centre of the lobby. The receptionist quickly dialled to announce his presence, clearly agitated.

'Can we get you anything, sir?' the security guard asked, dashing back towards Simon but not standing too closely.

'No, thank you,' Simon replied. A warmth thawed Simon's soul as he once again remembered his encounter with Beth and he felt momentarily happy.

Mr Peterson suddenly appeared from the lifts towards the back of the reception. 'Simon, thank you for coming in at such short notice.'

'Nonsense,' Simon replied, standing up to shake Mr

Peterson's hand, 'that's what we're here for.'

Mr Peterson led the way to the sixth floor where a rather large meeting room already prepared with sandwiches, biscuits and a coffee pot awaited them.

'Just water for me, thank you,' Simon ordered as a small, young man appeared at the door. He nodded and scuttled off to get Simon his drink.

Mr Peterson took his suit jacket off, bringing full attention to his beer belly which was visibly pushing through the bottom of his shirt. He threw it roughly on the back of a seat and sat down. Simon more carefully and precisely hung his dark grey, tailored suit jacket on the back of a chair opposite and, after pulling a Bird Consultants branded pad and pen out of his bag, he joined Mr Peterson at the table.

The young man came back. He nervously placed the glass of water in front of Simon, nearly spilling it on his lap, before scuttling back out as quickly as he could, closing the door behind him.

'I'll get right to it,' Mr Peterson started. 'Like I said to Damien, things haven't gone quite as we expected.'

'I need to know everything,' Simon said.

'We've used your services many times now and I've never had any reason for concern, but this time things have gone... well completely to shit.' Mr Peterson was clearly agitated as he fidgeted in his seat.

'Things don't normally go wrong, Mr Peterson. I need to know exactly what's happened.'

'It's just not worked! They've gone beyond threatening legal action, we'll be seeing them in court. It's going to cost us millions. And we've already coughed up enough for your services. We want our money back.' As soon as he said it, Mr Peterson closed his mouth regretting the words. He shifted again in his seat.

'Let's take it a step at a time. There's no sound reason for this not to have worked. It was a fairly simple deal.'

'It couldn't have been!' Mr Peterson snapped.

'Mr Peterson, I assure you my contracts are always, without any question, faultless,' Simon asserted. 'The other side to it, as you well know, is never to be called into question either. Clearly something else has gone on here. Something we couldn't have factored in. Is there anything you need to tell me? Anything at all you've kept from me that I should have known about?' Simon's eyes were glowing as he studied Mr Peterson looking for any reason to doubt him.

'No, nothing. I learnt early on that we need to be honest with you.'

'Then it's something that even you don't know about. Don't worry, Mr Peterson, I'm yet to be failed by anything. May I have complete access to all your staff, all your resources?'

Mr Peterson sat up, flustered. 'I don't want anyone knowing what we did. You've always promised me absolute discretion.' He took his handkerchief out of his pocket to wipe his now perspiring brow.

'I assure you, Mr Peterson, Bird Consultants only operates with complete discretion. We're all wanting the same thing here, and we have far more to lose than you should that discretion be compromised. Leave it with me, I'll get to the bottom of this and it will be resolved. It's what I do best and why I make us all a lot of money.'

'Right. You can have anything you need, that's no problem. Probably best to start up in Birmingham. That's where the customer's based and it's our Birmingham operation that was supposed to be handling it.'

'Fine. I'll look at my diary for next week and I'll be in touch. Please be assured Mr Peterson, this will be resolved.'

* * *

Saturday morning soon arrived and it couldn't have been more welcomed by Beth and Simon.

Beth enjoyed a well-deserved lie in before she decided to make her first trip out into her, now local city of London. She sat on the bus heading to the tube station, an excited bounce to her every movement. This was her first ever time to Central London.

The move had cost her dearly, leaving her very little spare cash to spend, and with the fact that she knew no one at all in the whole of the south of England except for her new work colleagues, she'd decided to tackle London each weekend coming up in the cheapest way possible. She'd take a tube line a week and visit all the famous spots, the ones she'd seen on the telly and longed to breathe in for herself.

First up was the Piccadilly Line, it was a no brainer. She couldn't wait to see the lights of Piccadilly Circus. It was surely a magical place. Then she'd head for Leicester Square, Covent Garden, Kings Cross and Arsenal. As she studied her tube map, she saw there was also Green Park, Knightsbridge, Earls Court, and she'd heard of Hammersmith too. Maybe the Piccadilly Line would have to cover two weeks.

She'd chosen to head to Ealing, a zone closer to London and with a station that she knew the Piccadilly Line went from. The red double decker bus dropped her off just down the side of the Underground Station and she headed straight down the steps of the entrance not wanting to waste a second more.

The station was fairly small but was made tinier by the large amounts of fellow travellers bustling about. She waited in a small queue at one of the ticket machines, impatient to get on her journey. When it was finally her turn, she pressed the touch screen as instructed and her Oyster Card appeared in the ticket slot below. Her joy was palpable; she was now the proud owner of an Oyster Card and everything felt far more real. She beamed at the pale blue card in her hand.

Ready for action, she headed to the ticket gates, only to

find there was no sign for the Piccadilly Line, just the Central or District Lines.

'Excuse me,' she said to a passing family. 'Where's the Piccadilly Line?'

'You won't get that from here. Probably best to change at Earl's Court,' the young woman said.

'But my tube map says Ealing is on the Piccadilly Line,' Beth argued, pointing it out to them.

'That's Ealing Common. That's a different tube station.'

'What? Well how do I get there?'

Rolling her eyes, the woman pointed left out of the station. 'It's a good twenty minute walk, but it's easy enough. Just follow the road round and then keep going straight.'

'Thank you so much, that's very kind of you. It's my first time here and I've got a plan. I can't jump ahead to the Central Line too early!' she giggled to the disinterested looks of the family.

Beth headed back out of the station and followed the road she'd been instructed to go down. She marched on confidently, the mistake not throwing her at all.

Beth was incredibly independent. She came from a close-knit family and had been virtually inseparable from her parents and her brother when she was young. But in more recent years Beth had felt a growing distance from her family. She'd started to realise that maybe her true calling in life was somewhere else. As her independence increased, so did her confidence, and with that came ambition. And it was this insatiable ambition that had brought her on her solo voyage to London, and she was loving every second of it.

Fifteen minutes later she found the much quieter station of Ealing Common. She headed straight for the ticket barriers, pressed her Oyster Card hesitantly on the yellow pad and passed through the grey gates as they flung open. She had just a short wait on the outdoor platform and then the Piccadilly Line train finally arrived.

She entered one of the middle carriages and sat down, now very eager to arrive at Piccadilly Circus. Just two other people shared the carriage, it was pleasantly quiet.

The train pulled away and she sat bouncing along with its rhythm in her energised eagerness, thrilled that she was soon to be at her much desired destination.

Five minutes in, though, and the journey seemed to be taking forever. The anticipation was scratching away at her and she was starting to fidget. She was yet to go underground, as the tube network in her part of London was outside, and the sites around her weren't even interesting. It just looked like any old city.

What seemed like a lifetime, but actually just fifteen minutes into her journey, the train arrived at Earl's Court, and Beth was ready to burst with expectation. The carriage was getting quite busy now, and all the seats were taken. But finally, for the first time, they were heading underground.

The names of stations started to become far more appealing and she felt a little starstruck as she passed through Kensington, Knightsbridge and Hyde Park Corner. She knew she should finally be enjoying herself as she was so soon to set foot in the city of her dreams, but her pleasure was still compromised. With each stop the carriage seemed to shrink more and more with the abundance of fellow travellers cramming their way in, and it was becoming quite uncomfortable.

Then suddenly, approaching Green Park, the train ground to a halt in the tunnel and Beth was left trapped in a heaving metal tube with very little else to look at other than people and blackness outside.

The lack of momentum set her mind wandering. She needed to think about something else other than this unpleasantly packed carriage, and soon images of Simon flashed into her head. His strong, handsome body and potent presence left tingles on her skin just thinking about him. She could see how some might say he was scary, but to her he was like a sweet delicacy that had seduced her taste buds and she couldn't wait for another chance to see him.

She then realised, with great disappointment, that it may never happen. If none of her peers had ever even spoken with him then it must have just been a fantastic twist of fate that she was lucky enough to have had that chance at all. He'd be back in New York soon and it would be over.

Her deliberations were disrupted by the crashing waves of even more people entering the carriage at Green Park. She'd barely even noticed that they'd started moving, but now she felt quite claustrophobic.

A stiflingly uncomfortable couple of minutes later and Piccadilly Underground Station finally came into view. She squeezed her way out of the carriage to find herself in a stream of people, all flowing down the platform like water, still yet to escape the tremendous impact of the crowds.

Reaching the escalator, she stood obediently on the right hand side and rose up with her fellow travellers to ground level, where she finally felt the welcome tickle of cool air around her face. She fought her way to a ticket barrier and freed herself.

The tube station was massive and utterly manic, Beth didn't know where to look. There were so many people with so many different things to do; it was a million miles from her country upbringing. Rather than the tension she'd felt on the tube, though, this bustle sent a rush of adrenaline through her. She tried to get to grips with her surroundings, excitedly looking at the many exits to choose from, not sure which one was best.

Just to her right she saw one that was signposted to the Trocadero and Shaftsbury Avenue, and quite a few people seemed to be going in that direction. Feeling it was as good as any, she headed that way, along a subway section and up a draughty stairway.

At the top, she breathed in the spring air. The warmth of the sunlight hit her along with the smell of smoke, congestion and food. It was intoxicating, her senses were overwhelmed.

When she reached the top a smile burst on to her lips. She was right beneath the image she'd thought about so much over the past few years. It was the lights of Piccadilly Circus. But it wasn't as she expected. They weren't the lights she'd seen online or in films, it was now three video screens on top of one another wrapped around the semi-circular building, and it brought the chaos of the circus around her to life.

She was surrounded by huge, decorated buildings, advertising so many things, and there were people absolutely everywhere. In the centre of the circus lay a complex road network that was brimming with endless streams of cars. It was a never-ending cycle of busyness, and it was the most exhilarating environment she'd ever been in.

She made a mental note that she had to come back at night to see it properly come to life. Surely the night time would bring its own version of this magic. As she breathed in the pollution, she felt a massive sense of achievement. The polluted air was far more freeing and satisfying to her than anything she'd experienced in the confinements of the acres of land that she used to live around. Life had now truly begun for Beth.

Roughly forty miles away, in a mansion in the Buckinghamshire countryside, Simon sat casually in his living room reading the Financial Times. The whole house was silent, but Simon was used to being alone, it was just normal life.

He sat on one of his three beautifully soft cream sofas in the artfully yet sparsely decorated space.

He put the paper down next to him and picked up the remote control from the arm of the settee. Switching the telly on, he flicked through the endless channels, but he wasn't really interested in watching anything at all.

The truth was he was bored, fed up and utterly alone. He refused to acknowledge that he was feeling any of these emotions, though, and he pushed all negative thoughts far to the back of his mind. But the emptiness of his life continually niggled at his subconscious, and the nagging was getting harder for him to ignore.

He heard the front door open and his butler poked his head into the room. 'I'm back, sir,' he announced. He was a smart, yet casually dressed man, perhaps just a little older than Simon, with short mousey hair. 'Your suits will be ready for early in the week.'

'Thank you, Jim,' Simon nodded.

'Can I get you anything? How about a nice English cup of tea?'

Simon stopped looking at the TV and momentarily lost himself in a daydream. His encounter with Beth had been the best moment of the week. Scrap that, the best moment of the decade.

'Yes please, Jim, tea would be lovely. Strong, white and no sugar.'

'I know, sir, I'll get on to that right away.'

Finding a smile creeping up on his lips, Simon picked up his laptop from the coffee table before him and opened his email. Nothing had made him smile in such a long time, maybe it wouldn't hurt to see if he could make the smile last a little longer.

FOUR

Just like the week before, Beth actually welcomed Monday morning. She arrived into work eagerly and straight away flicked on her computer, trying to piece together where she'd left things on Friday.

She'd had one email over the weekend, and as it popped up on her screen she froze. All she could see was that it was from Simon Bird and the subject said 'Thank You'. She grabbed control of her senses, rationalising that it was most likely an email to everyone in the company thanking them for their great work or something equally vague, as she was finding commonplace. She double clicked on it to find out what he had to say, and was left frozen again as it was, in fact, a personal message to only her:

Dear Beth

Thank you so much for the cup of tea you made me last week. It was the best cup I've had in a long time and it was very kind of you to offer. Maybe I'll be lucky enough to try a second sometime in the future.

I hope you had a nice weekend and perhaps I'll see you around the office on Monday.

Kind regards
Simon Bird

Thrilled and amazed, Beth didn't know what to do. He'd been so short on words when they'd met, but this was a lovely email. Despite all the excitement of her weekend, he'd never been far from her thoughts, and now the electric desire to speak with him again raced through her body.

Standing up, she urgently caught Gayle's attention.

'Everything okay, love?'

'You know how you said last week that I didn't need to worry about going upstairs?'

'The Executive Floor? Yes, love, don't concern yourself with that.'

'But are we, like, banned from going up there? I mean could I get the sack or something?' Beth asked.

'What are you talking about?'

'Say I got lost and went to that floor by accident? Or something else?'

'It's not banned. But why would you ever need to go up there?'

'Right. But I wouldn't get the sack?'

'What are you going on about?'

Beth didn't answer, instead she found herself turning around. Then she stopped and sat back down, berating herself for her foolish, impulsive decisions. She had to stop being so silly. Then a flash of Simon's velvet eyes came into her mind and her legs took over.

Before she knew it she was in one of the lifts and had pressed to go to the tenth floor. Her breathing was now erratic and the exhilaration of seeing Piccadilly Circus paled into insignificance.

The lift doors opened and she entered into a similar white corridor to her floor, only this one had a small red sofa against the wall.

She turned left and headed to the glass doors where she found another open plan office, but it was far classier than hers. The walls were crisp white, everyone had designer chairs and large desks, and there were hints of scarlet around the place that really brightened it up. It felt executive.

She pulled open the door and the room stopped. Seven men all sitting at their individual desks stared back at her. At the end of the room was a massive segregated office with the words 'Simon Bird, CEO' etched on a plaque on the black door. The walls of his office were floor to ceiling glass and Beth saw Simon sitting at his desk. She suddenly wondered what on earth she was doing; this was crazy.

She smiled and waved unnecessarily at the seven male faces, none of whom she recognised, as they watched her slowly and awkwardly walk towards Simon's office. She stood at the door, feeling fourteen eyes burning into her back, and knocked quietly for his attention.

'What?' Simon snapped from within. Regretting her ridiculous decision, but now at the point of no return, she slowly opened the door and took one step in.

Simon didn't even bring his head up from his computer, still typing purposefully.

'Sorry to bother you,' she murmured in a sweet voice, feeling a little breathless from the warm glow that radiated throughout the room. Simon instantly stopped what he was doing and looked at her. His whole body language softened. 'I got your email.'

In typical form, Simon remained still and waited for her to continue. She was now starting to feel very uncomfortable, wishing she could read that mind of his.

'I was making a cuppa for the girls and thought maybe you wanted one too? Silly I know. Sorry I shouldn't be bothering you like this. You've probably been here for three hours already and you're all caffeined out, but I didn't want to deprive you of a cuppa if you were too busy to get one. Or something stupid like that. Sorry.'

Simon pushed back his 'big cheese' chair and stood up. Beth nervously swallowed as his impeccable black suited body effortlessly walked towards her. 'Please Beth, don't apologise. This is incredibly thoughtful of you. On any other occasion I would jump at the chance for another one of your divine cups of tea, but unfortunately I am due to leave in a few minutes to meet a client in London.'

'Sorry, I shouldn't be here. Of course you're busy.'

'This situation is my loss, and I appreciate your visit more than you can know.'

'Thank you. Well, any time you feel like one of my magical cuppas, you be sure to let me know.'

'Magical?' Simon replied, a wry smile creeping up on his lips.

'I'm here at your disposal.'

'Thank you, Beth.'

'See you later.'

As she headed back to the lifts, a tall, lanky man stopped her, holding out his long, skinny fingers for her to shake.

'And who might you be?' he asked.

'Hi, I'm Beth Lance. I'm an Admin Assistant working for Trisha Clock down on the ninth floor.'

'Such a pleasure to meet you. I'm Damien Rock, Sales Director. We so seldom get visitors up here, especially such pretty ones. You've brightened up our day.' Beth looked round to see that she was no longer of interest to his peers. They all seemed to be busily getting on with their work, except for the man closest to Simon's office, who was rubbing his head in frustration.

'Nice to meet you,' she smiled, turning back to Damien.

'And what, may I ask, brings you up here today?'

'I just needed to see Simon about something. I mean, Mr Bird.'

'Simon... indeed. Such a busy man. I'm sure you've

been a great help to him. What was it you were helping him with?'

'Not much on this occasion, unfortunately, but it's always good to offer.'

'I take it you're new, then? Such an eager attitude! I do admire enthusiasm.'

'This is my second week.'

'And you're already on the Executive Floor! I'm very impressed,' Damien smirked. 'Well I do hope you'll grace us with your presence again soon, Miss Lance, we always welcome beauty up here. It is Miss isn't it?'

'Yes. Thanks so much, it's great to meet you too. It's not so scary up here after all.' Damien sneered at her comment before placing his hand on her back and leading her to the lifts.

'Do let me know, Miss Lance, if you need anything. We're one team here at Bird Consultants. You scratch my back, I'll most definitely scratch yours.'

'Thank you, Damien. That's very good of you.' She stepped into the lift and they remained staring at each other until the doors closed. Finally alone, Beth let out a huge sigh, both of relief and achievement. Although her offer had been declined, it had been worth the trip.

Back in his office, Simon waited until Damien returned to his desk before taking his seat again himself. There was perhaps the slightest hint of jealousy present in his heart as he watched Beth interact with Damien; not that he'd ever admit it. He was growing wildly fascinated by this woman, but he was trying not to admit to that either.

He thought back to the two hours on Saturday afternoon when he'd drafted and redrafted those few words in his email to her. It was the hardest thing he'd ever written, but it was the most genuine thing he'd ever said to anyone.

The confidence that shone through her last week hadn't been quite so fierce on this interaction, and she was clearly out of her comfort zone, but this made her even more attractive to him. He thought about kissing her, how that might feel, and then stopped himself before he could think too much.

He'd stayed far away from any source of potential pain for over ten years, and it had served him well. This was just a flashing fantasy and as much as she mesmerised him now, it would never last. He lived in too different a world for anyone to ever really get close. It was his fortune and his downfall, but that was just what he had to accept. He decided to enjoy the fantasy while it lasted, but be sure to keep it at just that – a fantasy. He would try and stay away from her whenever he could and just let her play in his dreams until she was all forgotten about. He was back to New York in a couple of weeks, and that would be the end of it.

Despite all his great efforts, though, by the time the day ended the thought of Beth was hounding him. It was seven thirty and he was back in his office, now alone in the entire building except for two security guards sitting in reception, and he could think of nothing else. He'd found it hard to concentrate in his meeting that morning, even more difficult in his afternoon one, and by the time he'd got back to the office he could swear he could smell her sweet skin still at the door. She was consuming him. He'd never felt like this before about anyone and it needed to stop.

He grabbed his jacket from the back of his chair, locked his office door, slipped the keys into his trouser pocket and headed for the lifts. He needed some fresh air.

A couple of minutes later he welcomed the cool evening air and he found relief as it wrapped itself around him. He gained clarity of thought as he rationalised his feelings. He so longed for human connection and now it was being given to him, forcefully, by a stunningly beautiful woman. It was breaking down the stone cold barriers he'd built up and it was changing him. It would never and could never last, though, he took comfort in that. All he had to do was survive for the next couple of weeks and he'd back on a plane to his solace on the Upper East Side.

He'd often seen a smart looking bar a few hundred yards down the road from the office and he decided that now was the time to make his debut entrance. He walked on and before long he could see the gold letters of its name "The Rose" shining beneath an LED glow.

He pulled open the heavy oak doors, the taste of whiskey already tempting him. The cosy, well-kept room was virtually empty, with just one other customer and a female bartender who was eagerly examining the bottles of spirits.

She suddenly turned around and placed her eyes on directly on him. Simon was brought to a sudden halt as he realised it was Beth.

FIVE

Beth could have sworn for a moment Simon looked like he was going to leave, and then, to her relief, he moved forward towards her. She couldn't believe he was there, she felt tingled with excitement.

He sat firmly on one of the stools at the bar, the whole time never taking his eyes off her.

'Hello!' she said through a smile that had well and truly gripped her face as she welcomed the warm essence that he always brought with him. 'You're the last person I expected to see.'

'Am I a disappointment?' he replied. Beth was delighted that he was engaging with her, it had been so hard until now to get him to speak.

'Quite the contrary. A familiar face is always welcome when you move to a new place.'

'Moved?' Simon queried, but Beth was already starting her next ramble.

'What can I get for you? But be kind to me, it's my first day. Although the boss said I am a natural. I suppose it's not my first bar job, so that helps, but I'm still trying to get to grips with it all, so don't order anything too difficult. No, please, how rude is that, order whatever you like.'

'Is a whiskey okay?'

Beth turned round to look at the array of whiskeys on offer and bit her lip. Simon watched her, a glint in his eye. 'Any preference?' she asked.

Simon looked across the range then a dry smile curled up on his lips. 'Chivas Regal will do just nicely.'

Beth served him the drink and then paused awkwardly, the adrenaline of his presence now growing in power as she realised he wasn't leaving and they were virtually alone.

He looked at her thoughtfully. All the millions of things she always had no trouble talking about now betrayed her and her mouth was left dry and motionless.

'Enjoying your whiskey?' she asked, desperate to break the silence.

'As good as the tea,' he responded playfully and it made her giggle.

'Do you come here often?' she asked, trying to keep the silence at bay.

'Never before. It's been an unusual day, I needed a drink.'

'I know that feeling.'

'You've been with us a week now haven't you?'

'This is my second week.'

'Are you settling in okay?'

'I love it. The best job ever!'

For the first time, a brilliant smile spread across Simon's face and Beth saw his gleaming white teeth. 'Are you always so infectiously cheery?' he asked.

'I didn't know I was. Maybe I am.' Beth then considered his question. 'The first twenty-five years of my life have been a bit dull; I don't suppose I was very cheery growing up. My mum and dad wanted me to be part of their incredibly boring coffee shop business. I waited tables for three years, but I knew I wanted more, so they let me do the books and stuff which helped me get to grips with admin and then that gave me the step up to fulfil my real dream. I guess that's why I'm so cheery now. I'm living the dream.'

'Living the dream?' Simon queried, not a flinch to his face.

'In London! The city life! I want to be like you. I want to be a big business woman, making a million pounds, never having to answer to anyone and never worrying again about anything. I want to feel alive and live through every moment to the absolute max.'

'Is that how you view my life?'

'I guess so,' Beth mumbled, suddenly worried that she'd crossed a line.

Simon looked back at her silently for a moment, giving no clue as to what he was thinking. Then he just asked, 'And that's the dream, is it?'

'To me it is. My parents think I'm crazy. No one in my family has ever left Stonheath. Generation after generation of Lances have never amounted to anything, but I'm changing all of that. I'm going to make the most of every day from this moment on.'

'I hope all your dreams come true.'

'It's partially thanks to you that I'm already on my way to success. I applied for dozens of jobs in and around London and this was the only interview I got. So thank you Bird Consultants!'

'I'm delighted we could help.'

'Well that's what you do isn't it, you help people.' Beth suddenly stopped, worried again that she'd said too much. She was warned to respect the secrets of the company and now she was lecturing the CEO all about it.

He didn't bat an eyelash, though. 'We help wherever we can,' he simply responded.

'Beth, how you doing?' a man in his late thirties suddenly appeared from a door in the back of the bar.

'Good thanks, Sam. Only got a couple of customers, so it's nice and easy today.' Sam stopped and stared at Simon, a chill clearly teasing his skin.

'I'm just starting on the accounts, but don't hesitate to

call me if you need me.' He disappeared again and Beth turned round to see Simon's whole persona had changed, the relaxed, calm spirit now far more rigid and uncomfortable.

'I better get going. Thank you for the drink.'

'Oh really? Okay, no problem. Well, thank you for your custom, please come back again soon.' Beth waved like an idiot as Simon walked smoothly towards the door. He turned around just before he left and nodded towards her. As soon as he was gone, Beth exhaled hard, as if she'd been holding her breath the whole time he was there. She felt that emptiness once more that always came just after his departure and she wished he'd come back.

Beth was very tired the next day at her desk. The second job was necessary if she wanted any sort of life in her new city, and it wouldn't be forever, but she could see it would be much harder working two jobs here than at home.

'The damn cheek!' Gayle snorted from her desk, bringing Beth straight back to reality.

'I know, I just saw it too,' Diane agreed.

'What is it?' Beth asked, poking her head up over the partition to look at her disgruntled colleague.

'Have you see the newsletter?' Gayle replied.

'What newsletter?'

'Oh Gayle, she's such a bitch,' Michelle chipped in.

'Open up the email from Caroline,' Diane explained. 'She's from marketing, the people who can't stop telling us stuff. I don't know why they feel the need to all the time.'

Beth looked in her inbox and saw an email that had been sent to the whole company with the subject 'The Chirp'. She opened it up to find a PDF attachment with the same title. She clicked on it to reveal a four page newsletter, which explained itself to be the employee newsletter for Bird Consultants.

'What's wrong with this?' she asked.

'Look at page two,' Gayle mumbled.

Scrolling down to said page, Beth saw a picture of Trisha looking smug next to an article about how she'd singlehandedly revolutionised the filing system at the company. It explained that after weeks of research, Trisha had found an ideal electronic filing system that was soon to lead Bird Consultants into the new millennium where for the first time they could achieve a truly paperless environment.

Beth chuckled. 'Paperless? It would take half the world's resources to clear the paper out of Trisha's office!'

Seething, Gayle rolled her chair round to Beth's side of the desk so she could speak to her quietly. 'That's just for starters,' she began. 'Not only is Trisha the most disorganised person on the planet who wouldn't know what an invoice was if it bit her on the nose, she also doesn't have a clue what an electronic filing system is. She's never even used it.'

'Then how can she talk about it?' Beth queried.

'Have you not noticed Trisha's one and only skillset yet?' Diane responded. 'The only thing that lazy cow is good at is taking credit for everyone else's hard work!'

'My daughter started to use this system at her company,' Gayle explained, 'and she said it was fantastic, so I mentioned it to Trisha. I should have known better, but I'm sick of never being able to find anything. Anyway, she asked me to put together a proposal for us to use it, which took me days, on top of all the other work I've got to do, and then the next thing I know they're implementing it and Trisha is taking all the credit.'

'What a bitch!' Beth hissed.

'Tell me about it!' Gayle nodded. She saw that Trisha was staring at them through the window of her office. Gayle glared back nastily, before wheeling her chair back round to her side of the pod, leaving Beth to carry on reading the misinformed article.

It was just then that Beth felt that familiar warmth

sweep the office into silence, and a strong presence graced them. Knowing exactly what this meant, she felt a thrill race through her. She waited for the wave of Simon's scent to tickle her nose so she could melt away in it, but when the scent arrived, it stayed. She could feel his warmth behind her and it was the most potent aphrodisiac.

'Good morning, Beth.' She snapped around in her chair to find his gorgeous eyes bearing down on her. Her back was now facing away from all the shocked eyes of her peers, who were fearfully and astonishingly catching a glimpse of this monumental man speaking to one of their kind.

'Morning Simon. How are you today?' she asked, trying to hide her delight.

'Very well, thank you. I hope you don't mind me bothering you, but we seem to be out of tea bags and I thought you may know where I could get some from. I wouldn't normally ask, but I'm really feeling like a cup of tea this morning.'

'I'm sorry I haven't a clue. Hang on.' Beth turned to Gayle. 'Do you know where the tea bags are kept?'

A little startled, Gayle grabbed a set of keys from her drawer. 'They're in the locked cupboard at the back of the kitchen. Here,' she said passing Beth the keys, a small, barely noticeable tremble to her fingers. She held out a small silver one in particular for Beth to use.

Beth led Simon to the kitchen. She could feel him looking at her sharp black stilettos, then working his way up her thin, shapely legs and finally to her grey pencil skirt, and she enjoyed how attractive he made her feel.

The cupboard easily unlocked and inside was an enormous bag of PG Tips. 'There we go, will that be enough do you think?' she giggled.

'How was the rest of your night?' Simon asked as Beth started to fill up the tea jar.

'Ooh, so boring! We had two more customers after you left and that was it. I shouldn't complain too much as at least I got to learn the ropes on an easy night, but I just can't function padding out time. I'm a go getter. I bet like yourself.'

'You make a lot of assumptions about me, don't you.'

'Sorry, I never know my place,' Beth backed down.

'Don't apologise. You're perhaps the first person ever to make the correct ones. Please continue.'

'I just say what I think. Not that you're, like, really transparent or anything. It's only going on what I know about you. Like that you're rich and powerful and run this business and stuff.'

'And I'm apparently sweet and strong,' Simon smiled, his eye brow raising ever so slightly.

'I knew I was right about the sweet bit!' she chuckled. 'That was pure intuition.' She put the remaining tea bags back in the cupboard and turned to Simon. 'Now, let me make you a cuppa.'

'One of your magical cups?' Simon smirked. Beth giggled as she grabbed a pristine branded mug. Simon watched her, a small smile now permanently etched on his lips, as she made his brew.

'There you go, Mr Bird,' she said, handing out the mug to him. 'One of my finest, I hope. Made with extra loving care.'

'So I saw. Thank you, Beth. I really appreciate it.' He took a second before reaching out to take the mug, this time more purposefully letting his fingers brush against hers, sending shockwaves through her body.

'I may pop in for another whiskey later, if you're around?'

'I sure will be, second day of training. If you manage to pop by, it'll definitely be the highlight of my night.'

'I'll take that as a compliment,' he said, flashing a dazzling smile her way. 'See you later.' He walked away, taking the whirlwind with him, leaving Beth once again feeling utterly spent from speaking with him.

She made her way back to her desk after she'd caught

her breath, but this time it was her presence that caused the silence. This time all eyes stared right at her.

'What the fuck was that?!' Michelle screeched as Beth sat down.

'What?'

'We've never heard his voice before. He never speaks to us. I didn't even know he drank,' Gayle exclaimed.

'I thought he drank blood,' Diane muttered.

'Don't be ridiculous. I made him a cup of tea the other day.'

'You did what!' Michelle screeched again.

Before she knew it, Beth was surrounded by pretty much everyone on the floor, all except the management team who seemed quite oblivious to what had happened in the safe havens of their offices.

'He just wanted tea. I don't get what the big deal is,' she argued, feeling quite defensive.

'He knew your name,' Michelle stated.

'So? I know his.'

'Fuck, I've just remembered, you called him Simon.'

'So?'

'I think you'll find most people here wouldn't have a clue what his first name is,' Gayle explained.

'Don't be ridiculous, it's on his office door.'

'You've been to his office!' Michelle shrieked, now getting more excited by the second.

'What's the big deal?'

'The big deal, Bethany,' Diane started to explain, 'is that before five minutes ago this man had been a silent, scary, unapproachable yeti, who we were all terrified of looking in the eye in case he sacked us, or killed us, or worse. Now suddenly he's a friendly, tea drinking bloke that appears to be best mates with you. I think we have a right to know what's going on.'

'Oh for Christ's sake. I saw him in the kitchen the other day and made him tea. Then he told me he'd like me to make him more tea, so I went to his office to offer. I suppose he just sees me as the tea making girl, that's all. He's not a vampire, he's just a normal man with a, no doubt, extraordinary bank balance and a lot of power behind him. And I'm just his tea person.' Beth's explanation seemed to satisfy the inquisition, although she could tell this event had still shook the office quite substantially.

It was a lie, though. She hated herself again for being deceitful, but she couldn't tell them the truth. How would they ever understand?

She knew he hadn't just come down to find tea bags. She knew he'd wanted to see her, she could see the glint in his eye and she felt thrilled by his playful tones as they chatted. Whether it was a break from his busy life or whether he actually really liked her, she'd probably never know, but she was loving every second of his attention, and she was certainly going to enjoy it for as long as it lasted.

SIX

Beth had loved getting ready for work that night. Driven by the excited anticipation of seeing Simon again, she'd allowed herself to get lost in the buzz of beautifying herself. It had been a long time since she'd adorned herself for a man.

She was starting to feel like it was all a waste of time now, though, as it was after nine o'clock and Simon was still nowhere to be seen.

The bar had been drastically quiet all night with just a few customers staggered throughout the evening, and currently there were just four men playing pool in the back room and that was it.

She tried to remain positive, after all she'd not really lost anything, he was never hers to lose. At least she'd been able to enjoy the moment while it lasted.

The door to the bar slowly opened and before she even saw who it was, she felt his presence. At last!

He smiled straight at her as he made his way to the same stool he'd sat on the night before.

'So glad you came,' she grinned, trying to hide her ecstatic joy. 'I thought you might have gone home.'

'Never ending work demands. That's the problem I

always face when I'm back in the UK.'

'I'm so sorry. I bet you need that drink tonight! Have you eaten? You must be starving.'

'It's all right, Jim brought some food into the office.'

'Oh that's good. Who's Jim?'

'My butler.'

'You have a butler?! I don't even have a cat,' Beth stated with shock, as if the two were somehow related.

'I don't have a cat,' Simon responded, a slight smile edging up on the corner of his mouth.

'Are you a cat person?' Beth asked, trying to disguise her shock by changing the subject. She didn't even know people had butlers in real life, this was quite an immense revelation for her. 'You're not a dog person, are you? I don't get dogs. I mean they're cute and everything, but there's something lovely about the independence of a cat.'

'I'm definitely a lover of the feline.'

'Oh that's so great. I always find it easier to chat with cat people. It's nice that we have that in common. Anyway, listen to me gibbering on, do you want another... what was it... Chivas Regal?'

'Actually I think a pint tonight might be nice. It's been a long time since I've had a proper English Ale. Take your pick, I'll leave the choice to you.'

Grinning wildly, Beth grabbed a pint glass and poured "The Fiddler's Hand" into it. 'It's seemed quite popular with the regulars, so you'll have to let me know.'

'Are you an ale drinker yourself?'

'Oh yes! I drink anything me. My ex was a bit of a beer lover, we always used to go to these beer festivals and things, and I definitely wasn't going to miss out.'

'Your ex?' Simon asked as Beth placed the golden pint in front of him and he slipped a note into her hand.

'My one and only ex,' she explained as she popped open the till. 'We were high school sweethearts. He was nice, good looking and all that, but he was a farmer, destined to a life of fields and vegetables, and when he asked me to marry him I ran for the hills.'

She placed his change next to him and continued thoughtfully. 'It wasn't love; not really. We weren't compatible. He'd never leave Staffordshire. That's where I'm from, a little village in Staffordshire called Stonheath. It's where he's meant to be, he's so happy in the countryside, but I've been itching to leave for years. I knew I wasn't the one for him. Bloody hell, he would have had kittens at the thought of me living down here! I think he's engaged now, so my mother tells me, and I'm really pleased for him. The only thing that I've been focussed on ever since is my career. I've been saving up, applying for jobs, learning as much as I can. It's a career in itself looking for a career, I can tell you!'

'You're very open,' Simon observed.

'Say it like it is, that's my motto. I always believe in absolute honesty. I've nothing to hide, I hate secrets-' she quickly regretted those words, and backtracked, recalling the locked offices of Bird Consultants. 'Unless they're absolutely necessary. Like white lies, or trade secrets. I just meant I hate secrets in, like, normal life. Do you know what I mean?'

Totally unflinching, Simon smiled. 'I hope you take me as you find me, Beth. Secrets do have their place in this world, but they should never cause pain or upset, that should never be their purpose.'

'Yes, I completely agree,' Beth lied, frustrated that he was practically admitting that he was keeping stuff from her. Then she felt very confused.

She hated dishonesty of any kind. Being open and truthful was a deep and fundamental part of her moral code. She'd never before even felt the slightest urge to lie, but her morals were suddenly getting very hazy. She felt mad with him for being secretive, but at the same time she was lying to him by saying that she thought deceit was okay in certain circumstances, when that was absolutely not what she thought. How hypocritical could she be!

Then it occurred to Beth that, in reality, he wasn't being deceitful at all, he was actually being completely honest with her.

She started to feel even more confused. Her black and white view of the world was being contested greatly and she didn't know quite how to deal with it. Instead she decided to try and find out something that he would tell her and move on. She'd tackle her inner honesty debate another time. She could see Simon was going to challenge her.

'Do you have a girlfriend?' she finally asked.

'No,' he answered, quite plainly.

A thought flicked in her head. 'Are you married?'

'I wasn't being cryptic, I'm free and single. Like yourself, my career has left little room for anyone else.'

'What if you met the right person? Someone who fitted in with your career?' she asked, trying to feign nonchalance.

'If that were ever possible, things would be very different.' Simon took the first few sips of his beer.

'Is it good?' Beth asked, feeling the need to change the subject.

'It's very fine. Beer and chocolate are the two things I miss most of the UK.'

'Not big enough things for you to stay, though?' Beth enquired, continuing with her free spirited approach.

'Nothing has ever made me want to stay.' He took a few more sips and an uncomfortable silence started to grow. The air was thickening and it felt quite stifling, Beth needed him to relax again.

'So we're both young, free, single and destined to be millionaires!' she beamed, trying to brighten the mood.

'Is that so?' he smirked, lighting up again.

She studied him for a moment, trying to work out what else she could discover that he might be willing to share. 'Can I ask how old you are?'

'I'm older than you.'

'I'm twenty five.'

'I know that.'

'How? Have you looked me up? Have you Googled me?' she asked, her eyes wild with fascination.

'I haven't Googled you. I have looked through your file at work, though, I hope that doesn't bother you? I suppose that's the old fashioned, man in charge, privileged version of Googling. But I know how old you are because you told me last night.'

'Did I?'

'You talk a lot,' Simon dryly stated before the hint of a smile sweetly curled his mouth. If Beth had noticed, she might have seen how much he obviously adored her great verbal skills, but, ironically, she was too busy with her next lot of chatter.

'I don't mind that you've looked me up. It's quite nice that you've taken an interest. I'm going to Google you tomorrow. I'll be doing it in the twenty-first century, girl with no other power than the internet kind of way. I bet I'll find loads!'

'You may be surprised.'

'So am I going to have to guess your age?'

'Very well. I'll let you know when you're right.'

'What? You're not serious, I have to guess? All right then,' she sighed, rolling her eyes. She studied him hard, taking a little longer than necessary to do so, enjoying the pleasure of scanning him carefully. 'Twenty-nine?'

'No.'

'Well am I warm or cold?'

'I only promised to tell you if you were right.'

'You're infuriating! This could be a long game.'

'I'm not fifty,' Simon helped, looking firmly into Beth's eyes.

'Well obviously! Okay, thirty?' Simon remained silent. 'Thirty-one?' He still didn't flinch. 'Thirty-two.'

'Yes.'

'Woo hoo, I got it right!' she cheered, doing a silly little celebratory dance. Simon burst into laughter. It was the first time she'd heard it. It was a wonderful sound and the whole place seemed to lighten up alongside him.

He took the last gulp of his beer and she gestured to make him another one, just as a middle aged couple entered the bar and walked straight over to Beth for service. They went to stand near Simon, but after smiling at him they felt the need to move aside, like his presence chilled them.

Simon remained silent, looking down at the empty glass he grasped in his hands. When their drinks had been served and the couple finally walked away, Beth placed her hand gently over his and slipped his glass away.

'One more?' she asked, noticing how his mood had changed the ambience once again. He nodded in reply. 'So, tell me something else about you,' she encouraged as she poured the ale.

'What do you want to know?'

So many questions buzzed through Beth's head but she didn't dare ask any of them. She needed to keep it simple. 'What's your favourite colour?' she finally asked after a short pause, opting for an ultra-safe choice.

She placed the pint down in front of him as a slight smirk dashed across his lips. Suddenly realising how lame a question it was, she quickly added more. 'Mine's pink. Not because I'm really girly or anything like that, more because I love things that are feminine. I love skirts and high heels and lipstick and all the wonderful things that only women get to experience and enjoy. And I love the way wearing all those things makes me feel. Pink is such a fabulous colour that us girls get to celebrate in a way that a man never could. But I still drink pints and I'm very good at darts, so I'm far from your average stereotype. Now your turn,' she nudged, taking another note from him for his beer.

'My favourite colour is red.'

'Like Bird Consultants? Was that all your idea?' she queried, putting the change down by his pint again.

'No, the branding was all my uncle's idea. He's the real owner of the company, I just head up the UK.'

'So it's just a coincidence?'

'I guess not. I've never thought about it until now, but maybe I like red because I associate it with the company. The company is all I've really got.'

'What does that mean?'

'I live and breathe work. It's sad, I know, but that's just the way it is.'

'You must have hobbies?'

'No,' Simon replied sincerely.

'Of course you do. For starters, you must be a regular down the gym,' Beth stated, looking at his strong physique.

'No,' he replied.

'Okay, so you have a gym at home. But wherever you work out, it classes as a hobby.'

Simon was hesitant before he responded. 'I've actually never been to the gym a day in my life.'

'So you play football or tennis or something then? What do they do in New York?'

'I don't work out. Not at all. Never have.' Simon was clearly getting agitated by this line of questioning. 'I'm just lucky. Must have a good metabolism.'

It was a rare occasion that Beth was lost for words, but she was finding this new life of hers was leaving her mute more often than she cared for.

Beth's manager, Sam, broke the tension as he popped his head out of the back office. 'You all right out here?' he asked.

'Yes, all's good, thanks,' Beth grinned. Sam looked directly at Simon and, after a moment's awkward silence, he quickly disappeared again.

'I don't have any hobbies, either,' Beth uttered, trying to lighten things up. 'I used to work all day for my parents at the coffee shop and then I did a bar job four nights a week to try and save money for my move. My weekends were spent seeing friends and applying for jobs and that's been my life for years. I guess we have quite a bit in common.'

Their conversation was broken again as three lads entered the pub. Chatting joyfully, they walked straight up to the bar. Like the couple before, they gave Simon a wide berth, then they wasted no time flirting playfully with Beth.

As Beth poured them all a pint of lager each, she could sense Simon's pensive stare, but it didn't bother her. She enjoyed every second that he looked at her. She wondered if he was jealous of the lads' flirtatious jest and she delighted in the idea that she could make him jealous.

'Thanks, sweetheart,' one of the lads said when all their pints had been served. She went to hand him his change but he put his hand up and shook it. 'No, keep that, have one for yourself, beautiful,' the young man winked.

'Thank you so much, that's very kind of you,' Beth grinned.

'I better get going,' Simon suddenly announced.

'Already?' she asked, worried that she'd pushed him away by engaging too much with the lads.

'I have a very busy day tomorrow.'

'Okay. Well, I'm really glad you stopped by,' Beth smiled, accepting their time together was over again.

Simon pulled his phone out of his jacket pocket and dialled a number. 'Ready, Jim. Great. Thanks.'

'I hope we can do this again sometime?' she asked, optimistically.

'Me too, Beth.'

She watched him walk to the doors, looking back just once as he left. The vacuous chill that always greeted her upon his exit once again replaced Simon's warmth, and she knew he'd gone.

Wednesday had been torturous for Beth, she was so tired. The day had been filled with silly mistakes and general clumsiness, and she was now working hard pulling pints again, feeling the stress of a busy bar as the mid-week quiz night had drawn in the crowds.

There weren't many seats left empty and those who just wanted to drink were standing around the bar making it very hard for Beth to see who needed serving. Everyone had been very pleasant, and she'd survived the night with few errors so far, but she couldn't help the niggling disappointment that she was yet to see Simon.

Shortly after nine, when the quiz was in its second phase and Beth was mastering a pint of Guinness, she felt the welcome wind of the man she desired swirl through the place.

She could see his hands placed at the other end of the bar, but there were too many people around for her to see his face. She then had to be fair and serve two more patient punters before she could make her way down to him.

'Sorry! Are you okay? What can I get for you?' Beth asked as she approached him. She could see him visibly uncomfortable by the busyness of the bar and she wanted so much for everyone to suddenly disappear and leave them alone.

'Whiskey please,' he ordered, a sternness to his face she'd not seen in a while.

'What sort are you up for trying tonight?'

'Whatever I had last time is fine, thank you.'

'Okay.' Beth reached for the bottle of Chivas Regal and poured his drink, wishing it could be more like the night before. He handed her a twenty pound note and told her to keep the change, trying to smile.

She was quickly distracted by more eager customers and when she finally managed to catch sight of Simon again she found him warily standing in the far corner. Praying for a break in the crowds, she carried on serving. She looked up again a short time later but he was nowhere to be seen. She knew she could no longer feel him, but his aura hadn't left such a gaping hole in the ambience this time, just a gaping hole in her heart. She felt awful.

She barely slept that night, so worried that she'd somehow let Simon down. She consoled herself that she would make it up to him tomorrow, and first thing she'd make him a cup of tea; she wouldn't even ask.

She got in early the next morning, before anyone could see, and went straight to the kitchen. By half past eight she was in the lift heading to the tenth floor with a strong, hot cup of tea in her hand.

She left the lift, walked through the glass doors and headed towards Simon's office. Only he wasn't there.

She stood in the middle of the Executive Floor, suddenly feeling like such a fool. There were only three directors already at their desks, the noisiest of which was the man that sat closest to Simon's office. He was ranting on the phone demanding an extension for a deadline. Beth looked to the plaque on his desk and saw that his name was Eric Rogers.

'Mr Bird, or Simon as you call him, is on the road now. We don't know when he'll be back in,' Damien chirped up, grabbing Beth's attention.

Beth was so full of disappointment, she could think of nothing to say.

'If there's a cup of tea going, though, I'm more than happy to help you out,' Damien offered through a greasy smile.

'Yes, of course. Please. Just trying to keep the boss happy and all,' she justified.

'I thought Trisha was your boss?' Damien teased.

'Making her one next,' she lied. There was no way she would ever be making Trisha a cup of tea, that lazy cow could make her own. Then it hit her again, that pang of guilt at how she'd felt compelled to lie. But what was she supposed to say? She hated her current boss so would never even dream of making her a cuppa, and the real reason she was up here was because of a growing infatuation with the CEO of the company. They were hardly things to share with a director. She thought, on this occasion, her lie was justified. What did Damien matter anyway? Surely it was okay to mislead a virtual stranger?

She wanted to always have the moral high ground but it was getting increasingly difficult in her new life.

Damien took a sip and screwed up his face. 'Ugh. Well for the record, I take two sugars. Just in case you want to suck up to me too. I'd always make time for such a pretty face.'

'It's not like that. I just... Never mind. I tried. His loss, your gain!' she fumbled. 'Do you want me to go and put sugar in it?'

'No bother, I prefer sweeteners anyway, I have them in my drawer.'

'I better get going,' Beth mumbled.

'Come back soon!' Damien sniggered as he watched her shuffle towards the lift.

She arrived back at her desk feeling quite silly and very down beaten. She stared at her monitor, the Bird Consultants branded desktop looking uninvitingly back at her. Then the little blue 'e' of her Internet Explorer pricked her thoughts.

She opened up the internet and went straight to Google. In the search box she typed in "Simon Bird". The top results showed there was an actor with that name, which was no good, so she looked on through the many pages. She could barely believe it but nothing came up about her massively wealthy and powerful business man. She clicked in images to see if anything came up there, but still nothing.

Trying a different tactic, she typed in "Simon Bird CEO Bird Consultants".

Links to people on LinkedIn and some business directories came up, but still nothing about her Simon Bird. Flicking through the search pages, six pages in, she finally found one mention of him having attended a charity ball three years ago, but it was a list of attendees in part of a local newspaper, hardly breaking news. Other than that, she found nothing.

How could such a wealthy and powerful man not exist on the internet? All she could think of was that he'd made sure he couldn't be found. She'd heard of people doing that, wiping themselves off the online world. He did have a lot of secrets. No, he must have an immense secret. What on earth was he trying to hide?

She heard the chattering voices of Gayle and Diane behind her and she quickly clicked off the internet and went straight to load up her Outlook.

Maybe she'd just ask Simon tonight. She believed so strongly in being honest and upfront, asking him directly was the right thing to do.

That night, though, her plans were to be fruitless. She waited and waited. Her thoughts of trying to quiz Simon to get to the bottom of whatever it was he was hiding had all but left her mind, and now she just felt utterly miserable that she wasn't even going to see him.

The bar was the busiest it had been yet and that caused in itself extra stress for her, on top of all of her other worries. His secrets were a niggle, but they were barely noticeable compared to the longing she now had to feel the thrill of his whirlwind again, and she was left with the slightly heartbreaking fear that somehow she was to blame for his absence.

Let him have his secrets. All she cared about was that she would someday see him again.

SEVEN

The next morning Simon was making the short journey from his city centre hotel in Birmingham to MB Solutions' regional office.

He was fighting his tiredness and so wished he didn't have to face this client's problems today. He'd barely slept all night. It wasn't the fact that he was in a hotel, he'd never felt anywhere to be a particular home for him, so being away never bothered him at all. No, his insomnia had been caused by his constant thoughts of Beth.

He was supposed to have spent yesterday pouring through paperwork in his penthouse suite, but instead he'd spent hours worrying about what this girl had done to him.

He still couldn't find out why the MB Solutions contract had failed and he was far from prepared for today's employee interrogation, it was so unlike him.

He'd managed so successfully for years to block things out. He didn't want any complications in his life, he was quite content with keeping everything at bay and living a simple, quiet life. Nothing hurt that way, and he couldn't deal with any more upset. This girl, though, she'd somehow gotten under his skin and it was driving him mad. He wanted to brush her aside but she kept popping up and bewitching him.

He reached the little industrial park just outside the city and parked his Aston Martin. Then, with his black bag in hand, he headed straight to the sky blue door.

Mr Peterson was already eagerly awaiting him and Simon was swiftly led through a manic call centre to a small meeting room, set up ready for the morning with coffee and pastries.

'You'll be in here, if that's okay?' Mr Peterson instructed.

'That's fine.' Simon took off his black suit jacket and deliberately placed it neatly on the back of the only chair that faced out into the main office. He then reached into his bag and laid out his paperwork. 'I've made a list of all those I'll be wanting to see and in which order,' he said. 'This is not to be changed in any way. I've carefully selected these people based on the information you sent to me. Do you understand?'

Mr Peterson scanned through the five sheets of paper. 'There might be a problem with-' he started.

'No, Mr Peterson. I'd like to remind you that several million pounds and the reputations of both our organisations are at risk here. This must be done efficiently, effectively and discreetly. Please do exactly as I say and we might just come out of this as winners. Can I rely on your full support?'

Mr Peterson reached out for his handkerchief and patted the back of his neck. 'Yes, Simon. Whatever you need. Just make this go away.'

'You have my word, I will not rest until this is a problem of the past.'

Three days later, forty seven people interviewed (with some of them even having to come in at the weekend) and nineteen folders of paperwork examined, and Simon was still at a loss. His normal calm exterior had long since started to crack and he was getting excessively tetchy at the thought of yet another dead end.

It was now the middle of Monday afternoon and Simon had just twelve employees left to speak with. There was still lots of time for him to find the culprit, he just needed the drive.

If only he could stop thinking about Beth. She'd plagued his thoughts now for days and he was growing intensely aware that he was falling deeply into a place that he'd avoided for so long. The fact that he'd missed her so much had been a sobering issue. He'd assumed that as soon as she was out of sight, she'd be out of mind. But her absence had, in fact, just driven him wild with desire. All he could do was think about her and dream about her, and his dreams were getting more exciting every night. He was sure he could smell her scent on him and he longed to press his lips against her neck to take in her riveting sense for real.

His deep thoughts were cut short as his next interviewee entered his prison. He was a young looking man named Liam. He had proven to be a real high flyer in the sales department, and although he wasn't directly related to the issue at hand, hence his late listing, he was still a customer facing member of staff and it was still worth the interrogation.

The young man was clearly tetchy as he sat opposite Simon, unable to look at him directly. Although Simon was used to awkwardness in his presence, this was something else. This man was noted as a cocky young lad with the gift of the gab, yet he now seemed very unsure of himself as he rubbed his fingers together nervously. This had the stench of guilt, and Simon's ears, for the first time in days, pricked to attention.

'Do you know why you're here?' Simon asked, expecting the same 'no' that the previous employees had given him; but Liam remained silent, and Simon's suspicion grew.

'Who have you been speaking to?' Simon quickly asked.

'No one.'

'I'm going to ask you again,' Simon stated, so much power in his voice that the table trembled between them.

'I don't know, sir,' Liam mumbled.

'Don't know what?'

'I don't know anything.'

'Anything about what?'

'I don't know.'

'If you don't know why I'm here then how can you be so sure you don't know anything?'

'What?'

'Why am I here?'

Liam was now stumbling for words. He was clearly confused and was trying not to slip up.

'Tell me what you've been told!' Simon blustered, so harshly Liam jumped a little.

'I was told it was something to do with Broadway Stores. That's all.'

'What to do with Broadway Stores?'

'That's all I know, sir, I promise,' Liam protested, for the first time daring to look Simon in the eye. This was also the first thing that Simon believed.

Simon sat back in his chair, carefully selecting his next line of questioning. The lad was clearly guilty of more than just knowing what the questioning was related to, he most definitely had something to hide, Simon was sure of it. There was no evidence that he'd had any working dealings with Broadway Stores, therefore it had to be outside of work hours. A relationship tree had been triple checked before the contract was put together, so this was something that was either new or had been very well hidden.

'Who do you know at Broadway Stores?' Simon asked.

'No one. I don't work on their contract.'

'Who do you know at Broadway Stores?' Simon repeated in a slightly firmer tone.

'I just told you,' Liam affirmed a little shakily.

'Who do you know at Broadway Stores?' Simon repeated again, a deeper strength growing in his voice this time.

Liam hesitated now.

'Am I going to have to keep asking you? I've got an endless amount of time, and you're not going anywhere until we find out the truth,' Simon stated.

Liam looked across at Simon, for the first time offensively. 'It's got nothing to do with you anyway!' he snapped.

'What hasn't?'

'It was in my own time and we never chatted about work once. I didn't even know she worked there until the next day.'

'She?' Simon queried, seeing the first glimpse of hope in days.

Not an hour later, a relieved and impatient Simon found himself knocking on Mr Peterson's office door. With great satisfaction, he handed a file over to Mr Peterson who opened it carefully and read the report inside. 'How on earth did you find out this? I could kill him.'

'His intention was totally harmless. The loophole is so fine, it's a wonder it even made a difference,' Simon replied.

'Are you sure this is it? It seems so flimsy.'

'This is it. Everything else is perfectly locked tight.'

'Is he going to do what he needs to?'

'I have ways of persuading people. You just need to ensure a full cover up, and keep the pressure on him.'

'This is unbelievable. I can't get my head round the fact that something so stupid could cause so many issues,' Mr Peterson remarked, shaking his head.

'That's the field I work in. Although this was rather unusual to say the least. Will there be anything else?'

'No, thank you Simon. You've been fantastic. I might sleep tonight.'

'Let's speak soon. I'll see myself out.' Simon then turned around and, wasting no time, he made a beeline straight to his car, knowing exactly where his first port of call was going to be when he got home.

The M42 was a nightmare. Between a mixture of roadworks and a small crash, he knew it was going to be a very slow journey. He was an hour in and he still hadn't made it to the M40, which was where the bulk of his journey was to take place. He looked at the time and worked out it was about midday in New York. He dialled his phone through his car Bluetooth and waited for the answer.

'Simon, mate, tell me good news,' a rough cockney voice on the other end of the phone answered. It was Simon's uncle, the global Chairman and owner of Bird Consultants, and Simon's only remaining family.

'All sorted, Paul. We've got a little time before we know for sure, but I'm not anticipating any further issues,' Simon replied.

'Great. What was it in the end? I'm hoping it wasn't our fault?'

'I'm happy to say no, we live to fight another day. It was some young idiot who couldn't keep his pants on at a totally unrelated event. The chances were minute and the loophole was even smaller. But that's the way it goes.'

'How on earth could that break the contract?'

'I'll tell you all about it tomorrow. For now I'm shattered and fed up with it all. I just want to get back to London.'

'Why don't you just come straight back here? You're not needed in the UK anymore.'

Much to his surprise, Simon felt the unusual sensation of a knot in his stomach at the thought of leaving the UK. For the first time he actually didn't want to go. The dread of the UK and the problems it brought with it just seemed to fizzle away from his head and all he could think about was seeing Beth. New York could wait, his house could wait, everything could wait. Until he saw her he was making no decisions.

'Actually, Paul,' Simon said after his considered pause, 'I still have a few things to do.'

'What? No, come back. Let them lot deal with the rest. You've done your bit.'

'No, it's fine. I'd feel better tying up the loose ends myself.'

'What you talking about, mate?'

'I'll be back soon,' Simon assured his uncle.

'What aren't you telling me?'

'Nothing. I'm just tired. Very tired. And there are a few things that need my attention. I am CEO over here, I do have a responsibility.' Simon could barely hide the desperation in his voice.

'Right,' Paul responded, hesitantly. 'Keep in touch. If I find out you're keeping anything from me, I won't be happy.'

'Believe me, Paul, you have absolutely nothing to worry about. Go and get some lunch.'

Simon hung up the phone and closed all other thoughts from his mind except for one beautiful girl. That was all that mattered now. She had become more than just an infatuation, she was opening up the world around him that he'd kept so tightly shut for far too long. Just the thought of her made him want to be a better man. He wanted to take a risk again and feel life again. Things had started to improve more recently for him, but Beth made him want to take the leap once and for all.

After a torturous journey, he finally reached Heaningford at eight o'clock. Despite a rawness to his eyes from his fatigue, nothing was going to hinder his plan. He parked in the small car park at the back of "The Rose", relieved to see it was virtually empty, and quickly got out of his car.

His heart was pounding as he reached the entrance, an unfamiliar sense of excitement and exhilaration radiated through his whole body. He'd never felt like this before in his life, ever. This wonderful, amazing girl had swept into his world and had saved him. He didn't know what was going to happen tomorrow, nor any time after that, but all that mattered was that she had given him hope.

He pushed open the door and saw Beth turn quickly round, as if she'd sensed him straight away. He saw her hair blow delicately around her shoulders in reaction to his exceptionally strong entrance and he looked lovingly at her glowing face. She was far more beautiful than he'd remembered, she was exquisite.

He felt the urge to kiss her, to take her into his arms, to make passionate love to her just then and there and kiss every inch of her incredible body, and it drove his senses wild. He took a deep breath and then a second one to help him regain his composure, and he walked towards her.

EIGHT

Beth remained motionless. Her breath was taken away, both by the passionate wind that seemed to blow through the bar and also by the relief that he was here; he'd come back.

'Hi,' she whispered as he approached the bar and took his usual seat. 'Welcome back,' she added, desperately trying to mask the exhilaration she felt by his long-awaited presence. 'I was worried I wouldn't see you again.'

'What are you talking about?' Simon queried. 'There's nowhere else I'd rather be.'

'Where have you been?' she asked, feeling a lustful rush of excitement at his words.

'I've been to Birmingham, visiting a client. I've just got back from there.'

'Must have been a tiring few days. You look exhausted. You look like you need a drink.'

'I definitely need a drink, but you're right as ever, it has been a very tiring few days, so I'll just stick with a coke for now, thank you.'

As Beth poured him his cola she noticed a glint in his eye she'd not seen before. He was troubled by something. She placed the drink in front of him and waited quietly, sensing that he was about to tell her something. Her heart started to pound and she hoped it wouldn't be bad news. He was surely due to leave for New York soon, maybe this would be their last encounter. She felt so sad and worried all of a sudden as she eagerly watched him prepare himself to speak.

'Beth,' he finally said much to her relief.

'Yes?' she replied, her hands now shaking. It was more than just the anticipation of what he was going to say, of what she'd physically seen him building up to, she could actually feel the tension emanating from him and it shook her.

'Would you like to go to a party with me on Friday night?'

This had been the last thing Beth had expected and it took a while for his words to truly sink in. She looked back at him trying to work out if he was serious but she could see it was now him who was waiting eagerly for her to speak.

As reality set in, Beth's face visibly lit up, and any efforts she should have made to play down her excitement were non-existent. 'I'd love to!' she replied. 'What sort of party is it?'

'It's a customer's party.' Beth's face dropped, suddenly fearful that he was merely asking her to a work event. 'It's not quite that boring,' he quickly added, misreading her reaction. 'Have you heard of Layfields?'

Beth was a little hesitant. 'As in that mega online retailer?'

'Yes, the very same. This week is Frederick Layfields' birthday.' Beth's mouth dropped open a little as she anticipated what was to come next. 'Every year he has a major party and as he's one of our clients, I get an invite. I wondered if you'd like to join me?'

'You want me to go with you to the birthday party of one of the richest men in the whole wide world?' Beth clarified, elation building through her body.

'Only if you want to go.'

Her joy was suddenly halted again as a thought hit her. 'I have to work on Friday!' Then a hopeful smile crept back on her face as she saw some salvation. 'But only until nine! Oh my God, how lucky is that! Sam told me tonight that Katy, who usually covers the afternoon shift, has to leave early on Friday cause of some thing or other, I can't remember, but Friday is mega busy on the after work shift, so I'm coming here straight from work, well my other work, you know where I work with you, and I only have to work till nine. So I can leave at nine. Is that too late?' Beth was full of confused excitement, not sure whether this turn of events had saved the day or ruined the night.

'The party doesn't start until eight, so that's perfect,' Simon confirmed.

'Oh wow, how exciting! Where is it?'

'I'll send you all the details. I'll sort everything out for you. You just need to find something to wear.'

Worry now reigned Beth's eyes, she was all over the place. 'Oh God! I have nothing!'

'You must have a party dress?'

'How fancy a do is it?'

'It's black tie.'

'What does that mean? I've never been to a black tie event before. What do people wear? The only really dressy clothes I own are my work ones and a few going out tops. What should I wear?' Her distress was getting more visible as she started to flap her arms around with concern.

'All the ladies normally wear cocktail dresses,' Simon explained, trying to be helpful.

Beth's expression now quickly turned to panic. She didn't even really know what a cocktail dress was. It sounded expensive. She could only just about afford her rent at the minute, how was she supposed to afford a new dress?

'Let me buy you a new dress,' Simon offered, trying to alleviate some of her anguish.

'No!' Beth argued. 'Absolutely not. I make my own way in this world, thank you very much.'

Simon was clearly impressed by her response. 'Then let me loan you the money.'

'No! No Simon, it's very kind of you, but I'll get my own dress with my own money, it's no problem at all. I just need to do some budget juggling. And anyway, what's the point of a credit card if you're not going to use it!' Beth chuckled, now trying to hide her whirlwind of emotions with faux nonchalance.

'I respect your independence, Beth. It wouldn't be charity, though, I'm allowed to buy you a gift, surely, you'll be my date.' Beth felt joy race through her body at the confirmation that it was a date, but it didn't waver her standpoint. 'I'll leave the offer out there if you need it,' he resolved.

'That's very kind of you, Simon, I appreciate it.'

'Can I take your number?' Simon asked. She looked down as he pushed a white business card topped with the scarlet letters of "Bird Consultants" her way.

'You want my number?' she asked, delighted.

'It might make meeting you on Friday far easier. I'll have to meet you there, unfortunately, they have their annual conference in the day which I must attend. I hope that's okay?'

'No problem.' She grabbed the card as she pulled her phone out of her pocket. 'I'll phone you so you have my number.' She typed Simon's number into her phone and they waited for it to ring through on his device.

They spent a few seconds just looking at each other enjoying the fact that they were now far more connected. Then Simon was beaten by a yawn that he just couldn't contain and for the first time he looked away from her.

'I'm so sorry, Beth. I'm going to have to go home. I'm sure I'll see you before Friday, but either way I'll get all the details of the party to you. I'm really looking forward to it.'

'Me too, Simon. I'm so glad you asked me. And a

wonderful excuse to go dress shopping!' she lied, feeling deeply sick now about the whole event. Simon stood up, took a final last look at Beth's face and walked out of the bar. The vacuum of his exit wasn't quite as powerful as she'd known before, but he still left her breathless as always.

* * *

Sitting in his office the next day, Simon pressed send on his computer and the email he'd just finished typing vanished. The satisfied smile quickly dropped from his lips, though, when he saw what the time was. It was just after midday and he still had to prepare for that afternoon's meeting. He was getting less enthused by his work with every passing day.

He looked for his black bag so he could scan through his notes, but it was nowhere to be found. Then he remembered he'd left it in his car, all the way down in the car park.

Ever since Beth had come into his life, things had definitely swerved at a major tangent. He used to think of nothing but work, he was so in control, but now he was spending his time daydreaming and planning things to please her. He was even going to attend one of those dreadful parties that he used to find any reason to avoid. It was such a great thing to take her to though, and he wouldn't have to face her alone. Their time together had been so fantastic to date, but he was still very concerned that something might go wrong. He didn't want to push it too soon.

He stood up and left his office, locking the door behind him. As he made his way across the floor, trying to avoid eye contact with all seven of the company directors that surrounded him, he was brought to a halt when he heard his name. Standing by Damien's desk, he turned his head slowly to find out what the Sales Director wanted.

'I just wanted to ask you about that meeting you have this afternoon with FLD Designs,' Damien started, a little edgy at having to ask. Simon didn't move, he just waited patiently for Damien to ask him an actual question. 'As they're my customer and I've done all the work on the Stock Termination project, can I join you?'

'It's just a courtesy meeting, Damien. I'm not there to talk about the project in particular.'

'I know that, but when you're not around I'm their main contact. I thought it just keeps that consistency. I won't speak, I promise. They're not the brightest bunch, I think we could have a fruitful relationship with them.'

Simon considered Damien's question. It made business sense as far as consistency was concerned, but there was something about Damien that had always left him feeling very cautious. Damien's ambition was greatly known, and he'd trodden on everyone he could to get to his position on the board of the company. To date, his shareholding was very minimal, with Paul owning nearly half and then Simon taking up the vast majority of what was left. The seven remaining directors owned just a small percentage each, but he could smell Damien's desperation for more. Still, how harmful could it be letting him attend one customer meeting? It was, technically, Damien's account after all.

'Very well,' Simon responded after his thoughtful consideration. 'We're leaving promptly at two fifteen.' Simon then walked on to the lifts so he could collect his bag, not even looking back for a reaction from Damien. If he wasn't ready then Simon would go anyway, it didn't really matter.

Down on the ninth floor, Beth had just finished processing details of an order for 'Extra Curricula Issues' when she saw the little envelope icon appear in the corner of her screen. She opened up her Outlook to find an email from Simon. She swiftly clicked on it, her heart skipping a beat.

Hi Beth

As promised, these are the details of the party on Friday. I'm so looking forward to spending the evening with you.

The party is in Hertfordshire at a hotel, so I've arranged for Jim to pick you up at 9pm from The Rose and I will see you there. Please call me when you get there and I'll come and meet you. I'm staying at the hotel for a couple of days, but Jim will come back and collect you whenever you're ready to leave.

I hope that you have a good night. I also hope that you have no issues getting a dress. I'm sure you'll looking stunning whatever you wear.

See you soon.

Kindest regards
Simon

She secretly smiled, trying not to bring too much attention to the thrilling anticipation that bubbled inside of her at the prospect of Friday's date. There was no way she could tell anyone else. Her colleagues overreacted at her making him a cup of tea, how would they cope with the news that she was going on a date with him? An actual date!

She'd made peace with the fact that she needed to buy a dress, and her friend, Ellie, from back home had been really helpful in advising her on what sort of dress to buy and where to shop. As this was her only night off until Saturday, she was making her first trip to Oxford Street straight after work, going on the Central Line directly from Ealing Broadway - as she had noted in her London scrapbook the night before. It might be skipping forward on her tube journey plans, but Simon was throwing everything out, so this was just another thing she'd have to sacrifice to have one of the most anticipated dates she could ever dream of.

Feeling her stomach grumble, she looked at the time and saw she could legitimately eat lunch without the fear of being hungry by mid-afternoon. How her sandwiches tempted her so much during the day! She reached down to look in her bag under her desk, but her sandwiches weren't there. She looked on the floor and around her desk to see if they'd dropped out, and then she realised she'd left them in her fridge. She chided herself for being so dopey, but it wasn't far to walk home.

A flyer on the edge of her desk that she'd not seen before suddenly caught her attention. It was advertising the little tea shop, just two doors away, saying that they had fifty percent off all sandwiches for that day only between twelve and two. There was a baguette on the front bursting with fresh salad and it looked incredibly tempting. Beth felt a pang of guilt as she had two perfectly edible sandwiches sitting in her fridge at home, but the more she looked at this flyer, the more the idea of being naughty and buying lunch seemed appealing.

Deciding that life was too short to turn down such a great offer, she grabbed her bag, checked with her colleagues that they didn't want anything (who all declined politely) and made her way down to the sandwich shop.

As she passed Trisha's office she looked in to see her chatting away on the phone to someone happily. It didn't look like a professional call and Beth shook her head in frustration. She'd been lumbered with the worst manager in the world. Trisha was a big hurdle in her career progression.

It took just a few minutes for her to get to the tea shop. It was a small shop, nicely decorated with tea cups on the wall, but despite their fantastic lunchtime offer, the shop wasn't really that busy.

'Excuse me,' Beth said to the middle aged lady behind the counter who was busy buttering bread. 'Are you still doing that fifty percent offer today?'

The woman appeared momentarily confused until she properly absorbed the flyer that Beth was waving in the air. 'Why yes,' she responded, 'of course.'

'Great!' Beth smiled. 'Can I have a chicken salad baguette then, please?'

'Of course, dear. Oh, and congratulations, you're our one hundredth customer today, and that means you've won our prize.'

'What!' Beth exclaimed, feeling that it really must be her lucky week.

'Yes, as part of our four year, three month and one day anniversary special, we are giving the one hundredth customer today one thousand pounds,' the lady stated, in a fairly lifeless tone considering the occasion.

Beth's jaw dropped open. She was expecting a free sandwich at the most. This was incredible. 'Are you sure?' she asked, positive that there must be some sort of mistake.

'Yes, dear. Congratulations!' Before the lady started Beth's sandwich, she clicked the till open and from underneath the cash drawer she pulled out an envelope that contained the one thousand pounds. She handed it to Beth, who was now shaking with disbelief. Barely able to wait for the sandwich, she raced home to check if it really was all real.

Sitting on the edge of her bed, she opened the envelope and counted the fifty twenty pound notes inside. She felt like all her prayers had been answered. And she already had a shopping trip planned that night!

Adrenaline raced through her body as she shakily reached for her phone. She had to tell someone, and she could think of no one better to share this amazing news with.

As Damien and Simon approached the Aston Martin just after two fifteen, Simon took his phone out of his dark grey trouser pocket to check on his communications and was delightfully surprised to find that he'd received a text from Beth. He didn't want to react and let Damien see his happiness, but he could barely help the smile that dashed quickly across his lips.

Hi, hope you're well? Thanks for the email. Amazing news, I've just won £1000! Dress shopping definitely on tonight! Hope you like what I get. Have a good day. Beth. x

Simon quickly texted back as Damien waited impatiently by the car.

That's fantastic news! You must be very special! Can't wait to see the outfit on Friday. Hope you have a good day too. x

Tapping his foot now, Damien sighed as Simon eventually unlocked his car so they could get in.

'It's a rare treat getting to ride in the Aston,' Damien purred as he slipped into the soft, black leather seat.

'If I'd known I was going to have company, I would have brought the Lexus,' Simon stated in reply, bringing Damien's enjoyment to a swift halt.

Simon threw his black bag on the back seat and they pulled out of the car park. It wasn't too far to their meeting, about half an hour to the north-east of the office, but it was far from a pleasant journey. The silence was icy cold between them.

The atmosphere cracked a little when Damien's phone started to ring. He pulled it out of his black jacket pocket.

'Hi, mum, everything okay?' he answered. Simon's ears pricked up. He knew Damien's family very well and he'd heard that his mother had been in hospital quite recently.

'Great news, mum,' Damien continued. 'I'm just with Simon at the minute, we're heading to a client... Yes I will do. Yes he's good, thank you. No, I don't know that. No. No. Yes. Look do you want to just speak to him yourself!'

Damien snapped.

Simon smirked to himself. Damien's parents had looked out for Simon so much when his parents had died, when Simon was just a teenager. Damien hated the attention they gave to him. Damien was an only child and had always been the focus of his parent's attention, but when Simon came to visit Damien was put in second place and it had always been a sore point.

Simon thought back to when his parents were alive. They'd tried to protect him from the world, and from himself, so much. His uncle Paul had been Simon's first exposure to the bitter truth, and as much as he hated the darkness that surrounded him, at least he now had the freedom of knowing who he really was.

Simon's thoughts quickly diminished when he heard Damien mention a party. 'No, it's Friday night, mum. Yes, it's at this hotel north of London, should be good. I'll probably be a bit worse for wear on Saturday, so I'll come and see you on Sunday. Okay. You too. Love you.' Damien hung up the phone and slipped it back into his pocket.

'Are you going to the Layfields party on Friday?' Simon asked, still looking hard at the road ahead.

'Yes, looking forward to it.'

'Since when do you get an invite to these events?'

'Since you stopped going. I've been to the last two. They said they know how busy your schedule is but they're keen for representation from Bird Consultants – as you can imagine – so they now ask me.'

'Are you going to the conference too?'

'No, you can still do that.'

'I'm doing it all this year,' Simon said, a little pleased to be rubbing Damien's face in it.

'You're going to the party?'

'Yes.'

'Haven't you got to get back to New York?'

'No. I won't be leaving any time soon, I'm spending

some time in the UK.'

'What?'

'I understand what disappointing news that is,' Simon retorted, hearing the discontent in Damien's voice. Simon was under no illusion that Damien pretended to be in charge when he wasn't there. He knew that Damien was after his job, although the chances of that were non-existent. It was Bird Consultants after all. It was a family business. Damien was an exceptionally hard worker, that was true, but he worked hard so he could earn lots of money and gain lots of power, not so he could help customers out.

There was a time, when he was young, that Simon had enjoyed the power and status that money could bring, but it all seemed so empty now that he was older and wiser. He had a lovely house, fabulous cars, a dream lifestyle in New York's Upper East Side, but he was also lonely and detached and it was very ungratifying. He longed for so much more.

In more recent times he'd been far more determined to give his customers satisfaction and keep the strong relationships alive. He wanted to properly earn his money, not to take it regardless. Dealing with people was incredibly difficult for him because of his cursed life, and he'd avoided human contact in all social arenas for so long, but at least he could be himself at work. People may fear him, but at work at least they respected him. That was a reason to get up each morning.

Damien had refused to respond to Simon's quip, and the two fell back to silence.

When they were just a few minutes away from the customer's office, Simon couldn't resist making a final dig at Damien, he had to optimise on the few pleasures that he had. He also wanted to make sure he'd see as little of him as possible that Friday. 'I hope you won't be expensing a night at the hotel.'

'What do you expect me to do?' Damien replied

snottily.

'I'm going to pretend that you didn't expense a room last year, as you clearly did. Get admin to arrange a car for you, we can expense that.' A thought suddenly clicked in Simon's head. 'And ask one of the more experienced staff, not that new girl, Beth. Give her a break.'

Damien rolled his eyes, assuming that Simon couldn't see. Simon gritted his teeth, he found Damien so irritating. He stuck in one more point as they pulled into the car park. 'I'm staying at the hotel, though, as I'll be at the conference during the day. And I'm the boss.' Inside he felt a moment's achievement at getting one over Damien, it was a rare occasion. Thinking forward to the week ahead, Simon was growing hopeful that maybe this really was going to be an exceptionally good week for a change.

NINE

Thankfully, Friday had flown by and Beth was now waving goodbye to Sam, her manager at The Rose, and was heading straight out the door where she hoped to find Jim waiting for her. She caught her breath as she stepped outside and saw a black Lexus glint under the lamplight with Jim standing beside it, just as promised.

She'd expected Simon's butler to be wearing a classic black suit, maybe more of a uniform, but instead he was, far less stereotypically and far more casually, wearing black trousers and a blue shirt. He still looked smart, though.

She stepped forward, feeling the most glamorous she'd ever felt in her life. She'd settled upon a sleeveless, straight, red satin dress with a V neck just low enough so it left a squeeze of cleavage, and the hemline just tinkering above her knee, enough so it was tasteful but still showed off her shapely figure as a teaser.

To complete the outfit she'd bought gold sparkly stiletto heels with a bag to match. The whole ensemble was let down slightly by her trusty brown jacket, but she figured that she'd be leaving that in a cloakroom anyway, so it didn't really matter.

Jim opened the door to the back of the car and invited

her in.

'Miss Lance?' he asked as she approached. She nodded as she slipped onto the cream leather seat and relaxed into the softness ready for the journey ahead.

As they pulled away, she toyed with the idea of chatting with Jim, not quite sure what the etiquette was with regards to speaking to one's date's chauffeur, this was all very new territory for her. She decided against it, not wanting to make him feel awkward, and instead just sat back and watched the world go by.

It was the first time she'd relaxed all day, it had been manic. She'd had so much work to plough through at the office before racing over to the bar where she'd had a frantic night serving drinks. She'd then, in just minutes, tidied up her hair and make-up (she'd worn her hair up for ease) and had thrown on her clothes before dashing out to meet Jim.

She was finally so happy to be sitting in the back of this luxurious car looking forward to a wonderful night ahead. She knew nothing of what an A List party would actually be like, but all she cared about was seeing Simon and nothing more had really entered into her head all day.

Before she knew it they were exiting the M25 and heading into Hertfordshire, and then the nerves started to rumble inside. The realisation that she was on her way to a massive, exclusive, glamorous party with a man she barely knew in the middle of nowhere suddenly hit home.

Sighing apprehensively, she unclipped her clutch bag and reached in for her lipstick. The increasing edginess to her hands made the bag fall to the foot well and, cursing, she was forced to bend down in the darkness and feel around for everything. She clumsily piled everything back into her bag and, holding it awkwardly on her lap, she tried to top up her soft pink lipstick, ensuring the vibrations of the car didn't jolt her too much and make a mess.

She put her lipstick and vanity mirror away and sat back, getting more nervous with every passing second. She could take the silence no longer. 'Are we nearly there yet?' she asked Jim who sat in front of her in the driver's seat.

'Yes, Miss Lance, just a few minutes away now.'

'I'm so nervous, Jim, it's crazy.'

'What have you got to be nervous about?'

'It's a massive party and I won't know anyone but Simon, and I suppose I don't really know him. God, what am I doing?'

'Mr Bird will look after you, I'm sure.'

'Do you know him well, Jim?' Beth asked, taking the rare opportunity to question someone who knew him.

'I have worked for him for three years now, Miss Lance, and he has been a fantastic employer.'

'But do you like him?' Jim remained silent. 'Please be honest with me. I'm not asking to report back, I'm asking as I'm about to go on a date with him but I know so little about him.'

'The honest truth is,' Jim started, 'Mr Bird takes a lot of getting used to, but once you get to know him he's a kind, fair and generous man with a good heart.'

Beth accepted this response with delight. Although she knew Jim was never going to bad mouth his employer, he spoke with such conviction she was sure that she was doing the right thing.

They were now travelling down a pitch black country lane and Beth had no clue as to where they were. Then right up ahead she saw lights. They turned left into a softly lit, tree lined side road and then headed down towards the vast grounds in the distance. As they neared the massive hotel, Beth marvelled at the size of it. It was a grand building, clearly very old but it looked immaculate. They passed by dozens of parked cars and made their way towards the entrance. It was hard to see just how expansive the grounds were, as the black of the night hid so much around them, but Beth could sense that they were pretty much in the middle of nowhere.

The actual hotel entrance was backed into a courtyard

that cars couldn't get down to. Jim had to stop at the end of a little pathway. He walked round to let Beth out the car, but she was already opening the door in awe of the beautiful place ahead of her.

Despite the fact that the party had started nearly two hours earlier, there were plenty of people around and Beth suddenly felt very small. The ladies wore beautiful long gowns, dripping with diamonds, and the air was tinted with expensive perfume. All the men around her were spotless in their dinner jackets.

'Are you all right?' Jim asked.

'Oh yes, fine. Just getting my bearings.'

'Very well. I'll meet you just back here whenever you are ready to leave. Mr Bird will give me a call.'

'Thank you so much, that's so good of you.'

'My pleasure.' Jim then got back in the car and Beth watched him drive away. She suddenly felt very alone.

She headed on up the pathway to see the courtyard in all its beauty. It was a pristinely decorated area, but Beth's eyes were drawn to the red carpet that paved the way to the main entrance, guarded by two black uniformed doormen.

She'd never been greeted by a red carpet before, and she suddenly felt so lost. Then she remembered that all she had to do was call Simon and he'd come to meet her. She opened her bag to get her phone out, but it wasn't there. She looked again, but the bag was so little there was nowhere for it to hide. She checked on the floor around her before realising that it must have dropped out in the car. She turned round quickly to see if Jim was still in sight, but he was long gone. She was now properly alone.

Sighing, she stood up tall. She told herself that getting to this party paled into insignificance compared to her starting a new life for herself in London, and she needed to just get on with it.

Feeling a renewed inner strength, she walked up to the front doors, sure she would find Simon as soon as she got inside. She went to walk past the two doormen when one stopped her.

'Sorry, love, it's a private event tonight,' the one closest to her said. He was a tall, hefty built man with very short hair and a fierce looking face. His colleague was slightly slimmer with spiky black hair and he looked far more approachable, although he too was nearing six foot tall.

'I know,' she replied. 'I've been invited. I'm on the list.'

He looked her up and down, paying extra close attention to her slightly scruffy brown jacket. 'You're on the list are you?' he smirked. 'And what would your name be? Cinderella?'

'It's Bethany Lance,' she answered confidently.

The man looked sarcastically at his hand pretending it was a notepad. 'Nope, sorry, your name's not down. I can't let you in.'

Beth looked at him, utterly bewildered by how difficult he was being. 'I've been invited,' she confirmed.

'I suppose you're friends of the family?'

'I know exactly whose party this is!' she insisted. 'It's for Frederick Layfield.'

'Ahh, you're one of them. We had more than enough trouble with you lot last year,' the doorman mumbled, catching the attention of his colleague who moved over to see what was going on.

'Sorry, love,' the slimmer man chipped in. 'It's an exclusive event, no press allowed.'

'I'm not the press!' Beth exclaimed, feeling increasingly frustrated.

'Whatever, you're not getting in, and that's that,' he simply replied.

'Look, I'm with Simon Bird, if you could just get him-' Her assertion was cut short as the doormen started to laugh.

'That's a new one!' the fiercer one chuckled.

'Do you even know who Simon Bird is?' she asked.

'Everyone knows Mr Bird, love, I don't know what

you're trying to pull.'

'I'm his guest. If you could just go and find him, he'll vouch for me, I'm sure.'

'You want me to go in there, find Mr Simon Bird and then ask him if he'll come and vouch for some...' the man looked her up and down, '...little tart out here. I don't think so.'

'How dare you! Simon will vouch for me!'

The doormen just looked at each other and then the quieter one spoke up again. 'We're going to have to ask you to leave now, love. Nice try, no hard feelings, but this is an exclusive event and not for you.'

'But!' Beth was almost lost for words. 'This is an outrage. I'm an invited guest, just ask Simon.'

'Stop it now, you're embarrassing yourself.' More well-dressed guests entered the party, the doormen barely even glancing at them, and Beth felt a deep pang of indignation. She raced through ideas in her head as to what she could say or do. She was so close to getting in and spending an amazing night with an amazing man, but it was all starting to crumble around her.

'Move along now, or we're going to have to call the police.'

'Call them! Then they'll go and get Simon and they'll be able to ask him.'

The doormen were now getting impatient with her and their tetchiness was showing. 'No one is going to be bothering Mr Bird, is that clear? You obviously have a story you want on him or something, but I'd stay well away if I were you. Mr Bird is not to be messed with, and for that matter neither are we. Please leave or we will have to make you.'

Beth sensed how the tone was far more threatening this time and she found herself walking away in disbelief. She had to find a way around this. This was ridiculous. The fury and desperation in her started to grow in equal measures as she realised if she didn't get in then she'd lose her chance at a date with Simon.

Up ahead she saw a group of people heading towards the entrance, there must have been about eight of them. She figured that if she tailed behind them she could probably nip in quickly and not be seen. All she had to do then was find Simon and it would all be over with. He'd tell them. They weren't going to chase her around the hotel, after all... were they?

She timed it well, keeping her distance from the doormen, and reached the entrance. Suddenly, though, her hope was all gone when she felt a hand on her arm and she was pulled forcefully to the floor. She landed just to the side of the red carpet on the concrete with a bang, the pain in her backside shooting up through her. She wanted to argue, to make her case again, but before she knew it she was being dragged to the side of the entrance, more out of sight, and then her arm was twisted round so her face fell flat on the floor. Now pinned down with her arms being held behind her back, she heard her assailant tell the other doorman to phone for the police.

She lay with her cheek against the cold concrete, utterly unable to move, and all hope drifted away. As she thought to Simon and how he'd probably believe she'd stood him up, and as the utter humiliation of the last few minutes drained through her, the sting of a tear hit her eye and she bit her quivering lip, devastated. Beth couldn't remember the last time she'd ever cried in her life, but she was now absolutely broken and completely out of her depth.

Not fifty metres away, at the back of the hotel, in a huge function room, stood Simon. Dressed in a stunning dinner jacket, he was sipping at a glass of champagne while keenly staring at his phone, now feeling very anxious.

The huge room was made up of two floors. The top balcony area, where Simon stood, held a bar and casino, and the bottom area was more for dancing and eating.

Simon checked his phone again and sighed. It was now

just after ten. Maybe they'd got caught in traffic, he deduced. He so wanted to phone Beth up and find out where she was, but he didn't want to seem too eager. If there was a problem, surely Jim would have let him know.

He scanned the room behind him, in case she'd just forgotten to call, and he set his eyes straight on Damien who was just entering the party. Simon made his way over to him.

'Evening,' Simon greeted.

'Good evening,' Damien replied not even looking at Simon but instead skimming the room for people to suck up to. The slight slur to his tone gave away his already inebriated state.

'I don't suppose you've seen Beth Lance at all, have you?' Simon asked, trying not to seem too bothered.

Damien finally turned to him and sniggered. 'You mean our admin girl?' Simon nodded in response. 'Now there's a girl who's desperate to succeed. She's going to go far, that one. You have to give her ten for effort.'

'Have you seen her or not, Damien?' Simon repeated, growing impatient with Damien's ramblings.

'Yes I have. Last time I saw her she was being man-handled out front. Don't know what she thinks she's playing at,' he sniggered again.

Without thinking, Simon thrust his glass of champagne into Damien's hand and headed towards the main entrance. It was quite a way there, and Simon found himself almost running as he headed out of the function room, down the stairs, along the corridor, across the lobby and towards the main entrance.

He sprung out into the cool night air and saw nothing but one doorman standing there, whose eyes suddenly blackened with fear. Simon stepped around the man to find another doorman pinning Beth to the ground. A violent anger raged through him as he stepped forward and threw the doorman aside, letting Beth free.

The doorman was knocked back quite a distance,

absolute shock tearing across his face. He quickly gained his composure and jumped to his feet ready to fight back. Then he looked straight at Simon who was glaring back with fiery eyes and he instantly backed down, all of a sudden very timid, just like his peer.

Simon leant down and helped Beth to her feet, placing his arm around her for comfort. 'Are you okay?' he asked, guilt surging through him as he looked at her flustered face. She just nodded a little shakily.

Not leaving her side, Simon glared back intensely towards the man who'd pinned her down.

'Sorry, Mr Bird. We didn't know. We thought she was trouble. You know what happened last year with all those press lot getting in, our jobs would be on the line if anything like that happened again. We panicked,' the man whimpered.

'Name!' Simon ordered.

'Barry Fitzgerald,' the man replied without a second's thought.

Simon turned to the other doorman standing much more closely, the slimmer one of the two, and before he even had chance to open his mouth, the man gave his name. 'William Brown,' he said.

Simon repeated the names back to himself, making a mental note of these terrible men and promising himself that he'd make them pay for what they'd done to the woman he was so clearly falling in love with.

Simon turned back to Beth and tucked a little piece of escaped hair behind her ear. He couldn't believe how beautiful she looked. She was stunning, especially in that striking red dress. He lost himself in her sparkling emerald eyes. She was so clearly fighting a battle with the sting of tears and it pained him. He wondered how she could ever forgive him.

He made a pact with himself in that instance that he was always going to look after her, and he'd never let anyone hurt her again.

TEN

Don't cry, don't cry, don't cry, Beth repeated to herself as she looked back into her saviour's velvet eyes. She felt a complete fool as she leaned against his safe arm and breathed in his strong, masculine musk. She wondered what on earth he must think of her. Whatever, though, she was so grateful he'd come out when he did.

'Let's get you cleaned up,' Simon said, glancing at her grazed knees. Beth just nodded and she let Simon lead her into the hotel, a wave of relief pouring over her as she crossed the threshold.

Inside the entrance was the main hotel reception. The spotlessly clean marble floor was cluttered with glamorous people and Beth held tightly onto Simon as he led her across the lobby, down a corridor and then up some carpeted stairs. The upbeat music from the party could finally be heard as the entrance of the function room came into sight.

Beth felt so embarrassed as she looked down at her grazed knees and she winced at the ache across the top of her back. She was sure her dress must be smeared from her ordeal, but she daren't look. She kept her head down, trying not to make eye contact with any of the glamorous people milling around. She was utterly ashamed of herself.

Stopping just inside the door, Simon called over a security guard standing watch in the corner of the balcony area. Simon whispered something in the man's ear, then the man nodded before promptly disappearing into the ladies toilet near them.

Within a few seconds, four ladies all came out of the toilet together, followed shortly by two more, and then the security guard held the door open for Beth and Simon to enter. As they did, he waited for the door to swing slowly shut and he stood guard.

The toilet was like nothing Beth had ever seen. There was a reception area that had three full length mirrors and two pink chaise longues, and then sparkling clean cubicles and marble sinks were found towards the back.

Simon placed Beth between two sinks and studied her. They could hear the muffled sound of the disco outside and Beth hoped it would stay away. Her lip quivered slightly, but she was determined not to cry. He looked down at her grazed knees; the skin was clearly broken but there were only specks of blood. He picked up a flannel that was neatly folded in a wicker basket and then dampened it before bending down and dabbing at her knees.

Despite his ever so gentle touch, it stung, and Beth could hold on no longer. She felt so stupid all dressed up with grazed knees, like an idiot child playing at being a grown up. A single tear escaped down her left cheek and her mouth quivered again as she fought to keep her full sob at bay.

Simon looked up at her with touching sympathy. He stood up slowly and placed the towel aside, and for a moment they awkwardly watched each other, not quite knowing what to do next.

Despite how safe she felt in Simon's presence, Beth couldn't stop a second tear falling down her cheek as the heady emotions of the night took their toll. Simon focussed on her, clearly troubled by her sorrow. His chocolate eyes fixated on her and then, moving his hand slowly, he ever so gently cupped her face, softly wiping away her tear with his thumb.

They remained still, staring into other's eyes, for the first time properly breathing each other in. Beth felt so at peace yet so enthralled under the touch of his hand. It was one of the most intoxicating moments of her life.

He was now so close, she could see how perfectly flawless his skin was and she could almost taste the irresistible softness of his slightly parted lips. She let herself relax in the mesmerising beauty of his deep brown eyes. She had never met a man so handsome.

She wanted him to kiss her so badly. Every inch of her was screaming out to feel the touch of him against her lips. Then, causing her heart to frantically throb, Simon slowly leaned in towards her.

Closing her eyes, she lost her breath as she felt the gentle warmth of his lips against hers. It sent an electrifying ecstasy race through her. The soft yet adoring power of his spellbinding kiss spread its enchanting glow through her face, then it melted down her neck before finally radiating through her whole body. She felt every inch of her skin tingle with desire and it left her helpless in the bliss of his tender embrace.

His lips slowly parted from hers and the air was instantly cooling against her mouth. Moving his head back slightly, he gazed lovingly at her face, still holding her cheek with his hand.

Lost in his eyes, Beth totally forgot where she was. As she stared deep into his soul she was sure she could see a glint of a flame burning passionately back at her. It was a crazy notion, but as all the world around her had seemed to disappear, she didn't question it, she just enjoyed their first intimate encounter and yielded to the incredible impact of his touch.

He leaned in to kiss her once more, their reverie taking

them further away from reality. Beth was spinning with desire as Simon's more ardent kiss this time captivated her every pore and sent a lascivious blaze surging through her whole body.

His embrace slowly softened and he brought his hands down to hers. Touching fingers, the pair of them stayed lost in their entrancement.

After what seemed like hours but was just a few minutes, the music from outside slowly penetrated its way back in, and the reality of the bathroom they were standing in dissolved away the velvety dream.

Beth caught her breath for the first time. It felt invigorating, like she hadn't properly breathed for a few minutes. She noticed that the pain at the bottom of her back and on her knees had completely disappeared, and the awful events of earlier that night seemed like a distant memory.

They smiled at each other, words not needed, and they both enjoyed the warm sensual connection that they now shared. Something incredible had just happened, and Beth felt breathless, overwhelmed and overjoyed.

'Do you want to go to the party?' Simon whispered. Beth just nodded, still trying to regulate her breathing. Simon helped her take her coat off, revealing her beautifully slim figure underneath for the first time.

'You look absolutely stunning,' he said as he placed her coat neatly across his arm. He then took her hand and led her out of the bathroom.

The guard was still standing outside, and as they passed him Simon stopped. He gave the guard Beth's coat, whispering instructions in his ear, and then he smoothly and subtly placed a note in the guard's hand, before leading Beth across to the champagne bar.

They didn't let go of each other's hands as Simon ordered two glasses of champagne, then they made their way over to a table in a dark corner of the room overlooking the casino area. They couldn't take their eyes off each other, the memory of that amazing kiss still reeling through them both. Beth had still not said a single word, but the broad grin that helplessly covered her face told Simon everything he needed to know.

She coyly looked down as she replayed the kiss over and over in her head. It had been fantastic and singularly the best moment of her life.

Then her expression turned to one of confusion as she glanced at her knees. 'They've healed!' she exclaimed.

'What have?' Simon asked, following her stare, seeing too that there was now not a mark visible from her attack.

'My knees. The grazes have gone. How can they just have got better?'

'Don't be silly,' Simon replied, totally overlooking the miraculous cure as if it hadn't happened at all. 'They weren't that bad, and it's dark in here. It must have seemed worse than it was at the time,' he justified.

'Yeah, of course,' Beth nodded, perplexed by the miracle, but ready to believe that her new happy state had thrown fresh light on everything. Maybe it hadn't all been as bad as she'd thought. She squeezed Simon's hand, thankful for his rational, clear mind.

She sipped at her champagne and, for the first time, took the room in. It felt so alien to her. There was so much money around her, so many designer outfits and priceless accessories, and she dreaded to think what each of the chips on the Black Jack table were worth. It was dwarfing to her and it left her feeling very much like she didn't belong there, a sensation she'd never thought she'd experience. She'd always been taught that everyone was her equal, but seeing such opulence around her made her unusually self-conscious. She quickly questioned what Simon was really doing with her; they lived in such different worlds. She never thought that she'd ever admit it, but maybe people weren't all equal. Maybe her life back at home hadn't really been a true reflection of life elsewhere.

'Is there something wrong?' he asked, noticing how the grin had disappeared from her face.

She shook her head. 'I've just never been to a party like this before. Or anywhere like this before. It's all a bit strange.'

'Are you not enjoying yourself? That is, ignoring the terrible start to the evening.'

'It's not that. The last few minutes will take a lifetime of beating, believe me,' she simpered. 'I just don't think places like this are really... well... me.'

'Thank God for that!' Simon laughed. 'I hate these parties.'

'Why did you invite me, then?'

Simon shrugged. 'I thought you might like to go. I just wanted to ask you out.'

Beth bit her lip through her grin. 'I'm glad you did.'

They both looked out across the room. It was now quite full with guests, all enjoying themselves, oblivious to the loved up couple in the corner.

'What's your room like?' Beth asked, meaning it as a perfectly innocent question, not thinking once about the underlying suggestion it made. All she wanted to do was get away from these people.

'You want to see?' Simon responded, just as innocently; he too was very ready to leave.

He took Beth's hand as they stood up and she squeezed it tightly, making sure it was all really real. They took their champagne back out towards the lobby. This time, though, they stopped at the lifts.

Stepping in to the lift, Simon pressed for the fourth floor and it suddenly dawned on Beth where she was going. Her heart now started to thump wildly as the realisation that she was going to his bedroom sunk in.

They got out on the fourth floor and headed to the room right at the end of the corridor. The door clicked after Simon waved the card in front of it and he opened it up for Beth to enter.

It was a beautifully large room. The queen size bed was the main feature but it still hardly filled up half the space.

At the far end was a giant window but all Beth could see was her own reflection against the black night. She stepped forward to shut the huge brown curtains and took a moment to compose herself, wondering what would happen next. The truth was, she felt such deep-seated urges for this man, she secretly hoped for more. But she told herself not to push it and to behave like a lady.

She turned round to see Simon looking in the mini bar, his jacket now taken off and placed neatly on the back of the chair. 'We've got beer, wine, vodka, whiskey... whatever takes your fancy,' he said.

'Any chance of a white wine?'

'There's a Pinot Grigio?' Simon offered, taking the little bottle out of the fridge to show her. She nodded her head, downed the last of her champagne, and held out her glass for Simon to fill up. He shook his head lightly and grabbed a white wine glass from the top of the mini bar.

'You can't drink white wine from a champagne flute,' he smirked.

'Sure you can,' Beth argued.

Simon shook his head again and grinned. 'The shape of the glass affects the flavour of the wine. Trust me. Flutes for champagne, large glasses for red wine and these,' he said, holding up the glass in his hand to show her, 'for white wine.'

'You're quite the connoisseur,' she giggled. 'I'm happy to play along.' She put down her flute on the desk and took the glass from Simon. He opened the screw top of the wine and poured half of it in her glass. Then he placed the remainder back in the fridge and reached for a bottle of Peroni for himself.

Beth made her way to sit on the bed, unable to resist the soft Egyptian cotton. They both sipped at their drinks and the room fell silent. The tension of what would happen next was now slowly building between them.

Then Beth got concerned. This devastatingly handsome man who stood before her must have had dozens of partners, and she was just a naïve little girl from the countryside. No matter what was going to happen, she wanted to set Simon straight so his expectations weren't high. She felt a strange comfort in laying out the truth about herself to him. Her honesty had always served her well in the past.

'I need to tell you something,' she started, and Simon came over to sit next to her. 'I'm not saying I expect anything tonight, this isn't about that. We've only just had one kiss and this is our first date. It's wise to take these things slowly. I just want you to know something about me, okay? I think it's important you know.' Simon looked at her with a mixture of confusion and worry.

'You know I told you how that ex-boyfriend of mine asked me to marry him and I ran for the hills?' Simon nodded in response, waiting for more. 'Well, that was two years ago now. And that was the last time I...' she paused, choosing her words carefully. 'That was the last time I was with a man. I've not had a single date, kiss or anything more since I left him. Until tonight.'

Simon didn't react for a second, and Beth felt very concerned, terrified he was going to ask her to leave. She imagined that he wasn't even going to phone up Jim, he was just going to throw her out on to the streets. Then he stood up.

'I need to tell you something too, Beth,' he suddenly said, much to her surprise. 'You're so honest and open. That's new territory for me, but I'd like to always be honest with you too, wherever I can. I know how important it is to you.' It was Beth's turn to feel the churn of expectation as she watched Simon pace around nervously.

'When I was just eighteen I made my first million. I was young and rich, but also very lonely. Then I met a girl.' His face darkened as he turned to Beth. 'I don't know if you've noticed, but people don't always take to me. Not you, you're somehow immune to me, it's extraordinary; it's liberating. Other people, though, don't warm to me quite as you have.'

Beth screwed up her face, feeling very defensive towards her man. 'People don't feel that way!' she argued. Simon just raised his eyebrows in response. Then she thought to the office and to the horrible things that people had said about him. And then she thought to The Rose, where people had stood out of his way when they came to be served. He had the most amazing presence about him, it was undeniable, but she'd always felt it magnetising, not uncomfortable.

'Okay, people in the office act a bit weirdly around you,' she conceded. 'I suppose I've seen other people be a bit weird too. Why is that?'

'Oh Beth, I wish I could tell you,' he answered sincerely.

'Can I ask you something?' she started, a little hesitantly. 'You don't have to answer.'

'You can ask me anything, and I'll give you the best answer I can,' he replied, cryptically.

'My friends in the office. They told me you'd sacked people and you'd done terrible things. They said you'd killed someone. Why would they say that?'

Simon moved back to Beth's side and sat down, reaching out for her hand. 'None of that is true,' he declared with deep conviction. 'People are afraid of me; it's hard to explain.' He paused as he considered how to make her see his point of view. 'When people don't understand something, they fear it, and that fear changes people and makes them act differently, cruel even. Trust me, Beth, there have been many, and far worse things said about me in my life, but none of it's true. That's why I've always kept people at a distance. Until I met you.'

Beth marvelled at his tolerance for the rumours that had been spread about him and for the nasty things that people had said. He was so brave and level-headed.

'Beth, you look at me in a different way to anyone I've ever met before. You treat me completely differently. You've given me something I've never had from anyone. But that's not the only reason I'm sat here with you today,' he told her. 'I think you're amazing. You're, without any shadow of a doubt, the most beautiful, fun, kind, fascinating woman I've ever met.' Beth exhaled a little at the sensational words he bestowed upon her. She felt exactly the same way about him.

'And that's why I need to be honest with you,' he added, standing up again nervously. Beth waited for him to continue.

He walked towards the curtained windows, as if he wanted to look out, but not quite sure what to do with himself. 'When I was nineteen I met a woman. She was about three years older than me and we met at a party, somewhat like this one. She chatted to me all night, and for the first time I felt a real connection to someone. I could see that she was a little uneasy around me, but she seemed captivated by me regardless and I let her in. We started dating and for a while it was really enjoyable. Then I started to... well, I thought I fell in love with her; I'm thinking that wasn't the case now. Anyway, as I grew closer to her, she backed away from me. It got more and more about the materialistic things I could do for her and less about the closeness a couple should have.' Beth looked at him sadly.

'I was twenty-one when I finally saw things really for what they were. I found her one night in our home with another man, all over him. She thought I was away on a business trip with my uncle. The truth is I cancelled it. I wanted to see what she was up to, so I surprised her. It was the most heart-wrenching thing to see her, especially when she just blamed me and my apparent coldness for her disloyalty. Not trusting her was the best thing I ever did and that's stayed with me ever since.'

'Oh my God, Simon, that's awful,' Beth said, wanting so much to comfort him.

'She moved out the next day and I never saw her again. Since then I haven't let anyone in. I've kept all that hurt and heartache far away from me.'

Beth smiled sympathetically, and then the maths dropped in her head. 'You were twenty-one when you broke up?' she asked, waiting for his nodding response. 'And now you're thirty-two.' He nodded again. 'So you've not been with a woman in eleven years?' she exclaimed.

Simon shook his head. 'A bit more than your two.'

Beth couldn't believe that such a tender, wonderful, gorgeous man, who emitted such a warm and powerful essence, could have not been with a woman in such a long time. Her hunger for him went into overdrive and, wasting no more time, she stood to her feet, threw her arms around him, careful not to spill the wine she still held in her hand, and kissed him. It was a far deeper, more heated kiss than before, driven by their mutually heightened sexual desire.

Simon pulled away and took her glass, placing it with his beer on the desk. Then he wrapped his arms around her and they locked lips once more, kissing fervently. Losing themselves for a moment in their impassioned embrace, their arousal spiked and an intense lust took charge.

Breathlessly they broke away, not sure how far they could go, not wanting to upset the other one. Simon tucked Beth's freeing hair behind her ears and stared lovingly into her eyes.

'We don't have to do this, you know,' he said.

'There's nothing more in the world I want right now than you,' she whispered. 'But only if you want it too.' Simon didn't move for a second, and Beth waited agonisingly for some indication of what he wanted.

Then he picked up her carefully in his arms and placed her on the bed. He lay next to her and then he kissed her again, deeply and seductively.

Catching his breath, he slowly unpinned the silver clip from her coiffure, releasing her soft wavy hair so it could fall freely to her shoulders. He placed the clip carefully on the bedside table next to him and then gently tucked her brown waves behind her ears so he could properly see her face.

Beth reached down to kick off her shoes and Simon did the same. He then loosened his bow tie so it fell around his shoulders, leaving Beth to pull it away. She threw it to the floor behind her and they kissed again, both of them a little more nervous now with the realisation of what was to happen. Despite their inexperience and concerns about pleasing one another, the single reassuring factor was that their relative innocence was mutual. It was yet another thing that they had in common, and Beth was starting to believe that Simon could well and truly be her soulmate.

Simon slowly reached back and unzipped Beth's dress. With her help, he pulled it off her before carefully letting it slip to the floor beside them. He then absorbed with delight her slim, shapely body, and her pale skin that shimmered against her black satin underwear.

Beth unbuttoned Simon's shirt, now desperate to see what lay beneath. As he yanked his arms out and threw the shirt to the floor, she touched his silky skin, stroking his lightly toned chest. There were just a few dashed hairs, enough to make him manly, but too few to be that noticeable. She couldn't believe how perfect he was. He was strong yet tender; masculine yet vulnerable. She couldn't wish for more.

Simon edged up to be on top of her, undoing the button of his trousers for comfort, revealing blue boxer shorts underneath. He looked down into her eyes and kissed her softly on the lips. Then he kissed her cheek and moved slowly down to her neck. She could feel his warm breath tickling her skin and it sent waves of desire crashing through her. He took her breath away again, just as he did the first time he kissed her.

He carried on to explore more of her body with his smooth caresses, working over her chest and down her torso. Beth felt herself melting away with every euphoric stroke, gradually losing the reality around her. It had been so long since she'd been touched in such a way, but more than that, Beth had never felt so strongly and so passionately for anyone in her life. She had never even imagined such intense feelings of ecstasy were in fact possible, and as he worked his way down passed her belly button, Beth lost all her senses.

The deep craving she had for him took over and she felt herself falling. She was falling far into the night, into a place she'd never been before. At that moment she realised she was in love. This went far past lust or desire, this was incredible, deep-seated love that she had never even been close to before.

The world as she knew it was gone, and she was now in very new territory. As she found herself lost in a blissful reverie, far away from the reality around her, she realised that not only was she experiencing immense pleasure but she was also scared to death.

Ever since she'd met this wonderful man, he'd managed to, somehow, wield such an intense power over her. He'd become everything to her, it was as if she was hypnotised by his commanding presence; but it was exactly where she wanted to be. Nothing had ever felt so right.

The only question left to answer then was why, if it was all so perfect, was she so terrified of what was to come? She was absolutely in love with everything she knew about this man, and she was convinced that he was, in every way, her soulmate. She just needed to find out what he was hiding, and she hoped, so desperately, that it wouldn't be bad. Surely nothing could affect how she felt for him now... could it?

ELEVEN

Simon and Beth woke the next morning wrapped up in each other's arms. They had both shared the deepest, most satisfying sleep of their lives, despite the fact that neither of them were accustomed to sharing a bed.

Beth slowly opened her eyes, nestled in against Simon's shoulder. She was so comfortable. Simon gently kissed her forehead, and he then moved to kiss her nose and, before they both knew it, that burning desire was taking over again. Simon moved his warm body on to hers and they locked their arms around one another. He just left her for one second to reach for the contraception he'd placed on the bedside table the night before (he'd seemed to magic them from nowhere much to Beth's surprise and delectable relief), and then they enjoyed their exploration of each other's bodies all over again.

They moved softly together, the intensity of their feelings heightening at their love making. Beth once again felt that explosion of feeling, like her body was being shattered into a million euphoric pieces with every thrust he made, and her climax literally took her breath away.

Once they'd both calmed down, Simon slipped away from her. He took one final kiss and then pulled his boxer shorts on and headed to a cupboard next to the minibar. Inside, he pulled open a drawer revealing the tea and coffee making facilities. 'Can I do the honours today?' he smirked, picking up the kettle and waving it in the air.

'That would be lovely.'

'Do you take it strong, white and sugarless as well?' he asked confidently.

'I'd say well remembered, but we're just like two peas in a pod, you and me, so it was an easy guess!' Beth giggled as Simon moved to the bathroom to fill up the little silver kettle.

Once full of water, he placed it back on its base and flicked the switch to turn it on.

'You're really telling me you don't work out?' Beth asked, relishing in the view of his flawless body.

'No,' he simply answered, awkwardly folding his arms.

'You can't be serious. How on earth have you managed to get a body like that?'

'Like I said to you before, I'm just lucky I guess. Do you work out?' he threw back at her.

'Not really, but I am always on the go.'

'You have a stunning figure, so there you go. It's not always about time in the gym.'

'No, I guess not,' she replied, secretly smiling at the wonderful compliment. No one had ever called her stunning before.

Simon was now scanning the clothes strewn on the floor. He reached down to pick up his suit trousers and placed them neatly on the armchair in the corner, and then he made his way around the bed to pick up Beth's red dress.

'You looked absolutely beautiful last night,' he said, looking at the satin garment in his hand.

'Thank you. I'm glad you like the dress,' she responded, not quite believing the compliment was aimed at her and not the dress. She wasn't at all used to being adored in such a way.

'Where did you get it from in the end?' he asked, folding it neatly on the back of the desk chair over his suit jacket.

'Debenhams. It was the bargain of the century. Cost just fifty pounds.'

'Fifty pounds!' Simon spat, looking straight round at her.

'Yes.'

'I thought you won a thousand pounds?'

'I can't spend a thousand pounds on one dress! Even if I wore it every day, I'd never spend that sort of money on one outfit. No, I spent fifty pounds on the dress, which was reduced from eighty I might add, and then the shoes cost me sixty pounds and the bag was twenty. Then I did spend a little more on the underwear, but that was worth it. Overall, though, not too bad. Although when you actually think about it, over a hundred pounds on one outfit that I might not wear again is a hell of a lot.'

Simon chuckled, more to himself, and then sat down next to her on the bed. 'We'll just have to find somewhere else for you to wear it to then, won't we.'

A thought clicked in Beth's head and she looked around the room. 'Where's my jacket?' she asked.

Simon stood up and walked to the wardrobe in the corner of the room. Opening the mirrored doors, he revealed her brown jacket hanging neatly within it.

'Is that what you asked that guard to do?' Beth queried, grinning.

'People will do anything for the right price.'

'I'm starting to think people will do anything for you. Those doormen last night looked pretty terrified when you came to my rescue.'

Simon's face dropped at the mention of those terrible men. 'I'm so sorry about that.'

'It's not your fault. I'm the one who lost my phone. Will Jim still have it in his car?'

'Of course he will. Let's not think about that now,'

Simon said, but Beth could tell his mind was still processing the event.

'Do you want to do something today?' she asked, more to change the subject.

Simon looked to the bedside table and clocked the time. He then closed his eyes as he remembered a meeting he had.

'I'm so sorry, Beth,' he said, coming back round to sit next to her again, 'I've just realised I've got lunch with Fred Layfield. He asked me yesterday, I didn't think you'd be here.'

'That's fine, don't worry, I'm sure we'll see each other soon.'

'What about tomorrow? Could I take you out somewhere?' he asked hopefully as the kettle finally made its accomplished click.

'I wish. I have to work tomorrow at the bar. I'm so sorry.'

Simon brushed her hair aside with his fingers to get a proper look at her face. 'You just let me know when you're not working and I'm going to take you out somewhere, anywhere you like.'

Beth knew exactly where she wanted to go. It was silly and very unexciting, but she knew she wanted to share it with Simon. 'There is somewhere I'd like us to go together,' she told him.

'Anywhere, you name it. I'd take you anywhere,' he sweetly smiled as he walked back over to the kettle. He placed a tea bag in each of the two plain white mugs that sat next to the device.

'Don't laugh. It may seem silly to you, but I'm just a country girl who's never been to London before and has always dreamed of the bright lights of the city.'

'So where are we going?' Simon asked, pouring the boiling water into the mugs.

'Piccadilly Circus,' Beth stated.

Simon couldn't stifle his laugh as he placed the kettle

back down. He turned to look at her. 'Piccadilly Circus?' he checked.

'I really want to go and spend a night in Piccadilly Circus. I want to see the lights, soak up the atmosphere, maybe take in a show, go for a drink, and then stagger home in the early hours of the morning. I want the London life, I want to experience it for myself; and I can think of no one better to share it with than you.'

Simon stayed silent for a second, clearly touched by Beth's simple dream. He stepped back over to the bed to sit next to her and squeezed her hand. 'Piccadilly Circus it is. But if you want to stagger home in the early hours, then maybe we make it a weekend?'

'I'm not working Monday, Tuesday and Saturday this week, so maybe we could do it next Saturday? That's if you're not busy?'

'I'm definitely free. Saturday it is. I'll take you to the bright lights of Piccadilly Circus. But can Jim drive us?'

'No!' Beth asserted. 'I want to feel like a Londoner, so we're going on the tube. That's non-negotiable.'

Simon grimaced and then laughed. 'Do you know how many years it's been since I've been on the tube!' he stated, going back to take the stewed tea bags out of the mugs.

Beth watched him lovingly. A sense of completion relaxed her body and the fear she'd felt the night before now seemed a distant memory. At that exact moment in time, everything was just perfect.

* * *

The following Monday, Simon had virtually leapt out of bed with excitement knowing he was going to see Beth again that day. He was carefully straightening his navy blue tie in front of his bedroom mirror when his phone rang. He saw it was his uncle calling.

'Hi Paul,' he answered.

'I know it's early mate, but we've got a problem,' the

voice on the other end said.

'It's not that early here,' Simon responded, looking at his bedside alarm clock that read four minutes past seven.

'I need you back here,' Paul said, a tenseness to his voice that Simon didn't hear very often.

Simon felt a sickening twist in his stomach at the thought of leaving now. 'I'm needed here, Paul, I can't.'

'What are you talking about, Si?'

'I have some stuff on.'

'Like what?' Paul demanded.

'Some stuff to do with Layfields,' Simon lied, then he felt terrible as he never lied to his uncle.

Paul was the only person in the world who knew the real Simon. Their bond was very strong, and it was something Simon respected greatly. It was the exact feeling he was developing for Beth. How could he leave her now? What would she think?

'Let Damien take care of it,' Paul instructed.

'It's more-'

'God damn it, Simon, what are you playing at? I'm your boss and I'm telling you to get your butt on a plane out here asap. We've got major contractual issues and I need your brain on it. Do I make myself clear?'

No one ever spoke to Simon in the way that Paul did, and Simon always responded to it obediently. He was far more than Simon's boss, he'd been Simon's guardian for many years and he was Simon's only remaining family. Simon knew his duty was to go back and help Paul out as requested, even if it meant sacrificing his future with Beth; or at least his immediate future.

'Of course, Paul, no problem. I'll get the first plane I can. I'll call you from the airport.'

Simon hung up. The excited feelings that had bubbled through him just minutes before were now gone. He was thoroughly disheartened at the thought of going back to America. The timing couldn't have been worse. He feared so much that Beth would just think he was using her.

He phoned downstairs where Jim was making them breakfast. 'Yes sir,' Jim answered.

'I need you to look at flights for me, I have to get back to New York today.'

'No problem, sir, leave it with me,' Jim replied.

Simon sat down on the bed and stared at his mobile. He really wanted to go and see Beth to explain it all, but there just wasn't time. He had to start packing and he had an important meeting that he couldn't postpone. He reluctantly dialled her number, hoping she'd be awake.

'Morning!' her thrilled voice sang on the other end.

'Hi Beth,' Simon said, trying to keep his voice light. 'I didn't wake you up, did I?'

'Don't be silly. Although I am still in my pyjamas! How are you today?'

'I have bad news, I'm afraid.'

'Oh no! Is everything all right?'

'My uncle Paul's just called me and I have to go back to New York. There's some sort of problem and I need to get on the next flight.'

Beth fell silent for a second and Simon prayed that she wouldn't be mad with him. 'That's so rubbish!' she said after a few moments, the disappointment in her voice palpable.

'I'm so sorry, if there was any way I could get out of it.'

'Don't worry, Simon. It's your job. That's more of a home to you anyway isn't it,' she replied, unintentionally stabbing Simon right in the heart.

'It has been,' Simon corrected, now wishing that he'd never been there at all. There was another awkward pause. 'Look, Beth, I'll be back as soon as I can. I don't want to go; if there was any way I could stay, I would. Saturday was the most incredible night. It was the best night of my life. It wasn't just a one night thing for me, you have to know that.'

'Do you mean that?' she asked.

'Most definitely.'

'I'm so glad you said that. It was the best night of my life too. I can't stop smiling!'

'Me too. Well until about five minutes ago when Paul called me back to the States.'

'Listen, as soon as you're back, you're taking me to Piccadilly Circus, you hear me! You're not getting out of it that easily,' she giggled, lightening the mood.

'No question, it's a date. I'll even spend all night on the tube if I have to, just to be with you.'

'How long will you be gone?'

'To be honest, I have no idea. I don't even know what it's all about. But I tell you what, as soon as I get there I'll find out and I'll give you a call. I'll make it the shortest trip I possibly can, I promise.'

'That means so much to me, Simon. I can't wait to see you again. I really hope it's soon.'

'Me too,' he responded.

'Speak to you soon?'

'As soon as I get there. I'm going to speak to you every day, I swear. The Atlantic isn't going to get in our way.'

'You mean that?'

'Every day.'

'I look forward to it. Have a safe trip.'

'Will do. Speak to you later.' Simon hung up the phone and sighed. He was mixed up with feelings of elation from hearing that she hadn't been able to stop smiling and then unbelievable depression at the fact that he probably wouldn't see again her for weeks. Everything in his life had completely changed and he felt exhausted.

Jim knocked on the door and entered. 'Excuse me, sir. I've looked and there's a flight at five o'clock, will that be okay?'

Simon just nodded. 'That's perfect, actually. I'm supposed to have lunch with Derek Field in Croydon and I'd like to still make it if I can. Could you see if he's free at noon and then we'll head to Heathrow after that?' Simon asked.

'Derek Field? As in the CEO of Point Security?' Jim asked.

'Yes, the very same. I need to have a word with him about some of his staff. A couple of men disappointed me on Saturday night, and I'm sure Derek won't like to hear that I'm disappointed.'

'Of course not, sir, I'll give him a call now to move the meeting forward.'

Following a very successful lunch and unusually light traffic on the M25, Simon was now walking into the Heathrow Terminal 5 Departures at a nice and early half past two. Dragging his suitcase behind him into the light, sophisticated departures hall, he checked the board and saw that his flight was on time. Having not spoken to Paul since first thing, he felt he should keep him posted, although Simon was still mad with his uncle for forcing him to return to the States.

'What's the news then, Si?' Paul answered.

'I'm getting the five o'clock. I should be in about half seven your time if you can send a car.'

'I'll come and pick you up, we need to talk about this contract. It's all gone to shit here.'

'Can't you just tell me now?'

'I don't want to talk over the phone.'

'Don't bother then,' Simon retorted, frustrated with the game that his uncle wasn't playing, but that he'd built up in his head that he was. He really didn't want to go back to New York at all.

'What the fuck is it Simon?' Paul snapped. 'What's going on? For years now you've moaned when you've had to go back to the UK, and now I give you a golden reason to come back here and you're having a tantrum.'

'I'm not having a tantrum.'

'Tell me what's going on, Simon. Don't mess me around. Are you in trouble?'

'Of course I'm not.'

'Then what is it?' Paul demanded.

Simon sighed, looking around him to make sure that no one was listening. 'I've met someone,' he muttered after a short pause.

'What do you mean you've met someone?' Paul asked.

'A girl.'

Paul remained silent for a few moments, clearly not expecting Simon to say this. 'You've met a girl?'

'Yes.'

'When?'

'Since I've been back. She works in admin.'

'It's not like before, is it? Is she serious?'

'I can't explain it, Paul. She's not afraid, not repelled. Quite the opposite, she actually enjoys being around me.'

'For real?'

'She started speaking to me, like it was the most normal thing in the world. She's attracted to me, it's amazing.'

'Don't get sucked in Simon. Be careful.'

'If you could only meet her, Paul, you'd know. She's incredible. And beautiful. She's the most perfect girl in the world.'

Again, Paul felt silent. These were unusual words from his nephew and Simon had a passion to his tone that Paul could never have heard before. This was all very new. 'Is it mutual?'

Simon chuckled quietly. 'I think so.'

'But how do you know?'

'The incredible night we spent together kind of gave it away,' Simon replied, not able to resist the broad grin that took over his face.

'You've slept with her?!' Paul gasped.

'It was the best night of my life. I'm in love, Paul.' The broad grin evolved into a warm, affectionate smile as he spoke the words out loud for the first time. He felt a sense of euphoric relief unlock the darkness that had been kept inside of him for so long as he acknowledged his true feelings. 'I'm in love.'

'Does she feel the same way about you?'

'I know she cares for me.'

'Have you told her how you feel?'

'Not completely.'

'Oh for fuck's sake, Simon. Get your butt back over to her and tell her. I've never heard you like this, you sound so different. You're acting so different! Don't let it go.'

'But what about the urgent need for me to get back to the States?'

'Sod that! You're more important. Don't bugger it up now, you tell her.'

'What?'

'Look mate, I just want you to be happy. That's all I've ever wanted. It's broken my heart seeing you so sad and lonely for all these years, and there's nothing I've been able to do about it. The rest of all this shit can wait. I'll see if there's a way you can help us remotely or something, but don't even worry about that at the minute. You just focus on being happy and you make sure you don't let this girl slip away.'

'You don't need me anymore?'

'We always need you Simon, you're the best mind we've got, but you need to worry about yourself right now, you hear?'

'Thanks, Paul. Thank you so much.'

'Doesn't this teach you a lesson?'

'What's that?'

'Be honest with me. If you'd just told me this earlier then I wouldn't have got so mad. For fuck's sake, is this why you were being weird last week? Si, you need to be honest with me!'

'Sorry, it's just been a lot to take in.'

'Tell me, what's her name?' Paul asked.

'Beth. Beth Lance.'

'She's a very lucky girl, I hope she knows that.'

'I'll let you know how it goes,' Simon beamed as he hung up the phone. Wasting no time he redialled his phone to speak to Jim. There was only one place he needed to be now.

TWELVE

Beth knew Simon couldn't possibly be in New York yet, there just hadn't been enough time. It was only the middle of the afternoon, but she couldn't resist checking her mobile every few minutes on the off chance that he might have called. Or texted.

Her thoughts were interrupted by the ringing of her work phone. She saw across its little screen that it was Trisha calling.

'Hello,' Beth answered.

'Can you come to my office?' Trisha ordered.

'Of course,' Beth said, hanging up the phone. She headed behind her and walked into Trisha's office, looking for somewhere to sit.

Her office was the usual mess and Beth had to move a stapler off the chair to make herself comfortable.

Beth felt irritated that everyone praised Trisha so highly for all her hard work, but in reality she wondered how on earth anyone could be good at their job in such a disorganised, chaotic environment. The more Beth thought about it the more she realised that she didn't actually know what Trisha did at all. This was only the second time they'd spoken since Beth's arrival, and

Trisha's betrayal of her employee had left Beth feeling quite bitter.

'Our Sales Director, Mr Rock-' Trisha started.

'Damien?' Beth interrupted.

'That's very familiar of you, Bethany. Where did you hear his name?'

'He introduced himself to me when...' Beth took a second to consider whether she should tell Trisha that she'd been up to the infamous tenth floor or not. Trisha had omitted it from her first day tour and she was nervous about whether she could trust Trisha with anything. However, she was feeling exceptionally empowered today; she was sleeping with the CEO after all. 'I had to help Mr Bird out with something, and Damien introduced himself to me.'

'What are you doing helping Mr Bird out with anything?' Trisha snapped, clearly peeved that her lowly employee was mixing with the big boys.

'It was nothing,' Beth suddenly backed down, her confidence dwindling under Trisha's icy glare. 'I saw Mr Bird in the tea room and he asked me to make him a cup of tea.'

'He spoke to you?'

'Did you not know? He came down to the office and asked me to help him out a second time,' Beth informed her, trying to hide the smile that was so desperate to burst across her face.

Trisha was fuming. 'Why would he ask you to make him tea?'

'I suppose I was just closest to the door,' Beth lied. And this time she meant it.

Trisha's vexation at how Beth was making a name for herself in the office was tangible. 'I want to know why Mr Rock has requested your assistance with a big project he's working on,' she demanded.

'He's what?'

'Don't get too big for your boots, Bethany. Remember

we're a team here; teamwork is all that matters.'

Beth bit her lip, aggravated by Trisha's hypocrisy. In no position to argue, Beth took a second to let her anger subside before she returned to the issue at hand.

'What does Mr Rock want me to do?' she asked.

'I haven't got a clue. Seems I'm not privy to such information, unlike yourself,' Trisha snarled. 'He just said you'll need to work late. Is that going to be a problem?'

'No, Trisha. That's fine, I can work late.'

'I'm glad to hear it. He said he'll ring down for you when you're needed, but it will be after five o'clock. He's a busy man, Bethany, don't mess him around.'

'I wouldn't dream of it.'

'And don't ask too many questions. I've been told you're very nosey. You'll get a bad reputation if you don't start minding your own business.'

'Who's said I'm nosey?' Beth asked defensively, very much hurt by Trisha's accusation.

'Brenda reported back to me after your embarrassing string of questions in the induction. You need to toe the line. You're paid to do your job, if that's not good enough for you, you're free to go elsewhere.'

'Is that a threat?'

'It's a suggestion. Now are you willing to do as Mr Rock asks of you and nothing more?'

'Of course' Beth nodded, roaring anger building up inside.

'You're representing the admin department, remember that. And I'd call him Mr Rock to his face if I were you.' Beth went to argue with her, but realised it was futile. She forced a smile and walked back to her desk, keeping in mind that she had Trisha's ultimate boss as an ally.

The reality of what had just happened then hit her as she sat back down in her seat and a new sense of status poured through her.

Damien - as he had introduced himself - had noticed her. A slight doubt played with her thoughts as she considered that it was somehow related to Simon. She wanted to make her own way in the world and get noticed for her own achievements. But what could Simon have done, she reasoned, he wasn't even in the country, he was half way around the world. This was her moment. As the rage from her encounter with Trisha subsided, she felt very pleased with herself.

Simon was, in fact, now stuck on the M25. He sat in the back of his Lexus, being driven by Jim, but they hadn't moved for quite a while. The traffic report had informed them that the M25 was actually closed up ahead due to a four car pile-up and there was nothing they could do but sit and wait.

Simon checked his watch and saw it was four thirty. They weren't that far from their exit at junction sixteen, but there was no way they were going to get back to the office for five o'clock.

Jim glanced in the rear view mirror at Simon biting his nail anxiously. 'Do you still want me to go to the office, sir?' he asked.

Simon thought through the options in his head. He knew Beth wasn't working that night so he could easily phone her up and agree to meet her somewhere, but that would ruin the surprise.

He was going to tell her that he loved her, it needed to be special. He wanted her to miss him and then it would make his declaration mean so much more. He'd also then know how much she felt the same. It was this that worried him the most. Every inch of his body told him that she felt the same; there was no way anyone could fake such intense emotion. It had to be real, but he needed to see it for himself plain and clear. He wanted to hear either the delight or displeasure in her voice first hand as he told her, not only that he was going to be staying put in the UK more permanently, but also that he was in love with her.

He started to bite his nail again at the thought of the

task ahead of him. He'd dealt with some of the biggest companies and most powerful people in the world without batting an eyelid, but telling the woman he loved that he wanted to be with her was the scariest thing that he'd ever done. This could break him. But he had to do it.

If only he knew her address. He knew she wasn't far from the office, but he couldn't very well roam the streets shouting out her name. Then he remembered flicking through her file in the office. Her address was there.

'Straight back to the office, please Jim. We're going to make a short stop and then on to Beth's.'

'Excellent, sir,' Jim nodded, a slight smile evident on his lips. He was clearly happy with the change in his boss.

It was well after five thirty and Beth was still waiting for Damien's call. The office was now eerily empty and all that could be heard was the whirr of electronic equipment and the tapping of Beth's fingers on her mouse.

She was using her time to try and find more out about her beau. She was now on page twenty-two of her Google search of "Simon Bird CEO Bird Consultants", but other than that one mention of him she'd found the other day, there was nothing. It just wasn't right. He must be somehow manipulating this.

She thought back to that dreadful doorman she'd battled with on Friday night. He'd told her that no one messes with Mr Bird; he'd warned her to keep away, that somehow Simon wasn't good news, and she could tell he really meant it.

Beth felt a chill as she suddenly started questioning who this man really was. Then she thought to his honest declarations about how people treated him. It was blatant to Beth that she wasn't the only one who felt the atmosphere change by his presence, but maybe she was the only one who liked it. There was far more to Simon than she knew, and she suddenly felt knotted at the prospect of finding out.

At the same time, though, the thought that she wasn't going to see him anytime soon devastated her. There were many unanswered questions, but the one thing she knew for sure was that she was in love with him. What on earth could be so bad that she could ever feel differently? To her, he was magnificent. Maybe she was just the only one to be brave enough to see it. He was probably right; whereas the rest of the world had run away in fear of his brilliance, she had taken the time to understand it. That's what made her stand out.

At last her phone rang and she saw it said "Mr Rock" on the screen. This was it.

'Hello, Beth speaking,' she said.

'I'm ready for you now, Beth. If you could join me upstairs.'

Beth clicked off the internet and made her way to the lifts. She took a deep breath as she waited, her imagination now running wild as she fantasised that he'd have a very important job for her with a client. Then she'd meet the client and massively impress them, and then they'd insist that she was the best administrator that they'd ever come across, and suddenly Trisha was being led out of the front door and Beth was being moved into her office as Administration Manager.

The lift chimed and she stepped in, holding back her motivated smile as she pressed for the tenth floor. She could feel this was going to be a vital step towards achieving her ultimate dream.

The tenth floor soon arrived and Beth stepped out into an equally eerie corridor. The silence was very unsettling.

She walked through the glass doors to see Damien typing away at his computer. He immediately stopped when he saw her, brandishing his greasy smile. 'Thank you, Beth, I'm really glad you're here.'

He walked to the desk next to him and rolled his colleague's chair over so they could sit together.

'You're eager to succeed, aren't you Beth?'

She nodded, sitting forward in her chair, ready for action. 'Yes. I'm willing to work as hard as I can and do whatever is needed to achieve great success.'

Damien nodded along, enthusiastically. 'I see a lot of myself in you, Beth. I like it. I wish more people were as eager to succeed as you.'

'Thank you, Damien. How can I help?'

'It's more how I can help you, Beth.' She looked confused, not really sure what he meant. 'I have an opening in sales and you were the first person I thought about.'

'Sales? Wow! That would be incredible.'

'You're up for giving it a go, then?'

'Yes, definitely. Thank you so much.'

'Hang on a second. It's not as easy at that. People don't just get handed jobs like that, do they now. You need to earn your right to it. Otherwise you won't appreciate it, will you Beth?'

'No, of course not. I have some sales experience. It's in the retail world, so it's a bit different.'

'No, no, no, I already know you'll be a perfect fit. You've got passion and drive, and that's what it takes.'

'I don't understand.'

'I just need to know how much you want it. It's a job hundreds would kill for. How far would you go?'

'I don't want to kill anyone!' Beth exclaimed.

Damien laughed. 'I'm glad to hear it. No, I was thinking more of how you could persuade me,' he finished. Then he placed his hand on her thigh.

She knocked it off. 'What are you doing?'

'You scratch my back, Beth, and I'll scratch yours.'

'What are you saying?' she asked, astonished.

He placed his hand on her thigh again. 'If you please me, there's no saying how far you'll go.'

Beth stood up, knocking the chair back behind her. 'How dare you! That's harassment. I'll have you know I'm very good at my job and would make an excellent sales person, and I don't need any special favours from you, thank you very much!' She went to walk off, but suddenly her arm was yanked back behind her.

'Don't be so naïve. How do you think any of us make it in this world?' Damien twisted her round to face him, clutching her arm tightly.

'Most people do it on merit!' she shouted back, trying to pull herself free from his brutal grasp.

'You're so stupid. Of course they don't. The whole of Bird Consultants is built on the very fact that people like to cheat the system. Why be good when you can find a way around it?'

'What do you mean?'

'You don't know anything about what you're getting yourself into. Turning up at parties you're not invited to, making tea for a man you know nothing about. This is a dark world you're trying to worm your way into, I'm just offering you a friendly leg up. You pitch up in my camp and I'll make sure you're taken well care of.'

'I don't need anything from you,' she cried, still trying to break free from him.

'I'll look after you, Beth. Keep you away from the darkness, keep you away from the icy terror.' He grabbed her other arm to hold her still, trying to get her to see sense. 'You want it Beth, I know you do. I can make all your dreams come true. Don't fight it, I'll change your life.'

'Just you wait till I tell Simon about this,' she warned, realising it was futile to struggle against his grip.

'What's he going to care? When he's gone I'm in charge. He's miles away in New York, and he doesn't give a shit about the likes of you. He's in a world of his own, you don't matter to him. You're so stupid.'

'No I'm not!' Beth shouted. 'I'm not! Simon is ten times the man that you are. You just wish you could be like him!'

Damien slapped her hard across the face and Beth fell to the floor, partly against the force, partly due to the shock.

'What the hell is going on here!!' a voice bellowed from the doorway. It was so loud and tempestuous, it shook the room around them. Damien stepped back as he saw Simon's fierce eyes glare at him.

Beth found her feet and ran to Simon. She wrapped her arms around him, so relieved he was there. Her cheek was raw from the slap and confused tears were now pouring down her face. She hid herself against Simon's chest, taking comfort in his secure embrace.

'What's going on?' he repeated, more softly this time.

'Damien offered me a promotion if I slept with him,' Beth sniffled, shaking. She suddenly felt waves of anger physically surge through Simon and it pushed her back. Bewildered, her eyes were drawn to his hands. They were physically pulsating, as if something was bubbling up beneath his skin, like his anger was tangibly taking control.

'Wait here,' he whispered to her, gently moving her aside.

'Is that true?' he said to Damien, who was standing stock still in the middle of the office.

'Of course not,' Damien shouted back. 'This stupid little girl was begging me for a promotion, I was trying to set her straight.'

The fury in Simon took charge and he stepped up to Damien. He grabbed him round the neck and threw him backwards, sending him hurtling through the air with impossible force. He crashed into the glass of Simon's office window and fell sharply to the floor.

Beth stood agape. The force in which Simon had thrown Damien was immense.

Simon strode over and, reaching down in a single, easy movement, he picked up the glass covered man by the neck and raised his legs completely off the floor. It was an incredible strength.

'Leave her alone,' Simon commanded. He threw Damien back towards the middle of the office leaving him to crash to the floor awkwardly on his arm. 'Do I make myself clear?'

Damien just nodded, breathlessly. Beth watched with fear as Damien seemed to take this beating completely in his stride.

Simon was now standing over Damien. He appeared taller and bigger than ever before. 'I never want to see you again. Pack up your things, you're fired,' Simon charged.

He turned to look at Beth and caught the stark astonishment on her face. Her terrified eyes quickly abated his anger and he walked over to her, leaving Damien to fend for himself in a heap. Simon took Beth's trembling hand and led her to the lift.

'What the hell was that!' she gasped, feeling the fury physically pulsate through Simon's fingers.

'Go down to reception. Get in the lift and wait for me down there,' Simon ordered. Beth was desperate to argue, but the ferocity in his eyes told her to listen to him. Utterly confused and scared, she did exactly as he asked and stepped in the lift. She made a short stop at her desk to collect her things and then, not wasting a second more, she headed on to reception as instructed.

She was petrified at the idea of what Simon was going to do. All those rumours about him now circled round her head and she prayed it was going to be all right. As she reached the ground floor she stepped out, shaking, and waited.

Part of her wanted to run away as far as she could. She'd just witnessed something so peculiar, she couldn't make any sense of it. No matter how scared she was, though, her feet refused to budge. No matter how terrifying it had all started to get, there was, strangely, still nowhere else she wanted to be other than with Simon. It was like she was addicted to him.

The lights of the lift finally sparked and she saw the LED above it count up to the tenth floor. She eagerly awaited its return. It slowly started to count back down and, after what seemed like an age, the doors finally opened to reveal Simon, alone. 'Let's get out of here,' he said.

THIRTEEN

'Where's Damien? What have you done with him? Are you just going to leave him up there?' Beth shrieked, following Simon out of the building.

'It's fine, Beth,' Simon shouted back.

'You've just...! Is he hurt? What about your office? There's glass everywhere!'

'It's fine.'

'What was that?' she shouted again, the adrenaline of the past few minutes now taking control.

They walked out into the cool breeze of the evening to find Jim waiting at the end of the footpath. He promptly opened the back door of the car.

Beth stopped still. 'Tell me what that was all about.' She was still terrified of the situation, but she wasn't the slightest bit scared of Simon. She could never be frightened of him. Right now all she wanted was an explanation.

'Damien crossed the line,' Simon stated, turning round to see Beth's fierce glare. 'He hurt you.' He went to touch her red, sore cheek, but she slapped his hand away. Jim suddenly stood up straight, clearly not expecting this turn of events.

'Don't mess me around, Simon.'

'Can we get in the car?' he pleaded.

'I'm not going anywhere until you tell me how you managed to throw him across the room like that. It was crazy!'

Simon looked around, hoping no one could hear them. There were a couple of people across the road, and lots of traffic, but no one was in earshot.

'Get in the car, Beth. I'll talk to you in the car.'

'No!' she asserted back.

'Please Beth. Get in the car,' he calmly asked again.

'Tell me, Simon!'

'I'll tell you everything in the car. I just want to get away from here.'

'Where are we going?'

'I want to take you back to my place.'

'I only live down the road.'

'Yes, and Damien is only a few feet above us. Let's just get away from here, away from him. Then we can talk.'

'If I go with you, will you answer all my questions?' Beth snapped.

'If you get in the car, I will answer any questions you have. I promise.'

Beth hesitated for effect, and then strutted towards the car. She sat down on the soft leather seat and Jim closed the door. Then he walked around to let Simon in beside her.

The car pulled off in the opposite direction to her flat, away from London. Beth looked out of the window, not daring to face Simon. She was furious. But then it occurred to her she didn't know why.

Simon had just turned up and saved her. Again. It was the second time in three days she'd been put in an awful situation, and the second time he'd been her knight in shining armour. Shouldn't she at least be a little grateful?

She took a few breaths and let her anger towards him subside. Then she turned her head to find him staring at her. He was waiting for her to say something.

'How did you manage to throw Damien so far across the room?' she asked, determined to get to the bottom of the irrational event.

Simon considered his response. 'You know you hear about those people who have inner strength when they need it. I guess that's what happened. It made me so mad that he hurt you.'

'Inner strength? It was more hulk-like.'

'Don't be silly, Beth. You're just stressed. It wasn't that far really.'

'You crashed him through your office window!'

'It was an accident.'

'Is he even alive?'

'There's nothing wrong with him. I made sure of that. That's what I went back for.'

'You could have killed him.'

'I knew what I was doing.'

'Did you, though? I felt the rage. It was like it was physically surging through you. I could actually feel it.'

'Of course you couldn't!' Simon snapped defensively.

'What if you'd killed him?'

'He's absolutely fine. Please stop it. I saw him hurt you, I felt quite mad, we had a fight, I came out on top and now he's out of our lives forever. What else do you imagine happened?'

Beth couldn't answer. Maybe she was all confused. Damien had hit her quite hard.

'Okay, answer me this,' she started, gripping on to something that she wasn't at all confused about. 'Why is it there are practically no mentions of you on the internet? You're rich and wealthy, and that doorman at the weekend told me everybody knows who you are, yet I can't find anything out about you.'

'You Googled me?' he asked, a hint of flattery to his tone.

'I tried. You just don't exist.'

'I know. But I don't know why.'

'Of course you don't!' she retorted sarcastically. 'Have you been manipulating it? Do you pay people to erase all mention of you online? What sort of world do you live in? What are you trying to hide?' She was now getting quite angry again.

'Right, Beth,' Simon asserted, staring straight at her. 'Firstly, I have never paid anyone to erase a mention of me online. People have, and often do say what they like about me. It's just part of my life. However, if they don't choose to say it online, that's their business. I told you the other day that people seem to fear me, so maybe that's the reason. But I can only guess at that, Beth. I know as much as you do.' Beth kept quiet, processing his firm response.

'Secondly, why do you think I'm trying to hide something? What is it you want to know? Can't you just take me as I am? Am I not enough as I am?'

His question silenced her. He was enough. She didn't even know why she was so mad with him anymore. She tried to search for a reason why she felt so angry. She knew he had secrets, but maybe they were all connected to his job and they didn't affect him as a person at all. Then she remembered what Damien had told her.

'Damien said that you live in a dark world. He told me that Bird Consultants was about helping people cheat the system. He talked about an icy terror. Why would he say all that? I know you're hiding something, because none of us are allowed to know anything about the company. We're not told and we're not allowed to ask. What do you do, and why is it so bad that it's all so confidential?'

Simon took a second to consider his response carefully. 'It's true, our clients do ask us to help them in ways that some people may see as, perhaps, immoral. Power and money give people options that others may not have. When I first started at the company I'd do anything the client wanted. I loved the rush of helping people and the rewards they'd give to me in return. But not anymore.

Everything I do now is for the greater good. I wouldn't do anything bad. And as questionable as some things I've done in the past have been, I've certainly never done anything illegal. I swear.'

'What does all that mean? How do you help them?'

'I have a gift, Beth. I can... I don't know. I can work problems out for clients in ways they couldn't possibly manage without me. I'm very intelligent and have a unique way of looking at the world.'

'What sort of problems?' she asked, calming down as she was finally getting some answers.

'Anything. It could be they have a problem with a member of staff; or they're being sued by a disgruntled customer. It could be absolutely anything. I just come in as a consultant and... help magic their problems away.'

'That seems quite reasonable. So why all the secrets?'

'Trust me, most of these customers don't want anyone knowing their business. They just want their problems gone. It's on a need to know basis only.'

'That's sort of what the induction video I was made to watch said.'

'There you go.'

Beth turned to look out of the window again to process all the information that had just been thrown her way, but something still niggled at her. She couldn't help feeling it didn't all add up.

Her mind was suddenly cleared when she saw them arrive at a house. She looked around to see very little else, just a couple of similar looking houses much further down the road. They waited for the big iron gates to slowly open and they drove into the large driveway.

The house was massive. It was fairly modern and beautifully symmetric in a gorgeous orange brick colour.

The car stopped right outside the front door and Jim came round to let Beth out. Simon then let them both in the house and they entered the hallway.

She stepped in slowly and absorbed his home for the

first time. It was magnificent.

The whole essence was gleaming white and the grand staircase that arched across the reception area was breathtaking. There were doors off in all directions, but it was to their right where Simon led Beth.

Behind the door was his lightly decorated, cream living room.

'Take a seat,' he offered, heading towards the back of the room to find the drinks cabinet. 'Can I get you anything?'

Beth felt bemused. 'Why am I here?' she demanded as Simon poured her a glass of wine before helping himself to a whiskey.

He handed her the glass, but she refused to move. 'Why am I here?' she repeated.

He placed the glasses on the coffee table and looked back at her. 'I just want you to be safe.'

'I wish you'd taken me home,' she muttered. Her head was fuzzy with all the commotion of the past hour. She couldn't work out how she'd managed to find herself now standing in this massive house that left her feeling so small and insignificant. He had so much money. She'd never really considered how much until now. What was she doing with him? This was all so drastically out of her comfort zone.

She couldn't remember a day in her life that she'd felt scared before moving to London. Nothing ever used to bother her. She'd always seen life as an adventure that you had to go and make happen, and her move to London was supposed to be about making dreams come true. But now she felt trapped in a world that she didn't understand and she just wanted to go home. She could sense herself changing with every second that she spent with Simon, and she wasn't sure whether it was a change for the good.

'Please can I go home?' she asked.

'Beth, please stay. I don't want you to leave like this. Have a drink with me.'

A new thought then entered her head. 'Why are you even here? Aren't you meant to be in New York?'

'I didn't go. As you can tell.'

'Why not?'

Simon walked away and pretended to examine the drinks cabinet again. 'I needed to come back.'

'What for? Damien? Did you know?'

'Of course I didn't.'

'Then what? A customer?'

'No, nothing like that,' he answered, still not able to look at her.

'What then? Why don't you tell me anything? What was it? Work? Your car? Your house? Another woman? What is it? Why won't you tell me! Why do you never tell me!' she shrieked, now absolutely at a loss with this man.

'It's you!' he shouted, turning to face her, for the first time really losing control. 'You! I came back for you!'

Beth was silenced. He walked over to her and looked her straight in the eye. He looked so vulnerable, almost scared. The stern expression that so often struck his face had vanished, leaving the exposed scrapings of a helpless man behind, and she swore she could see the ghost of a tear in his eye. It thawed her heart.

'I'm in love with you, Beth. I love you.' Beth's breath was extinguished as the words hit her soul.

'You love me?'

'I'm crazy about you. I couldn't go back to New York.'

'You came back for me?'

'Yes. I love you.'

'I love you too,' she told him, feeling the sting of tears in her eyes. She reached up and kissed him gently on the lips. It was a loving kiss, the lust of the other night now replaced with far more tenderness and meaning.

They enjoyed a few moments of their silent embrace before Simon tucked her straggled hair neatly behind her ears and whispered to her, 'Come and sit down.' She took his hand and they sat on the middle of his three sofas. 'I'm not easy, Beth, I know that. It's a rollercoaster for both of us. But I want to start this journey with you, if you'll have me.'

'You want to start a relationship with me?'

'I'd love to call you my girlfriend.'

Her lips bounced into a smile as the thought spiralled through her delightfully. 'I'd like that too.'

'I know you're so confused and have so many questions. My life is very complicated. I'd give anything to change that, but it's the hand I've been dealt. But I won't ever hurt you, Beth. You can trust me.'

Beth nodded. Maybe she had been a bit harsh. After all, he'd answered all her questions, what was she expecting? Just because they weren't the answers she wanted, it doesn't mean they weren't the truth. She wanted some sort of incredible declaration that gave her absolute explanations as to all the craziness, but sometimes things weren't that black and white. She was learning that quickly.

He worked in a corrupt world, that was clear, but that didn't make him bad. People strangely feared his presence and so they didn't write about him on the internet; that wasn't his fault. In fact it was his very presence that Beth found so intoxicating. She couldn't have it both ways. She suddenly felt foolish for being so angry.

'I'm sorry,' she whispered.

'For what?'

'You came to my rescue – again – and all I've done is shout at you.'

'You were scared, I understand. I'm just so sorry these awful things keep happening to you. But don't worry, Damien's gone now, you'll never have to see him again.'

A thought then struck Beth and her face dropped. 'If I'm your girlfriend, does this mean I'll have to leave Bird Consultants?'

'You better not leave! Look at it this way, no one knows the first thing about me, they all hate me.'

'They don't hate you!' Beth corrected.

'They don't like me. So it's none of their business. And who are you going to tell?' He paused for thought. 'You work for Trisha, don't you?' Beth nodded. 'And she works for Gus, who works for Eric, the Administration and Contracts Director. Then he works for me.'

'Woah, I really am sleeping with the boss!' Beth chuckled.

'My point is, we're so far apart at work, it doesn't matter.'

'And you're barely there,' she added, sadly.

'That's going to have to change. I'm the CEO of the UK office, I think it's time I take up the role more permanently, don't you?'

'Really!' Beth squealed, and then she hugged him tightly.

'Please don't leave, Beth. And please say you'll be my girlfriend.'

'There's nothing more in this world I want. Or for that matter, have ever wanted. But if I'm going to stay then we definitely need to keep it a secret at work. You sent ripples through the office the day you asked me to find tea bags.'

'Ripples?'

'It was the biggest thing that had ever happened, I'm not kidding. And did you hide those tea bags? There were plenty of them a couple of hours before.'

'No!' Simon insisted. Beth looked at him disbelieving. 'I binned them. They looked old and like they'd gone off.'

'I knew it! Well you can't come into the office to speak to me anymore, not like that. I don't think Michelle can take it. But I can still come and visit you and make you tea, can't I? The tenth floor is tabooed after all.'

'It's what?'

'Trust me, people don't like going up there. But the other directors don't seem to care when I'm up there.'

'That's sorted then. But I need at least ten cups of tea a day,' Simon informed her, pretending to be deadly serious.

They kissed again, warmly and softly, and this time it

was the easiest kiss they'd had, now both safe in the knowledge that their feelings were definitely mutual. They were now officially in love.

Late that night, after they'd made love again, Simon lay wide awake, troubled. Beth was curled up in his arms, but Simon couldn't sleep. He stared at the ceiling, listening to the soft breathing of her slumber. She was the first woman that had ever shared this bed with him, but his joy was tarnished with fear.

She'd seen him at his worse that night, and although she was still there he felt terrified that she was going to leave him.

She was right, he was keeping something from her. But how could he tell her? Surely it would be the last straw. She could only just about cope with everything believing it was her stress that had made it seem as bad as it was. How was he going to explain the truth to her? He didn't want to lose her, and she'd have to know one day if they were going to stay together. He just didn't want the truth about him to be the reason she left.

He grappled with anxiety until the early hours, trying to work out the best way to tell her who he really was. But every time he played it out in his head, she always ran off screaming. How could he ask anyone to deal with this? It was his burden and his curse, and he was so afraid it would hurt her. But he was too far in, now, he loved her too much just to walk away. What was he going to do?

* * *

About ten miles away, in a house a bit smaller than Simon's, Damien sat at the desk in his bedroom. It was a brown room, dimly lit against the darkness of the night. He held a small black metal box in his hand and he was studying it thoughtfully.

The events of that night were racing through his mind -

how Simon had turned up, how angry he'd been, how softly he'd looked at Beth; it was all so very telling.

Then he thought to the party, when Simon had been asking about Beth, then how she'd been making him drinks in the office; it was all so obvious. Simon had a weakness. The glorious, unbreakable CEO, who was blessed with such power and such wealth, finally had a weakness. It was too good an opportunity to miss.

Damien placed the metal box on the oak desk before him and opened it up. Inside was a mound of red power that mystically radiated a gold blaze. Damien looked at it hard, and then a broad, sinister smile spread across his face. Now was his time. At last.

FOURTEEN

As Beth rubbed her eyes the next morning she was momentarily confused as to where she was, not at all able to make sense of her surroundings. Then, as the unexpected tenderness to her cheek stung against her touch, she was quickly dragged back to reality.

It had been a tempestuous night before, but Beth felt very satisfied by how it had ended and she couldn't resist the smile that crept on her lips as she replayed the moment in her mind when Simon declared his love for her.

She looked at the digital alarm clock on the bedside table and it said nine forty-five. She jumped out of bed, suddenly very aware that she was naked, and panicked. Simon was nowhere to be seen. She thought about going to look for him, but the realisation that Jim could be lurking about deterred her.

She got back under the soft blue sheets and reached down for her bag which was laid on the floor beside her. She pulled out her phone and called Simon.

'Good morning!' he chirped. 'What are you doing?'

'Where are you? Why have you left me on my own? Do you know what time it is?!'

'Stop worrying. I'm just downstairs making you

breakfast. I'll be up in a second.'

Beth hung up, half her panic gone, but she still couldn't believe she was in bed at this time on a Tuesday. What was Trisha going to say?

She looked around for her clothes, but she couldn't see them anywhere. Simon was such a neat freak, she guessed he'd probably tidied them away somewhere. She had no choice but to wait for him.

She breathed for a second, telling herself that she was with Trisha's boss's boss's boss, so at least she wouldn't be getting the sack. But she was still quite miffed that Simon hadn't woken her earlier.

She waited impatiently, feeling once again dwarfed by Simon's enormous bedroom. This room alone was bigger than the whole of Beth's studio flat.

Simon finally returned sporting a tray of breakfast delights in his hands. 'Tuck in when you're ready,' he said as he lay the tray on the desk at the back of the room.

'Thank you. This is lovely, but why didn't you wake me? I'm so late. Trisha will be fuming. And I don't have anything to wear.' Beth spoke as calmly as she could, trying not to seem too ungrateful for his gesture of breakfast in bed.

'First things first,' Simon replied reassuringly. 'I called Trisha earlier and said that you'd be helping me out with a few things for the next couple of days so you wouldn't be in. At least when it comes from me, no one questions it.'

'You shouldn't have done that! She wasn't happy when Damien wanted to see me, she'll have kittens over me doing work for you. Why did you do that?' Beth's calm demeanour had quickly vanished.

'Don't be mad, I felt guilty. You were so deeply asleep and you've had such a rough few days. I insist, as the boss, that you take a couple of days off. Trisha will understand; surely you helping me out is a good thing?'

'She'll want to know why you didn't ask her! Trust me, I'll pay for this.'

Simon looked at Beth with confusion. 'You'll pay for this? What does that mean?'

'Trisha! She's not very nice.'

'She just takes some getting used to, I'm sure she'll be fine.'

Beth rolled her eyes and shook her head, annoyed that Simon couldn't see Trisha for who she really was. There was nothing she could do about it now, though, she'd just have to face the backlash when she returned to the office. At least she had Simon's support; that counted for a lot.

'You look like you're ready to go into the office,' Beth countered, pointing out Simon's fully suited state.

'I'm only popping in for a short while. I have to sort out all this crap with Damien and then I'll be straight back, I promise.'

'He's still fired isn't he?'

'Very much so. That's why I want to go in this morning and make sure it's all finalised and official. I just need to sign the paperwork and then I'm coming back to take you out to lunch. Is that okay?'

'What a life! You can turn up late and then take the day off, just like that,' Beth stated through a cheeky smile.

'One of the perks you'll no doubt enjoy when you're running your own business,' Simon grinned. 'Anyway, I've lived and breathed nothing but work for the last decade. I think it's more than about time I had a day off for me, don't you?'

'When you say it like that, I suppose it's okay. That just leaves one problem, what on earth am I going to wear? I don't really fancy going for lunch in your clothes, or worse, naked!' Beth smirked.

'That's all in hand. Jim has already washed all the clothes you were wearing yesterday. You can pop them on for now and then he's going to take you out shopping to get something else to wear.'

Beth considered this. 'I suppose I could use some of my winnings from last week to get some new stuff. And I have just been paid as well.'

'Nonsense, Jim will get it on my card.'

'Do we have to have this discussion again?!' Beth warned.

'Yes we do. You're going to do as you're told for a change and you're going to let me buy you a couple of new outfits.'

'But-'

'You can leave them here if you want and just use them as outfits for when you visit. I don't care what you do with them, but you have to accept my offer and I won't hear another word about it. Now you're my girlfriend, you're going to have to get used to being spoilt! What's the point in being rich if you can't spend it on the woman you love?' Simon's commanding tone was laced with kindness.

'You don't have to do this.'

'I want to. And I want you to let me.'

Beth nodded sweetly, so genuinely touched by Simon's lovely gesture. Although she was already working out the cheapest places to shop so as to not take advantage of him.

It was nearly eleven when Simon parked his Aston Martin in his reserved space at the back of the Bird Consultants office block.

He walked round to the entrance and opened the glass doors into the reception area, straight away greeted by the usual icy silence from the staff that surrounded him, a reaction he'd become almost immune to over the years. He, in return, just ignored everyone else, it had made life so much easier for him.

He reached the tenth floor and headed towards his office, not at all acknowledging the miraculously fixed windows, not a piece of smashed glass in sight. Business all seemed to be carrying on as normal. That was, however, until he saw Damien sitting cheerily at his desk, typing away.

'Morning, Si!' Damien sang, a slime to his tone that

aggravated Simon even more.

'In my office, now!' Simon ordered, striding across the floor and unlocking his office door.

'Can I help?' Damien asked, following Simon as if everything was just fine and dandy.

'What are you doing here?'

'I work here.'

'Not any more you don't. Didn't I make myself clear last night?'

'Ohh!' Damien chuckled with weighted pretence. 'I didn't think you were serious.'

'You're fired, Damien. Get your stuff and leave.'

'No,' Damien simply responded.

'Get your stuff and leave,' Simon commanded, the power of his voice now starting to shake the room.

'I'd say make me, but we both know you can. Does your lovely little Beth know about that?'

'Leave her out of it.'

'Does she know how far you could really go?'

'I said leave her out of it,' Simon demanded again.

'I think maybe it's time she knows the truth, don't you?'

'Don't!'

'She and I could have a little chat. I think she needs to know what sort of man she's desperate to get into bed with... so to speak.'

Simon didn't respond. He stared hard at Damien trying not to react, but it was too late. Damien's flow was halted as he caught the fiery glint now evidently burning in Simon's eyes at the mention of getting into bed with Beth.

'Why are you looking like that?' Damien asked, confused. 'I don't think I like that look. No. You couldn't have. That's not possible!'

'Leave,' Simon ordered.

'I knew she had ambition, but...'

'I'm not going to keep asking you.'

'I have to admit, I didn't see that coming. Well done

you.'

Simon was now breathing intensely as his anger escalated.

'She must be more desperate than I gave her credit for to fuck such an icy freak like you,' Damien stated, shaking his head. 'She definitely deserves a promotion, I have to hand it to her.'

'Get out now!!' Simon bellowed, sending shivers across the room again, the atmosphere charging with his rage.

'You only have to ask. I'm not Beth, you don't have to beg,' Damien said before suddenly exiting Simon's office. He paced out across the main floor and started to grab paperwork from all the other directors' desks, throwing the items messily around. He then opened a cabinet in the corner and threw files out in all directions.

'Get out!' Simon demanded, his rage now peaking at Damien's callous, ridiculous behaviour.

'Why?' Damien asked, looking at Simon innocently.

Simon stood still, not sure what his next move should be, so strange was Damien's behaviour. He couldn't let Damien dominate him. No one ever got the better of Simon like this. He took a few calming breaths to consider his options, although he could barely cool his fury.

'Okay. Say please and I'll leave,' Damien offered, very seriously.

Simon didn't respond. He stood still, trying to work out what Damien's game was. This was more than just random behaviour, Damien had an angle, but Simon could not see what it was. 'Pretty please,' Damien continued.

Simon felt trapped. He didn't want to lose his temper like the night before, especially not in front of the other six directors, who were now staring agape at the performance being played out in front of them, but at the same time he needed to assert his authority. Then he saw what he needed to do.

'You're fired, Damien. Don't act like such a fool. I've asked you to leave, and if you don't leave in the next hour there will be consequences.'

'I'm so scared!' Damien responded sarcastically.

Simon turned to Eric, the usually stressed out Administration and Contracts Director, who also oversaw personnel issues as part of his remit. 'Eric, I want Damien gone by close of play today. Do whatever you need. You have my full authority to do anything that's required. I want him gone and with all the paperwork sorted by nine am tomorrow, do I make myself clear? I do not want to be disappointed.' Eric nodded, knowing he had no choice.

Damien stood still in the middle of the office and glared at Simon. Simon simply turned back into his office, picked up his bag, then came back out, locked the door, strode across the floor and left.

He headed straight back into the lifts, not stopping all the way to the ground floor. He walked out across the reception area, so totally lost in the confusion of Damien's shameful behaviour, he didn't even have chance to acknowledge the standard icy silence that always met his presence.

The more he thought about what had happened, the angrier he became. By the time he got back to his car his fury was flaring. What game was Damien playing at? He'd managed to wriggle right under Simon's skin and scrape viciously at his nerves.

Simon suddenly felt very flustered. He wasn't used to feeling such intense anger and it was grating at him. He suddenly started scratching his right harm ferociously, barely reaching the itch beneath his suit jacket and shirt.

He knew he just had to get home. He started the engine, still scratching at his arm, and headed away from the office, from Heaningford, and back to his house.

As he drove on, he couldn't stop the thought of Damien's behaviour playing round and round in his head. The rage within him exploded as he recalled Damien's words about Beth. Would Damien really tell her the truth? Simon knew it would be so much worse coming from

Damien than from himself. He couldn't let that happen.

His frustration and panic grew, and along with it so did the intensity of his itch. He scratched on with intent, still not quite getting to the core of the irritation.

He finally reached the welcoming gates of his home, the itching now unbearable. He stopped the car right outside the front door and raced straight inside, making a beeline for his bedroom up the stairs.

He charged into the room, now jittery against the force of the irritation. He paced around, not sure what to do next, his head a jumbled mess.

Beth suddenly appeared at the bedroom door having heard the commotion. 'Simon, what is it?' she asked, full of concern.

'Just that prat, Damien. He was there. He was refusing to leave.'

'What? What's he playing at?'

'That's what I'd like to know!'

Beth noticed Simon itching his arm ferociously. 'Have you hurt yourself, are you okay?'

'I'm fine, I just can't believe him. His behaviour last night was shocking, I was so mad with him anyway, and then this morning it was just humiliating.'

'Has he left now?'

'Someone else is dealing with him now,' Simon mumbled, becoming wholly distracted by the itchiness on his arm. He needed to try and do something about it. He yanked his suit jacket off and threw it to the floor, before quickly unbuttoning his shirt to get to the core of the problem. He needed to relieve this discomfort once and for all.

As his shirt hit the floor, Beth's gasp was alarming. He looked at her, not sure what was so wrong.

'What is that?' she shrieked, pointing to Simon's arm.

He looked down to his right arm, where the itch had been so terrific, and saw in its place a bright red feather poking out from his skin.

FIFTEEN

Beth couldn't work out what unnerved her more, the fact that Simon had grown a feather or the fact that he didn't seem that freaked out by it. She sat on the bed startled.

'Beth,' Simon said, coming to her side. 'It's fine.'

'What the hell is that?' she gasped, backing away from him. 'Have I just not noticed that before?' She was now getting panicky.

'I don't know what this is.'

'How can you be so calm? You've sprouted a feather!'

Simon looked down at it. As far as random, abnormal growths went, it was beautiful. It was a bright scarlet colour and felt like satin to the touch, like no bird either of them had ever seen. It shimmered against the sunlight that poured in through the window.

'I don't know what this is, Beth,' he repeated, flustered. She knew he wasn't flustered by the feather, though, he was far more worried about her reaction.

'This is very weird, Simon. What's going on? Is this something you've been hiding from me?'

'No! I've never had a feather. I've never seen anything like this before in my life, I swear.'

'Then why aren't you freaking out? I don't get it. It's just another of part of the random, bizarre, utter fucking craziness that I've had to deal with since meeting you.' Beth was properly agitated now. She walked towards the window, looking for an escape that she didn't really want but that she couldn't really not want either, and tried to fathom some logic from all the recent events. She felt sick.

'Beth, you have to believe me, I don't know where this has come from.'

'Is there something wrong with you? People just don't have moments like this in their life. Is it me? Am I losing my mind? What's going on?'

'Okay,' Simon interjected, but it didn't help, the ramble continued.

'I can't take this. This is all too much. I want to be worried about you, I want to help you, but I see something that's so far off the wacky scale it's practically unbelievable, and you don't even seem that bothered. If I wasn't looking at the fact that a feather was sticking out of your skin right now...!'

'Okay,' Simon repeated a little louder, standing up to try and regain some sort of control on the situation.

'Not stuck in by accident, either. Not that you've fallen on it somehow or you've been playing with a bird and part of it's got caught on you. Not anything reasonable or logical. You've actually spontaneously grown a feather overnight. I just wouldn't believe it if I wasn't looking at it.'

'I said okay!' Simon was really losing his temper now.

'And you seem far more concerned with how I'm going to react than the fact that you've got plumage. Why is it that that's not the thing that weirds you out? I can't cope anymore Simon. I can't. Too much craziness in too little time. I can't!'

'Sit down!' he bellowed. Beth felt the ground beneath her shake. Rattled now by the force of his voice, she did as she was told and sat down on the bed facing him. 'You want to know?' he shouted, 'You want to know? Then I'll tell you. I'll tell you everything. I'll tell you what I'm so desperately hiding, I'll tell you what Bird Consultants is really all about and why we try so hard to not let the secret out. I'll tell you every sordid detail. But you have to promise me one thing in return.'

Simon was actually now close to tears and Beth felt terrible for her selfish rant. This man was clearly going through something enormous and all she'd thought about was herself. He looked more stripped back and more exposed than she'd ever seen him before, and she knew that he was about to bear all. This was it.

'What?' she asked.

'No matter what I'm about to say, no matter how much it scares you, promise me you won't just leave; you won't just run away. If you don't want to be with me anymore, that's fine. I'd hate it, but I'd completely understand. But let's at least leave each other amicably. Let's at least honour the love we've felt and say goodbye properly.'

Beth's heart pounded at his desperate plea. What was he about to say to her? She felt petrified, but she needed to know, and she'd give him a fair hearing, whatever it was. She owed him so much respect, and she'd honour that truthfully.

'You have my word,' she said, anxiously awaiting his admission.

As sick as it made her feel, as she sat and waited for him to find the words to begin, she found herself transfixed with his new growth. She couldn't take her eyes off it. Seeing her unable to look at anything else, Simon went to his wardrobe and pulled out a black jumper to cover it up. Using the moment to gather this thoughts, he finally found where to start.

'I'm part of a group,' he said, like this explained a lot.

'Like the Masons?' she asked.

'No, nothing like that. It's something I've been born into. It's called the Malancy.'

'Never heard of it,' she clarified.

'You wouldn't have.' He sat down next to her and tried to explain it better.

'A few hundred years ago there was a family. They were good, honest people who suffered a terrible tragedy. After losing much of their property to a theft, their house then burned down one night and in it their two sons were killed.'

'That's awful. What happened?'

'No one's ever known for sure, but everyone's always suspected foul play.'

'Everyone?' Beth asked.

'The Malants. As we're known. The couple were devastated, as you can imagine, feeling the pain of losing everything they had. Hitting absolute rock bottom, they disappeared for a few days. No one knows what happened to them. Some conspiracies believe they sold their souls to the devil, others say they were killed and reincarnated somehow; I don't really know what I think. You see when they turned up again, completely out of the blue, they had some sort of... power. They could harness the elements around them and... do magic.'

'They were magicians?'

'Not really,' Simon smiled. 'This power started a new timeline. They had another son and they passed the power on to him. Then, when he married, he passed it on to his children, who passed it on to their children, who passed it on and passed it on, and to cut a long story short, today thousands of people possess this gift and have these magical powers.'

Beth snorted, not sure if it was a joke or not. 'So you're telling me there are thousands of magicians living around us?'

'Not magicians.'
'Wizards?'
'No!'
'Oh no, sorry, warlocks?'

'Beth, this is not some fantasy fiction where I wear a black cloak and wave a wand around, I just am what I am.'

'So you have this gift?' she asked, still dubious.

'Yes... but more than that. Oh Beth, I didn't want to tell you this so soon. I don't want you to hate me. Please don't hate me!' The distress on his face was now glaringly apparent.

'What is it?' she asked, uneasily.

'There's a very good reason why people don't take to me. It's not in anyone's imagination, it's real.' Beth waited fretfully for his confession. 'My parents were part of the Malancy, so inevitably I am too. But I was born with a gift that no Malant has ever had before. I was born differently to anyone ever. Every other Malant can harness nature around them and make things happen; cast spells if you like. They can use the wind or the rain or coal or insects; the possibilities are endless, but it's all about their surroundings. I, on the other hand, was born with the power locked deep inside.'

Beth screwed up her face, not sure what he meant, the whole story seeming massively implausible to her.

'I was born with the ability to create magic autonomously. I don't need other elements, I can just do it. Yes, for some things I need external resources, like when I require a large amount of power, but mostly I have the gift within me. And that's a unique characteristic. Nobody has ever existed with such power before.'

'What are you talking about? Are you saying you possess magical powers?'

'Yes. Hence the fact that I could throw Damien halfway across the room, I just used my spiritual strength. I could have thrown him much further, believe me, and my anger doesn't help much in controlling it all.'

'You can move stuff, like, with your mind?'

'Let me show you,' he said. He looked at the pillow lying on the bed beside him and it promptly flopped on the floor.

'You kicked the bed!' Beth argued.

Sighing, Simon tried again, this time upping the ante. He looked to his desk and concentrated. It obediently shifted, levitating a metre in the air, until Simon nodded his head and gently brought it back to its position on the floor. Beth's jaw dropped open.

'What the hell was that?' she gasped.

'I told you, I have a gift.'

'And you're on your own?'

'Not as a Malant, just with the power to do these things without the need of any other element to help me. You've seen how people react to me, Beth. That's the power.'

'But you said there were other, whatever you call them.'

Simon paused for a second, finding a way to help her understand. 'There are probably dozens of Malants you've met in your life. We're just like normal people; we are normal people, but we have a gift for invoking the elements. Damien's a Malant, for example. So are all the directors of Bird Consultants.'

'What?'

'You couldn't tell could you? They're not different. Just me. I was born with this power and it oozes from me, there's nothing I can do about it. Everyone I go near feels it. I know I change the ambience of every room I enter, and I know it scares everyone I meet. People sense the power that radiates from my pores and it terrifies them. It's not natural, it's not meant to be this way. You can't blame them for not understanding it, and as they don't understand it, they fear it. They fear me.'

'I don't fear you,' Beth confirmed.

Simon's faced softened and he gently curled a tuft of hair around Beth's ear. 'You're the first person I've ever met to not fear me. You don't seem to find my presence overwhelming or intimidating, and that's such a breath of fresh air. Even my parents found me hard to be around. So does my uncle Paul. They learnt to tolerate it, granted, but no one's ever accepted it as you have. Beth, you're amazing.'

Beth remained silent. The information she'd been hit with during the last few minutes had been engulfing and she needed time to process it all. Her boyfriend was not only part of a secret magical organisation, but he had the unique attribute of being the only ever truly magical one with the exclusive ability to channel power with only his mind. That about summed it up to Beth. She wanted to be scared and she wanted to be mad and she wanted to declare that none of this could possibly be true, but deep down inside she was just relieved. This explained so much. She was finally scratching that niggling itch herself, and it was liberating. She had so many more questions.

'So this explains your crazy presence and why people detract from you so much,' she uttered, 'but where does Bird Consultants fit into it all? And what has any of this got to do with your feather?'

'Let's get to Bird Consultants,' he started, then he looked around the room. 'Come on, shall we go downstairs, I need a drink.'

Simon led Beth out of the bedroom and they headed down towards the living room. He went straight for his drinks cabinet and looked inside. 'You want anything?' he asked.

She thought hard. It was only just the afternoon, but something to help calm her nerves did seem appealing. It was way too early for whiskey, though.

'Would it be possible for me to have a beer?' she asked.

'Of course,' Simon responded. 'Actually, a beer sounds great.' He walked to the stylish black sideboard at the back of the room and dialled the phone.

'Can you bring us two beers, please? We're in the lounge, thanks.' Simon hung up and invited Beth to sit down next to him on the middle sofa, where they'd sat and made up the night before.

The silence was awkward. The sound of the brown clock ticking on the wall was all that could be heard as they waited for their beers to arrive.

Jim soon entered the room and placed two bottles of Budweiser on coasters on the coffee table before them.

'Is there anything else you need?' he asked politely.

'I don't want any disturbances, Jim. For the rest of the day.'

'Of course, no problem.' Jim then left, quietly shutting the door behind him.

Simon took a sip of his beer and considered where to start.

'Bird Consultants,' he said after a second. 'I suppose I should start at the beginning. When I was born my parents didn't know what to do with me, my power was so strong. They could see how it repelled people and they got scared. They made the hard decision to turn their backs on the Malancy and to raise me with no knowledge of my heritage at all. We moved out of London, where I was born, to the Kent coast. There are very few Malants that way, and they thought we could start afresh.

'I could feel – can feel – the power inside me, but without knowing any different, I just assumed it was normal and never questioned it. People always took an instant dislike to me, but my parents kept me away from the hurt as much as they could. Kids get bullied, I just thought I was unlucky.'

He paused and took another sip of his beer. Then he took a deep breath. 'When I was fourteen my parents died.'

'Oh Simon, I'm so sorry,' Beth said, squeezing his leg in sympathy.

'They went out to a restaurant one night. It was a trendy French place out in the sticks and I'd been allowed to stay at home alone. There was a gas explosion at the restaurant and...'

'You poor thing, I had no idea. You only ever talked about your uncle Paul, but I assumed it was just because he worked with you. I'm so sorry.'

'Paul is my only remaining family. I'd never met him before. Obviously being a Malant too, my parents wanted to keep me away from him. He disagreed with their decision to hide me away and so they sort of fell out. I had no choice but to go and live with him in Clapham, back in London, after it happened, and he opened my world up. He told me everything and helped me understand my power and who I am. He also helped me control my strength. He was, and still is, everything to me.'

'I can't imagine what you must have gone through.'

'I was quite mad with my parents at first for hiding the truth. I suppose it helped with the grieving too, feeling they'd wronged me; I could reject them completely. But over the years I've learnt to respect their decision. I was their little boy and they were scared. I understand.'

They both took a second to reflect upon his words. This was a lot of information to process, and Beth was quickly getting through her beer, which she was now grasping tightly in her hand.

'Before I even went to live with him, Paul was in the process of starting up his own business. He was a keen entrepreneur and had done a few things here and there, but he was starting to see how the power of the Malancy could be of real benefit to non-Malants. And, let's be honest, he could see the tremendous amounts of money that it could make him. Others had tried to do something similar in the past, but Paul was clever. He knew how to do it so it worked. He had to get approval from the Malancy first, though.'

'What do you mean, approval?' Beth queried.

'Oh right, I forgot to tell you that bit. Over the years, it became necessary for rules to be put in place by the Malancy. A hierarchy, or I suppose government grew, very diplomatically, and everyone agreed that they'd only use their magic for good. You can use it for your own or anyone else's benefit, but not at the demise of anyone or anything. It has to be for good.'

'That's very noble.'

'It needed to be. Not all Malants have been moral over the years, and something needed to be put in place to handle it. We have our own law and order, if you like.'

'So Paul needed their approval?'

'Yes, but it was very easy. As long as everything we do falls into the rules of the Malancy, we're fine.'

'Even though you charge people to do magic for them?'

'It's just using your skills to make money,' Simon justified. 'It's no different to an accountant who's good with numbers, or a journalist who's good with words. I've never seen it any other way. If a company or a person needs a problem solving then we step in to help. We only work with certain people, though. They have to have a stable business with a good track record, and they have to sign hefty contracts to protect us all. Everything we do is based around detailed, carefully produced contracts.'

Beth wasn't so convinced about how ethical a business like this really was. 'It sounds very dodgy to me. It's wrong to change people and make them do stuff,' she argued, unimpressed, 'no matter what the reason is.'

'No, that's the one thing we can't do. We can't change anyone's thoughts or emotions, we can only change physical things around them. Yes, by default it might alter a person's mind or perception when things around them change, that's the cunning part to the job, but we can't actually change anyone's personality in any way.'

'I'm glad to hear it!' Beth confirmed. 'So you and Paul just started your own magical company?'

'Not quite. I was studying for my A Levels one night and Paul was struggling with a client. It was a tricky case and he felt he'd got in way above his head. I went to help him and it just seemed so obvious to me. It turns out I have a great gift for sifting through problems, for finding ways around things and for soaking up information. He offered me a job then and there. It had never been a set thing for me to join the company, but my skills fitted perfectly and there was nowhere else I wanted to be.'

'So you've never worked anywhere else?'

'No, I've never needed to. By the time I was eighteen I was his number one employee, working all my own cases, and raking in the money. It was incredible.'

'And that was all based in the UK?'

'Yes. Paul only moved to the States six years ago. He could have happily retired on his earnings, but he wanted more. So he set up a branch in New York and now he just sits back and only gets involved when he has to. I sort of do the same now, too. Or I did. I came back when I was needed, and then spent the rest of my time just overseeing things from afar, spending as much time with my uncle as I could. Let's face it, he's all I've got. I'm not a natural friend-maker.'

'You have me!' Beth pointed out.

'Do I?' he asked, sheepishly.

'I love you, Simon. I'm going to need some time to get my head around all this, but nothing so far has made me feel any differently about you. If anything, it's like a weight's been lifted. Unless there's something else to come?'

'You don't know how happy that makes me,' he smiled, reaching in to kiss her softly on the cheek. 'You know the bulk of it now. Let me think.'

It was all so strange. The more he told her, the safer she felt around him. As weird as her head told her it all was, her heart felt like everything was slotting into place. At that moment she felt more comfortable and relaxed than she had in weeks. It made no sense, but she thought it best to trust her gut and go with it. At least for the time being.

Then it struck her, the biggest question of all had still not been answered. 'What has all of this got to do with your feather?' she probed.

'I don't know. That's the truth.'

'After all that, and you don't know? How can you not know?'

Simon rolled up his sleeve to take a look at it, but the feather had gone. There wasn't even a mark left in its place.

'Where's it gone?' Beth asked, confused. 'It was there, wasn't it?'

'It was most definitely there. That's the thing, Beth, that's why I wasn't freaked out. If you knew the strange things that have happened to me over the years, you'd understand. Imagine being at school and suddenly sending your pen shooting across the room and not having a clue how it happened. Or imagine seeing your skin bubble with rage as you find out your girlfriend has been sexually harassed by your employee at work.'

'That did actually happen? I knew it!' Beth's head then raced through all the other strange things that had happened that she couldn't explain. 'You get fire in your eyes when you're turned on!' she exclaimed.

'Do I?'

'You definitely do. I thought I was hallucinating. And my knees! They were grazed, weren't they? After we kissed for the first time, all that pain I'd been feeling just disappeared. Was that you?'

'I didn't actually mean to do that. It was just that kiss, it was incredible. I got carried away and when I saw your knees had healed I didn't know what to do. I was kind of hoping you wouldn't notice.'

'You can heal?'

'I don't get ill and I don't get injured, it's a benefit for sure. Also, to answer your many questions on the subject, I don't need to work out, my body just takes care of itself.'

'I knew it! I knew there had to be another reason as to why you have that gorgeous body. Not that I'm complaining,' Beth smirked.

'The feather's just a new chapter in my bizarre little world. I can't explain where it came from, and I can explain even less where it's gone. I told you it was a rollercoaster ride with me.'

'So things like this could happen again?'

'You know as much as I do. I'm unique, it's all a guessing game. Does that scare you?'

Beth wanted to say yes. She felt so much that it should scare her, but it didn't at all. She was so ready for the journey with Simon, none of it mattered. She was now even more in love with him for being her strange little freak. It made no sense to her, but she felt a happiness inside like she'd never experienced before. She wasn't going to let it slip away.

'I think I can live with it, as long as from this moment on you're honest with me. No more lies, no more secrets. And that works both ways.'

'I'll never hide anything from you again,' Simon sighed.

Beth looked at the clock on the wall, it was now one thirty. She felt hungry.

'What happened to you taking me out for lunch?' she said.

'I don't much feel like going out now, do you?'

'No. But I am hungry.'

'Shall I get Jim to run out and get us some chips?'

'He'd do that?'

'That's what I pay him for!' Simon smirked, a clear weight now lifted from his shoulders.

This was a new beginning for the two of them, and Beth was ready for a simpler time ahead. All of her worries were surely behind her, now that she knew the truth.

SIXTEEN

Simon's alarm chimed loudly the next morning and woke Beth up from her sweet sleep. She opened her eyes, a little confused at first with what the sound was, and then where she was, but as Simon's bedroom came into view, she remembered.

She closed her eyes again and thought back to the day before. She'd been overwhelmed with information, most of it very unusual, but none of it had left her cold. She'd accepted everything, much to even her own surprise, and she felt a pleasing completeness for the first time since the whirlwind of Simon came into her life.

Simon broke her thoughts as he sat up in annoyance. 'I'm so sorry, Beth, our day together is going to have to be postponed.'

'What's happened?' She turned over to see him looking at his mobile phone, frustrated.

'I've got a customer demanding an urgent meeting. I'll have to go.'

'Oh no! Can they just demand you see them like that?' Beth asked.

'If we want to keep their business they can! I want you to stay here, though.'

'No, that wouldn't be right,' Beth responded, now sitting up to join him.

'You don't have to go in. I'll cover it with Trisha.'

'I don't want any special favours.'

'I know, but you've been through a lot.'

'And the best way to deal with it all is to throw myself back into normal, everyday life.'

'If you're sure. Whatever you think is best.'

'Can I get a lift with you, though? Will that be wrong? People will notice, won't they? I don't want to start lots of office gossip.'

'I don't see how else you're going to get into work!' Simon grinned. 'I'll drop you off just down the road, if you like. I'm going to have to go straight to the client's in North London anyway, so I can drop you off surreptitiously and be gone. No one will ever know.'

'Thank you! It would be utterly scandalous if anyone found out we were dating.'

'I'm not that bad, am I?' Simon asked, a little hurt.

'It's not personal. But you're the big, mega, overall, don't get any higher, boss of all the bosses, and I'm right at the other end of the scale in the no frills admin job.'

'You don't see it like that, do you?' Simon asked.

'Sadly, that's just the way it is. As much as I hate to admit it, we live in a snobby world where we aren't all equal, and I feel like I've got a mountain to climb ahead of me. That's something Bird Consultants has definitely taught me.'

'How can you say that? You're at the start of a wonderful career, you have so much potential ahead of you. I see it as I'm the owner of a successful business but without invaluable members of staff like yourself, then I'd be nothing.'

'That's so sweet,' Beth smiled, touching his hand.

'We've got a really good team at the office, I'm very lucky.'

'It's mostly good,' Beth nodded. 'One exception does

come to mind, though.'

'Who?'

'Have I told you about my useless manager?'

'I'm getting the impression you don't like her very much!' Simon smirked, getting out of bed. 'Now are you going to join me in the shower?'

Showered, dressed and full of a wonderfully unhealthy English breakfast, Beth was allowed for the first time to step into the Aston Martin. Although far from a car connoisseur, she could appreciate its beauty and its expense.

Beth slipped into the soft, black leather seat. It was like a little drop of luxury and she felt a hunger to one day own a car like this herself.

They waited for the gates to open and then pulled away on to the remote country lane, heading towards London. Beth's mixed emotions were tossing inside of her. On the one hand she was very excited to be travelling to work with her new boyfriend in his stylish, expensive car, it was all like a dream come true; but she was also weighed down with the fear that someone might see him drop her off.

It plagued her as she so wanted to not care what people thought. She'd gone against all her family's wishes moving to London and she'd always stood tall for what she believed in, it had never bothered her before to be different. But now she was finding herself trying to hide from people that she barely even knew. That dark worry that her move to the city had really changed her disturbed her once more.

She consoled herself with the justification that she wasn't quite ready for the questions. Anybody would be cautious about their colleagues' reactions to finding out they were dating the boss, but this happened to be a bit more. She was dating the scary boss that everyone thought was some sort of insane, blood sucking killer. As ridiculous as it all was, this was what Beth was having to deal with.

She knew at the very least she had to get used to it all herself before she could even consider anyone else finding out.

She sighed heavily as millions of thoughts, questions and fears inundated her mind, utterly overwhelming her.

'What is it?' Simon asked, placing his hand affectionately on her leg.

'Just processing everything, that's all.'

'Like I said last night, if you have any questions, and I mean anything at all, you must let me know. And I promise I will give you an honest answer.'

Beth knew she had more questions, but there were so many, she didn't really know where to start. She sifted through her thoughts quickly in her mind, trying to get to a question that niggled her the most. Then she thought of something important.

'I have got a question, if that's all right?' she started.

'Go ahead.'

'When we were talking the other day after Damien had... you know... you said that you'd never broken the law, or done anything illegal, but you've done questionable things at times. What exactly does questionable things mean?'

Simon paused for a short moment, choosing his words carefully. 'You have to understand, Beth, that the person I am now is very different to who I used to be. My ethics are much stronger now.'

'So you don't do questionable things now?'

'I certainly like to think not. My past is different, though. When I was young I used to get such a kick out of helping people. I'd spent my childhood as an outcast, and suddenly, when I started working for Bird Consultants, I was being respected and treated well. Yes, people still acted weirdly around me, but they made the effort. It was like I'd been set free. So I did whatever I could to help them. I never broke the law, but I pushed it as far as I could. To be able to interact with people and gain such respect in return was like a new start for me. It gave me a life I never thought I'd have.'

'And you don't feel that way now?'

'It's suited me better in more recent years to keep my distance. And being more ethical about how I do business has definitely helped me sleep better at night.'

'What have you done?'

Simon thought for a second. 'When I was about twenty we were working for a man at this giant tooling company. We'd helped them with issues they'd had in their repairs department. It was fairly simple and they weren't exactly big business for us, but we were starting out. Then the MD called me back in. It was his and his wife's thirtieth wedding anniversary and he wanted to do something special for her. He asked me to help him get a very expensive necklace for the night for her to wear. It was from some fancy jewellers she'd seen in New York, but there was no way he could afford it, yet it was her dream to wear it.'

'You stole the necklace for her?!'

'No, of course not. I just borrowed it. He had it for twenty-four hours and then it just magically went back. He couldn't afford to pay me, but I contracted that he had to get me five more jobs worth at least a million pounds in total and I'd accept that as the payment.'

'What if he didn't get the jobs?'

'He had one year to do it in, or his wife would get a permanent rash where the necklace had been to remind him of what he'd done.'

'Simon, that's awful! How could you do such a thing?' Beth was horrified.

'It sounds worse than it was. I knew he had several friends that could benefit from our unique consultancy, he just needed to encourage them. I wouldn't have asked for what I couldn't get, and none of it was technically breaking the law. I just borrowed a necklace that I made sure no one missed for one day and he agreed to my terms willingly and openly. I suppose you could say it was all ridiculously immoral, but at the end of it no one was hurt, she got the necklace of her dreams for a day, and I got, as it turns out, five million pounds worth of contracts, and two new long-term customers.'

'I'm sure that is illegal. I can't believe you did that. How did that not break the Malancy rules?'

'It's all in the way I word the contracts. I can see the loopholes and write the small print that always guarantees success but never really gets anyone hurt. I have a very special gift. Other people have tried and failed at what I do, even Paul at times. That's why we don't have any big competitors. They just can't do it.'

'No wonder you don't tell the staff! I can see there are certainly grey areas to your work,' Beth said, feeling increasingly uncomfortable at Simon's confession.

Simon reached over to touch her knee again.

'Do people like Trisha know all about it?' she asked after a few moments.

'All the management teams are allowed a certain level of knowledge, depending on their role, but they're also forced to sign contracts that control what they can and cannot do with this knowledge. There's a reason so few people know about the Malancy, it's not good for the general public to find out.'

'No kidding! I can't imagine getting a promotion and then being told all that. It would blow your mind.'

'We do it gently, believe me. Trisha probably knows very little, especially in comparison to someone like Gus, her boss. That's why we have so many levels, it's all about control. Need to know basis.'

'So I know more than Trisha?'

'Most definitely. I think you probably know more than anyone at the company who's not actually a Malant themselves.' A satisfied smile crept up on Beth's lips as she enjoyed her elevated status. 'I completely trust you, Beth. This is a huge step for me. I'm so relieved you're not running for the hills away from me, I appreciate how massive a thing this is to grasp. You're still okay with it all, aren't you?'

'I'm not going anywhere, don't worry.'

'I'm so glad to hear it. And don't hesitate to ask as many questions as you need to.'

Another question was now beating heavily in her mind, but it was one that she doubted he could answer. She so desperately wanted to know why, with every strange detail or unnerving confession he made, she didn't feel that perturbed. Logic was telling her to scream and run away as it was all such peculiar, and potentially dangerous territory. But with every word Simon spoke, her heart just yearned for him more. She felt such a strong bond with him and she knew that there was no one else better for her to be with than him.

The edge of Heaningford came into view and for the first time Beth recognised her surroundings. And for the first time she started to panic at thought of her peers seeing her.

'Drop me off here!' she ordered, suddenly.

'Don't be silly, we're a good five minute drive from the office yet.'

'Please, please! I don't want anyone to see us together.' Her heart was now pounding at the thought of someone like Diane walking past. She didn't know how she could explain being in his car, she couldn't explain it to herself. She might be deliriously happy in so many ways, but she knew there was no way her new friends would match her enthusiasm for him.

Simon indicated and pulled in to the kerb of the busy street. 'No one is going to see you. I was going to pull in to the car park of that restaurant a few doors down from the office,' Simon reasoned.

'That's ridiculous! We'll get caught for sure! No, it's fine here.'

'It's not that bad being seen with me, is it?' Simon

questioned, now clearly upset by her desperation.

'I just need time. You've changed my world, Simon. I'm not the same person I was a month ago. I'm not even the same person I was twenty-four hours ago. You weren't kidding when you said it was rollercoaster with you. I'm only just coping with everything as it is, I couldn't possibly deal with having to explain our relationship to anyone else. I think it would send me over the edge. Please, Simon, it's not about you, I love you so much, I just need to feel comfortable with everything myself before I can feel comfortable explaining it to others.'

Simon squeezed her hand and nodded. 'That's fair enough. I know I'm asking a lot of you.'

'You're not, Simon. I'm just a simple girl from a simple village and suddenly my life has been turned upside down in the most bizarre way. But it hasn't changed the way I feel about you.'

'Oh Beth, you're anything but simple. I think you're remarkable. But are you sure I can't drop you off at least a couple of minutes closer? It'll take you twenty minutes to walk to the office from here.' Simon looked at the car clock which read eight forty-five. 'You'll be late.'

'I feel so much better like this. Please.' Beth opened the car door and got out. She stood still for a second and breathed in the city air, hoping it would clear her thoughts.

A flash of guilt then stabbed her. It wasn't his fault she was having a flap about her colleagues, he wasn't the judgemental one. She couldn't leave him like this.

She looked back in the car sporting a cheeky grin. 'It doesn't really matter if I'm late anyway, does it? It's not like I'm going to get the sack, I'm sleeping with the boss!'

Simon laughed and the atmosphere instantly changed. His warm essence dissolved away all the tension and Beth felt herself suddenly relax. 'I'd like to see them try,' he sniggered. 'Now get to work!'

'Call me later? Oh no! I've just remembered I've got to work tonight at the pub. Will you drop by for a drink?'

'There's nowhere else I'd rather be,' Simon smiled.

Beth shut the door and watched as Simon pulled away. She then turned and virtually jogged her way into the office, for the first time cursing her stilettoed feet.

She finally got to her desk, gasping for breath, at two minutes past nine.

'Bloody hell,' Gayle laughed, 'run to work this morning did we?'

'An unexpected delay you don't think you'll have when you live so close to work!' Beth cryptically explained, deliberately not muttering a single dishonest word. She then quickly took her coat off and flicked her computer on simultaneously before daring to see if Trisha was in her office. A shower of relief rained over her when she realised Trisha was nowhere in sight.

'Here' Gayle said, handing Beth a pile of papers. 'These are all the orders that need processing today.'

Beth took them from her and sat down. She studied the descriptions for the orders, her newly acquired knowledge now making them appear very differently. One said "miscommunication elimination" and Beth considered what this could really mean. She guessed that Simon had to simply eradicate a problematic miscommunication for the company, perhaps in relation to its customers. Maybe they'd sent out a letter by mistake offering one hundred percent off their products rather than ten percent, and Simon had to make it so the letter never existed.

Another said "resolve staffing issue." This one was easy. She assumed that Simon had to resolve some problem that the company was having with its staff, like a problem with an over-zealous employee who was making difficult demands. Although, she recalled, he could only change situations and circumstance, not actually anyone personally.

She pondered what he actually achieved and how much it meant to all these companies. A bad miscommunication or a major staffing issue could be very damaging. Hiring someone like Simon was a very simple way of, quite literally, magically erasing all their issues from existence. It was slowly starting to make far more sense to her.

She scanned the room around her and realised that very few of her peers had any clue as to what the real purpose of the business was, and nobody but herself knew the full truth. With everything that had happened in the last day, the one thing that she hadn't considered at all was how her life at work would change. She was now in the know. She now had exclusive knowledge that even her own boss wasn't privy to. She wanted to be delighted, but as she looked at her colleagues she actually felt more alone than ever.

She'd slated the company in her own mind for being so secretive, and now she was part of it. A deep dread weighed her down as she feared things were going to be far more difficult than could have ever imagined.

SEVENTEEN

Simon had only been on London's North Circular for a few minutes and he was at a complete standstill. Thoughts of Beth circled his head and he smiled. Then he remembered that he needed to catch up with Eric to make sure that the situation with Damien had been dealt with as requested. He dialled the main office switchboard through the Bluetooth in his car.

'Good morning, Bird Consultants, Margaret speaking, how may I help you?' the voice greeted.

'This is Mr Bird, put me through to Eric, please.'

There was a moment's silence. 'Of course, Mr Bird, transferring you now.' Margaret's tone had become far more serious and wary. Simon waited, listening to their upbeat on hold music.

'Simon,' Eric suddenly answered.

'I want good news,' Simon said.

'Damien's gone. We sorted the paperwork out not long after you'd left. I don't know what the performance was all in aid of.'

'Thanks Eric. I appreciate it.'

'When are you in next?' Eric asked, a slight anxiety to his tone.

'I don't know, I'm on my way to see Flaremore at the minute.'

'We need to talk. It's getting too much.'

'I got you a PA,' Simon responded.

'She's fantastic, don't get me wrong, but there's just too much to do. We're growing faster than we can deal with and we need to react.'

'We can't keep bumping up your department, everyone will want new staff. For now, I need a new Sales Director, and he has to be a Malant. Let's focus on that.'

'But Simon-'

'Get working on a finding a new Sales Director and we'll talk about your situation. Prepare me a proposal and we'll take it from there.'

Eric paused for a few seconds. 'Yes boss. I'll try and fit it in.'

'Finding Damien's replacement is a priority. I want a candidate list by Monday for initial review.'

'Monday! Simon, you've got to be kidding me.'

'Monday, Eric, will there be anything else?'

Eric sighed. 'No.'

'Thanks for your help.'

Simon hung up the phone. He knew how stressed Eric was and he was well aware of the enormity of Eric's workload, but he couldn't afford to seem weak. He'd known four of the directors since he was a teenager and he had to make sure he emphasised his authority wherever he could so it wouldn't all be too familiar.

He knew he'd have to look for a way to help Eric out and he knew there was little chance of Eric coming up with any viable candidates for Damien's job by the next week, but he'd learnt very early on that people will take advantage if they can and being a tough boss had always paid off in the end.

The traffic finally started to move and he was soon at his destination. The receptionist of the large, grey office block had been expecting him and he was escorted straight to a meeting room.

He sat down on one of the blue chairs in the centre of the room, took out his branded pad and pen from his bag and waited for the arrival of his customers.

Finally, a very smart lady, perhaps in her forties, dressed in a sharp suit, entered the room. 'Sorry to keep you, Mr Bird,' she said in her high class accent as she firmly and confidently shook Simon's hand. 'I'm Veronica Hambleton.'

Veronica glared at Simon as she sat down on the opposite side of the table. 'They weren't kidding about you, were they?' she declared. Simon refused to respond, not used to having his presence brought to the forefront in quite that way. He just glared back at her silently. 'I don't know how much Damien has told you about this new job we have for you?' Veronica asked, getting straight down to business.

'I'm sorry, where's Charles?' Simon asked. Flaremore Publishing was one of the first clients that had ever worked with Bird Consultants and it was a client that Paul Bird himself had found. They were a rather large publishing house that had a portfolio of business magazines covering a variety of different subjects, from medical practices to accountancy. Charles was the man in charge and Simon knew him very well, but he'd never even heard of this Veronica before, although he could see she meant business.

'Charles is taking a back seat in the business now. He's close to retirement and he's looking for an easy last few years. Can't say I blame him. He's hired me to take over the day to day running of things. Like yourself, I'm now CEO. I have a strong background in this game, Mr Bird, and I know how to make businesses thrive. That's why we've called you in.'

'Please explain.'

'I was under the impression that Damien was going to fill you in, but that's no issue at all,' she stated. Simon went to open his mouth to inform her that Damien was no longer employed by Bird Consultants but she carried on. 'First of all, I feel I must tell you that I have been made fully aware of what you do and how you have helped Flaremore in the past. Don't worry, I've signed the necessary non-disclosure agreements, your secret is safe with me.' She forced a smile on her face at this point but it didn't suit her. 'I have to say, I was a little surprised at first, but then I realised how useful your services could be, especially with the small problem we're currently facing.'

'That's what we're here for.'

'Apparently that's what you're here for,' Veronica continued, much to Simon's confusion. 'Damien came to see us last week and I put forward our proposal. At first he said that Bird Consultants couldn't help due to a legal loophole, and I have to say I wasn't happy. However, out of the blue, he phoned me up yesterday to tell me that he'd realised there was a way that you could help us. He told me all about your special skillset, Mr Bird, and it's clear he wasn't joking.'

Simon glared back at her, trying not to react to her second comment about his presence. When he was young he'd often been taunted by his peers about the way he made them feel because of his powerful essence, but as an adult he'd that found very few people ever actually mentioned it. They'd look at him, they'd keep their distance, they'd certainly talk about him behind his back, but it was rare anyone actually commented on it to his face. He really didn't like it.

'You bring with you quite an intimidating aura, don't you Mr Bird. I thought Damien was just being metaphorical, I see now he wasn't. You're not dangerous are you?' she asked, quite to the point, clearly not comfortable with Simon but not inhibited by him either.

'You're quite safe. What else did Damien tell you?' Simon asked, both peeved by her rudeness and nervous about Damien's actions.

'He said our problem is a tricky one but you have the unique ability to help us.'

'And he told you this yesterday?'

'Yes, yesterday afternoon,' Veronica confirmed.

Simon's wariness of Damien now spiked and he was very cautious about where this meeting was heading. 'What exactly do you need Bird Consultants to help you with?'

'We want Derek Quigg,' Veronica plainly stated.

'Who's Derek Quigg?'

'He's the owner of Quigg Media. He opened his doors for business about five years ago and has been hugely successful. He has several titles that compete with our own, but, I hate to admit, he does them all better. He's a very clever man who has a real entrepreneurial flair and an excellent understanding of his customers. So we want him to join us.'

'Have you asked him?'

'Of course not, Mr Bird,' Veronica sneered. 'You can't very well go to the competition begging them to join you; that shows weakness.'

'Why is he going to want to join you if he's already running a successful company?'

'He wouldn't. It makes no sense.'

'Then I'm not sure how I can help you,' Simon explained, quite confused.

'Make him want to join us.'

'I can't make people do things, Veronica.'

'Of course you can.'

'This isn't really what Bird Consultants is about.'

'Damien explained that. He said that he wouldn't be able to do that. He said that no other Malant has the power to change people's thoughts but you.'

Simon felt adrenaline race through him as they hit the heart of Damien's new game. 'No, Veronica, Damien was right to begin with. No Malant has the ability to change anyone's thoughts or feelings.'

'Don't bullshit me, Mr Bird. I'm willing to pay

whatever and sign whatever, just make this happen.'

Simon's anger continued to build at her brazenness. He took a deep breath to try and control himself. His head was unusually foggy against the upheaval of recent events, but he forced himself to think around the problem as best he could. 'What about a merger?' he suggested. 'Surely you could offer Mr Quigg a generous proposal for your companies to come together.'

'He's not going to sell, he's doing a better job than us and he knows it. You need to make him change his mind.' Veronica was clearly growing with frustration.

'There are probably things we could do to encourage Mr Quigg to take your offer, such as make life difficult for him or put his business under threat, but that's not what we're about.'

'I don't want his titles to go under, they're strong publications. We want him to bring them with him.'

'Veronica, what you're asking me to do is either illegal or completely impossible.'

'What can we do for you, Mr Bird?' Veronica suddenly asked, sitting back in her seat, changing her tack. 'We'd be willing to pay a very generous bonus personally to you for any inconvenience our proposition causes. Or is there something else you want?'

Simon was getting enraged now, and he started to scratch his arm. 'I can't help you, Veronica. There's nothing I can do.'

'I can't believe that after all the years that Bird Consultants and Flaremore have worked together, that you're suddenly so willing to let us down. I warn you, if you don't help us with this, you will never get a penny from us again.'

Simon didn't respond to this. There was no competition, he was used to threats like this. With nowhere else to go, Simon knew customers always came back when they needed help.

Their silent standoff continued for a few moments

until Veronica finally broke it with a small cackle. 'It's so funny. Damien said you wouldn't react to my threat to leave, even at the expense of what your uncle might say, losing such a big client.'

Simon exhaled deeply, still scratching at his arm. He was not happy that his uncle had been brought into the equation but he refused to engage with this vile woman anymore.

'I know Damien left your organisation this morning, Mr Bird.'

Simon raised his eyebrow at the fact that she believed Damien had left that morning. Damien was desperately trying to manipulate this awful meeting and Simon needed to get away.

'I bet you're gutted to lose such a strong talent,' she continued. 'He told me you were ready to promote him.' Simon's anger flared again and he started to tap his foot on the floor with frustration. The itching was getting increasingly intense. 'Too late, though. Either you help us out with this or we're going to join his new company.'

Simon hadn't expected this and he brought his feet together under the table with apprehension. Was Damien really going to try and compete with Bird Consultants? He lost himself for a moment as he tried to decipher whether Damien could, in fact, ever be true competition.

He was quickly snapped back to reality, though, when he felt Veronica's stern stare from across the table burning into him. He knew that he needed to find a way to bring this meeting to a close. He had nothing more to say to this woman; he was not going to let her bully him.

His silence had now peaked her patience and Veronica stood to her feet in anger. 'I can feel your power Mr Bird, just as Damien told me I would. He explained everything to me. He told me how your exceptional aura gives you unprecedented abilities and that what we want is a mere walk in the park for you. You're lack of willingness to help us gravely disappoints me, Mr Bird. You have one day to change your mind or Flaremore will never be doing business with you again. I'll let you explain that to the more senior Mr Bird.' Veronica then walked out the room, not looking back.

Simon was now ferociously scratching at his arm. He threw his pen and pad in his bag and left as quickly as he could. He finally got to his car and he slumped into it, the itching now unbearable. He took his phone out of his jacket pocket with the intention of calling his uncle, but he was quickly halted when he saw he had fifty-four missed calls. Confused, he looked at the missed call list. There were two from the office and the others were all from an unknown mobile number.

Suddenly, the mystery number called again.

'Simon Bird,' Simon answered, quite flustered. The other end of the phone remained silent. Simon could just hear movement and breathing. 'Hello?' he urged.

'Having a good day?' the voice sniggered.

'Damien?' Simon knew that voice all too well.

'I am. Seems I've already got myself a new client. It's only been one day and, guess what, it's one of Bird Consultants' oldest and largest customers. I guess it's not a good day for you.'

'You can't possibly be serious about starting your own Malancy business?' Simon asked, but it was too late. Damien had already hung up.

Simon breathed heavily, trying to process the whirlwind of recent events. Then he looked down and saw he was now scratching his other arm. Both arms felt on fire, the burning intensifying with every passing minute. He knew he needed to get home. All thoughts of calling his uncle were long forgotten, all he was now concerned about was getting to the safe haven of his house.

The journey was not a pleasant one. The traffic had been typically awful and every time it came to a standstill, Simon's heart pounded with vexation as the itching increased in concentration.

When he finally got home, just waiting for the gates to open was agonising, and Simon wanted to tear off his clothes to relieve himself of this excruciating discomfort.

He didn't even bother actually trying to park his car. He dumped it haphazardly outside the front door, bounded out, quickly let himself into the house, and raced upstairs.

He slammed the door to his bedroom behind him and threw off his suit jacket. In one jerking motion he was free of his tie, and then, finally, yanking at the buttons of his white shirt, he scruffily pulled it off his body and let it fall to the floor beneath him.

His urgency was frozen as he caught sight of himself in the mirror and he started to shake. On his arms he could see seven dotted feathers: four on his right arm and three on his left. Each one was the same beautiful, striking red fuzz as before, but it had just got seven times more terrifying.

'Sir, are you in there?' Jim asked, knocking at the door.

'Go away!' Simon ordered.

'Sir?' Jim responded, clearly taken aback by Simon's outburst.

'Just go away.' Jim did as he was told and Simon looked back to his arms. The pain was overwhelming.

Simon went to his bed and lay down. He knew he needed to try and relax, but it was so hard against the burning sting that was now consuming him.

After an hour of tossing disturbingly he finally managed to fall to sleep, but his dreams were even more disturbed. Images of Veronica and Damien crept into his head, and they were making him do things that were going to lead to his ultimate downfall. All of his fears were playing out in his restless drowsiness and it only served to increase his agony.

He was brought back to reality a few hours later by the sound of Jim's voice again. 'Sir, can I get you anything to eat?'

Simon looked at his arms, still covered in plumage, and

he was horrified. 'Leave Jim. Just leave,' he ordered back.

'Do you need me to get you something?'

'Get out the house now, and don't come back!' Simon shouted, the door shaking with his force.

'Very well, sir,' Jim replied, and Simon heard him walk away.

Simon lay back on the bed, the fierce torment on his arms still vibrant, and he prayed for peace. He felt utterly alone and absolutely petrified.

EIGHTEEN

Feeling very downbeat, Beth grabbed her jacket at The Rose and got ready to head home. It was nearly midnight and she'd not seen or heard from Simon since she'd said goodbye to him that morning.

It had been an exceptionally busy night and she was exhausted, but the worry of why Simon had not made any sort of contact with her bore down on her even more.

She knew he wasn't good in crowds, and she completely understood that now, but he could have at least called or texted to say he wasn't going to visit her after he'd promised he'd be there.

She'd texted him when she'd left the office earlier on, then she'd called him in her break that evening, and she'd just tried to call him again. She really didn't want to seem desperate, but she hated not knowing what was going on.

Her tired mind was convincing herself that he'd lost interest. She worried that he'd had his fun and that was that. Their paths would never really cross at work and if he didn't want to see her, he wouldn't have to. He could even sack her if she was trouble, he really was in control. She fussed about what she could have done that was so bad that he suddenly didn't want to speak to her anymore.

'You ready?' Sam asked, standing at the till, counting money.

'Yes,' Beth answered, snapping back to reality.

'Just give me two minutes and I'll let you out.'

'No problem,' Beth said, resuming her cycle of misery as she leaned up against the bar and waited.

She looked to the stool where Simon had sat so many times, deliberately to come and see her, and logic finally kicked in. She rationalised that there was no sound reason why he would just suddenly lose interest in her. He was a very busy man and he'd probably got stuck at some client meeting, or maybe he'd been summoned back to New York at very short notice and he will call her soon.

Then other thoughts popped into her head that brought new hope. Maybe his phone had broken. Maybe he had come to see her but she'd been too distracted with customers and he'd hated it there so much he'd left. Maybe he would call her up to his office tomorrow and all would be revealed and they'd laugh, and she'd feel so silly for ever worrying. There was definitely a logical explanation, Beth sighed, trying to keep her spirits up.

'Right, come on,' Sam said, putting a wad of cash in a bag and laying it down. He walked to the front door, pulled the bolt at the top and bottom, and let Beth free.

'Thanks Sam,' she smiled.

'Thanks for your help tonight, Beth. See you tomorrow,' he said.

She walked out into the cool, still night, ready make the short walk home, but her steps were quickly halted by a familiar and very welcoming view. A smile burst onto her face. She knew he wouldn't let her down!

Right in front of her, parked on the road, was Simon's black Lexus with Jim waiting by the side of it. She surmised that Simon had to be in the back as she made her way towards the car, but as she got closer the look on Jim's face told her otherwise. She suddenly felt very anxious. His usual greeting smile was nowhere to be found and he looked uncharacteristically sombre.

'Jim?' she asked, not sure what was going on, a gurgle of concern turning over in her stomach.

'Miss Lance, how are you?'

'What's going on? Where's Simon?'

'Would you come with me?' Jim asked.

'Where? Where's Simon?'

'I'll explain on the way, Miss Lance, but Mr Bird needs your help.'

Beth felt sick with worry. She needed to know what was going on. 'Where are we going, Jim? What's going on? Why haven't I heard from him?'

'He's at home, Miss Lance, and he's not very well.'

Beth sighed, at least that gave her a semblance of an explanation. 'Can I just get my work clothes for tomorrow from home?'

'Of course. You are okay to come with me, aren't you? He really needs you right now, I don't know who else I can ask.'

'I'd do anything for him, Jim.'

'Thank you, Miss Lance. Get in and I'll drop you off at home first.'

Jim opened the back door and Beth got in the car. He then jumped in the front himself.

'Where to?' he asked, pulling his seatbelt across him.

'About two minutes down the road on the right hand side,' Beth answered. Jim indicated and pulled off, and just as instructed, about two minutes later, Beth stopped him.

'Just there, that block on the right. There's a car park just before it, you can pull in there.' Jim did as he was told, and pulled into the car park just before the small, modern block of flats. The car park had about twenty spaces, all of them taken, so Jim just dropped her off at the entrance.

She jumped out the car and ran round to her front door. She needed to see Simon so badly and she needed to know he was okay. Her nerves were shattered as she shakily let herself into her home.

She grabbed her rucksack from under her bed and threw in some clothes, anything she could quickly access. She'd already bought some toiletries to keep at his place, and she wanted to waste no more time, so without thinking any more she headed straight back down the staircase and into the night.

'What's wrong with Simon?' Beth asked as they pulled off. 'He told me he never gets ill.' Then it suddenly occurred to her that she had no clue as to whether Jim knew about the Malancy or not, or, more so, whether he knew about Simon's exceptional gift. She couldn't very well ask him in case he knew nothing. She realised she'd have to consider her questions carefully until she could speak to Simon.

'I have no idea,' Jim replied. 'He came home earlier, about lunchtime, and ran straight upstairs. He's shut himself in his bedroom ever since. He's refusing to let me see him, he's asked for nothing, and when I knocked on his door a few hours ago to check on him he asked me to leave. I mean completely leave and get out of the house.'

'That doesn't sound like Simon.'

'It's not like him at all, Miss Lance. He had such desperation in his voice, like he was in pain. I wanted to help him but he wouldn't let me.'

'He'll have no choice but to let me!' Beth asserted.

'I hope you don't mind me coming to get you?' Jim asked. 'Obviously Mr Bird hasn't got a clue. He doesn't know where I've gone at all. I had to do something, though.'

'I'm really glad you came to get me,' Beth confirmed.

'We're all he's got,' Jim added.

'I know Jim. But we're enough. We'll get him sorted out.'

Beth sat back in the seat, her eyes now sore and heavy. She felt very worried about Simon, but much better for being on her way to see him, and she was sure she could help him out.

The twenty minute journey to Simon's house seemed to take forever, despite the very light traffic, and Beth was fighting hard to stay awake against the soft vibrations of the car.

'Are we nearly there?' she asked, seeing nothing but blackness around her.

'Yes, Miss Lance, just a few minutes now.'

Finally, the gates to Simon's house came into view. Beth rubbed the corners of her eyes, trying not to smudge her light make-up, desperately resisting her fatigue. She wanted to look her best for Simon, she couldn't help it.

They went through the gates and Jim parked the car. He walked round to let Beth out and as she stepped on to the driveway, the cool air against her face helped to refresh her, ready for action.

They entered the house and Jim nodded for her to go upstairs. 'I'll wait down here,' he whispered.

She walked up the stairs to Simon's bedroom, feeling quite nervous as she approached the closed door. She knocked gently, looking at her watch. It was now after half past twelve.

'Simon?' she called. There was no answer. 'Simon, I'm coming in,' she said, softly pushing down the firm silver handle.

'Beth?' his voice finally called back. 'Don't come in!' His voice seemed so weak, his resistance was meaningless.

Beth walked in to the pitch black room. 'I'm turning on the light,' she whispered, feeling for the switch on the wall.

'Beth don't,' Simon feebly pleaded.

She found the switch and pushed the silver knob, illuminating the room. She squinted against the bright light, but she could just make out Simon sitting on the side of the bed, his head hanging down in shame.

As her eyes adjusted, she gasped with fear. His arms were covered in red feathers. It was the most unnerving sight.

'What are you doing here?' he asked, not moving a

muscle, too mortified to look at her.

Beth breathed hard for a second trying to absorb the alarming situation ahead of her, but it was all too incomprehensible. There were at least twenty feathers spread across both his arms, it was like nothing Beth had ever seen before; it was horrific. They were part of him. They weren't just stuck to his skin, they were actually growing from him, like they were, indeed, his very own plumage.

Her immediate reaction was to run away, it terrified her so much, but, out of nowhere, her inner strength kicked in and took charge. She couldn't leave him now, what sort of person would that make her? He needed her and she loved him, that was all that mattered. She took another deep breath and strode to the bed to sit next to him.

'Jim picked me up, he's worried sick about you.'

'You don't need to be here, Beth,' he whispered sadly.

'I absolutely do!' she exclaimed. She knew she had to try and find a way of controlling herself. She had to make sure she kept her emotions completely out of it, they weren't going to help either of them. 'You might be used to doing things on your own, mister, but you've got me now. You said you wanted me to be your girlfriend and that means we're partners. Your worries are my worries; your problems are my problems. If you're going through something difficult, then the issue is immediately halved by having me by your side.' Her words may have been firm but they seemed to strike a chord with Simon and for the first time he raised his head to look at her.

He looked withered, like this affliction had severely eroded away at his soul. She knew he needed her strength to get through it. There was no way he could go through this on his own, and he shouldn't have to.

She kissed him softly on the side of his head, but she couldn't bring herself to touch him anywhere else. As selfish as it made her feel, the silky red feathers impaired his beautiful arms left her quite nauseous.

The more she stared at the horror in front of her, the more the reality of it set in, and her fear turned to upset. The sting of tears finally pricked at her eyes and she could restrain her emotions no more. The man before her had gone from a strong, powerful being to a weakened, tarnished wreck and it pained her so deeply. It was one of the saddest things she'd ever seen.

'I love you, Simon,' she whispered earnestly as the trickle of tears set themselves free.

Simon could hold back no longer himself now and a single tear rolled down his cheek. 'Beth, what's happening to me?' he whimpered in despair.

'I don't know.'

'I'm so scared. I've been through a lifetime of weird experiences, but this is so painful and so overwhelming.' Simon rested his head on her shoulder and sobbed.

Beth put her arm around his back. She wanted so much to help him but she had no idea what to do. Suddenly his feathers brushed softly against her side and she gritted her teeth at the discomfort. It left her grappling with such uneasiness, but she knew she had to find the strength to deal with it. She was determined that nothing was going to prevent her from loving this man. She would not be selfish.

'Tell me everything. You're a logical man, let's try and find out what's causing this and then we can find a solution,' she reasoned, searching for any way to end this horror as quickly as possible. 'I'm sure if we put our heads together, we can get to the bottom of this.'

He looked back up at her, calmer. He definitely needed her strength. He exhaled, bringing his tears to a stop, and he sat upright.

'Okay,' he nodded. 'I went to the client meeting, that's where it started. It was awful, Beth. They wanted me to do things that either couldn't be done or were illegal.'

'Is that unusual?' Beth asked, still getting to grips with what Malancy was all about.

'Not in itself, but this was different. Damien had set it all up. He'd made them believe I could do all these things, so when I said I couldn't help them, they thought I was being deliberately difficult. I think he's trying to poach our clients.' Agitation was growing in Simon's voice as he told his story, and as it did he started to scratch his arm again.

'Stop it!' Beth ordered, and Simon immediately did as he was told. She looked to his face, thinking through the events in her head. 'I think there's a pattern here,' she explained.

'What do you mean?'

'Last time this happened...' she pointed to his arms, unable to say it, 'you came home stressed. And this time it happened, you came home stressed. Was this time worse?'

'Definitely. This woman was so insolent. She knew exactly how to rile me. Or rather Damien had set it up that way.'

Beth thought for a second. 'You know how some people get worked up and then get a rash?' she began. Simon nodded dubiously. 'Let's think of this as your rash. It could be, you are a little different.' She looked at Simon's beaten eyes, the velvety strength now washed away.

'First things first, we need you to relax,' she continued. 'You're in safe hands now, I'm here with you. Let's lie down together. I love you, Simon, think of that. Think of the fabulous life we're going to have together. Now, come on, take your trousers off and get comfortable.'

Simon stood up and did as he was told, placing his trousers neatly on the back of the desk chair. He then got into bed and Beth tucked the sheets up around him so he was comfortable, before stripping off and getting into bed herself.

'I won't come near you,' he said.

'Don't be silly,' she lied, seeing how much he needed her. 'Come here.' She held her arm out inviting him in, ignoring the tension that grasped her at the very thought of touching him.

'No, it's too much.'

'Are you going to do as you're told?'

'Are you sure?' he asked.

'Get over here!' she grinned, breathing deeply at the horrendous prospect of feeling his arms.

After a second's pause, Simon slowly moved towards her. He rested his head on her shoulder as she lay on her back. Hesitantly, he picked his arm up and placed it very feebly on her side, trying to keep the impact to a minimum.

For the first time she felt the silky feathers against her bare skin. It took her breath away. They were like warm satin, it was the most incredible and foreign sensation that had ever touched her. Within minutes Simon was asleep, but all Beth could do was lie facing the ceiling, trying not to move so that she minimised the impression of the feathers against her.

Time ticked by and Beth struggled with sleep as the thoughts of everything that had happened over the past few weeks raced through her mind. Although she'd found the whole night quite distressing, as the hours passed by she started to realise something quite surprising; something that had been going round and round her head for days, but she hadn't until now fully acknowledged. She knew that, with no uncertainty, despite all the bizarre occurrences and crazy events, despite all her fears and concerns, there was absolutely nowhere else she'd rather be and no one else she'd rather be with.

It was like in the jigsaw of her life, she'd finally managed to slot together all the pieces. No matter how hard she'd tried before, things had never quite fitted together; she'd always been the odd one out. But suddenly everything fitted together so perfectly. She felt complete.

The final picture may be a little strange, but it didn't matter. For reasons far beyond anything she could explain, deep down inside she felt true happiness. Her new life in

London and her new life with Simon was finally where she belonged. She was on the road to fulfilling her dreams and she'd developed a very strong bond with such a wonderful man.

She looked to Simon who was sleeping peacefully beside her and the anxiety started to melt away. She was in love and she was happy. Surely such intense emotions could help them conquer anything. What did a few feathers matter anyway? They were so irrelevant in the big picture.

A new sense of faith that they were going to get through this lifted her heart and, as her thoughts finally relaxed, a smile settled on her lips, and within minutes she drifted off to sleep.

NINETEEN

The alarm finally brought morning. Beth switched off Simon's alarm clock, not wanting to disturb him too much, and saw it was seven o'clock.

She looked to see if he was awake to find his eyes slowly opening up, their strong, chocolately glow far more vibrant than the night before. All she could see was his face at that moment as his body and arms were still tucked under the duvet, but she knew that he was getting better.

'Morning,' she smiled, feeling closer to him than ever.

'Morning,' he smiled in reply.

'How are you feeling?' she asked.

'Loved,' he replied sincerely. 'Thank you so much for last night.'

'I'm always here for you.'

Simon hesitantly pulled the duvet down to look at his arms. There were just four feathers left. There weren't even marks where the other ones had been, it was as if they'd never existed at all.

'Thank God!' Beth grinned, relief washing through her. 'See, I told you. It's just your stress rash!'

'Thank you, thank you so much,' he said, sitting up to kiss her.

'You have to stay here today, do you understand? I don't want you going anywhere until you're back to full health,' Beth ordered.

'Will you stay with me?'

'I can't, Simon. I've already had a day off and I have to work at the bar tonight. I've only just started, it doesn't look very good.'

'Bird Consultants is very lucky to have such a conscientious employee.'

'Will Jim take me in?' she asked hopefully.

'Of course he will.'

'Thank you. Can I come back tonight to see how you're doing?'

'I'd love that. You just tell Jim what you need from him and he'll take care of you.'

Jim certainly did take care of her. He cooked her a flavoursome English breakfast and then he waited patiently for her to say goodbye to Simon, before letting her in the Lexus and driving her to the office.

Beth sat back and thought to how Simon had seemed so much calmer that morning. As she'd kissed him goodbye she'd noticed the weariness still weighing down on his face, but he was on the mend and they'd gotten to the heart of the problem, so at least the worst was behind them.

'Jim, would you mind dropping me off a few minutes down the road from the office, please? I'll show you where. I think Simon's butler dropping me off may raise a few eyebrows.'

'Of course, Miss Lance, anything you require. I can't thank you enough for last night.'

'I'm glad you came to get me. I think the worst is over.'

'If you don't mind me saying, Miss Lance, I'm so glad you came into Mr Bird's life. You've been very good for him.' Beth couldn't help but smile at Jim's admission, the feeling was quite mutual.

Her happiness was challenged during the day, though, as it dragged slowly on. Even then, at five o'clock, it was far from over. She had about ninety minutes at home before she had to leave for her second job at the bar.

Not knowing where the energy was coming from, Beth forced out her characteristic charm as she served the Thursday night crowds, even though it was the last thing she felt like doing.

Beth's feet were aching with exhaustion when Sam finally rang the bell for final orders. The last of the rush was served and slowly, with a little encouragement, the customers departed one by one as Beth hurriedly cleaned around them, desperate for the night to end, both so she could get back to see Simon and also so she could get some rest. At about eleven forty-five Beth was finally set free and, as planned, Jim was waiting for her outside.

'How's he been today?' Beth asked as they pulled away.

'Happier, Miss Lance. He's pretty much just watched films all day and relaxed, I'd say he's well on his way back to his old self.'

'That's such good news,' Beth smiled, now relaxing for the first time that day herself.

'It's thanks to you, Miss Lance. I was very worried last night.'

Beth thought to the night before, although it seemed like a lifetime ago now. If he was getting better then her stress rash theory must have been right. It was only then that the implications of this occurred to her. Did this mean that he could never get angry or frustrated again? Was this a short term issue or a problem that would plague his life forever? How would they deal with that? It wasn't like they could go and see a doctor or anything and ask for medical advice, it was too strange a situation. But then again, Beth pondered, maybe there were Malancy doctors that he could visit. She knew so little about his world.

Remembering how unique he was, she thought to how it was highly improbable that anyone had suffered this affliction before, so how could anyone really help him? She suddenly empathised with how lonely he must feel. She was so glad she could be there for him.

Fatigue was really setting in now and her eyes started to sting. It was a worthless battle, and the next thing Beth heard was the engine switching off and she awoke to find Simon's house next to them. She rubbed her eyes and yawned as Jim walked round to let her out of the car. She followed him into the house and headed straight for Simon's bedroom.

Simon looked much better. He was sitting in bed watching television in a black V-Neck jumper, his arms hidden from view, and he looked thrilled to see her.

'How are you?' she asked as she sat down next to him.

'So much better. It's all thanks to you,' he replied, kissing her lovingly on the lips. He pulled up his sleeves and revealed just two feathers on his right arm, the improvement was remarkable.

'I'm so happy.'

'You look shattered,' Simon stated, brushing her hair behind her ears.

'I'm all right,' she lied.

'Come on, let's get you comfy,' he said, edging the duvet up as a signal for her to get under.

She stood up and threw her clothes on the floor as Simon flicked the television off with the remote, then they both curled up next to each other. Beth lay her head on Simon's chest and she enjoyed the feel of his arms wrapped warmly around her, taking solace in the fact that they were covered in his cotton shroud. Within minutes she fell asleep.

The alarm soon came again at seven o'clock. Beth had had a much better night's sleep, albeit only just over six hours of it, and she rubbed her eyes slowly trying to prepare herself for yet another long day ahead.

She got up, then showered and dressed, before flicking a splash of make-up on her eyes. She enjoyed her cooked breakfast, kissed goodbye to a much more peaceful looking Simon, and got in the back of the Lexus to start the madness all over again.

Requesting Jim drop her off down the road as before, she darted her way to the office only to be greeted by a vile tempered Trisha.

A few mistakes she'd made the day before were being wildly escalated out of proportion by Trisha's already bitter state of mind towards her. Beth had to spend an hour of her morning being patronised and lectured by her worthless manager. It left her reeling at the utter hypocrisy. She may have made a few mistakes, but at least Beth did some work.

When five o'clock eventually struck, she had the usual ninety minutes at home before an even more punishing and long Friday night at the bar. This had been her busiest night yet, and it took all the strength within her to stay charming and friendly to the customers.

Sam had a let a couple of locals have a last cheeky pint, and it was well after midnight when Beth was finally set free. She staggered to the car to meet Jim and prayed for sleep, ridiculously relieved that she didn't have work again of any sort for nearly forty-eight hours.

Jim didn't disturb her in the back, he just let her sleep through the entire journey home.

Hearing the car pull onto the drive, Simon opened the front door to greet them when they arrived. Jim parked the car and gestured for Simon to join him. 'She's fast asleep,' he said.

'I'm not surprised. Thanks Jim,' Simon smiled. Simon opened the back door of the car and helped Beth out. She stirred, but only enough to say hello, and then he carried her carefully up to his bedroom.

He placed her softly on the bed. 'I'm so grateful for everything you've done for me this week, Beth,' he whispered. Then he flicked off her shoes and tucked her in to his bed, not wanting to disturb her any more. He looked at her peaceful face and curled her hair behind her ears. 'You mean the world to me. I love you.'

* * *

All that could be heard against the silence the next morning in Simon's bedroom was Beth's soft breathing. She'd slept straight through for over ten hours, and was only just starting to stir.

Her eyes slowly opened to meet her now far more familiar surroundings. She suddenly sat upright, realising that Simon wasn't there, then, looking to his clock, she saw that the time was nearly eleven o'clock. Her immediate panic was that she was late for work. It took a second for her brain to click that it was, much to her relief, Saturday, and she had nothing at all to do.

Sighing, she snuggled back down under the covers and let her heart relax once more. She looked around the room. It was so quiet, not a single sound could be heard, and it reminded her of being back at home in Staffordshire, so far from the noisy street her flat was on. She could see the bright morning sun penetrate through a gap in the curtains and she felt momentarily complete.

Wondering where Simon could be and feeling the need to see him, she got out of bed. She was still fully dressed in her work clothes and, spying Simon's fluffy dressing gown on the back of the door, she decided to leave her workday behind and get comfortable.

When she got to the bottom of stairs she heard music filtering through the slightly ajar door of the living room. She walked in to find Simon sitting casually on one of his sofas with his laptop across him. She couldn't believe how adorable he looked in his checked pyjama bottoms and sweatshirt. She'd never seen him looking so laidback, it was a lovely sight.

'Morning!' she grinned.

'Morning,' he replied, clearly very pleased to see her.

He placed his laptop on the coffee table as Beth snuggled in next to him. He held her tightly in his arms and rested his head on hers. Beth felt a glow of wonderfulness within her.

'You shouldn't have let me sleep so late!' she said a few minutes later, looking up at him.

'After the week you've had and after the way you've looked after me so well, there was no way I was going to wake you up. You needed the sleep.'

Simon suddenly pulled away from Beth and quickly rolled up his sleeves, revealing just skin across his arms. 'Look!' he said proudly.

'I'm so happy! See, you're completely relaxed at the minute and your stress rash is nowhere to be found. You are a funny one, you!'

'Thanks so much, Beth. I dread to think what would have happened if you'd not been here.'

'I'm always here for you, Simon,' Beth confirmed, moving back in for another cuddle.

'Well, today it's time for me to do something for you. It's all been arranged, we're going out to Piccadilly Circus tonight, just as you wanted.' Beth pulled back to look Simon directly in the eye, utterly thrilled. She kissed him warmly on the lips.

'We're going to have the best night!' she beamed.

TWENTY

At half past six that night, Jim drove Beth and Simon to Uxbridge Underground Station. It was one of the nearest tube stations to where Simon lived that could take them directly into Central London, just as Beth wanted.

The entrance was in the middle of a busy shopping area and so Jim dropped them off as near as he could and they made their way hand in hand to the station.

Beth looked beautiful in jeans and a short sleeved, pink satin top, and with Simon in his smart jeans, black shirt and charcoal blazer, they made a very attractive couple.

They headed into the large station hall and made a beeline straight for the unoccupied ticket machines. Beth excitedly topped up her Oyster Card, whereas Simon opted for a more traditional travelcard.

'You've not got an Oyster Card?' she asked as he put his credit card into the machine to pay.

'It's been years since I last went on the tube. Jim just normally drops me off around London and picks me up again.'

'Wouldn't the tube be easier?' Beth asked, watching Simon surreptitiously type in his pin number on the pad.

He looked across at her, a glint of vulnerability in his

eyes. 'You'd think,' he whispered. 'Anyway,' he then smirked, 'who would actually ever choose the tube if they had a chauffeur!'

'Me!' she argued. 'I love it!'

'That's because you walk to work!' he gibed, taking his travelcard from the slot at the bottom of the machine. They headed through the barriers and towards the outdoor platform where the Piccadilly Line train was already waiting.

'Come on!' Beth said, worrying they'd miss it.

'It's all right,' Simon replied, 'it's not due to leave for six minutes.'

'What?'

'It's the end of the line. Or start if you like.'

'This isn't proper London!' Beth argued.

'You are funny,' Simon teased, lovingly.

They walked to a carriage near the middle of the train and stepped on. They both sat down in a very quiet section. After a few moments a young man entered the door right near them. He went to sit down opposite Simon, but he hesitated, staring at Simon uncomfortably. He quickly left the carriage and moved further down along the platform. Another two people did exactly the same about a minute later, and by the time the train pulled away not one person had attempted to sit near them.

'What's wrong with these seats?' Beth innocently asked, searching for what they'd noticed and she'd missed.

'It's not the seats, Beth,' Simon calmly explained.

She looked a little confused for a second before placing her eyes directly on Simon's. He looked both nonchalant to the behaviour of the fellow passengers and equally worried about how she was going to deal with it. 'Then what?'

'I told you. People feel uncomfortable around me.'

'That's so rude.'

'It's not their fault, Beth,' Simon reasoned.

She couldn't fathom it. To her, he felt so warm and

lovely to be around, it was a joy. 'Well I think it's very rude. You must feel awful!' she announced, feeling incredibly defensive towards him all of a sudden.

'I'm used to it, but if it makes you feel uncomfortable at any time-'

'With you, I feel like I'm the luckiest person in the world. They're just ignorant sods.'

'They're not ignorant, they just don't understand.'

'That's ignorant in my book,' Beth stated, folding her arms defiantly.

Simon smiled and kissed her on the cheek. 'You are remarkable,' he whispered.

It was over half an hour later when they finally saw the first sign of a tunnel, just leaving Earl's Court. The train was now very busy, and people had been forced to sit near them, although it had created an uneasy tension. The silence was tangible as people stared around, trying to figure out what the strong, prickly sensation was. Beth could physically see people doing up their coats or pulling their partners in closer to them to counteract the discomfort that Simon's essence so clearly emanated.

She was astonished by the reaction. She'd been exposed to it somewhat in the office and had witnessed it a little at the bar, but this was a new experience, and something she couldn't empathise with at all. How could his desirable warmth create such an adverse reaction?

She looked to him and saw the blankness on his face. If she hadn't have known better she would have believed that he was completely oblivious to the effect that he so obviously had on his surroundings; but she did know. It then became clear to her that his way of dealing with it was just to ignore it. She couldn't imagine a lifetime of this tension around her every time she was near people. She felt so sorry for him.

The journey continued with the same tense surroundings, and by the time they reached Piccadilly Circus Beth felt completely humbled by Simon's courage.

'How can you bear it?' she asked as they stood on the escalator, heading towards ground level.

'I know no different. The only blessing I've had in the last half of my life is that at least I've been able to understand their treatment of me.'

'You had so many strange looks and confused stares.'

'I make them feel uncomfortable. Anyone questions what they don't understand. Wouldn't you?' Beth considered this, but she couldn't relate to their disdain towards him.

'I can see now why you avoid the tube,' she consoled.

'The advantage of going out on a night like this is that people don't tend to notice so much when they're drunk,' Simon smiled.

'I think we need to get drunk!' Beth exclaimed, hopping off the top of the escalator, finally feeling the draught of the tube station.

Beth was suddenly brought to a standstill by the view ahead of her. She thought it had been busy before, but now it was heaving. People were everywhere. They were bumping in to one another, crossing each other, all going in different directions, and it was all so noisy and hectic.

It was now just after eight o'clock and the atmosphere was buzzing. Beth grabbed Simon's hand and tried to navigate her way through the crowds to the same exit as she went to last time; heading straight up to see the lights. She felt exhilarated, all the concerns of the journey quickly flittering away.

They walked up the stairs to feel the cool, still night finally touch their skin. At the top, Beth stood aside, moving out of the way of the torrent of people, and then she pointed up to show Simon the lights of Piccadilly Circus, her face blazing with joy.

'You like the lights?' he asked, grinning broadly as he looked at her enchanted expression.

The sun had yet to set on the early May evening, but Beth was still dazzled by her surroundings. Whereas before it had been busy, it was now electrifying. There were thousands of people clogging up every street, walking in and out of every establishment, some even queueing ages for service. The noise of the tourists and the locals against the endless stream of traffic gave Beth a renewed sense of life.

The exhaustion of the week she'd just had now extinguished itself completely as the thrill of the life around her and its diverse contrast to anything she'd known from her past stirred her senses.

'What do you want to do first?' Simon asked, kissing her lovingly on her head.

'Eat!' she chuckled, rubbing her stomach.

'Sounds good to me. Can I make a suggestion, though?'

'Anything.'

'I don't really mind, but I normally opt for nicer places where the staff are more diplomatic to their surroundings, if you know what I mean?'

'Not really.'

'Can we go somewhere where I won't be given the cold shoulder, so to speak?' Simon clarified.

'Oh right, I never thought about that. You really suffer, don't you?'

'It's not the end of the world, I just think we'd both relax a bit more if we weren't being glared at or avoided.'

'Where do you suggest, then?' Beth asked, feeling very defensive again towards him.

Simon thought for a second before finally grabbing Beth's hand. 'Follow me,' he said.

They headed to the other side of the circus and down a much quieter, albeit massive road. At the bottom of that road they turned right and finally stopped at a little black door. It was barely noticeable unless a person was looking for it, and Beth couldn't believe how small it seemed compare to the majestic buildings that occupied the rest of the street.

'A lot of Malants eat here, that's all right with you isn't

it?' Simon asked before attempting to enter.

'Why wouldn't it be?' Beth asked, but now standing at the door she felt uneasy. She suddenly had a flashback of her first day at Bird Consultants when she stood outside the building and a darkness seemed to envelop her. That strange cloudy manifestation now eerily prickled her skin once more.

'I just want to make sure you're comfortable with everything,' Simon checked, worried by the sudden reflex of her folding arms. 'We'll be able to relax in here, we'll have a nice time,' Simon assured her. 'Do you want to go in?'

As chilled as Beth felt, it hadn't stopped her entering Bird Consultants and it wasn't going to hinder her date with Simon. If he felt comfortable here, that's exactly where they going, she was determined. 'Let's do it!' she smiled.

Beth didn't know what to expect as they stepped in to the cream corridor behind the door. At the end of the walkway there was a glass door with 'Marco's' etched on in fancy lettering. Simon opened that door to reveal a very chic, stylishly designed restaurant.

As soon as they'd entered the room a middle-aged man in a black suit came striding over to them, his hand held out.

'Mr Bird,' the man greeted in an Italian accent, shaking Simon's hand. 'Nice to have you back. Are you staying long this time?'

'Indefinitely this time, Leonardo, I'm pleased to say.' Simon replied with a glint of a smile in the corner of his mouth.

'Wonderful news!'

'This is Miss Lance.'

'Nice to meet you,' Leonardo said, kissing her on each cheek. 'I have your favourite table, Mr Bird,' Leonardo said, then he led them through the busy restaurant.

Despite the fact that most of the tables were occupied,

the atmosphere was tranquil with everyone just politely eating and enjoying themselves quietly. It was serene and Beth could see why Simon liked it.

They were led to a table in the far corner of the restaurant, and, once they'd taken their seats, Leonardo placed a menu in each of their hands.

'What can I get you to drink?' Leonardo asked politely.

'Dom Perignon,' Simon practically whispered, and then Leonardo swept away.

'Did I hear that right?' Beth asked, shocked.

'I knew you'd argue if I suggested it, and I want us to have the best. It is a special night. I hope you don't mind.'

'That's very sweet of you,' Beth capitulated, letting Simon have his moment. Then her eyes widened at seeing the prices on the menu. 'I was actually going to say that I was buying dinner, but you're most definitely paying now. But I'm getting the first round of drinks wherever we go afterwards, though.'

'That's good with me.'

Beth scanned the menu. The majority of it was like a foreign language, she didn't even know what some of the ingredients were. It was Italian in style, she could tell that, but the dishes were far from the well-known favourites she was more accustomed to.

'What is all this?' she asked, feeling very out of her depth.

'Sorry,' Simon replied, putting down his menu to look at her. 'The chef, Marco, likes to challenge the palate. His food might be a little unusual, but it's never anything but excellent.'

'Do they not do Spaghetti Bolognaise?' she asked, much to Simon's amusement.

'You're going to have to get used to this living when you're a millionaire boss of your own major corporation,' Simon teased.

'Nonsense. When I'm rich I'll still be eating Spaghetti Bolognaise.'

'But you'll also be able to experience far more of what the world has to offer. Doesn't that interest you?'

'I've never thought about it,' Beth answered truthfully, before returning to study the menu.

Leonardo came over and elegantly poured them their champagne.

'Tell me about living the dream,' Simon asked as Leonardo smoothly walked away again. Beth was considering her response when a young waiter suddenly appeared at their table.

'Are you ready to order?' he asked in a distinct Italian accent.

'Have whatever you like, Beth. Try something different,' Simon encouraged.

'You go first,' she said, her eyes darting around the menu in a frenzy, not one clue what to order.

'I'll have the pork for starters and then the salmon for mains, please,' Simon said, not even attempting to pronounce the fancy names of the items.

Following his example, much to her relief, Beth chose the first things she could see that she kind of understood. 'I'll have the soup for starters, please.' She paused to rescan the mains. 'And then the chicken, please.'

'Excellent choices,' the waiter nodded, and then he whizzed away out of view taking the menus with him.

'So?' Simon probed, reminding her of his question.

'The dream?' she clarified. Simon nodded. 'To be rich. And powerful.' Simon waited for her to continue, but she just smiled and shrugged her shoulders.

'Nothing more specific?' he asked.

Beth considered the truth. 'When I was young I saw my parents work so hard to run their little coffee shop. Don't get me wrong, they're doing really well, but it's never going to make them millions. They're comfortable and they're very happy, but I don't get it. Why work so hard to achieve just comfortable?'

'Maybe that's all they want.'

'It is! That is all they want! It just seems silly to me. I've worked with them since I was eighteen and I've had so many ideas as to how they can make improvements, how they could grow. I used to feel like I was bursting at the seams with ambitious plans, but they've always told me I'm being ridiculous. They make a modest turnover and that's all they want. It drives me crazy.'

'Do you get on with your parents?'

'More as I was growing up than I do now. I love them to pieces, I really do, but I've never fitted in quite as they wanted me to. Their dream is to have me and my brother one day take over the business, but it's just too small a dream for me. They think my moving down here is foolish and they're all waiting for me to turn up one day back at home having got it out of my system and for everything to go back to normal.'

'That's not very nice.'

'It's the truth. My parents were so mad at first when I said I wanted the London life and I wanted to make something of myself. They felt like I was stabbing them in the back, letting them down.'

'That's unfair.'

'Us Lances have lived in Stonheath for a very long time. We don't venture far as a family; until now. I'm the first Lance to ever spread their wings and it's gone down like a lead balloon.'

'Surely they must be proud of your ambition?'

'They don't understand it. Like you said, people fear what they don't understand. Why would I want to risk it all in London when I have a secure, stable job for life at home? It seems ludicrous to them.'

'I'm so sorry.'

'Don't think bad of them. They're good people. In the end they appeared to support me, but I know for a fact they believe it all to be a crazy phase I'm going through and, very soon, I'll be running back home begging to part of the family business again.'

'You don't see that happening?' Simon asked, a hint of concern in his voice.

Beth looked Simon directly in the eyes. 'Can I tell you something?' Simon nodded. 'I've never felt more at home and more like I belong, ever in my life, than I do right at this moment in time. I'm not going anywhere.'

Simon reached across and squeezed Beth's hand lovingly.

'My family will just have to get used to it,' she continued. 'I know they will one day. They definitely want me to be happy, they just don't understand how this sort of life could ever make anyone happy. They think they know best, but they'll see.'

'Do you speak to them a lot?'

'Maybe once a week. They make me feel awful about myself as I can hear them waiting for me to breakdown or admit that I regret my decision, so I've avoided some of their calls. It's bad, I know, but I suppose they've brought it on themselves.'

'I can't believe it, Beth, I feel so terrible for you.'

'It's a lot better than what you have to go through. I have it easy in comparison.'

'Maybe, maybe not,' Simon shrugged as he squeezed Beth's hand once more. 'Well, I think you're incredibly brave, not at all ridiculous. You're one of the most amazing people I've ever met. I admire your ambition very much.'

'Thank you, that means so much to me.'

'So tell me more. I want to know all about this thriving ambition. Is the plan to run your own business?'

'I want to run one of the most successful businesses ever! I want to be hugely wealthy and powerful and have offices all over the world. I'm willing to work, and work very hard, but what's the point if it doesn't ultimately bring you great success?'

'We are so alike. Back when I started out all I could think about was power and success, and when I made my first million it just made me hungry for more.'

'See!'

'It's not everything, though. It's been very lonely at times,' he added.

'I hope not so much of late,' she smiled coyly. They shared a small moment looking affectionately at one another.

'So what's your business going to be, then?' Simon asked.

'I haven't quite got that far yet,' she admitted. 'I've helped my parents run their business, so I know quite a lot about looking after the books and I'm very good at admin, but I guess I've still got a lot to learn. London has definitely fuelled my ambition, though.'

Their exchange was interrupted by the arrival of their starters. Beth glanced enviously at Simon's juicy pork loin, noting how colourfully it was decorated by a diverse mix of vegetables and finished with a dark orange sauce. It looked delicious. Far more so than her white, creamy soup.

'What flavour is it?' he asked, tucking straight in to his dish.

'I don't know. Some sort of bean?' she answered, unsure.

She picked up her spoon and dipped it in cautiously, blowing on it a little before trying her first, small taste. It was delectable. The flavour was completely new to Beth, although there was definitely a hint of vegetables, but the seasoning and creaminess of it melted in her mouth and warmed her insides as it slowly delighted her throat.

'Good?' Simon asked.

'Amazing!'

They enjoyed a moment's peace and quiet while they devoured their tasty meals.

'Do you think you're learning a lot at Bird Consultants?' Simon asked, eventually breaking the content silence.

'Oh yes, definitely. It's great experience.'

'Well I hope Trisha's looking after you,' he added, not expecting the immediate scoff that emanated from Beth's mouth like a reflex.

'Something wrong?' he enquired.

'You don't have a clue do you?'

'What don't I know?'

'Oh Simon,' Beth said, shaking her head. 'A good boss should know everything that goes on in his company.'

Without losing a beat, Simon responded. 'I thought I did. I pay my staff very well to keep me up to speed with things. What am I missing?'

'To be fair, I think Trisha has most people fooled.'

'Fooled?'

'Oh yes! You get to know her and you find out she's utterly useless at her job and takes the credit for everyone else's work.'

'Trisha?' Simon queried in disbelief.

'She's a complete waste of space and she's a really horrible person.'

'I've never had any bad reports about her before.'

'Who have you asked?'

'I've seen it for myself. I've always been impressed with her.'

'How? How could you be impressed with her? Have you seen her office?'

'What is it she's done that's so bad? Enlighten me,' Simon asked, curiously.

Beth considered a good example. 'Take this new electronic filing system.'

'Yes.'

'Trisha has taken all the credit.'

'It was her idea,' Simon stated.

'No it wasn't! It was Gayle's idea. Gayle's daughter recommended the system after she'd started to use it at her company. Gayle went to Trisha and Trisha made her put a proposal together and then the next thing Gayle knows, Trisha's taking all the credit for it.'

'Trisha didn't write that proposal?'

'You read it?'

'Of course I did. They needed to get my approval to go ahead. Trisha even came to one of our board meetings to present the idea. You're right, she claimed it all as her own.'

'She doesn't even know how to use it, it's just embarrassing.'

Simon took a second to process what Beth was saying. Leonardo suddenly reappeared to refill their nearly empty champagne flutes and just seconds later he was followed by the waiter who removed their completely empty plates.

'That actually makes so much sense,' he confirmed when the waiter had disappeared. 'She didn't really know how to answer our questions. She just kept repeating facts from the proposal, not able to talk around it at all. I assumed it was because she was nervous, clearly she just didn't have a clue.'

'She's horrible, I hate her. Can you sack her?'

'No,' Simon smirked. 'Despite the rumours, I don't go around sacking people. Damien's the first person I've ever sacked, and he really deserved it. Anyway, it would have to come from her manager, Gus. I can't interfere without good reason. And my girlfriend not liking her is not a good reason!'

'She's not capable of doing her job, that's the reason! Sack her and promote me!' Beth grinned.

'Hang on, I thought you wanted to make your own way in the world, now you want to sleep your way to the top?' Simon teased.

'To gain true success one must know how to utilise their assets to best effect,' Beth stated with a wry smile.

'I'm an asset now, am I?' Simon chuckled.

'You certainly are!'

'I'll tell you what. I can't sack her, but I can make sure she has enough rope to hang herself. Leave it with me. If she's as bad as you say, I'll make sure she gets caught out.'

Before Beth could add any more, their main meals appeared and they once again fell silent as they enjoyed their mouth-watering dishes.

The rest of their night continued with great conversation, lots of fun and dozens of passionate exchanges. It was nearly three o'clock in the morning before they considered going home.

After leaving the restaurant, they'd tried a couple of different bars on their way back up to Piccadilly Circus, before finally opting for a late night venue in Leicester Square. It had been like nothing Beth had ever experienced, not only in music, but in size, atmosphere and decoration. She'd found the whole night thrilling, in every possible sense.

They were now walking east through Leicester Square, making the short journey towards Trafalgar Square, nearby where Jim was due to collect them. Despite the fact that Beth now felt very tired, the buzz of the busy streets around them was keeping her quite alert.

They walked on, hand in hand, giggling about what a wonderful time they'd both had, and before they knew it, they saw Jim waiting for them. He was parked, ever so slightly illegally, on the side of the road. They quickly jumped in the car and, wasting no time, Jim pulled away.

Within minutes, Beth was asleep, but the smile was still very present on her face. Simon sat back, not letting go of her hand, and watched the world race by in front of him. For the first time ever he felt at peace in his heart, and, just like Beth, a smile couldn't help but spread upon his lips. At that moment in time, everything was perfect.

TWENTY-ONE

After devouring Jim's delicious Sunday roast the next day, Simon drove Beth straight to work at the bar. It was another busy shift for her, and when she got home, just after nine o'clock, she revelled in the chance to curl up in her own bed, something she'd not done for days.

Despite the fact they'd had just one night apart, though, they'd missed each other tremendously, and they certainly made up for it on Monday morning. By the time midday arrived, Beth had made Simon two cups of tea, they'd exchanged three texts, four emails, one furtive phone call and they'd made plans to have dinner together that evening, taking advantage of Beth's rare night off.

Simon was now sitting in his office in the process of typing an email to Gus, Trisha's manager, putting into play his promise to Beth from Saturday night. His flow was cut short, though, when a very unwelcome sight appeared right outside of his office. He paced to the door to make sure he'd seen it correctly and locked his eyes directly on Damien, who was very smartly suited up, talking to Eric.

'What are you doing here?' Simon demanded, standing in the doorway of his office.

'I could ask you the same thing!' Damien spat with

anger, spinning around quickly to meet Simon's icy glare.

'What do you want?'

'I was told you were off sick. You haven't been in for days. What are you doing here?'

'So when I'm not here, you think you can just waltz in the place and take over? Is that your plan, Damien?'

'We all know you never get sick, Simon. This lot may be too scared to say anything, but we all know the almighty, powerful Simon never gets sick. So where have you been?'

'You need to leave.'

'Where have you been, Simon?' Damien pushed.

'Leave!' Simon shouted, the room quaking at his tone.

Damien breathed heavily for a few moments scowling as fiercely as he could at Simon, although it looked so feeble against Simon's immense presence. Then, realising his attempts to get an answer were futile, he turned around and headed straight for the door, his head held high.

Simon glared straight at Eric. 'Was he here last week while I was off?'

'No, but he did call. Twice, I think. He seemed delighted that you weren't in.'

'Why didn't you tell me?'

'It was nearly a week ago, it just slipped my mind. I've got a lot on my plate,' Eric bit back defensively.

Simon looked out across the room. 'If he calls again, to any of you, I want to know. Do you understand?'

The room all agreed in return, and Simon went back into his office, closing the door behind him.

One floor down, Beth was heading out for lunch. She'd made sandwiches that morning, but had deliberately left them in her fridge so she could go home and grab a few minutes' peace and quiet. The mania of her life at present was draining her completely, and she knew that she needed to optimise on every relaxing moment she could find.

Feeling bright and happy, she made her way down the

street towards her home, completely oblivious to the fact that Damien had spotted her. She innocently walked on, completely unaware that Damien was now following her, his eyes widened by the opportunity ahead of him.

She entered her flat and headed straight for the fridge, fully intending to eat her sandwiches to alleviate her grumbling tummy before anything else.

Just then her buzzer went. Her flat was connected to the main door downstairs via an intercom system, and so far in all the time she'd lived there she'd not heard it ring once.

She walked to the cream interconnecting phone near the front door. 'Hello?'

'Delivery for a Miss Lance,' the male voice answered.

'Delivery?' she questioned, knowing she wasn't expecting anything.

'Yes, for Miss Beth Lance,' he clarified.

Shrugging her shoulders, Beth pressed the button just beneath the phone to let the man in. 'It's just up the stairs,' she instructed before opening her front door and waiting for him.

She'd barely had chance to poke her head round the door when Damien burst into her flat, knocking her backwards. He quietly closed the door behind him and Beth felt uncomfortably trapped.

'Hello Beth,' he said, trying to grab her hand. She backed away from him, boldly. She was angry, confused and frightened by his sudden appearance in her home, and she prayed it would be a short visit.

He calmly took off his jacket and threw it to the end of the bed before taking a seat on the pink, rose patterned duvet himself.

'Please join me. We need to talk,' he smiled suggestively, patting the covers next to him.

Hesitantly, she walked over and sat down near her pillows, sitting as far away from him as she could. Her heart was now pounding. 'What do you want?' she firmly asked, trying to hide her growing fear.

'I told you before, we're very alike, you and me. Although I have to admit, I'm a little in awe of your efforts. You really will stop at nothing to get what you want. It's a very admirable quality.'

'What are you talking about?'

'Come on, it's just you and me now. I know the truth. A player knows a player. You may fool the idiots, but I know better.'

'What am I supposed to be playing?' she asked, her firmness now dwindling as her concern for his presence increased.

'The system. And you're very good at it. I like the way you use your feminine charm, that's obviously something I've never been able to do.'

'I don't know what you're talking about. I'd like you to leave,' Beth requested, her breathing now intensifying at the agitation of her uninvited guest.

'That's not very nice, Beth, is it? I'm here to offer you a proposition.'

'I didn't like your last proposition, I don't want another one.'

'Maybe it was a little beneath you, just a basic sales role. I understand that. So I'm aiming higher this time. This time I'm going to make all your dreams come true,' Damien grinned, reaching out to touch her hand. She swiped it back out of his way.

'What do you know about my dreams?' she asked, her panic now evident.

'I told you. Everything. We're very alike. You scratch my back, remember?'

'You need to leave. I'll call Simon.'

Damien started to laugh at this. 'I love it! The damsel in distress card. He seems to like that. You really have got him measured. I don't know how you do it, he's normally so distant and unapproachable. You must make a fucking good cup of tea.'

Beth scanned the room for her bag, knowing her phone was inside, but she couldn't see it anywhere.

'Call him if you like. Suits me just fine,' Damien shrugged, not at all bothered by her threat. 'But wouldn't you like to know what I'm offering first?'

'What do you want?'

'You!' Damien smirked. 'I want you to join me. Simon's on his way out, trust me. You're sucking up to the wrong man. He won't be CEO for long, and then where are you going to be? I, on the other hand, am just starting out. There are big things ahead for me, I promise, and I think we could be good together.'

Beth's panic had now turned into fear. She eyed the door, trying to compute whether she could make it and what his reaction would be. She stood up, but within seconds he'd grabbed her wrist and had yanked her back down to the bed.

'That's a bit rude,' he said quite firmly, all of his humour now gone. 'I come all this way to offer you a fantastic opportunity, and that's your reaction. I thought you wanted to go far?'

'You don't know anything about me!' Beth seethed, trying to pull her wrist free.

'I know that within a few days you managed to thaw the heart of one of the biggest freaks on the planet. I know that you managed to score an invite to Frederick Layfield's birthday; now that takes some doing. I know that you've fucked that cold hearted bastard. That takes even more doing. You must be willing to go very far. What's he offered you? Because whatever it is, I can give you so much more.'

'Get off me!' Beth shouted, finally pulling her hand free from his sweaty grip. It did no good, though, he quickly grabbed both her wrists in return.

Her heart was now thumping as she tried to pull free. Her wrists were stinging sharply and her hands were turning white against his fierce grip. All she could do was try and fight him.

Looking around again, she finally located her bag, but it was by the door. She had no hope of getting it. Damien was now staring hard at her face waiting for her to concede, and she could feel his warm breath on her cheek.

Her head became fuzzy with terror and she was losing the grasp of what she needed to do to get away from him. This was all so terrifyingly unexpected and Beth could barely breathe at the prospect of what was to come.

'I could make you director. You could sit side by side with me. You could sit anywhere you like,' he leered

Beth had no desire to respond to him. She was sickened by the prospect. All she wanted to do was be free.

He finally let go of her hands, as if he believed she would go along with the proposal, but, instead, taking no time to think about it, she jumped to her feet to make a run for it. He stood up more quickly, though, and blocked her way, then he slapped her back down to the bed. He stood over her menacingly, his anger at her obstinacy now increasing.

'You're starting to piss me off. I don't know if you're just stupid, or maybe Simon has offered you something that I don't know about?'

Now quite terrified, Beth scrambled to the other side of the bed hoping she might make it out that way, but Damien walked round effortlessly and blocked her again. He grabbed her by the neck this time and threw her back down to the bed, leaving her a little choked.

'You bitch! You ungrateful bitch! When I say I want something, people normally oblige. How dare you!'

She tried to stand up again, this time with the plan to push him out the way, her desperation now intense. She went for his chest, but it was no good. He slapped her hard across the face and she fell awkwardly on the bed.

'You better start doing as you're told!' he ordered in a chilling tone, but with nowhere near the command that Simon had.

'Simon will be so mad!' she shrieked, hoping that would be enough to scare him off, remembering the last time she saw the two of them together.

Damien's glare hardened as he considered her outburst. He looked deep into her eyes. 'Don't tell me you've got a soft spot for him? For that cold, anti-social freak?' Damien seemed exceptionally maddened by this, and Beth froze with fear. She couldn't work out why this made him angrier. 'What is it about him? He's a complete outcast! He scares the crap out of everyone he meets. Half our clients can't stand to be around him. I've had to soften the blow on so many occasions, you wouldn't believe, but the people around me, they all seem to think he's the best thing ever. He's got nothing on me. Nothing! Are you listening?!' Damien's eyes became wild with rage. 'You want to see how good he is compared to me?' he hissed. Then he kicked off his shoes and tugged at his belt.

Beth was petrified. Her breathing was now erratic and the sound of her own heart was pounding in her ears. She backed herself up towards the headboard to try and keep away from him. She just couldn't find it in herself to scream. It was as if she didn't want to make a scene, like it would somehow worsen the situation, and she hoped that if she just tried to remain calm it would, somehow, make it all go away. She just wanted him to go away.

'I won't tell Simon,' she begged, now realising his name was a major catalyst to Damien's crazy behaviour. 'Just let me go. No one will ever know.'

'On the contrary,' he uttered, kneeling on the bed in front of her, completely cutting off her escape. 'I want you to tell him everything. You tell him every sordid little detail.'

He grabbed her by the arms and forced her down on the mattress in an awkward diagonal position. She wriggled against him with all her might, but he just slapped her hard across her face again and then, utilising all his weight, he climbed on top of her, leaving her helplessly pinned against the covers.

She was now gasping for breath but she still couldn't find her voice. He ripped open her pink blouse, sending the buttons flying off in all directions, and he glared heavily at her lacy white bra below.

'No!' she begged with utter terror, the fear of what he was going to do now helping her to fight. 'No! Don't!' She was struggling so hard but it was all worthless against his grip. Her breathing increased intensely as he reached up and cupped her left breast viciously. 'Get off me!' she yelled hoarsely, but he just ignored her.

He smacked her across the face again, her cheek now swelling brutally against the beating, but it was the least of her concerns.

She tried to wriggle her legs, but she was completely at his mercy. So petrified now, she stared up at her adversary and saw his frightful grimace. Tears started to form in her eyes as she felt him move his cold, rough hands up her smart black skirt.

'No!' she cried, desperation now pouring out of her.

He yanked her skirt right up and it ripped a little against the force. 'Is this what Simon does to you?' he asked menacingly before he slid his cold, lanky fingers between her legs.

This was the final straw for Beth as the realisation of her worst nightmare set in and, with no warning at all, she screamed. It was a full bodied scream, finally letting out her shrill cry for help at the sheer horror of his impending violation.

He suddenly stopped, frozen by her outburst. She could see the shock on his face. 'Leave me, please, leave me alone,' she cried.

Damien's grip softened as he looked straight down at her, absorbing her terrified face, as if he'd not seen it before.

In one quick movement, he got off her and sat down on the side of the bed.

'I'm sorry,' he said after a few moments before quickly grabbing his shoes and jacket and racing out of the flat.

Beth rolled on to her side and sobbed, the relief and anguish of the past few minutes shaking her soul. Like a reflex, she leapt up and locked her door properly, her breathing still erratic, then she ran back to her bed and pulled the covers over her, like they were her safety blanket against the world. She pulled her duvet up over her head tightly, her body still trembling with fear, and she cried. It was deep, sad and uncontrollable, and no matter how hard she tried, she couldn't stop. She felt utterly ashamed and completely alone, and for the first time since she'd moved she wished she could be back home.

TWENTY-TWO

By mid-afternoon, Simon was starting to get concerned. He'd emailed and texted Beth a few times but he'd received no reply. Following the quick responses that morning, he was now worried that he'd upset her somehow. He was irritated that she was just downstairs but he knew he couldn't just go and see her without starting a whirlwind of gossip, and that was the last thing Beth wanted. He needed an excuse.

After much deliberation, he finally made his mind up to go and see Gus, who sat at the back of the ninth floor, and in a position where Simon would have to walk past Beth in order to visit him. He just needed to find the right reason to go. He'd already emailed Gus earlier that day and he didn't want to pressure him unnecessarily.

Simon had done as he'd promised and had given Trisha chance to either prove or expose herself. He'd requested that Trisha find the time to train him up personally on the new electronic filing system. He'd told Gus that he wanted Trisha to be proud of her hard work and that he wanted to reward her accomplishment by acknowledging it himself through a one to one training session. No other person would do. Feeling a little bit happy with himself, he wanted to share the news with Beth, but she was ignoring him.

With still no plan of action, Simon found himself walking towards the lift, making his way to Gus's office, praying for enlightenment.

Reaching the ninth floor, he walked through the glass doors and deliberately tried not to place his eyes on Beth straight away, hoping his aloofness would shine through. However, his act was all in vain as he immediately noticed Beth's desk was unoccupied. He could see her computer was still on as the screensaver bounced bubbles around her screen, and he surmised that she'd be back shortly, he now just needed to find something interesting to speak to Gus about.

Striding through the floor, ironically with purpose, he barely noticed the usual silence he summoned upon the room, and he forgot to see how no one looked him in the eye as he headed across to Gus's office. He was thinking of nothing but where Beth could be.

'Gus,' he said, entering Gus's small but exceptionally well ordered office.

'Mr Bird?' Gus replied from behind his desk, totally flummoxed by Simon's presence. 'I'm waiting for Trisha to get back to me,' he immediately spat out. 'She said she's got a busy diary but she knows how important it is to you. Could someone else not take you through the system?'

Simon leaned against a small cupboard on the back wall of Gus's office. It was a deliberate move as it gave him a clear view across the floor; he was so eager to see when Beth returned to her desk. 'Did she say she wanted someone else to show me?' Simon asked.

'She did, yes. She said that she didn't want to hold you up with her busy schedule.'

Simon tried to hide the smirk on his lips. He was seeing how right Beth was. 'If I ask for her time then she will make time, do you understand?' he stated quite plainly.

'Yes, Mr Bird.'

'Clear her diary. I want a date and time in my inbox by

five o'clock.'

'Of course, Mr Bird. I think she's just a bit shy, but the new system is proving to be a great investment.'

'She didn't seem very shy when she presented the idea to the board.'

'It wasn't a success then,' Gus added.

'No,' Simon replied, a little irritated by how Gus had so quickly jumped to her defence despite the fact that she was trying to evade the direct orders of the ultimate man in charge. That in itself was very telling. Just then, relieving him from the burden of padding out this visit anymore, an idea pinged in Simon's head.

'Tell me, Gus, how are things down here? Any problems?' he asked, recalling Beth's definition of good management and suddenly feeling that maybe he wasn't as well informed as he'd assumed.

'Not at all,' Gus replied, shaking his head,

'I mean with the staff. Is everyone happy?'

'Of course.'

Simon turned to face Gus, oblivious to the sweaty chill that now prickled at Gus's skin. 'Talk me through the floor,' he commanded. 'I want to know who everyone is and what they do.'

'Okay,' Gus nodded obediently, too fearful to question the motive. Gus stood up and walked to his office door looking out to the staff around him. Simon was determined to listen and properly learn about his employees, but within seconds his mind had wandered. He couldn't concentrate at all on what Gus was saying, no matter how important he knew it was. Instead, Beth's long term disappearance was still clawing away at him and he started to fear that she might actually be missing.

'No one's left or been fired today, have they?' he interrupted Gus.

'Not at all. No one's left this department in a while now.'

'Continue,' Simon ordered, and Gus did as he was told.

He explained in great detail every member of staff on the floor, what they did and how they were doing, to the best of his knowledge, but by the time he'd finished Simon had barely heard a word. The worry that Beth was still missing was now consuming him and he needed to find out the truth.

Realising his best option was to speak directly to her colleagues, Simon stood up. He knew Beth would be horrified by the very thought of him interacting with her peers, but he was doing it for her so she'd have to forgive him.

'Thank you, Gus,' he said. 'At our next board meeting I'm going to propose some changes to how we manage the staff. I want to make sure everyone is in the best position and everyone's needs are truly being met. I'm sure I'll be in touch to elaborate on the plans soon.' Then he exited the office as abruptly as he entered, and he focussed his attention wholly on his beeline towards Beth's desk.

'Good afternoon, ladies,' he said confidently as he reached Diane, Michelle and Gayle. Within a second three pairs of eyes were all staring back at him, aghast. They were amazed to hear his voice and none of them could find the words to reply.

Their shocked silence snapped Simon quickly back to reality, diminishing his confidence and bringing forth the stark realisation that he was completely unprepared for this interaction. All he could do was blurt out the first thing that came into his head. 'I'm going to be a more permanent fixture around the office moving forward... so... I'm here to properly introduce myself,' he garbled.

Again, the three ladies were muted by him. It was like they were in denial that Simon was actually speaking to them and they just gawped inanely at him as if he was talking in a foreign language.

'I'm Mr Bird,' he confirmed before feeling utterly stupid as they clearly already knew that. 'Thank you for your hard work,' he then added, as if to totally justify his reason for stopping. His brain was aching to find a reason to bring Beth into the conversation and he knew he had to think of something soon.

'Thank you, Mr Bird,' Gayle answered, forcing the words through her bemusement.

'You appear to be one person down,' he quickly observed. He was so relieved to be finally talking about Beth, but his respite was cut short by yet another befuddled silence. Then he considered how he'd actually made more of a statement that required no response than actually ask anything useful. He decided he needed to be unreservedly direct to end this torment once and for all.

'Is your colleague at work today?' he asked very plainly, now the hint of frustration peeking through his normally solid composure.

'Yes... No, Mr Bird,' Gayle started, her voice trembling. 'That is, she was here but she went home sick at lunch.'

Simon turned straight to Gayle, curiously. Why, if Beth had just gone home sick, wouldn't she tell him? Especially after the way she'd looked after him last week. He'd more than welcome the chance to look after her in return. It wasn't a question Gayle could answer, though, and Simon knew they'd helped as much as they could.

'Thank you, ladies,' he finally uttered, much to their clear relief. He could virtually hear them gasp for air as he walked away.

None of it seemed to make sense. Beth had been so happy and well that morning. The only person that could answer his questions now was Beth herself.

As he reached his desk once more he knew he needed to see her. The problem was, though, much to his embarrassment, he didn't know where she lived. He suddenly felt so selfish that all their time had been spent at his place and he was very angry with himself for missing such a fundamental detail.

He placed his hands on his head with frustration before the ping of realisation hit him once more. She was his employee, he had her full details on file.

He opened up the HR drive on the internal computer network. The perk of being the CEO meant he had the unique benefit of having access to absolutely everything across the company.

He found the personnel files and searched alphabetically for Beth's name. Wasting no time, he typed her address into Google maps and saw it was just a few minutes away down the road.

Now with great urgency, he grabbed his black suit jacket off the back of his chair, locked his office door behind him and paced to his car.

He jumped in his Aston Martin and headed down the road, knowing her block of flats was just on the right hand side not far away. Then he saw the small sign for 'Somerville House' peeking out from the side of the building. He turned right into the car park just before it and pulled into one of the spaces.

He walked round to the building's main door and pressed the buzzer for flat two. There was no answer. He did it again but there was still no answer. He was sure that she must be at home, nothing else made any sense. He was now growing wildly impatient as the concern raged warily inside of him.

'Beth!' he shouted up, not sure which window was hers, but not really caring either. He had to see her, it was becoming unbearable. He shouted her name again, this time much louder so that virtually everyone in the vicinity could hear.

Finally her voice came through the speaker by the door. 'Simon?' she asked.

'Let me in,' he insisted, perhaps a little too eagerly, but the desperation to know what had happened to her was now itching away at him. He waited cautiously, hoping she'd do something soon, but an age seemed to pass with nothing but more silence. Then the buzzer sounded and the door clicked allowing him to enter the building.

He saw a sign that directed him to flat two upstairs and he made his way up. He noticed her door slightly ajar to the left and he slowly pushed it open.

His first reaction was shock at the size of her very small home. He stared around in astonishment, noting how the bed absorbed most of the space, leaving just enough room for very little else. His bedroom alone was bigger than her whole flat.

Coming back to the task in hand, he gazed towards Beth who was completely tucked up in bed with the covers over her face. He could just see her soft brown hair poking out at the top and he immediately wanted to soothe her poorly state.

'Are you okay?' he asked gently, walking round to sit by her side; his irrational fears now dissolving away as he accepted her illness.

'What are you doing here? You shouldn't be here,' she said, her voice muffled by the duvet.

'I was told you'd gone home sick. Are you all right?' He tried to pull the covers down, but she was holding them tightly in place. 'Beth, what is it?' he whispered, his concern now reigniting at her determination to hide.

'I'm fine, please go.'

'I don't think so. It's my turn to look after you, I'm not going anywhere.'

He moved his hand up to stroke her hair but he was suddenly halted by the sound of her weeping from beneath her shroud. His heart started to pound. Something was very wrong. He'd been so sure that there was no way Beth would just go home sick without telling him; this was something different, and he felt quite panicky at the prospect of what was to come.

'What is it, Beth?' he asked, but she refused to respond. His worry for her was now spiking and he needed to know what she was hiding. He hated to see her like this.

He grabbed the duvet again, this time more forcefully to counteract her hold. Her grip was no match and he finally revealed her face. It left him speechless.

He looked down at her poor, tear stained face and his heart ached at the bruises that smothered her. She could barely see through her swollen left eye and the raw puffiness of her cheek made Simon wince. Then he caught the light marks on her neck and his blood started to boil at the thought of someone hurting her.

'Oh my God, Beth. What's happened?'

She looked up at him and the upset turned quickly to fury. 'You! That's what's happened! Ever since I met you I've encountered nothing but problems. I've been man-handled, pinned to the floor, used, exhausted, and I'm completely drained. I can't take it anymore.'

'What are you talking about? Who's done this to you?' Simon asked, confused by her outburst.

Beth buried her head softly into the pillow and cried. She wasn't able to look at him. He tried to stroke her head to soothe her, he wanted so badly to help her, but she knocked his hand away.

'No, Simon! No!' she yelled, snapping up to glare at him. 'You don't get to comfort me!'

'What have I done?'

'You live in a sick world, and I should never have got caught up in it.'

'You have to tell me what happened, Beth. You have to! You asked me to be completely honest with you, you need to do the same for me.'

A few seconds went by and then Beth conceded. She sat up straight for the first time, revealing her pink pyjamas, and then she took a deep breath. 'Damien...' she started, but that was all she could manage before the tears were freeing themselves again relentlessly down her cheeks.

Simon waited for her to catch her breath, his head spinning at how everything had so suddenly changed. The morning had been perfect but now she was sitting there so angry with him, he couldn't work out the logic.

'What about Damien?' he asked desperately.

'He...' The tears were making it so hard for her to talk. Instead, she nodded her head to a pile of clothes on the floor beside them. Simon looked across to see her shirt slightly torn, the buttons scattered all around it, and next to it her skirt lay twisted with a very clear rip up the side.

'What did he do?' Simon demanded, terrified of her answer. A rage was building inside of him at the notion of Damien's actions. Beth just sobbed again shaking her head, not able to talk about it anymore. 'Did he...?' Simon began, trying to find the softest words he could to not upset her further, but he had to know how far this had gone. 'Did he take advantage of you?' he finally asked.

It took her a second, but Beth found her words. 'He tried. I don't know what happened. He was asking me to join him. He got so mad at the mention of your name. The next thing I knew he was on top of me.'

'Oh Beth.'

'He didn't, though. He didn't. He just suddenly stopped and ran off.'

Then a new thought appalled Simon even more. He was completely to blame. He'd seen Damien earlier that day; he'd argued with him and then threw him out. Maybe he could have stopped any of this happening.

'When did this happen?' Simon asked, guilt now trembling his voice.

'Earlier,' she whimpered. 'Lunchtime'

Simon felt sick. He could have stopped it. He should have escorted Damien out himself, he should have made sure he'd completely gone. He should never have left Beth so vulnerable, especially after her last encounter with Damien.

Simon wanted to hug her, to comfort her, to somehow take it all away and make her happy again. He felt helpless and wretched.

'Please just leave,' Beth muttered, now much calmer having spoken about it.

'I'm not going anywhere,' he said.

'Please leave. I can't cope. The last few weeks have been too much, I need some time alone.'

'I can't leave you like this,' he persisted.

'Please!'

Simon felt awful and confused. He wanted to be there for her, he didn't know how to deal with her shutting him out. All he could do, though, was respect her wishes for now.

'I'm always here for you, Beth,' he muttered, standing up, but Beth had already pulled the covers back over her head. He didn't know how to find the strength to leave her like this. 'I'll call you later?'

'Please just leave,' she begged through her sob. He knew he had to go. It left him with a darkened, weighty sadness that pulled down on his body like the gravity around him had just tripled in strength, but he didn't know what else to do.

Forcefully, he pushed his legs to walk and he headed to the door, looking back one more time in the hope that she'd change her mind. But she didn't.

He returned to his car and sat still, completely defeated. His hands were trembling. He'd never seen someone so upset.

Her words played over and over in his head. Maybe he was all to blame. He'd introduced Beth, a young, innocent girl, to his difficult and dark world, how could he expect her to deal with it? He loved her so much, he felt so guilty for playing any part in her misery. He wanted to take it all away so badly.

A tear rolled down his cheek at the thought of never seeing her again. He was so terrified that she would never forgive him and the aching misery it brought with it tore away at him inside.

He recalled their wonderful weekend, and he tried to come to terms how it had all gone so wrong so quickly. Then his mind switched to Damien and anger instantly enflamed.

This hadn't just been an unfortunate event; Damien was to blame. He'd, yet again, stirred things up. It was one thing to mess with Simon, but it was another to mess with Beth. This time Damien was going to pay. Simon didn't care what his game was, Damien was now going to see how angry Simon could really get.

TWENTY-THREE

Sitting in his Aston Martin, Simon comprehended the terror that Damien had brought to Beth's home and his anger started to shake him. Damien had performed such an evil, cruel, senseless act and Simon could barely believe that anyone could be so inhumane. Damien had always been far from a saint, but to cause such pain and torment to another person was utterly unforgivable and Simon couldn't take the contempt that he now felt for, not only a former employee, but for someone who was considered a family friend.

Simon felt completely betrayed, distressingly angry and destructively vengeful. Damien would have to pay for what he did, there was no way Simon could let it go. Damien had picked on Beth deliberately; this was personal.

Breathing very heavily, Simon scanned his brain for where Damien could be, trying to think if he'd given away any clues as to his whereabouts that afternoon. But he could be anywhere. And he must know Simon would be looking for him; that must have crossed his mind.

Racking his overwrought brain, Simon suddenly realised what he had to do. It wasn't easy but it was very simple. He stepped out of his car and looked around the clean tarmac of the car park, but he didn't find what he needed. He moved to the edges and searched again before finally placing his hands on a medium sized stone.

He checked around him to make sure no one was in sight, but the car park was very quiet so he felt safe to continue. He sat back in his car and held the stone squarely in his hands before him.

It was the beginning of a very taxing location spell that would allow him to see Damien's exact whereabouts. It was a spell so powerful that Simon couldn't manage it alone without harnessing the energy of the stone in his hand. But all he needed was a little assistance, so exceptional was Simon's intrinsic force. It was at times like this he was so grateful for his supreme power.

He closed his eyes and summoned the strength within him. Another Malant at this time would be struggling far more. They'd need several extraordinarily powerful elements around them and words to incite their potency, not to mention the outstanding concentration, patience and vigour they'd have to have just to survive the might of the magic. But not Simon. He needed nothing else, it was all so inherent and all so easy in comparison.

All he had to do was sit back and picture Damien in his mind. He channelled the force within him, only utilising the natural properties of the stone to augment his innate ability, enabling him to reach the higher levels of magic that were required to achieve such an ambitious and difficult task.

Whereas most Malants would likely fail even an attempt at such a great spell, Simon took it all in his stride. The essence he emitted might have been his curse, but his remarkable power was a true gift.

As the images of Damien grew more vibrant in his mind, the stone started to take effect. A bright, golden glow erupted around it, soon turning to red. With each passing second its vibrancy intensified, and then Simon's whole frame mirrored it, a scarlet blaze now burning wildly in the front of his car. The heat increased as the inferno engulfed Simon completely, leaving a blinding sea of scarlet. Then, silent, dazzling beams shone out like the rays of the sun, illuminating the whole car park.

The image hit him.

The brilliant rays instantly vanished as Simon, barely even out of breath, threw the stone to the passenger seat and started his engine. He knew exactly where to find Damien.

Beth immediately regretted what she'd said. She was now sitting up in her bed with the duvet wrapped around her. Although the tears still hadn't stopped, she was far calmer.

She didn't really blame Simon for anything. He'd just turned up at the wrong time; her attack had still been so raw in her mind.

Beth looked down at her hands. Her beautifully painted nails were now all chipped away leaving just splodges of red in the middle of each finger. It was such an alien sight to her. Not having ever painted her nails before, she'd never had to worry about such trivial things as the upkeep of them.

At that moment her nail varnish symbolised everything. She'd changed. She'd once been a confident, strong girl and now she was just a splodgy mess on the floor. How could anyone change so much in just a few weeks of their life?

Did she even like this new person? She couldn't decide. This new Beth lied, that was something she didn't like. She'd always prided herself on being honest, it had always been so important to her. However, on several occasions of late, she'd not just omitted the truth, she'd actually told bare faced lies. To Simon even. The closest person to her. She hated herself for that.

Another thing she'd noticed was that new Beth was tired; she'd lost the bounce of the old Beth. But maybe that was a harsh comparison. New Beth did have two tiring jobs, a boyfriend who lived a fair distance away, the buzz of city life to contend with, and the shock of living all on her own for the first time, and in a brand new place. Then she was having to deal with all manner of new experiences on top of that, like being nearly arrested while attempting to go on a first date, solving outbreaks of random plumage growth, and then being attacked by her boyfriend's former employee who had recently been fired after a near first attempt of illicit behaviour. Anyone would find all that exhausting, surely?

Her old life couldn't have been more different. Nothing major ever happened in Stonheath. The greatest conflict she'd ever encountered was a squabble with her friends, and a busy shift at her old bar job consisted of about forty people spread across the whole night. Now she was dealing with manic, terrifying, emotionally draining and utterly stimulating events on what seemed like a daily basis. It was overwhelming.

She thought back to her concerns of how she'd started to lie. She could honestly say that she'd never told another person an untruth in her life before moving to London. She'd prided herself on that fact. But maybe she'd just never had a need. Her life was far more difficult now and these complex situations were calling for more complex ways to handle them.

She turned her mind to the fact that she hadn't been able to tell her colleagues the truth about her feelings for Simon. This was far more than omitting the truth, she'd completely lied to them more than once about what she'd been doing. Old Beth wouldn't have done that. But, to be fair, old Beth had never encountered such a difficult situation.

Her colleagues more than just hated Simon, they were frightened of him, and they'd made him a monster in their own minds. She wasn't just lying to be deceitful, it was a survival technique. They'd called him a blood-sucking yeti, it made it very difficult for her to just casually mention that she was in love with him. Maybe it made her weak. Maybe she shouldn't really care about other people's opinions. But, whatever, she'd never had to deal with anything like this before and she was taking it one day at a time, trying to work through it all as best she could. How could that make new Beth a bad person? How was that, in the eyes of old Beth, immoral? Old Beth was very naïve.

She then thought to how she'd lied to Simon about the true strain she'd felt the week before. Looking out for him in his feathered state had really taken its toll on her both physically and emotionally. The old Beth would have felt compelled to tell him everything in a misjudged state of mutual honesty. Yet the new Beth had realised how important it was for him to be completely relaxed to get better. What sort of selfish person would pile their own, somewhat lesser problems on to a sick loved one? Not new Beth, she'd decided not to. His needs had been much greater.

So, she considered, maybe her newly found dishonesty wasn't so bad after all. Maybe she was, in fact, growing up. They weren't deceitful untruths, in the more naïve way she used to view the world. Maybe 'white lies' really did have their place. Maybe it was okay to protect a loved one's feelings. Maybe life was far more complicated than she could have ever possibly imagined in the security of her family unit. Maybe this really was the best thing that could have ever happened to her. She really was growing up. It wasn't a change she was experiencing, it was a rite of passage. And the truth was, she felt so much better for it.

Then Beth realised she wouldn't swap her new life for the world. This new Beth was a far better person and she was so much happier.

Yes, she was very scared, and she didn't care for the idea of ever seeing Damien again, but at last her life was full. Rather than it making her want to retrieve back home, it was instead making her never want to go back again. She loved her family and she'd definitely visit, but there was no life for her there anymore. How could it compete?

It was then that she understood what she hadn't been able to see before: she hadn't changed at all. She was still the very same person inside, but her exposure to a brand new world had opened up her soul. She was far more alive and in touch with herself now than ever. It was as if this potential inside of her had been locked away since birth and it was only when she'd stepped foot into this new life that her true self had been liberated.

She found it absurd that she could find such great happiness after one of the darkest points of her life, but it was the vibrant contrasts in her life now that she needed. The black and white simplicity of her first twenty-five years were well and truly behind her and she never wanted to return to that Beth.

Far from being to blame, Simon was a marvel. He'd helped her to find herself. He was more supportive of her dreams than anyone she'd ever met and she was starting to believe that maybe he understood her better than she even knew herself. Simon was her future, she felt it deep inside. This was all her destiny and she'd gladly take the darkness if it meant she could taste that wonderful happiness as well.

Then guilt struck her. She'd been so nasty to Simon. She wanted to apologise but she felt too awkward to call him. She couldn't throw him out and then call him right back, the poor man wouldn't have a clue where he stood. She decided to try and get some rest and then she'd call him later. Rest was now definitely what she needed.

Simon was nearly at Damien's house. All thoughts had left his mind other than getting to his destination. His spell had revealed Damien sitting in his back garden sipping a beer. It made Simon so furious that he could perform such a vile act and then just relax in his garden as if nothing had happened.

Simon turned into Damien's road. It was a quiet road and Damien lived in a reasonably sized detached house at the end of a row of six similar houses.

He pulled on to Damien's drive and stepped straight out the car, barely waiting for the engine to stop. Knowing exactly where Damien was, he entered the side gate, kicking it out the way, and paced into the garden, his mission taking charge.

'Damien!' he shouted fiercely as he approached the man. Just as envisioned, Damien was sitting in his large, immaculately kept garden at his vintage metal table, drinking a Budweiser.

The ferocity of Simon's voice seemed to blow Damien to his feet and he stood to attention, staring blankly at Simon's intensity.

'Why did you do it?' Simon shouted, knocking Damien to the floor with a quick thud against his chest. Winded, Damien scrambled back to his feet, clearly ready to take the beating.

'I want to know what you were thinking!' Simon continued. He grabbed Damien by the head and shouted forcefully into his face. 'What has she done to you?'

Damien remained silent, now refusing to look into Simon's eyes. Simon once again threw him to the grass, desperate to shake him into action, but Damien just accepted the blow, this time not even trying to get to his feet.

'If you have a problem with me, you take it up with me. How could you bring her into it?' Simon roared, but Damien just looked to the blades below him not saying a word.

'She's just an innocent girl. You've ruined her, you bastard!' Simon's frustration was vastly increasing as he stared down at his opponent.

Still not getting a reaction, he picked Damien up by the arm in a single, easy motion and threw him back against the garden table, sending his beer exploding to the floor beside him.

'What are you playing at? Why the silence suddenly? Where's the madcap, jovial Damien I've had thrust down my throat so much of late?' Simon's voice plunged the whole garden into a physical throb alongside him.

Damien still refused to speak, but he did rise, struggling to his feet, touching his twisted, clearly broken arm in agony. However, he continued to look down, only fuelling Simon's fury even more.

His whole body now steaming with rage, Simon stood square on the grass before Damien and closed his eyes. All he wanted was for Damien to be sorry. He wanted an apology, he wanted reassurance that Beth wouldn't be hurt again and he wanted Damien to feel remorse. He needed to know why Damien had done such a horrendous thing, but all he was getting was a stony cold silence and the torment was sending Simon over the edge.

Simon couldn't bear the images of Beth being harmed that played on a loop in his head and he began to utilise his anger to fortify the power within him. He stood still, focussing on every element inside of him, bringing into force one almighty, powerful rush. Throwing his hands out sharply in front of him, he thrust everything he had in Damien's direction. Like a hurricane, Damien was blown over with such monumental force that he was left utterly breathless against the back wall of his house.

Simon then repeated the exercise of channelling his anger, but this time he focussed it all through one hand and a brilliant strength was propelled in Damien's direction. The power from Simon's right hand took hold of Damien, lifting him off the ground and crushing him; cracking bones throughout his body causing colossal damage. Damien screamed in agony as his body seemed to crumble against the force until Simon wickedly ended the torment, leaving Damien to crash back down to the ground, shattered.

Simon was now breathless and spent. He'd used all

he'd got, but Damien still refused to say anything. Angry tears built up in Simon's eyes as he approached Damien's crumpled body. He had nothing left now but sadness. He couldn't stop picturing Damien on top of Beth, hurting her and taking away her beauty, and it was crushing him alike.

'Why did you do it, Damien? What did you hope to achieve? She's just a young girl.'

Then Damien mumbled his first words. He was lying on the floor in agony, twisted up against the force of Simon's power, barely able to move, but he'd finally found his voice.

'What?' Simon asked. Damien mumbled his inaudible words again. Simon was now standing above him, needing so desperately to hear him. 'What?' he demanded.

'I'm sorry,' Damien uttered. If Simon had looked closer he might have seen the distant remorse in Damien's eyes. It was definitely there, and Damien had definitely accepted the punishment that Simon had so harshly thrown his way. But Simon couldn't see it, the compunction was buried just too deep. Damien wasn't used to being sorry and he wasn't used to admitting fault, therefore he certainly wasn't used to showing it to the world.

Simon shook his head, feeling completely bewildered and broken by Damien's wild, perplexing and unpredictable actions. The past few weeks had taken his already rollercoaster life on a whole new track. Things had always been peculiar, but they'd just managed to get insane and Simon was exhausted. Just then he sympathised with Beth. No wonder she'd told him to leave.

'You go near her again and I'll kill you,' Simon warned with far less vigour than he'd previously shown. Damien looked away, not able to face his guilt, and nodded his head in agreement.

'You can mend your own broken bones this time,' Simon spat. He walked off back towards the gate but paused before touching the steel bars to make his exit. He turned round and kicked a large stone Damien's way, the remorse now nagging at his own soul. 'That should help,' he said, referring to the power of the stone, knowing Damien's Malancy could utilise it. He then glared at it hard, transferring a little extra power to its already potent state, and left, confident that Damien would be fine.

Simon got back into his car and took stock of what had just happened.

He felt awful. His whole body ached from the anger he'd allowed to build up inside and he was still winded from Beth's harsh words. He felt like he'd lost everything.

As Simon started the engine he became suddenly aware that he was scratching his right arm again. Fearful, he tried to remember how long he'd been doing it for, but he couldn't think, such was the intensity of recent events.

He took a deep breath and tried to relax, heeding Beth's advice from before, but it was futile against his woes. The tension he felt was gargantuan.

The itching intensified and he knew he had to get home. It was about ten miles to his house, and he prayed for good traffic ahead. He drove as quickly as he could across mainly country roads, but with each corner the pain mounted. It wasn't just on his arms now either, it was on his chest, his legs, his head; just about everywhere. He was finding it harder and harder to tolerate. The itchiness had started to fuse with the rawness to create an agonising, tormenting hell that he needed to escape from.

The journey finally ended, and Simon could barely wait for the gates to open. He ran in and straight upstairs.

'Jim, I've had an argument with Beth. Can you please leave me be tonight?' he shouted through a gap in the door, desperately needing some space and knowing that Jim would be waiting not far, concerned.

'Of course, sir, sorry to hear that. I hope you're okay?' Jim called back from the bottom of the stairs, just as predicted, but Simon no longer cared as he hurriedly ripped of his clothes to try and relieve the torture.

Just down to his underwear he looked straight in the mirror and gasped. Nothing could have prepared for the sight in front of him. It was terrifying.

TWENTY-FOUR

By late Wednesday afternoon, Beth had still not heard from Simon and she felt dreadful. She could hardly blame him, she'd been so horrible to him, but she wanted it over now. She wanted to apologise and she wanted to make things up with him. The thought of him not being in her life was tearing her apart.

She'd tried to call and text him many times, but she'd heard nothing. The only thing left to do was to go and see him.

She'd not been in to work at Bird Consultants since Monday morning and had called in sick to work at the bar for that night. She'd told them she'd been mugged and was in a bad state. She knew she'd have to explain her face somehow and a mugging seemed enough for it to be a big deal, but not enough for her to be suffocated by sympathy. The perfect amount.

She walked round to her flat car park, putting the hood of her pink sweatshirt on her head and sunglasses on her face to mask her bruising. She got into her blue Ford Fiesta and pulled away. It was the first time she'd used her car since moving to the city, and she had questioned whether she needed it all. At that moment, though, she couldn't have been happier to have it.

Despite the numerous journeys she'd taken to Simon's house in recent times, she'd paid no attention, and now she was relying on her phone's GPS to guide her there.

It was a long and torturous journey, she just wanted to be there and to be with him. She needed him so badly and she wanted to be able to take away all the hurtful things she'd said the last time they'd seen each other. She ached more through the thought of losing Simon than through anything Damien had done.

Finally reaching his road, she pulled up towards the gates of his house and waited. Nothing happened. She'd always assumed that the gates just automatically opened upon the arrival of a car, but she supposed that made no sense. She had no clue how they really worked.

She looked around for inspiration and spotted a little buzzer to the left of the gate. She parked her car parallel to the steel bars, keeping well out of the road, and then stepped out to press the little silver button. She waited for something to happen. Nothing did, so a couple of minutes later she pressed the buzzer again.

'Beth!' Simon answered, to her complete relief.

'Let me in,' she said. He didn't answer. 'Simon?'

'I can't.'

'What? I'm sorry. I'm sorry for all the awful things I said the other day. I didn't mean them.'

'You were right, Beth. I can't drag you into my dangerous world. I'm no good for you.'

Beth wasn't expecting this. 'No Simon, no I was wrong. I love you, you're the best thing to ever happen to me.'

'Look at your face, Beth, it's all my fault.'

'You can see me?' she asked, then she noticed a small camera at the top of the gates. 'You're looking at me?'

'I feel dreadful. You deserve so much better than me.'

'Don't you love me anymore?' she asked.

'I'm always going to love you. That's why I can't put you through this. I've caused you so much pain.'

Beth suddenly turned to the gate. 'Jim!' she shouted, knowing he'd see sense and would let her in.

'He's not here. He's on holiday.'

'You've sent him away?' she asked, coming back to look at the camera, as if she was looking at Simon.

'I told him we'd broken up and I needed some time on my own. He understood.'

'We haven't broken up, don't say that!' she cried, tears now welling up in her eyes.

'I'm so sorry for all the hurt I've caused you.'

'No!' Beth sobbed. 'No, I don't want this. I love you. Don't do this, Simon. Don't I get a say?'

'This is the only way it can be. You have your whole life ahead of you, I can't let it be full of misery and hurt. I'm bad for you.'

'No! Simon, let me in. We can talk about this! This is what's going to hurt me!' she pleaded.

'I love you, Beth. Get home safely.'

'No Simon! Simon!!' She waited for an answer, but he was gone. 'Simon! I love you! This can't just be your decision!' She fell to the floor, crying desperately.

She'd had everything and in a flash it had all disappeared. She'd done nothing wrong, it was all so unfair. She sobbed on her knees, holding her stomach, feeling sick by the desperate loss that echoed through her soul.

'I love you!' she moaned. 'I want to be with you forever, why won't you let me in?' It was no use, though, Simon was gone. She looked up to the camera as if somehow it would bring him back, but all that existed was emptiness. All that was left was her deep, choking sobs. He was gone.

What Beth didn't know, though, was that Simon hadn't gone anywhere. He sat in his study and watched her, with great sadness, on his high definition monitor.

He'd had to let her go. Even though he loved her so

much. What option did he have? To ask her to stay and to draw her further into his dark, nasty world would just be selfish.

He could barely watch Beth so traumatised on the ground, her agony at his blunt decision so unbearable. If he'd let her in, though, surely her agony would be doubled, at least.

He looked down at his hands, covered in feathers, and felt certain of his decision, no matter how difficult it was. Then he looked to his arms, his chest, his legs and his stomach. Even his face and head had sporadic feathers thrusting up through his skin. He was now virtually covered head to toe.

His affliction was getting worse and worse and he couldn't involve her anymore. It was far more than a stress rash, this was who he was to become. The power inside of him had reaped its repercussions, but he didn't regret the force he'd used against Damien. He'd deserved it.

His life was already a rollercoaster without asking Beth to further deal with the shameful, hideous state that he now found himself in.

He watched Beth finally pick herself up and drive away. He'd been moved by her pleas and declarations of love, knowing every word she'd said was sincere. She always spoke with such honesty, he admired that quality. He couldn't offer her the same, though, and he knew he wasn't right for her.

No matter what he'd encountered, seeing her walk away was the hardest thing he'd ever done in his life. His lip quivered as he fought back the heart-rending tears that threatened to escape. He couldn't bear the thought of living without her, but he couldn't put her through the pain of being with him. He'd hit such a dark patch in his life. It was so grossly unfair that it had come at a time when he could have finally had true happiness.

No longer able to control the grief inside of him, he wept irrepressibly in his black chair. As the tears ran free and his body shook at the misery, a new feather reared its head through his stomach and he yelped in pain. All that lay ahead for him was torture and sorrow. But at least he'd known true love, he would be sure to hold on to that, no matter what.

Beth didn't sleep that night. She'd finally managed to stop crying, but she was still doubled up with the pain of losing Simon. She'd never known such hurt from anything in her life, the heartbreak crushed her inside.

She'd made the decision to go into work the next day. She couldn't face another day in her tiny flat, all alone, dwelling upon the woe of recent events; she needed to find a way back to her life, as empty as she knew it would now be.

Even if she managed to find a way past missing him incredibly, she still had to deal with the fact that she could never love anyone in the same way again. It ran deeper than love, they'd shared a special bond; but it had been ripped out of her violently, and she was left with no choice but to deal with the aftermath completely alone.

She dragged herself out of bed and slowly made her way to the office.

'Oh my God, Beth!' Gayle gasped when she saw Beth walk towards her desk. 'Your poor thing.' Gayle scanned the damage on Beth's face, alerting Michelle and Diane to her wounds.

'My husband got mugged once,' Diane said, almost sympathetically. 'Such a terrible world we live in.'

'Where did it happen?' Michelle asked, standing up to get a proper look.

'On my way home. I don't really want to talk about it,' Beth mumbled.

'Did you go to the police?' Gayle asked.

'No.'

'I don't blame you,' Diane exclaimed. 'My husband went to the police and nothing happened. These people fly in, take all your stuff, leave you for nothing, and then vanish off the face of the planet. All you're left with is the pain of repeating the story over and over again in the small hope that you'll get the justice that's inevitably never going to come your way.'

'Diane!' Gayle shushed.

'Can we just leave it!' Beth snapped.

'Of course,' Gayle nodded. 'Well, I'm very glad to have you back. I hadn't quite appreciated how much work you'd been ploughing through. You've been fantastic. Are you happy to get straight back into it?'

'Please,' Beth replied. 'Bury me with work, it'll be a great distraction.'

Gayle handed Beth a pile of invoices and Beth delved right in.

Five minutes past with complete silence and Beth found herself relaxing into her day. That was, though, until she was put on edge again by Gayle's unexpected outburst. 'Oh my God!'

'What it is?' Michelle asked, looking across at Gayle.

'Look who it is!' she said, pointing to Trisha's office. Beth turned round to see Trisha talking to an older gentleman. He was casually dressed in jeans and a checked shirt, but other than that all Beth could see was a full head of grey hair.

'Who is it?' Beth asked. Diane shrugged her shoulders, disinterested, but Beth's question was soon to be answered as the man was now following Trisha out of her office.

'That's her, there,' Trisha said, pointing straight to Beth. The man walked over and immediately glimpsed Beth's face.

'Bloody hell, what happened to you?' he asked in a strong cockney accent.

'Paul, hello!' Gayle greeted.

'Hello babe!' he answered, not seeing Beth's expression of sheer shock. He went to shake Gayle's hand. 'How've you been?' he asked.

'Really good, thank you. It's been a long time since we've seen you.'

'It sure has. You'll have to excuse me, Gayle, I've actually got some important stuff to attend to.'

'Of course,' she nodded, expecting him to walk off, but instead he looked straight back to Beth.

'Are you Beth Lance?' he asked. Beth just nodded, becoming increasingly sure that this was him, the only man that Simon actually looked up to. 'Good, you're coming with me.'

'Okay,' she said, standing up with respect. She followed him towards the lifts without turning back, and without seeing the startled looks of her colleagues, as once again one of the owners of the company had asked her, the new girl, for help.

Not saying a word to one another, Paul and Beth made their way to Simon's office.

'Take a seat, Beth,' he said, and she sat down on the sofa as instructed. 'Do you know who I am?' he asked.

'Are you Simon's uncle, Paul Bird?' she replied, praying that she was right.

'The one and only. Now where is my nephew?' he answered quite abruptly.

'What?'

'Simon's told me all about you, but that was well over a week ago and I've not heard from him since.'

'What do you mean you've not heard from him?'

'Where is my nephew?'

'He's at home. I think.'

'What have you done to him?'

'Nothing!' she shrieked quite defensively.

'Why are you smashed in? You look like you've been in a car crash.' Beth couldn't respond to this. She loved his nephew so much but she was hurting very badly and she didn't appreciate this accusatory tone. 'Well?'

Just that one, single word then pushed her over the edge. If he wanted to know, she'd tell him. She'd tell him everything. Besides, she needed to tell someone, she couldn't take the madness anymore.

'I don't even know how everything's happened,' she started, now freeing all her words and all her weeping simultaneously. 'It's all Damien's fault! That sick creep. Simon was so mad when he found out Damien wanted to sleep with me. He fired Damien but Damien went crazy. It was awful. Then Simon started to grow feathers. I didn't know what to do! Talk about random!'

Beth paused to gather her thoughts, but it wasn't long enough for Paul to ask the now increasing number of questions that must have been scaling his brain. Her release had started and she needed to tell someone all the terrible things that had been locked away inside of her for too long.

'He told me everything. I know all about it, all about the Malancy. It was freaky at first, but not as freaky as the feather. I still love him, though. We got through it and then the feather disappeared. It's his stress rash, I'm sure of it. But then Damien wound him up again and more feathers came back. That's what happens with stress, isn't it. It has to be his stress rash. He's so unique, it makes perfect sense. I mean what else could it be? So I got him to relax and all the feathers went away. See, I'm right, aren't I?'

Paul was now standing in the middle of the office, dumbfounded.

'Things were perfect at the weekend,' she rambled on. 'We were so in love. Then Damien attacked me and it all went wrong. I was so horrible to Simon, I shouldn't have been. I was such a bitch and none of it was his fault. He couldn't have been nicer to me. He lives in such a fucked up world, but none of it is his fault. He's just perfect, you know, he's everything.' Beth was really crying now. 'I told him to leave and now he won't speak to me. I even went to his house and he dumped me.' She put her hands in her face and heartily sobbed. 'He dumped me. He said he was no good for me, but I love him.' She looked up to Paul sincerely. 'I love him, Paul, he's my world, and he's left me.' Her words finally fell silent leaving nothing but crushing sobs in their wake.

Paul was left speechless, not quite sure what to do next. He looked around for a tissue, but Beth was already reaching for one from her pocket. She delicately dabbed her face, squinting against the soreness.

'I don't know where to start,' Paul exhaled. 'It seems a lot has happened.' He took a second to process the reams of information that had been passed his way. 'Right, first things first, we're going to see Simon to get this straightened out.'

Feeling momentarily happier at the news that they were on their way to visit Simon, she quickly used Simon's personal bathroom to tidy up her face, she collected her things, avoiding all eye contact with her colleagues, and then she followed Paul outside to his chauffeur driven BMW 5 series that was waiting at the front of the building for them. They both got in the back and the driver pulled away, apparently already knowing where they were going.

'You need to start at the start, love,' Paul said. 'That was a lot you just said. Damien's fired? Feathers? What are you talking about? And why on earth is your face so bashed in?'

Beth was now much calmer, a renewed sense of hope driving her forward as they headed on towards Simon's house together.

'Damien propositioned me, offering me a promotion if I slept with him. He's the reason for this too, but I don't want to talk about that,' she said, pointing to her face. 'Anyway, Simon caught him in the act and, after going a bit mad, he fired him.'

'That little git! That sordid little git. I can't believe he did that to you,' Paul seethed.

'But Damien wouldn't leave. He refused to leave the office and Simon got really angry. Then when Simon came home...' Beth stopped and looked at the driver. 'Can I talk in front of him?'

'Yes, of course, say whatever you need to.'

'Okay. Well, Simon had a feather poking out of his arm.'

'What do you mean a feather?'

'I mean a feather. It wasn't stuck to him, it was actually growing from him; it was part of him. Then it went, and then it got worse. His arms were covered in them. His stress rash.'

'It can't be a stress rash. Things don't work like that, Beth.'

'Not normally, no, but Simon's special.'

Paul smiled at this. 'He is definitely special, but not in that kind of way. Feathers don't just grow out of people, no matter who they are.'

'That's what I said, but Simon said he'd had a lifetime of weird stuff happening to him and this was just the newest thing.'

Paul sighed, frustrated. 'Oh Beth. I wish he could have known about himself since birth. Did he tell you that?'

'He's told me everything.'

'He has a power, but it's no different to what the rest of us could be capable of. He just has it within him. It's his gift and his curse.'

'It's not a curse.'

'At times it's been a great burden to him, but it's also been a great benefit. No matter what he is or isn't, though, no Malant has ever grown feathers, that is something just plain weird.'

'What's wrong with him, then?' Beth asked.

'You really love him, don't you?'

'I'd do anything for him. He's my soulmate. I know he is.'

Paul fell silent at Beth's statement and he watched her thoughtfully, but she didn't really notice. She was now staring into space thinking of Simon and how much she longed to see him again. She felt so grateful for this new turn of events that might bring them back together after their harsh, unexpected split.

To her relief, they soon arrived at Simon's house and the gate magically opened for them. 'How did you do that?' Beth asked, imagining it was some sort of spell.

'Remote,' Paul answered, pointing to the little black box in the driver's hand. Beth smiled to herself.

They pulled on to the drive and quickly got out the car. Paul reached for the front door key in his pocket and let them in, both of them immediately calling out for Simon. There was no reply, though, and they split up to search for him.

'I'll go upstairs,' Beth said, feeling his presence in that direction. She went straight for his bedroom and pushed opened the slightly ajar door.

She looked around but he was nowhere to be found. Giving up and ready to look elsewhere, she headed back for the door but was halted by a faint chirping sound. She looked around and saw nothing, then grabbed the door knob one more time.

The chirp came again, but this time it was louder, and this time its origin was brought straight to her attention.

She screamed.

Paul came running up the stairs. 'What is it?' he said, darting into the room.

He saw Beth standing open mouthed, staring wildly ahead of her. She started to shake.

'What is it?' Paul demanded.

'Simon?' Beth asked, edging towards the bedside table. Paul looked across and there, standing on the top, was what could only be described as a bird.

'Simon?' Beth asked again, and they both watched as the bird creature slowly nodded its head.

TWENTY-FIVE

The bird in front of them had the same stunning, scarlet feathers that had been growing on Simon's arms, but it was far from beautiful. Beth could barely look at it.

It was the same shape and size of a raven, but the remnants of man mingled into it were still very visible. There were patches of skin clearly stretched between the feathers, and one of the wings was actually nothing more than a finger with feathers on it. The legs were fleshy blobs that made it hard for the bird to stand and its beak was the colour of strained lips. But none of that freaked out Beth as much as the eyes. It was the eyes that gave this creature away to be Simon.

The eyes were much larger than one would expect to see on a bird and far more human. They were muddled in a mound of feathers and as Beth looked closely she immediately recognised the velvety chocolate sadness that swirled within the balls. The pain that Simon must be feeling was playing out in his frightened gaze and all Beth could do was freeze. The whole creature was a distorted jumble of man and bird. It was horrifying.

'This is all my fault!' she gasped, looking to the floor.

'How is it your fault?' Paul asked, utterly bewildered

himself.

'I was so horrible to him. You don't understand. I must have made him so angry, and then... this.'

'This isn't your fault. This isn't right. This has nothing to do with Simon getting angry, feeling sad or being stressed. This is magic. This is the work of a spell, Beth. Something or someone has done this to him, and there's nothing you could have done to stop it.'

'What?' Beth asked, finally looking up from the carpet.

Paul looked to the bird. 'Simon, buddy, can you speak, can you do anything?' Simon just shook his head.

'Oh my God! Who would do this?' Beth cried. 'This is awful. What can we do?'

'Oh believe me, Beth, we're going to do everything we can. No one hurts my family!' Paul affirmed. 'Si, are you going to be okay?' he asked, turning to the bird. 'You know where we've got to go.'

The bird creature just nodded.

'We'll be back as soon as we can,' Paul confirmed.

'Where are we going?' Beth asked. 'Can we just leave him?'

'Just come with me, Beth. Trust me.' Paul took one last look at Simon and then headed towards the door.

Beth forced herself to take a last glance towards Simon, but she couldn't think of what to say. She quickly turned to follow Paul, trying not to break down completely.

But as Paul led her down the stairs, Beth couldn't fight her emotions anymore and the tears freed their way down her cheeks. He stopped and looked at her.

'Don't worry babe, we're going to get this sorted. He's too good a lad to have this happen to him.' Paul placed his hand on her shoulder, feeling her shaking body.

They left the house where the driver was obediently waiting for them. Beth was let in the car first and then Paul followed, muttering a destination that Beth couldn't quite hear.

They pulled off, back through the gates, and back

down the country road. They both remained completely silent, individually worrying about the man they both loved, albeit very differently.

They drove on to the M40, a route Beth had grown very familiar with over the past couple of weeks, but this time they carried on, not stopping at the turning for Heaningford. They went right through the west of London, continuing through the zones and heading straight into the heart of the city.

They'd now been driving for an hour and Beth was still no wiser as to where they were going. They headed over London Bridge to the south of the river Thames, and then they turned right into a side street where the car finally stopped.

Beth had no clue at all where they were and it seemed like there was nothing but unnamed buildings around her. After waiting for the driver to safely let her out, she eagerly walked round to the pavement to join Paul.

'Where are we?' she asked, looking at a row of seemingly irrelevant buildings.

'Just in front of you,' Paul stated, pointing to a building Beth had not noticed until that moment. Just like the Malancy restaurant she'd been to, the building would have been unnoticeable had it not been pointed out.

It was a dull, grey brick building with no windows and just one dark wooden door in the middle.

'What is this place?' Beth asked as she followed Paul towards the door. Then a strange prickly chill crawled over her skin and she felt a dark cloud smother her. It was the same eerie sensation she'd felt both on her first day at Bird Consultants and at the restaurant Simon had taken her to. This had to be related to the Malancy.

'This is the Malancy Headquarters,' Paul confirmed. 'This is where we're going to get our answers.'

Paul opened the large, heavy door and Beth felt her breath extinguish with fear.

The door opened up into a light, bright room. Serene

shades of green and blue lifted the ambience in what was clearly a reception area. Paul greeted the timid receptionist.

'We need to speak with Jane, please,' Paul informed her.

'Do you have an appointment?' she asked.

'No, but she'll want to see us.'

'I'm sorry sir, Mrs Parker is very busy, you have to have an appointment.'

'Believe me, she'll want to see us.'

'I'm sorry sir.'

'Get on the phone and tell her it's about Simon Bird.'

'Simon Bird?' the girl asked, her eyes flickering at the mention of his name, much to Beth's surprise.

The receptionist did as she was told and dialled a number on her phone. 'Hello. I have someone down here to see you. He says it's about Simon Bird. Yes, of course.' The girl placed down the phone and looked back to Paul. 'It's fine. Mrs Parker is-'

'I know where I'm going, thank you,' Paul interrupted, heading straight for the lifts. Beth kept very close to him, all words now very far from her usually active lips.

The lift doors opened immediately and Paul pressed for the fifth floor as they entered. Beth suddenly felt dazzled by an explosion of questions, but she couldn't find the words to explicate any of them. She wanted it to all be a horrific nightmare. She wanted, at any moment, to find consciousness again and wake up lying next to Simon, no sign of a feather, no word of Malancy and magic, and for all of this to have been a bizarre fiction that she'd made up unwillingly in her sleep after a stressful day at work.

As the lift doors opened, though, the hope of it being a dream quickly faded and they stepped out to tackle more of the unnerving reality.

The fifth floor's serene green ambience mimicked the reception, and it helped to calm Beth's fears. They found themselves in a sparsely occupied, open plan office. The gentle whirr of electrical equipment was the only sound to be heard, with just two of the five desks in use.

'Paul!' a woman suddenly greeted. Perhaps in her early forties, she was dressed impeccably in a navy blue suit.

'Jane!' Paul greeted back, taking her hand and kissing her on the cheek, his lips brushing against her voluminous blonde bob.

'It's been far too long!'

'This is Beth Lance.'

Jane firmly shook Beth's hand, sporting a very welcoming smile across her heavily made-up face. 'Lovely to meet you. Are you okay?' she asked, studying Beth's bruises.

'She's fine. Work related accident,' Paul jumped in.

'Sorry to hear that. Anyway, come in.' Jane led them both into her rather large office.

The office had a maroon hue, with sophisticated black furniture, and it was spotlessly clean.

'So tell me, what's going on with our notable Mr Bird?' Jane asked, sitting down in her leather, executive style chair.

'It's a weird one, I'll admit,' Paul started, sitting opposite. 'He's turned into a bird.'

'What do you mean he's turned into a bird?' Jane queried quite plainly. Her face didn't flinch at all at hearing such bizarre news and Beth's skin prickled unnervingly at how this woman found the whole incident to be quite acceptable.

'I don't know what else to say. Beth knows more,' Paul said, looking to Beth for support.

Beth looked at Paul blankly. Words in general had escaped her, she had no hope at all of elucidating the madness of recent events. She didn't even know who this strange lady was.

Beth's brain now hurt as the mountain of questions kept building in her mind, but she was too afraid to ask any of them for fear of what the answers might be. She knew she had to find a way to speak, though. She was here for Simon and he needed her. Now was not the time for her to freeze. She took a deep breath and decided to stop thinking. She had to just let the words flow, saying whatever came naturally out of her mouth. All this lady wanted was the truth, she shouldn't need to overthink that.

She took one more deep breath and then shakily began. 'He's not a bird.'

'But Paul just said-'

'He's like a bird... man... mess. It's awful!'

Jane and Paul just glared at Beth, waiting for her to elaborate.

'It all started last week,' she began, now finding her flow. 'Simon came home from the office where he'd had some trouble with an employee and we noticed that a feather had started to grow on his arm. Then after another stressful encounter more feathers appeared. But when he calmed down they disappeared. But then something terrible happened and we had a huge argument and he refused to see me...' Beth's composure was in threat as she battled with her distress. She took a second to soothe her nerves. 'Basically, he's now this horrific bird thing!'

'This is most peculiar,' Jane stated. Her calm reaction to this nightmare was now irritating Beth. 'I know Simon has his issues-'

'What issues?' Beth snapped.

Taken aback by Beth's defensiveness, Jane looked at her inquisitively. 'Who are you?'

'She's Simon's girlfriend,' Paul explained.

'Girlfriend?' Jane spat, not even attempting to hide the surprise on her face. This was the bit that finally stirred her. This was, apparently, more shocking than Simon being a bird-man-like creature.

'Yes,' Beth confirmed, feeling now more uncomfortable, if that was even possible.

'I don't think you're a Malant either, are you?' Jane enquired.

'No.'

'You're his girlfriend?' Jane asked again, studying Beth curiously.

'Why can't he have a non-Malant girlfriend?' Beth asked.

'That's not the issue at all,' Jane clarified

'It's his presence she's querying,' Paul whispered to Beth.

'It doesn't put you off?' Jane probed.

'It's one of the things I love most about him.'

'Right,' Jane nodded after a few seconds, amazement widening her eyes. 'Well, you might like it, but people tend to steer clear of him because of said presence, not antagonise him. This is far from a clear cut case, as I'm sure you're well aware. It definitely sounds like magic, though. This isn't just a random act, that I'm positive of.'

Jane sat thoughtfully for a moment, searching her head for logic. Then she edged towards her computer and started typing. 'First things first, let's find out what magic we're dealing with.' She spent a few minutes typing something in that neither Beth nor Paul could see as they faced the back of her monitor.

'Oh dear God,' she finally exclaimed. 'This is quite unexpected.'

'What?' Beth asked, her heart now pounding.

'I've not come across this in years. I knew it had to be powerful to cause someone to physically change their appearance, but...'

'What is it?' Beth demanded, barely able to breathe now, petrified of what was to come.

'It's bicantomene.'

'What's that?' Paul asked, much calmer in appearance.

'It's a substance found in rocks in some African deserts. It's so dangerous, it can give users an incredible amount of power. It's been banned in this country for fifty years. I don't even know how it could enter the country without being detected.'

'I don't understand, is this bad? What does it mean?'

Beth pleaded.

'It means, Beth, that if this substance was in fact used against Simon then there may be no way of ever turning him back.'

TWENTY-SIX

Beth stood up, trembling. She didn't know quite how to deal with the news. She'd finally found her soulmate, but he'd turned into a monstrous bird thing, and now she was being told that he might be stuck in that state forever. Most people didn't have to deal with such issues. This was off the scale of weird and Beth needed some fresh air.

'Are you okay?' Paul asked, putting his arm around her. She took deep breaths and tried to find her equilibrium, not even sure where to start with comprehending this.

'Beth, please, we don't know anything yet. Let's find out what's actually gone on here before we start to worry,' Jane soothed.

'What do we do?' Paul asked Jane.

'I want you two to go and get a cup of coffee and I'm going to speak with Ralph. Okay?'

Paul nodded and then led Beth back to the lifts, his arm supporting her unsteadiness. Beth could barely take in her surroundings, she couldn't grasp the thought of Simon being a bird for the rest of his life. It couldn't possibly be true.

They got in the lift and she battled with tears that so wanted to escape down her face, but she knew she had to try and keep her composure. She'd spent too much time crying of late and it hadn't helped one bit. She now needed answers. She needed something more definitive to at least give her a fighting chance of making sense of any of it. There had to be a way of turning him back.

She didn't have a clue where she was in the building now, although she knew they'd gone down. Paul, with his arm still around her, led her out of the lifts, through a small corridor and into a large canteen.

Now mid-afternoon, it was completely empty with just the vague essence of beef and curry still floating through the air.

Paul took Beth to one of the plastic seats near the back of the room and then made his way to the coffee machine. 'What can I get for you?'

'Tea. With sugar. I think I need it,' Beth replied, slumping down in the chair helplessly.

'No problem.'

Paul pressed the button and a little white polystyrene cup appeared. The drink poured itself quickly and then he took it to Beth before going back for his own black coffee.

As soon as his coffee arrived he took his little polystyrene cup to the table and sat down opposite Beth. Beth was scanning the room, trying to catch her breath and calm her mind. She so needed answers.

Then, she decided she was going to get them. They were stuck here for some unknown reason for an indefinite amount of time in a place Beth hadn't even known existed until a very short time ago, and it was about time she got an explanation. She looked straight into Paul's eyes and let her mouth finally form words, the fear now all gone as pure determination took over.

'Where are we, really? Who was that woman? And what is going on?' she demanded.

Paul didn't blink, he stared straight back, confidently. 'We are at the Malancy headquarters. This is like our government. We have our own law and order that works hand in hand with the more general law enforcement of the country. Most Malants are good people, but there are some nasty sods in the world and this government was put together to combat them.'

'Simon told me about that.'

'That lady was Jane Parker. She's the Senior Law Enforcement Director here. I've known her for many years, she's a great lady. She was the one who approved Bird Consultants in the first place many years ago.'

'I gathered you knew her.'

'As she said, someone has done this to Simon. It hasn't just happened by accident or naturally, it's a malicious act that someone has consciously and viciously performed to cause Simon harm.'

'Did you know that straight away?'

'No, I didn't know what to think,' Paul confirmed.

'What made you come here, then? And why did they react so weirdly at the mention of Simon's name?'

'I don't need to tell you, Simon's very special. The government has always been very interested in him and his unique abilities.'

'Interested? What does that mean? Like they want to dissect him or something?'

'Don't be silly. Of course not. And anyway, even if they did, no one has the power to make Simon do anything.'

'Well that can't be true or we wouldn't be here, would we.'

'We don't know why we're here yet. Let them find out more before we jump to conclusions.'

'What are they doing? Who's Ralph?' Beth asked.

'Ralph is a very powerful Malant.'

'Like Simon?'

'No one is as powerful as Simon. Ralph is just very skilled at what he does, not like Simon. Si has a deep power held within him that he can manipulate in many different ways, probably more so than he even knows himself. Ralph, on the other hand, is more like a scholar who has learnt his craft through extensive studying. He understands our magic more than anyone. He's the best at what he does and he'll be able to track down this substance that Jane was telling us about.'

'How will that help?' Beth asked.

'There are quite a few substances banned for Malants in this country. Certain elements are connected to dark magic, something most of us try and steer well clear of. It's not wise to go down that route, it inevitably ends badly. No good magic could hurt Simon like this, so they need to track down where the bad stuff has come from.'

'Can they do that?'

'If anyone can, Ralph can.'

Beth knotted her hands together and thought hard.

'What are you thinking?' Paul asked.

'What if it's something else?'

'One step at a time, Beth.'

'I'm so worried.'

'You're not alone.'

'Is this punishment of some sort?' Beth queried, her mind starting to rationalise the madness.

'Punishment? For what?'

'His past?'

'What about his past?'

'You said that hurting other people was against the law. But Simon's done that.'

'What do you mean Simon's hurt people?' Paul asked, clearly confused.

'Simon told me about the case he had with the lady who wanted the really expensive necklace. If the man didn't meet his end of the bargain then Simon was going to mark the woman for life with the imprint of the necklace.'

'That was over ten years ago,' Paul exclaimed, shaking his head.

'So? Simon said he's done many questionable things over the years. They're not coming back to bite him now, are they?'

'Oh Beth. Simon is the best man I know. Nothing is coming to bite him.'

'But the stuff he did!'

'I don't know what Simon has or hasn't told you, but let me tell you this. Simon is as good as a man can possibly be. You have to forgive him for any indiscretions in his past, he's been through so much.'

'I know.'

'I don't know if you do.'

'Tell me then.'

Paul paused for a second and shifted in his seat. He looked quite uncomfortable all of a sudden.

'Has he told you that his parents died?' he started. Beth just nodded and this seemed to throw Paul for a moment. Then he continued. 'From the moment he was born, people were scared of Simon. None of us knew what the hell was going on at first, but then when he was about two he started to move things and change things without the need of any help. He didn't have to cast spells or harness the power around him like the rest of us, he just had a natural gift.

'It scared his parents so much, they didn't know what to do with him. Rather than trying to embrace it or understand it though, they ran. They were so worried about what the future might hold for him, they decided to just hide him away from it, never telling him anything about his true self, his legacy, or his right. It went against everything I believed in.'

'It must have been so hard.'

'It was the wrong decision! Anyway, it was so shocking the way they died. They were caught in a freak gas explosion, no one could have seen it coming. I felt so sorry for the poor lad, he was suddenly so alone. Even the social worker that came to take him away was scared of him. They called me up immediately, demanding that I collect him, I had to drop everything. It was so unsympathetic.

The most unthinkable tragedy had just happened to him and he was being treated appallingly. I knew straight away I had to tell him the truth.'

'That couldn't have been easy.' Beth tried to put herself in Paul's shoes. She didn't know much about Paul, but she knew he was a fun-loving bachelor, or so Simon had told her. It must have been such a shock to literally overnight become the legal guardian of a child he'd not seen in a decade. No matter how difficult it must have been, though, Beth could see that Paul would not have had it any other way. Family was clearly so important to him, and Simon was all that Paul had left.

'That night,' he explained, 'the first night we spent together, I sat him down man to man and told him everything. It opened up his world. It was shocking for him, sure, but it finally made everything add up. For a while it helped him cope, but it still didn't stop friends at school picking on him. He did the odd bit of magic for revenge, moving the bastards' items and showing them up a bit, but I quickly warned him off that track. He didn't want to get himself into trouble. How would I explain that to the head teacher?'

'It must have been horrible for him.'

'I suppose the only Godsend was that he knew no different, and at least finally being able to understand why people feared him gave him peace of mind. I don't know. Anyway, everything changed when he joined the business.'

'He told me he helped you with a tricky case?'

'That's right, he was studying for his A Levels. He's so incredibly bright, he could have done anything, but he was scared of going to University, for obvious reasons. He was completely confused about what he was going to do with his life. I was just starting out with the business, it was my fourth or fifth case, something like that, and I knew I'd taken on more than I could chew. I forget the details, but it was like one o'clock in the morning and I was stuck. Simon came to see me and he just saw it all so clearly.

Then he helped me again and again, and I started taking on bigger, more complex cases, and by the time he got his A Level results – straight A's I'd like to add – he was my junior contractor.'

'He told me he'd made his first million when he was eighteen.'

'That he did. He made us both millionaires in six months. I'd go and see the client and make the deal and Simon would do the hard work and make it all possible. He'd write complex contracts that ensured the client's problems, whatever they were, would just disappear, whilst never compromising the secrecy of Bird Consultants and our power. We had two spell workers at the time who'd do the magic, following Simon's intricate specification very carefully. We've got twenty-five now just in the UK. It's big business.'

'How could he get away with what he did to that woman with the necklace?'

'He never did anything. After a lifetime of being an outcast and being terrified about a future where people wouldn't even want to sit in the same room as him, suddenly people were asking for meetings with him, shaking his hand, inviting him to parties and paying him millions for the pleasure. His world was turned upside down and I suppose he felt a little surge from it all. He went off the rails a bit, but nothing other young men haven't done. He partied, spent his money frivolously, enjoyed exotic holidays, and he lived his new life to the max. When it came to that man with the necklace, Simon could smell the desperation so he used him a little to get some new customers. It meant no harm, and Simon knew that this man was good for his end of the contract. I see it that this man got a priceless necklace for his wife and the only cost to him was spreading the word of our work. Win win all round.'

'I suppose,' Beth shrugged.

'The big turning point in Simon's life was meeting that

awful bitch.'

'His ex-girlfriend?'

'He told you about that too?' Paul asked, pausing for a moment. Beth just nodded. 'Okay, we'll call her ex-girlfriend for the sake of this story as the words I often use aren't suitable for polite conversation. For years, Simon wanted for nothing except one thing, the one thing he knew he couldn't buy: companionship. By the time he was nineteen he'd never even kissed a girl. He was so desperate for love, and he never thought he'd have it. Then this silly bitch came into his life. I hated her from the outset, but Simon just couldn't see through her lies, he was so happy that a woman was actually giving him the time of day. I should have nipped it in the bud from the start, but I couldn't hurt him.

'For a time, despite everything, she was good for him, I suppose. But just for a very short time. I could see the despicable look on her face when he kissed her, but she put up with it all for his money. He spoilt her rotten and all she had to do was shag him every now and then. She could barely stand to be around him most of the time, but she did it all for a few lousy quid. Then she broke his heart.'

'He told me how he found her with another man.'

'It shattered him. It was like he came crashing down to earth with a vicious smack and it changed him overnight. He stopped going out, stopped partying, stopped going on holiday, stopped spending his money, everything. He became a recluse, only ever going out when he had to see people for work. Even then he'd only speak when he had to. It broken my heart to see, but he couldn't trust anyone anymore. He started to believe that no one wanted to be with him for him. They all just wanted his power and his money, that's all he could see.'

'Oh my God, that's awful.'

'He got a bit better just before he turned thirty. He started to buy nice things for his house and he bought his

Aston Martin. That was when Jim came on board too. I encouraged that.'

'Does Jim know about the Malancy?' Beth asked, suddenly realising that she still didn't know the answer.

'Not that I know of. I found out about Jim through a client and I knew it would be good for Simon to have someone looking out for him when I wasn't around. I hated the thought of him being so alone. To be honest, I don't know what Simon has or hasn't told Jim, I keep out of it.'

'I can imagine Jim would be very understanding. He's such a nice man.'

'I'm so grateful for him,' Paul admitted. 'And Simon's got someone to look after things when he's back in New York now, as well.'

Beth felt sickened by the thought of Simon going back to New York. She couldn't bear the idea of Simon leaving her now. 'Tell me about New York.'

'I only meant to move there for a year,' Paul explained, 'to set up the business, but I fell in love with it, so I stayed. Then Si came over to visit me and it was a break for him. Now it's his permanent escape. We've got a massive Condo, but he barely leaves it. I'm out all the time, maxing out my bachelor life, but Simon refuses to join me. It's such a shame, I miss us going out and having a few drinks. We have the odd meal, maybe once a month, but at the same old Malant places. That's it. The rest of the time he hides behind his laptop. He hates it when he has to come back here to deal with issues, but I've always made very sure he has an active role in the business. I can't have him shut off completely.'

'So he still works on all the contracts and things?' Beth queried.

'He's our best man,' Paul confirmed. 'Do you know why he came back here this time, before he met you?'

'Work stuff?'

'Yes, but do you know what he was doing for work?'

Beth shook her head. 'We had a client up in Birmingham,' Paul started.

'Yes, I knew he'd gone to Birmingham for a few days.'

'They're called MB Solutions, a massive software company with branches all over the UK. Their Birmingham branch had won a major job with Broadway Stores.'

'The supermarket?'

'The very same. MB had the contract to rework Broadway's stocking system. It was set to revolutionise the way they could manage their stock. It was, apparently, genius, and worth a lot of money to MB. But they cocked up. While the spec was being put together they went through two account managers and one tech guy. They don't keep staff for very long, I don't think they're a great company to work for. Anyway, when it all got signed off and went ahead it didn't work as expected and MB couldn't find out why, there'd been way too much inconsistency. Three months later with legal threats being fired their way they finally found out that some vital coding was wrong, but it was far from a simple fix. For a layman anyway. So they called us in to sort it out.'

'They called in Simon?'

'Not at first, the sales guys always go in first to see if we can actually help or not. Simon only gets involved at the contract stage when it's all been agreed. Which it was. So Simon wrote a very simple contract that said we'd sort out the coding and make it all work seamlessly, obviously for a hefty fee; and then he added in a few clauses.'

'Clauses? Like what?'

'This is where Simon has grown into a strong young man and I'm so proud of him. I never set up Bird Consultants so our magic could be exploited, I just saw a gap in the market where we could make some money and help a few people out. It's got a lot bigger, granted, but I never wanted a dodgy business.

'Anyway, when Simon hit rock bottom after that bitch

broke his heart he got a bit mad at our customers. He was sick of them just using us to magic away their problems. Sure, they'd pay a hefty price in financial terms, but it was business money so it didn't really matter to them personally. He felt it was completely unethical that they could so easily mess up with virtually no consequences, so he started adding in clauses to his contracts to make it a bit more... right, shall we say.'

'What did he do?'

'For MB Solutions, they had to agree to never do business with Broadway Stores again. It was phrased something like they couldn't again transact with the store or its employees in any way except for personal retail purposes. All members of staff had to agree to it, whatever their role.

'Simon didn't want them to have their major cock up magically washed away only for them to be free the next day to land another key contract with Broadway as if nothing had ever happened. It's not right that it could work that way. So he forced them to give up Broadway Stores as a future client. If they broke the contract in any way then the problem would reinstate itself and they'd be stuck with the same issue, but this time without any magic to help them.'

'So he came home to sort out the contract?'

'Well, yeah, but only cause it went tits up. It all seemed to be working and then suddenly, out of the blue, MB was being whacked with legal threats again and Broadway's stock management was in chaos.'

'What happened?'

'No one knew. Not one member of staff had even had a discussion with Broadway as far as anyone knew. The only man who could sort it out was Simon, so he had to come back.'

'And did he sort it out?'

'He always does,' Paul nodded proudly. 'He found out, God knows how, that some little git at MB had had a one night stand with the Purchasing Manager of Broadway Stores. This stupid boy had met her one night at a club or something and had bought her drinks, kebab and then, after they'd done the deed, he'd paid for her taxi to go back to her husband.'

'What?' Beth asked, confused. 'How did that matter?'

'Simon deduced that as far as the contract was concerned this stupid idiot had, in fact, transacted with this woman. He'd basically paid to have sex with her by buying her drinks, food and a taxi ride. It was like prostitution as he had no desire to ever see her again.'

'That's ridiculous, how could that make a difference?'

'These aren't just normal paper contracts that we sign and shove in a filing cabinet somewhere, they're sealed with magic. Once you sign them, you're forever at the mercy of what they say. Most of the time it works in your favour, but Simon plays a tricky little game and there's no room for error. As far as the contract was concerned, a transaction had been made and so it rendered the deal null and void. Broadway's computer system broke again and MB was having to deal with all the consequences.'

'Did he fix it?'

'Of course. He got the stupid boy to go on another date with the woman where he didn't pay for everything. She was unwilling at first, so I hear; she is married. But you don't mess with Simon, you do as he asks. So this boy somehow flattered her into sleeping with him again, and that was that. It all magically corrected itself and the problem was solved.'

'I can't believe it. I'd never think of all that.'

'He's a clever one, my Simon.' Paul paused for thought as a realisation hit him, and his mood became more sombre. 'You know the irony of all this, don't you?'

'What?'

'If I was trapped as a bird or you were, or anyone, Simon could probably fix it all. He always finds a way around stuff, nothing's ever got the better of him before.

But now he's the last person that can help.'

Beth sat up straight, a renewed sense of dedication and love towards Simon now fuelling her. 'It's our turn now!'

'For what?' Paul asked.

'He's done so much for both of us, so it's time we look after him. It's on us now, it's our turn to help.'

Paul's response was cut off as the door suddenly opened and Jane appeared. She stood in the doorway and nodded to them. 'You better come back up.'

'You know something?' Paul asked

'It was the bicantomene. We know when and where it was used, and we know who's done this to Simon.'

'Tell us!' Beth asked, not wanting to wait another second.

'You better come up,' Jane repeated.

'Tell us, Jane,' Paul pleaded.

She nodded, capitulating. 'All right. Does the name Damien Rock mean anything to you?'

TWENTY-SEVEN

Beth and Paul didn't say a word as they followed Jane back up to her office.

They sat down in Jane's office and waited eagerly for an explanation as Jane carefully took her seat.

'I take it from the looks on your faces you both know Damien?' she asked.

'Very well,' Paul confirmed. 'It can't be him.'

'Of course it is!' Beth exclaimed. 'It makes perfect sense. He's a horrible, horrible man. Who else would do this to Simon?'

Jane shook her head. 'The only facts we know at this present time are that Damien has somehow managed to place his hands on bicantomene and he used it last Monday to cast a dark spell aimed directly at Simon. There's a warrant out for his arrest and my team is on the way. Ralph's located him, that's what took so long.'

'Location spells are one of the toughest things that a Malant can do, they take enormous energy,' Paul explained to Beth.

'You're on your way to get him, definitely?' Beth asked, needing clarity.

'Yes, he'll be brought in as soon as possible,' Jane

confirmed.

'Why would Damien do this?' Paul mumbled.

'He's sick, that's why!' Beth insisted.

'This is such extreme action. He's a family friend, I can't imagine why on earth he'd want to do something so evil,' Paul stated, shaking his head.

'It's also highly illegal. Damien couldn't have thought that he was going to get away with it,' Jane added.

'You're going to make him pay, aren't you?' Beth seethed.

'Don't worry, this won't be dealt with lightly,' Jane confirmed.

'I need to know why he's done this,' Paul said. 'I want to see him.'

'This needs to be dealt with properly, Paul. You've got to leave it to us. The best thing you can do right now is go home and check on Simon.'

'This doesn't make any sense to me,' Paul muttered.

'When you bring him in, can we turn Simon back?' Beth asked, hopefully. 'Now you know who did it, can you undo the spell?'

There was a cold silence as Paul and Jane just looked at one another.

'What? Tell me? Please say you can undo it! Damien can undo it, can't he? You can make him!'

'Thanks Jane, we'll get on our way now,' Paul said, standing up.

'I want to know!' Beth asserted.

'I'll explain everything on the way home, we need to get back to Simon. Jane, you better keep us posted, I'm counting on you.'

'Of course,' Jane nodded.

'I'm not going anywhere until you tell me,' Beth declared.

'Beth, get your arse up off that chair now and come with me!' Paul commanded. 'You'll get all your answers, but Jane needs to get on with her job and we need to get back to Simon.'

Although his spirit was so weak in comparison to Simon's strong nature, Beth still knew she wasn't to mess with this man, and she did as she was told. She followed him to the lift, folding her arms for effect, performing a small tantrum at his refusal to give her answers. Her childish behaviour only masked the terror she was really feeling, though. She couldn't face the truth that he was inevitably going to tell her: that Simon was, indeed, stuck for life as a bird.

The car was waiting out the front for them. Beth couldn't be sure if the driver had been there all the time or whether he'd been summoned back somehow, but it didn't matter. She got in the back, shortly followed by Paul, and they headed on to face the early evening London traffic.

'Are you going to tell me?' Beth asked, not able to look at Paul for fear of his answer.

'You want to know what Simon's fate is?' he asked, knowing full well that was exactly what she wanted, but postponing the answer as best he could.

'Yes, please tell me. Can the magic be undone? Can he be a human again?'

'Without knowing the exact spell Damien cast, we can't know anything for sure.'

'Don't mess me around, Paul. Just tell me the truth.'

'All I know is that these spells are normally unbreakable. He didn't turn straight into a bird, so there might be some flexibility.' Paul then shook his head. 'The truth is, these spells are normally cast for life. They're set in stone and the only way they're ever broken is through the death of the person who cast them.'

'So what are you saying?' Beth asked, praying so hard that she hadn't understood.

'Basically, the only way Simon is ever going to be human again is if Damien dies.'

'Oh my God!' Beth gasped, tears filling up in her eyes. 'Is that what we've got to do, then? Kill Damien? We can't do that... can we?'

'Believe me, if there was any way of killing Damien and bringing Simon back, I'd do it. But we can't. Not only is he now being brought in, where he'll most likely spend the rest of his life in prison, but Simon would never forgive us. We're all he's got, bird or no bird.'

Beth sobbed quietly into her hands, hope now all lost. The desire for it to all be a nightmare now raged through her and she prayed to wake up next to Simon and to feel a sense of relief. She wanted none of it to be true. She felt utterly helpless.

'Why can't we be there to speak with Damien? Why does that bitch have to deal with it? She won't care, not like we do!' Beth shrieked.

'What bitch? Jane?' Paul asked, confused.

'Yes!'

'She's not a bitch.'

'She doesn't like Simon.'

'What makes you say that?' Paul queried, completely baffled.

'She said he's got issues and people like to steer clear of him. She didn't like the fact that I was his girlfriend.'

'She was just stating the truth, Beth. People do have issues with Simon.'

'Like who?!' Beth was getting quite traumatised now.

Paul looked at her stained face, the tears and dismay now so much in charge. Then a thought hit him. 'What do you feel when you're around Simon?'

'What do you mean?'

'You know what I mean. Tell me.'

Beth considered his question, and for a small moment of blissful relief she allowed herself to think back to the first glorious meeting she'd had with Simon, where she'd made him a cup of tea. She felt a warm glow wrap around her as she remembered his impactful aura. 'I feel warmth. He has a very strong presence, and I know that not everyone likes it, but to me he's warm and safe. I feel totally at peace when I'm with him, like there's been half of me missing for years and finally, when he's around, I'm whole again. It's a lovely feeling. How could anyone not feel wonderful around him?'

Paul remained momentarily stunned. 'That's what you feel? When you're in Simon's presence, that's how you feel?' he finally asked.

'Yes. Why?'

'That's not what anyone else feels. That's incredible. You two really do have something special, don't you?'

'What do other people feel?'

'To the rest of the world Simon emits an icy, painful chill.'

'No. He can't do.'

'He's not easy to be around. It's like a cold bitterness that burns your skin, it's so uncomfortable, and it can be very overwhelming. It's not so bad when Simon's happy or at peace, but when he's angry or excited it gets so much worse. It hurts to be in presence at times, he makes you feel very cold; blisteringly cold. It's not pleasant.'

'That's ridiculous!'

'Most people don't know it's him so they just get on with it. At best they assume it's a vicious draught from somewhere, but it never goes unnoticed.'

Beth thought back over the times they'd been together. She remembered the silent, frosty reception that her colleagues in the office always gave him. The people in the bar avoided him, too, and then there were those people on the tube that refused to sit near him. Beth couldn't fathom that anyone could feel such a way in his lovely company.

'I'm so glad he's met you, Beth.'

'Does he know how he affects people?' she asked, her tears now dried up.

'Not really. Well I've never told him, not to the full extent. Don't Beth. You tell him how he makes you feel, that's all he needs to know. He knows people feel uncomfortable around him and he's seen them wrap up or steer clear, but I don't think he knows he's painful to be around. None of that matters now, though, not now he has you.'

'How do you cope?'

'He's family, he's my blood. He's my brother's son, I have to find a way. I've got used to it over the years and I don't notice it so much anymore. I'd do anything for him. Tolerating a coldness that he has no control over whatsoever is a no brainer. He needs us, Beth. He needs you. You're the only person that feels differently around him, and so you can help him in ways that no one else can. Let's utilise that to get through this.'

Beth looked to Paul softly. He was a remarkable man, she could see why Simon respected him so much. But he was so different to Simon in so many ways. He had a strong build like Simon, but with nowhere near the height, perhaps just five foot nine. He was far more approachable, though, with playful eyes and a friendly face. She could tell he was a good salesman.

He and Simon together were the perfect team, no wonder the company had made so much money. Paul could win over anyone, his aura was undeniably affectionate, and then Simon had the brains. Unbeatable.

She thought to how lucky Simon was to have such a loyal guardian. Who knows what might have happened to him if Paul hadn't stepped up to take care of him when his parents had died. The thought chilled her.

In all the darkness of recent times, Paul was a definite light. She felt so confident that if there was any way to save Simon, Paul would find it. He couldn't be more devoted, it just wasn't possible. She knew she'd have to rely so heavily upon him to get through the next few days while they tried to find a solution. But together, they were Simon's family now, and she was proud to be part of the group.

It took them nearly two hours to get home, the traffic

was so bad. Despite his clear distress, Simon seemed very pleased to see them. They'd agreed to not tell him about Damien just yet, until they had more information, and instead they explained that Jane was still looking into things.

They'd moved down to the living room to give Simon a change of scene and Paul had found an episode of "Only Fools and Horses" on the television with the hope that it would bring some well-earned escapism; not that any of them could really concentrate.

Beth sat on the sofa nearest to the TV with Simon next to her. She so wanted to be supportive, but she couldn't face looking at him without feeling nauseous. She didn't know how Paul could carry on so normally.

'Anyone fancy a beer?' Paul asked, trying to cheer things up.

'That would be lovely,' Beth answered.

'Si, mate?' Paul asked, trying to be inclusive, but Simon just shook his head in response.

Paul left to get the beers from the kitchen and Simon turned to face Beth. Slowly, he crept in closer to her side, completely unaware of his appearance, and in desperate need of comfort. She immediately tensed, more so with every inch he got closer, but she couldn't move away. She didn't want to hurt his feelings, she so wanted to be there for him; she wanted to love him and accept all of this willingly and unconditionally, but it was too hard.

She closed her eyes and froze. She hadn't a clue how to deal with the situation so instead she found herself just closing up away from it.

Paul came back into the living room and placed the bottle of beer in front of her. She smiled up at him, and then looked to see Simon now just centimetres away from her. Their eyes met but she still couldn't move her body. Then they both just remained stock still, suddenly aware of how uncomfortable they were making each other feel.

Then the phone rang, freeing Beth from her cycle of

guilt and awkwardness. Paul walked over to it and picked up the receiver.

'Paul Bird. Yes. I see. Okay, we're on our way.'

He turned around to find the hopeful looks of Beth and Simon now burning into his soul. 'Apparently there's been a development,' he informed them.

'What does that mean? What's happened?' Beth asked.

'I don't know, but we've got to get back. I'm sure it's good news, Si, don't worry.'

Beth stood up quickly, unintentionally backing away from Simon as she did, relieved to be getting away.

It was now half past eight and any thoughts Beth had of being tired were long gone as she eagerly watched the trees race by once more on their journey back to London.

'Oh God!' Beth suddenly exclaimed. 'I had work tonight.'

'The office shut hours ago.'

'No, I work in a bar in the evenings. I totally forgot all about it. He's going to kill me! I'll get the sack for sure.'

'Why are you working in a bar?'

'We're not all millionaires! I needed that job.'

'Don't worry, I'll sort it out for you,' Paul soothed.

'With magic? How can you do that?'

'We don't do everything with magic, you know. We're quite capable of living our lives without magic as well. I meant I'll give your boss a call tomorrow and I'll sort it out. This classes as a family emergency, I'm sure, and I can be quite persuasive.'

'You'd do that for me?'

'Oh Beth, it's the least I can do. Us Birds are asking quite a lot of you at the minute. Most people would have run a hundred miles by now, but you're coping with it exceptionally well.'

'I don't feel like I am. I'm a complete mess.'

'Are you kidding me? You're incredible. Simon is one very lucky man.'

'I don't think so. He deserves so much more than me. But I'll always try, I promise.'

'How could he possibly want more than you?' Paul asked.

'I was so horrible to him the other day. I've been so horrible to him a few times. He's been through far more than I could ever dream about, yet I'm constantly playing the victim. I'm a selfish, pathetic, terrified excuse. Simon's ten times the person I am. I'm the lucky one to have him. That's if he still wants me.'

'What are you talking about?' Paul snorted. 'That's ridiculous. I don't know what happened the other day, but ever since I've met you you've done nothing but worry about Simon and you've done nothing but try and be there for him. You're the least selfish person I've ever met. And as for pathetic! I don't know anyone else who could deal with what you've had to. Even Malants would find this a leap. You're one of the bravest people I've ever met in my life. Trust me, Simon is so madly in love with you, and I can see exactly why. He's not going anywhere. And I hope you won't either. But we'll both understand...' Paul's voice trailed off and he looked away.

'What is it?' Beth asked, feeling unnerved by the sudden negative energy after such an uplifting speech. She'd never considered herself as brave. It had taken a lot of courage to make her big move to the city, yes, but ever since that day everything had terrified her. But maybe being terrified was part of being brave, she'd never thought about it like that before.

'I get the feeling that your love for him might be challenged tonight,' Paul muttered.

'Why?' Beth asked with growing concern.

'Something Jane said.'

Beth felt a flurry of panic as she saw the unease dance through Paul's eyes. 'Tell me.'

'We're going back at Damien's request. Apparently he's got a proposal to put forward.'

281

'That's good news isn't it?'

'I'm not so sure. It's a proposal for you. I get the feeling you're going to be drawn into this nightmare far more than you could ever have imagined. I get the feeling that tonight everything could get a whole lot worse.'

TWENTY-EIGHT

It took just an hour to get back to the Malancy headquarters, and Beth hoped it would be their last time there, although that was seeming highly unlikely.

They were greeted by a rather less than cheery Jane. 'Thanks for coming back,' she said, shaking their hands quite formally. 'He's this way.'

Jane led them down a quiet, green corridor that Beth hadn't noticed before. There were five rooms each side with closed doors, and they were taken to the middle one on the right.

Placing her hand on the silver door knob, Jane stopped and turned to Beth. 'No one has any expectations of you, Beth. There are no right or wrong answers here, we just have to do what we think is best. Okay?' Beth nodded, not quite sure what Jane was talking about but not caring too much either, she was just so eager to get inside and to find a resolution to this nightmare.

Jane slowly opened the door to reveal a dark grey interior. All that was in there was a large pine table with six black plastic chairs around it. In the middle sat Damien with a man to his left, clearly a law enforcement official of some description.

Paul went in first, glaring hard at Damien as he sat down on the other side of the table. Beth followed, more coyly, looking anywhere but at Damien, and took the seat to Paul's left, and then Jane, closing the door behind her, finally placed herself at the end of table. There was a tense silence for a few moments.

'You're probably wondering why we've called you back,' Jane started.

'Tell me you didn't do it,' Paul interjected, straight at Damien. Damien just glared back emotionlessly.

Beth studied her fingers with fascination, not sure what to do with herself. She felt nauseous at having to endure Damien's presence. She'd almost forgotten about their last encounter until she'd stepped into the room, so overwhelming had the last twenty-four hours been, but now it was all so vivid in her head again.

'Did you or did you not do this to Simon?' Paul asked more firmly, but Damien just looked at the table, nonchalantly.

'Mr Rock has confessed to everything, Paul,' Jane confirmed. 'He cast a spell last Monday on Simon that means every time he gets angry he'll turn into a bird.'

Beth gasped. This was nothing new to her in reality, but it was the first time it had been confirmed and she finally had nowhere to hide.

'Why Damien?' Paul snapped, banging his fist on the table, shaking Damien into action. 'What has Simon done to you?'

'He has everything!' Damien hissed back. 'I'm just as capable, just as clever, but I don't have the office, the flashy cars, the huge house. I don't have the trophy girl on my arm. I'm stuck as a Sales Director with nowhere else to go.'

'You did this out of jealousy?' Beth yelped, the anger now flipping inside of her.

'I'm sick of him. He's a freak that no one can stand to be around yet he's got everything he could ever wish for.

How is that fair?'

'Fair? You want to talk about fair?' Paul bellowed. 'Simon works ten times harder than you could ever dream about. And you're not as clever or as capable as he is and you know it. This isn't about jealousy, this is about you not getting your own way. Simon's told me quite a few times that you've been itching for more. You constantly want more money and more status, but you just want it handed to you without the effort. I know you've been squirming your way into the parties and exclusive events, sucking up to just about everyone, I hear stuff. You've got a directorship and a six figure salary, why is that not enough?'

'I want to be CEO,' Damien declared.

'That's Simon's job,' Beth stated.

'So? He can't do much as a bird, can he?' Damien sneered.

'You little shit!' Paul barked, standing to his feet.

'Sit down, Paul,' Jane ordered. Paul reluctantly did as requested, not taking his eyes of Damien for a second. 'Quite clearly Mr Rock has broken the law,' she stated, 'and in any other circumstance we'd be throwing him in jail and losing the key. However, Mr Rock has a proposal he'd like to put forward and I'm willing for it to be considered. Simon is an exceptional being and I'm sure none of us want to see him stuck as a bird forever, so I'm open to the terms of Mr Rock's proposal, as long as he agrees to our terms in return, of course.'

'What proposal?' Paul demanded.

'Please remember,' Jane continued, facing both Beth and Paul directly, 'this is open for discussion and it does not have to be accepted. Do you understand?' Beth and Paul both nodded in reply.

Jane picked up a piece of paper scrawled with her notes before taking a second to find her words. 'Mr Rock has cast a spell upon Mr Simon Bird that means every time he gets angry or upset he will, slowly and painfully, turn into a bird.'

'Let thine anger become thee,' Damien whispered to the fierce glares of Beth and Paul.

'There is no antidote to this spell, it's completely bound. As you noted before, Beth, Simon may find days where he gets better, but this is only in the case of him finding true peace and happiness. Then the second he gets angry again he will turn back into a bird, in a vicious, painful cycle. The only way for the spell to be broken is for Mr Rock to die.'

'So what are you proposing?' Beth spat out with urgency.

'Mr Rock will kindly agree to let us stop his heart for one minute, which will effectively break the spell and end Mr Bird's torture, but he wants two things in return.'

'Is that enough to kill him?' Beth quickly asked.

'No, it's just enough to sever the spell, that's all we need,' Jane replied.

'What does he want?' Paul demanded to know.

'Firstly, he wants the job of CEO at Bird Consultants UK and for Mr Simon Bird to leave the business for good.'

'You bastard, that's our company,' Paul seethed.

'What's the other thing?' Beth asked, her heart now practically beating through her chest.

'The second thing Mr Rock requires...' Jane paused and looked at Beth sympathetically. 'The second thing that Mr Rock requires is for Miss Bethany Lance to accept his hand in marriage and be his wife.'

'What?!' Beth shrieked, utterly sickened at the prospect. 'No!'

'What are you playing at?' Paul roared.

'Simon has had everything but he's enjoyed none of it. It's my turn now, he needs to give it up and move on,' Damien stated.

'I can understand you wanting the job, it's always what you've wanted, but why Beth?' Paul asked, fuming. 'You know that Simon rarely meets a girl, and he's finally found one that he can be happy with and you want to take it away? What's wrong with you? What sort of sick son of a bitch are you?'

'Simon doesn't know how to be happy! It's not his style. I see it that I'm freeing Beth of the burden of having to put up with him. Why would anyone want to be around that icy, cold hermit? He doesn't deserve her. I'm doing this for the good of the company and for the good of Beth.'

Damien paused and looked to Beth. He focussed on her closely, taking in her bruises – the ones caused by his own hand – and his face seemed to soften ever so slightly. 'I'm going to look after you, Beth.'

'That's how you've justified this?' Paul asked, baffled.

'You're not even half the man Simon is. How could you ever be good for anything?' Beth spat, utterly revolted by him.

'Mr Rock has very specific requirements. We need to discuss them,' Jane interrupted, clearly highly uncomfortable with the situation.

'I want a proper contract drawn up; a Bird Consultants specialty,' Damien explained. 'Before anyone's going near my heart, Beth will be my wife and I will have worked one, full, successful day as CEO of Bird Consultants, and all staff and customers will have been informed of Simon's resignation and my promotion.

'Simon is then not allowed in less than ten metres of me, Beth or the business. He can look from afar, I don't mind that, but that's it. And Beth, you have to stay as my wife until death do us part, and you must never even consider adultery. I want you always to be faithful to me, no matter what I do. Do you understand? If any of these conditions are broken the contract will state that the spell will be recast. And believe me, I won't be so willing for my heart to be stopped a second time.'

'You can't let him do this!' Beth cried.

'I don't want any tricks pulled, either. I want it that

when Beth marries me she's all mine and she can never leave. I also want it written that if any harm comes to me as a way of trying to wriggle out of the contract, like one of you trying to suffocate me in my sleep or something, then the terms are broken. If I'm not happy with the contract then we're going to hit a few problems.'

'Why are you letting him get away with this?' Beth fumed.

'No one is forcing you to do anything, Beth,' Jane clarified. 'But this is the only chance we have of getting Simon back. We can't just stop Damien's heart without his consent, it's completely against the law, and would be virtually impossible anyway. We'd need immense power and Damien would have to be completely still for at least a minute, it couldn't be done.'

'We could just kill him!' Beth stated, revulsion in her eyes.

'I'm going to pretend I didn't hear you say that,' Jane muttered. 'The truth is that Simon is a very important man and we have to find a way to get him back. I like this no more than you, Beth, but we need to find a way to protect him. It seems you're our only hope.'

'Why is Simon so important to you?' Beth asked Jane, suddenly feeling there was more to this than Jane was letting on.

'He's important to all of us,' Jane explained, but this didn't satisfy Beth's curiosity as to why Damien was literally breaking the law and getting away with it. Now wasn't the time to ask more about that, though, Beth knew that line of questioning would have to wait for another day.

'In a neat twist,' Damien smirked, 'I want you, Paul, to write the contract. You are well practised at this. And I know you'll have all our interests at heart.'

'You want me to what?'

'You are best placed for this, Paul,' Jane reasoned. 'You can make sure nothing else goes wrong.'

'What on earth would your parents say about this?' Paul asked Damien with disgust.

'You leave them out of this!' Damien snapped. This was clearly a sore point. 'When they see that I'm CEO of a massive company and I have a beautiful, successful wife then I'm sure they'll be proud of me.'

'They'd be shocked and disappointed more like,' Paul argued.

'Don't you dare bring them into this! They don't need to know any of this! I swear, you speak to them about this and the deal is off. You can explain that to your precious Simon.' Paul just nodded reluctantly, showing Damien he understood. 'You've got one day to decide,' Damien finished.

'The ceremony room here at the Malancy HQ is reserved at seven o'clock tomorrow night,' Jane explained. 'If you decide to go ahead with Mr Rock's proposal then you must bring the contract with you tomorrow and everything will be finalised. If you don't show up or if things aren't done to Mr Rock's satisfaction, then he will immediately withdraw his offer and it won't be up for discussion again for at least one year.'

'Basically, you either marry me tomorrow or you'll be stuck looking at your horrible little birdy man for a very, very long time. Any questions?' Damien clarified.

'You bastard!' Beth snapped.

'Come on Beth,' Paul said, taking Beth's arm, now very eager to get out of there. 'We'll be in touch,' Paul declared as he led Beth out of the room, not looking back.

'What are we going to do?' Beth cried as Paul escorted her to the lifts.

'I can't even start to think about this,' Paul mumbled.

Beth was utterly distraught. Each day in the past week she'd felt like she'd hit the worst it could possibly get only to find something even more impossibly bad was around the corner to knock her completely off her feet again. It was getting unbearable.

They reached the cool night air and breathed for the first time, letting the freshness clear their thoughts as best it could.

'Come on, we need a drink,' Paul stated, getting in to the car that was patiently waiting for them. Beth followed him and they were driven just a couple of minutes down the road to a pub.

Beth looked at the clock in the car as she waited for the driver to open her door. It was now quarter to eleven. It had been such a very long day.

Beth sat at a small table in the corner of the stale smelling pub as Paul ordered them their drinks.

He brought over a pint for himself and a large glass of white wine for Beth. They both took immediate gulps of their drinks, feeling completely lost as to what to do.

'It's so horrible,' Beth whispered, the tears stinging her eyes. 'I have to do it, though. I have to.'

'You can't, Beth.'

'I can't be responsible for Simon having to stay in that form, what sort of life is that? I have the power to take it all away and I could never forgive myself if I didn't do it. It's the most horrendous prospect in the world, but I must be brave. You said you thought I was brave.'

'You are brave. But don't be silly. By marrying Damien you'll be ending Simon's life anyway. Bird Consultants is all he's got. Then the only good thing to happen to him for years is you, and you're saying you're going to take both things away from him in an instant. How is he supposed to live with that?'

'How is he supposed to live as a bird?' Beth argued.

'There's got to be another way. There's always another way. Simon always figures these things out. He'd know what to do.'

'What's he going to do, chirp us the answer? Morse code? He can't help us. This is our only hope.' Then a thought occurred to Beth. 'But maybe when he's back he'll be able to find a loophole, he'll be able to fix it? Maybe this won't be the end?'

'It's going to be a Bird Consultants contract, Beth. They're pretty tight.'

'You said Simon always finds a way, we just have to have faith that he will this time. I don't want to be married to that sicko, it's a vile thought, but I'd do it for Simon.'

'You love him so much,' Paul smiled, touching Beth's hand. 'And he loves you. He's changed since he met you, and for the better. If we go ahead with this, I don't know if he'll ever forgive us.'

'He's going to have to. We're doing it for him.'

'We can't. I can't let you.'

'Can you think of another way?'

'I refuse to give in to that son of a bitch.'

'We're not giving in, we're just biding our time. We just have to pray that Simon will find a way out of it. Trust me, Paul, this is not the end.'

Beth wanted to believe so badly that Simon would miraculously come to save her again, but this time she knew he wouldn't be able to. She had to give Paul hope, though, she needed him to write the contract.

She could see her destiny now and it wasn't pretty. But how could she ever forgive herself if she didn't help Simon? She was the only one who could save him, it was all on her shoulders. She had no choice.

It was just then that she realised the true horror of her fate. Not only would she be marrying one of the vilest men she'd ever met in her life but she would also be truly and completely giving up Simon's love.

She'd never be able to touch him again, and she'd never kiss him or share a joke with him again. She'd never be able to make love to him again. It was the absolute, ultimate sacrifice, but how could she walk away?

She had just one day left to enjoy before her life would change forever.

TWENTY-NINE

Beth spent the whole of the next day with Simon. Her fear of him became a trivial insignificance as the knowledge that they were facing their final day together became a stark reality. No matter what form he took, she needed to enjoy his warmth for as long as she could. He was still her Simon, she could feel it.

She'd spent the night in his bed but had barely slept. The realisation of how much she truly loved him ached inside of her as she came to terms with the fact that it was all over. Later that day she was to be married to an awful, selfish man, and not only would she no longer be available to spend time with Simon, but she would literally have to sign her life away and agree to never interact with him again.

Every time she thought about not touching him again, not smelling his heavenly scent, not kissing his soft lips or even being able to share a conversation with him, she broke down into tears. It was an utterly heartbreaking situation but she was left with no choice. Her sacrifice meant Simon could at least live his life, the little that would be left of it.

Beth thought to his future and comforted herself with

ideas of how he might be able to salvage some sort of a life after Damien's attempts to take it all away. Maybe he could start up his own rival business, she thought. But then, she realised, it would mean him going up against his uncle and competing against the decade of hard work he'd already put in.

Then she thought that maybe he might meet someone else and still have a happy, loved life, but that hurt even more. As much as she wanted true happiness for him, she couldn't entertain the idea of him being with another woman. Then it saddened her again to think that he probably wasn't going to meet anyone anyway, such was his impact on people. Their relationship was truly unique.

Simon hadn't slept, he'd just watched Beth toss and turn from the bedside table, completely unable to offer any support. They'd told him the truth as soon as they'd got home. He'd been clearly distraught by the situation, it was the last thing he wanted, but with no words and no expression he was helpless to fight against them. He, forlornly, had to accept their decision.

The day had been a long and torturous one. Paul had worked tirelessly on the contract, desperately wanting Simon's advice and support, but for the first time he was completely alone. At the time when it mattered more than anything that he got it absolutely right, he was now forced to make all the decisions for himself and it horrified him; the pressure was almost too much.

As promised, he'd spoken with Sam, Beth's manager at The Rose, and had informed him that Beth was going through a family emergency. He'd then left a message for Trisha at the office that Beth was doing some important work for Simon so she would leave them both alone. Everything was sorted, they just needed to get on with the deed now.

At around four o'clock, just an hour before Beth was to leave Simon's house for the very last time, the gate bell rang. Beth had spent most of the day watching films with

Simon, trying to survive the lack of communication that had been thrust upon them. Putting it off for as long as possible, she was finally coming out of the shower and slowly starting to think about getting ready for the unthinkable night ahead.

Paul, already in the study, pouring over drafts of the contract and triple checking his work, looked up at the gate monitor and saw it was a delivery man.

'Yes?' he asked, pressing a button on the touch screen so the man at the gate could hear him.

'I've got a delivery for a Miss Bethany Lance,' the man replied. Hesitantly, Paul pressed another button for the gate to open and the man came to the front door.

Paul signed for a box and took it straight up to Beth who was sitting nervously on the bed in Simon's dressing gown.

'It's for you,' Paul said, passing the medium sized cardboard box to her. Simon watched from the desk.

'What is it?'

'Dread to think.'

Beth peeled the brown parcel tape up with her red splodged fingernails, further chipping away at the varnish, not that she cared. She eventually got into the box to find inside another white, shiny box, with a black organza ribbon tied neatly around it. She took it out and warily undid the bow, then, taking a deep breath, she opened the second box up.

Inside was a lacy garment, neatly folded with a letter on top. She read the handwritten note.

To my darling Bride to Be
If you are serious about the wedding then please wear this. I hope it resembles your dream dress just a bit, I do so want to make you happy. I know it's hard for you to believe at the moment, but I'm sure in time you'll see it's the truth.
See you at the altar,
Damien x

Beth felt sick. She stared at the ivory gown below her. She picked it up slowly and let it unravel to its full length. It was a fairly straight, strapless dress with a modest train. It was beautiful but Beth hated it.

'I'm not wearing it!' she stated, throwing it back down to the bed.

'I think you'll have to, Beth. We can't afford to piss him off if we're going to do this properly.'

'I don't want to be his bride!'

'None of us want you to. You know you don't have to do it. It's not too late.'

'How can I not? How can I let Simon be trapped like that forever? I couldn't live with myself.'

They both looked at Simon who helplessly stared back, shaking his head. They both knew he didn't want her to do it, but the alternative was just not an option.

'No one is ever going to think badly of you if you don't go ahead with this. Isn't that right, mate?' Paul said, looking to the bird. Simon keenly nodded, it was obvious how desperately he wanted to stop her but he was utterly powerless in his fragile state.

'I have to do this, Simon. I have to do this for you. There's no other way.'

Beth ran to the bathroom to get away from their sorrowful glances, it was too hard to deal with.

'I better get back,' Paul shouted through the bathroom door. 'The car will be here at five. If you really want to do this, we can't afford to be late.' Paul headed back to the study to quadruple check the contract.

Beth looked in the mirror and studied her face. It was damaged far more by the endless tears that had smothered her cheeks so much of late than the bruising. Her face seemed physically scarred with sorrow.

Forcing herself to move ahead, she picked up her black mascara and started to flick her eyelashes.

Her face was still so badly beaten, it was about all the

make-up she could manage. She couldn't believe she was to be married bearing the bruises of her new husband's hand, that about summed up the misery of this dreaded affair. It couldn't be further from how she'd imagined it.

Looking at herself, she saw how it could be any day. She was no different to when she was going to work or popping to the shops. She couldn't be bothered to make any effort at all.

She left the bathroom and slowly walked back to her dress. She took off the dressing gown, revealing her white lacy underwear beneath, items that Simon had bought for her, and she stepped into the garment. The only emotion she felt was one of contempt.

It slipped on to her slim figure elegantly and zipped up easily at the back. She turned to the mirror to view herself, but it left her cold. She was stunning, the dress fitted her so well, like it was made for her; but none of that mattered.

She turned to Simon who was still sitting quietly on the desk at the back of the room, and sighed heavily.

'This should be for you, you know. I should be marrying you.' Simon looked back at her glumly. 'I'm so sorry. I'm sorry for all of these horrible things that have happened to you. I love you so much, I want you to know that. You must remember that. I may be Damien's wife in name and by law, but that's all it will ever be. My heart will always belong to you.'

Beth glanced at herself once more in the mirror, tears now swelling in her eyes yet again. She could hardly believe what was about to happen, and the pain of losing Simon struck her hard.

She turned back to him, wiping the tears away, smudging her mascara ever so slightly in the corner, not that she cared. She needed to talk to Simon, it was her last ever chance. Anything she had to say, it was now or never.

'Paul told me how you make other people feel, how you chill them,' she began. 'I couldn't believe it. I don't feel that way around you, you need to know that. I never have. You feel warm and safe to me. You make me feel complete in every way and I love every second of being with you, it's the most ecstatic feeling in the world. The only thing that makes me feel uncomfortable is the gaping hole you leave behind when you're gone. You're my everything, Simon, and I'm so utterly devastated to not be marrying you.'

She walked over and looked Simon directly in the eyes, the tears now streaming down her face. She could see beyond his tortured chocolate gaze, deep into his stricken soul, and it wounded her even more.

A tear appeared in the corner of Simon's eye. He watched her in her beautiful dress, completely unable to say or do anything, knowing it was the last time he'd ever be near her again. It broke both their hearts in two.

'Don't cry,' she whimpered, not able to control her own intense sobbing. 'Please don't cry. I love you. No matter what happens in this world, remember that. I'm your soulmate. I choose you always and forever, and if there's any justice in this world then we'll find our way back together. I'll be your wife one day, Simon Bird, you mark my words. Nothing can stop our love. Nothing's going to stop me loving you. Ever.'

Despite all her earlier fears and putting aside any strange feelings inside, Beth seized her last chance and kissed Simon gently upon his head, the soft satin feathers tingling her lips as she did. 'Goodbye,' she whispered.

Then she turned around, stood tall, wiped the devastated tears from her face, and left the room, not looking back.

Simon waited helplessly behind. He wanted to run after her, he wanted to stop her, but he couldn't do anything. He listened for the last time to her voice downstairs, now so empty and sad, its joyful tone long gone, and he heard it disappear into the world outside, the door slamming shut behind it. She was gone. The love of his life was gone and there was nothing he could do.

He glanced out the window at the beautiful evening sun and let the tears fall. Everything was now so silent and everything was just so sad.

He looked down at himself with anger. How could he have let Damien get the better of him in this way? He blamed himself completely for everything that had happened, and he felt sick with guilt at the thought of Beth having to marry that awful man just to set him free. But what sort of freedom would it be? Damien was about to take everything from him, everything that mattered.

Then he thought to how beautiful Beth had looked in that dress. He took a moment to think of her soft, pale arms, her beautifully formed chest, her thin hips and her long shapely legs. She was gorgeous and that dress had suited her so much. He let his mind wander for a second as he imagined it was their wedding day and she was his bride.

The tears were suddenly halted as he realised it was the first time in his life that he'd ever thought such a thing. He'd never imagined his wedding day before. He'd never allowed himself to because, until that very moment in time, he'd never believed that anyone would ever want to marry him. He felt the ghost of a smile dash across his beak and his heart lightened. It was a glorious thought that someone actually wanted to be his wife.

Even with his ex-girlfriend, he'd never seen her as wife material. It had never occurred to him before, but, in reality, he hadn't been that serious about a future with her. It had hardly been real love. He supposed, looking back at it with a fresh perspective, that he'd used her as much as she'd used him. He'd wanted companionship so badly, he would have taken it from anyone, but he never loved her.

Suddenly he found peace for the first time. He was finally able to close the door on that painful break up as he realised that it would never have lasted anyway. Life had bigger plans for him, and he could now look confidently to the future.

Beth wanted to marry him. She really wanted to. And he wanted her so much in return.

Thoughts now of what could and couldn't be were suddenly less important as the enlightenment that his life had completely changed sparked through him. Then a new sense of fight surged through his soul. There was no way he was going to let Beth go. He'd find a way around this, there was always a way. He was far cleverer than Damien, and Paul. This couldn't be the end.

He thought back to the first time he'd met Beth, in the kitchen at work. Her joyful spirit had won him over straight away. He'd not been able to resist his feelings for her, despite his initial worries that he would only end up getting hurt. And now he knew that he was never going to get hurt by her. She'd called them soulmates, and he knew it was true.

His heart lifted again. He told himself that having a soulmate was far stronger than any stupid magic from Damien; far stronger than any contract. Their love for each other would combat this. How could Damien compete with that?

A new lease of life washed through him. He actually felt happy. As he breathed a sigh of relief, his heart found a state of complete contentment, and with it pain struck every inch of him. A sharp stinging sensation charged through his nerves.

He looked down at his red plumage and it was ruffling. Suddenly flesh poked through gaps in the feathers and he felt himself grow. As his body revealed itself, spurting up to his full six feet in height, the pain was overwhelming, every pore brutally and agonisingly stinging. Simon just breathed through it. Closing his eyes, he thought of nothing but Beth and the wonderful way she made him feel.

With one final, explosive shudder, thousands of feathers blew away from him into the air, shooting off in all different directions, before gently floating to their final resting place on the fluffy cream carpet. Then the pain vanished.

Simon looked down his naked body and saw the feathers slowly dissolve away into nothing around his feet. He was free.

He ran to the mirror, just to be sure, but there wasn't a feather in sight. He closed his eyes again, ensuring the image of Beth stayed strongly in his mind, knowing their love was the only thing to keep the bird at bay.

A broad smile spread across his face as he thought about her. She loved him so much. She was going to actually sacrifice herself, virtually sell her soul to the devil, just so he could be free. She was remarkable.

Now it was his turn to save her. He threw open his wardrobe doors to grab some clothes and headed straight down the stairs. There was just one destination on his mind.

THIRTY

Beth and Paul arrived at Malancy HQ at quarter to seven. The journey had been a sombre one and a sickening dread pulled at both of them.

They headed straight for the lifts at the back of the reception. The security guard just nodded in their direction, fully up to speed with the event.

'Do a lot of people get married here?' Beth asked as the lift doors pinged open. They stepped in and Paul pressed for the second floor. He was dressed in a smart black suit with a charcoal tie.

'I think so,' he replied. 'If people want to have a more magical ceremony, it's the best place to do it.'

'Oh,' Beth responded, but she wasn't really interested. Her forthcoming downfall was all that really occupied her mind.

The lift opened to the second floor and Paul led Beth to the ceremony room directly at the end of the corridor. The double doors were already open and she could see Damien in a smart black suit waiting at the front. He looked like he was going to a funeral, and Beth noted to herself how apt his outfit really was as she approached the end of her life as she knew it.

'You came!' Damien smiled, genuinely happy. Beth hesitantly walked down the aisle between four rows of chairs and headed towards a table at the front where the registrar stood.

'Do you have the contract?' Damien asked, still grinning inanely.

Paul presented a large white envelope in his hand.

'We're all here then,' Jane said, entering the room in a black suit herself. It wasn't really an odd coincidence considering the reality behind the occasion. She shut the doors firmly behind her before she joined them. 'Is that the contract?'

'Yes,' Paul confirmed.

'Let's do business then.' Jane led them to a small room hidden away behind a wooden door. It had just one table and four chairs inside and was beautifully decorated with paintings of different scenic landscapes.

They all sat down and Jane took the contract from Paul. She removed it from the envelope and Beth saw it for the first time.

It was made up of ten sheets of paper, all bound together with a single staple, but unlike anything she'd seen before, it glowed a tint of gold. It emanated a warmth and looked far more solid than paper should.

Damien gleefully grabbed the contract. He quickly flicked through the first eight pages, finally resting his eyes on the ninth. He read every word carefully and considerately.

'What's this bit?' he asked after a few moments.

Paul looked over. 'It's just to make sure it stays ethical. This is, after all, Beth's choice, do we not agree? It has to be based around Beth or her freedom may be called into question.'

'Fine, I suppose it doesn't really matter.' He read on and stopped again. 'Why have you phrased it like that?'

Paul looked again. 'Simon always insists our contracts

offer free choice for all parties. You might change your mind when you're married. In the end the power will be in your hands, it just offers flexibility.'

'In other words, you're hoping I'll change my mind. You wish! It's all irrelevant anyway, like you said, I'll have the power.' He carried on, nodding and grinning as he went along. 'It's fine,' he eventually said, folding the paperwork back as neatly as he found it.

Beth's heart raged in her chest as she realised it was her turn. Once her name was signed on the bottom of that golden document, there was no going back. She could feel the power it wielded and she feared more than ever the severity and finality of her signature. She hesitated when the document was passed her way, taking her last chance to run from it. Then she thought of Simon and she knew she had to do it.

'Have you see one of our contracts before?' Paul asked her. She shook her head. 'Right, well I'll explain. The first page is, obviously, just the header, and then after that there are a few pages detailing the magic. It says how Bird Consultants operates and who will perform the magic, if needed, and then the obligatory and definitive nature of it all when signed. Trust me on that bit, Beth, don't worry about it too much. Just go straight to the page that states terms of the contract. You have to be sure, Beth. There's nothing any of us can do once it's been signed.'

Beth nodded. She studied the front page that brandished the Bird Consultants logo and then detailed her name, address and the date. Then she opened the glowing paperwork.

As Paul stated, the first few pages were long, detailed paragraphs explaining the background to the contract and what it all meant. She skipped a few pages to 'Terms of the Contract', as instructed, and read on.

If agreed to, this contract is to be signed by Miss Bethany Lane willingly and voluntarily. Any undue force put upon her will break the terms making the contract null and void. Once signed, the listed actions are final and must be committed to, with no possible alternatives. No secondary contracts can be made to counteract this one and all parties must willingly partake in the agreed actions or face the consequences listed in section 2.

Section 1, the agreed terms:

1.1 Miss Bethany Lance will choose a husband voluntarily and willingly and will marry him legally in front of witnesses. Once married, she will be fully committed to said husband and will remain faithful to him in all ways until either one of their deaths. She will not be able to separate from or divorce him in any way, and only he may be able to end the marriage if he so chooses.

1.2 Upon successfully getting married, Miss Bethany Lance's chosen husband will automatically become CEO of Bird Consultants UK, taking up the role in place of the current CEO. At his discretion, he may banish the current CEO from the company and may further declare that the current CEO stay at a distance of his choice away from the company, its employees and his family (including his wife). This must be written as an addendum to this contract as and when it's decided upon after the wedding.

1.3 Miss Bethany Lance's husband, as CEO, will enjoy all the benefits of the role and this will not be compromised in any way.

1.4 The marriage of Miss Bethany Lance and her chosen husband will only end if the husband chooses to terminate the marriage or because of one of their deaths. Any attempt to end the lives of Miss Bethany Lance or her husband by any party even remotely associated with the husband or wife will automatically bring about the consequences as detailed in Section 2.

1.5 After Miss Bethany Lance's husband has successfully completed one day in the marriage and one day as CEO of Bird Consultants, when requested he will willingly go to Malancy HQ where, following their instructions, he will allow his heart to be stopped for one minute thereby ending any spells he has cast prior to this agreement. If Miss Bethany Lance's husband fails to agree to the terms set out by the Malancy HQ regarding his heart being stopped within a fortnight of the marriage taking place, all other parts of this contract become null and void and the contract will be eliminated.

Section 2, consequences:

If any of the agreed terms 1.1 to 1.4 are broken or changed in any way then the following consequence will take place.

2.1 The spell using bicantomene cast by Mr Damien Rock towards Mr Simon Bird will immediately be recast.

Once Miss Bethany Lance signs and dates this contract she and her freely chosen husband will be bound to these terms wholly and definitely.

Beth's hand was shaking now as she reached for the pen that Jane was offering. She was, in every sense, signing her life away, and she was doing it all for the man that she loved. But in signing it, like some sick ironic twist, she was, in turn, agreeing to never be with him. It was so unfair and so deeply saddening. Beth thought to Simon one last time, recalling how his red feathers had tortured his lonely soul, and she knew she had to go ahead. She carefully signed her name on the dotted line and wrote the date next to it. It was done.

She closed the paperwork and it immediately beamed gold light before sealing itself in a film that closed the sheets together once and for all.

'I'm so sorry, Beth,' Paul whispered.

'Let's get married!' Damien sang, the smile bursting from his lips. Beth stood up from her chair, all life in her now a distant memory, and she followed Damien back to the main ceremony room where the male registrar stood waiting for them.

Beth and Damien stood before him, their expressions and stances worlds apart. Paul glumly sat on the chair nearest to Beth and Jane sat nearest to Damien, happiness far from her face alike. There was nothing any of them could do now.

Suddenly the doors flew open and the warmth that Beth so longed to feel again soared through the room. Everyone turned to see Simon. His strong, well-built figure was swelling through his T-Shirt and his eyes were alight with a fierce glow. He moved to the middle of the aisle and stopped, glaring hard at Damien, furiously.

'What the fuck!' Damien shouted, grabbing Beth's hand. 'It's too late anyway, the contract's been signed.'

'Simon!' Beth squealed, yanking her hand free from Damien's sweaty grip. She ran to Simon and threw her arms around him. They kissed lovingly; a strong, deep kiss that they both never thought would come again. 'I love you, Beth,' he whispered.

'How is this possible?' she asked, delighted.

'How could it not be?' he whispered. 'Will you marry me?' he then asked, still holding her closely in a tender embrace.

'Yes!' she beamed, then they kissed again.

'It'll never last, Beth. In a couple of days he'll be wound up by something and he'll be a bird again. Do you really want that for him? Are you going to force him into a lifetime of suffering?' Damien shouted at them.

'Stand behind me,' Simon muttered to Beth, and she did as he requested. Simon stared firmly at Damien. It was a cold, stony glare that emitted a freezing hardness, chilling everything around him except Beth. All that she could feel was the warmth and safety of the man she loved.

'I warned you that if you ever went near Beth again, I'd kill you. Do you remember?' Simon hissed at Damien.

'You can't kill me! You're in the Malancy Headquarters

for God's sake, you'll be locked up for life,' Damien argued, but the tremble in his voice gave away the uncertainty of his words.

'I can do whatever I like.'

'You'll never be with Beth at all then, is that what you want?'

Summoning all his power, Simon thrust out his right hand and it brought Damien to a complete standstill. Damien was now at his complete mercy, unable to move at all. Simon was holding him so tightly just through the power of his fingertips.

'So, I warn you not to go near her, and instead you try to marry her. What were you thinking? I don't take kindly to people messing with me or my family, and, Damien, you have done both.' Simon was now focussing intently as he used all his strength to overpower his foe. His anger was visibly growing again and it was clearly challenging his body.

He tried hard to keep Damien in place, but a feather started painfully poking its red, shiny glow from his skin and his strength became compromised. He had to exert twice as much power just to keep the same level of force. He gritted his teeth against the agony.

Damien's eyes grew wide with terror as his muscles yielded to Simon's strong grip. Simon walked slowly towards the stock still man, trying to ignore the three more feathers that were forcing their way through the pores on his arm. He had to calm down to overcome the spell, but he needed the anger to channel his power and take Damien down once and for all. He had to find the strength to get through this.

With his right hand still freezing Damien's every move, he placed his left hand gently on Damien's chest, clenching ever so slightly against the raw stinging and itching that raged through his arm.

'You have no idea of the power I'm capable of,' Simon whispered into Damien's ear. 'Turning me into a bird is child's play compared to what I can do to you. Leave me, my family and my business alone or you will see how far I can go. You will never get the better of me, Damien. I'm smarter, better and so much more powerful than you could ever dream of.'

Simon then closed his eyes and pinched his left fingers, bringing Damien's heart to a complete stop. It took every ounce of his strength to not only freeze Damien's heart, but to simultaneously hold him in place whilst suffering the torture of the feathers that were increasingly tearing at this skin.

Simon's flesh was now burning at the stress, and the shocked faces of those around him could see him enflamed at the trauma of his actions. He didn't know how long he could hold on as his whole body trembled against the enormous power he was now emitting.

Damien screamed in agony. Everyone watched in horror as Simon exerted such great strength, subjugating his rival with more intensity than any of them had ever witnessed before.

Suddenly Simon yelled out in pain himself and both of them were flung back in their respective directions.

Damien hit the table behind him before falling to the floor. He grabbed sorely at his chest and tried desperately to catch his breath, not even noticing at first that Simon had been catapulted backwards in a ball of red.

Beth watched as Simon smacked to the floor stiffly, flat on his back. Just as the impact crashed around the walls of the room, thousands of red feathers exploded into the air. They appeared from nowhere, like they'd been locked inside of him and were now set free. He was now free.

The feathers individually and silently floated to the carpet, but this time they didn't dissolve. Instead they turned black and soggy, decomposing in front of their eyes; their power well and truly dying with them.

Beth ran through the feathers to Simon, who lay unconscious in the middle of the aisle.

'Simon! Simon!' she shouted, kneeling down on the blackened mess around him, no concern to the ruin of her white dress. Paul stood up and watched, and Jane shortly followed him to her feet. No one even glanced at Damien.

Beth gently stroked Simon's face, his soft skin and strong jaw skimming under her fingertips. Then his eyes slowly opened.

'Simon! You're okay!'

'What happened?'

'You did it. I don't know what you did, but it's gone. The feathers have all gone. It's all over.'

'And you're not married?' Simon asked.

'No! Not yet,' she smiled.

'But the contract's still been signed,' Damien coughed from the front. 'You still have to marry me or he'll turn back.'

'No she doesn't!' Paul argued.

'I think she does,' Damien coughed again.

'No, you can marry Simon,' Paul declared.

'What? What does that mean? We can't risk Simon turning back,' Beth said, her tone laced with worry as she tried to understand the situation.

'You have to marry Simon. And you have to marry him now,' Paul added firmly.

'What?' Beth asked, shocked.

'The contract's in play. It means that until you're married, Beth, it's open for anyone to take control of Bird Consultants. If you don't marry Simon then we're leaving ourselves vulnerable. Marry Simon now and he'll remain CEO of Bird Consultants forever.'

'I have to marry him with all the agreed terms of the contract?' she asked, her face now dropping.

'Is that a problem?' Paul asked.

'What did the contract say?' Simon queried, sitting up.

Beth looked to him. 'That I have to be fully committed to you forever.'

'Is that not what you want?' Simon asked, hurtfully.

'Of course, that's exactly what I want. But this is more than that. It states that all the power will be yours. You can do what you like and I'll be stuck at your mercy forever.'

'That's never going to happen, Beth,' Simon said, shaking his head. 'You're the strongest woman I know and I love that about you. I don't want all the power, I want us to be equal. Marry me, Beth, I promise I'll sort it out.'

Beth stood up and looked to Paul, bewildered by yet another crazy turn of events. 'What about my family? This isn't how I planned on having my wedding. Not one that matters.'

'Beth,' Simon started, standing up next to her and gently holding her hands. 'Do you want to marry me?'

'Yes. Absolutely, yes. Just...'

'Then let's get married now and nip this whole awful affair well and truly in the bud. Then we'll worry about the rest later. We'll re-plan a huge white wedding with all your family and we'll do it properly, I promise. That will be our real wedding, this is just logistics.'

Beth stared back at him, lost for words. She had no clue as to what to do.

'I promise, the first thing I'm going to do after this is look at that contract. I'm going to make sure that you're never in second place to me. I'm sure I've combatted tougher contracts in my life, it's not going to be an issue. I won't let it be. I can't lose you again. I won't lose you again.'

'You really want to marry me?' Beth grinned, touched by his words.

'More than anything,' Simon confirmed, then he kissed her softly on the lips. Beth threw her arms around him and they moved into a passionate embrace.

'Okay, but maybe looking at the contract won't be the first thing you do when I get you home,' she giggled in his ear before kissing him again.

'You can't just let him get away with this. He tried to kill me!' Damien squeaked from Paul's side, breaking the romance of the moment.

'Did he? Are you sure?' Jane asked. 'I don't remember seeing anything.' Shrugging nonchalantly, she raised her voice and called for security. Within seconds, two security guards entered the room. Following Jane's intensive stare, they walked straight up to Damien and dragged him moaning back through the doors.

'Don't worry about him anymore. He's my problem now,' Jane smirked. 'Let's just get you two married.'

'Just one thing first,' Simon said, gently turning Beth's head to face him. 'I don't want any memories of that awful man and what he did to you,' he whispered, then he placed both his hands softly on Beth's cheeks.

He moved in slowly and tenderly kissed her lips. Beth closed her eyes and enjoyed his gentle warmth. Then, just like on their first date, she felt an electrifying ecstasy race through her. A radiating glow spread through her whole face and melted across her cheek. She felt her eye relax and the swelling around it reduce. He was healing her, just like the very first time they'd kissed. The pain on her face quickly vanished and she was completely renewed.

He stood back to look at her. 'My beautiful Beth,' he smiled.

'Thank you,' Beth whispered, touching her cheek with relief.

'Now shall we get married?' Simon asked, taking her hand.

'Hang on!' Beth suddenly announced, stopping in her tracks. 'We're not going to be able to, are we? I mean people can't just get married willy nilly, it doesn't work like that does it? Don't we need a marriage licence? What about rings? That could take days to sort out, couldn't it?'

All four of the people around her broke into smiles. She felt very out of the circle, like they all knew the punchline but her. 'What? What am I not getting?' she asked.

'We're Malants, Beth. Small things like logistics never

get in the way,' Jane explained. 'How did you think you were going to get married so quickly in the first place?'

'I don't know,' she shrugged, feeling a little embarrassed.

'You've got a lot to get used to,' Simon said, kissing her on her head lovingly. 'Just you wait, you're going to love it!'

THIRTY-ONE

The newlyweds enjoyed the weekend as their honeymoon, saving the actual exotic break for when they repeated the ceremony with family and friends later in the year. There was so much to plan but it could all wait for now.

Paul had left them to it and had stayed in a hotel for the weekend, and by Monday morning he was waiting eagerly for their arrival in Simon's office.

The weekend had been particularly perfect for Beth and Simon, but their first little tiff came that morning in the Aston Martin on the way to work. Beth had insisted that Simon drop her off down the road so she could walk the rest of the way as she'd done before, but Simon wasn't so keen.

'You're my wife now!' he grinned, enjoying the battle, as he pulled into his space in the office car park.

'It's only for today. Don't you think it would be better if I tell people that we're married first before the gossip starts broadcasting around the place? It's me they'll be talking about, not you!'

'I understand that, but when they do find out that you're my wife, how does it make me look that I let you

313

walk halfway to work?'

Beth wanted to argue but she knew he was right. She was very worried about the forthcoming parade of questions that were inevitably going to charge her way, but she had to face it sometime. And, after all, she couldn't be happier to be his wife, so she should feel proud.

Simon stopped the engine and turned to Beth. He curled her hair behind her ear and then kissed her on the nose, making her smile.

'I suppose whatever happens today, it's going to be a walk in the park compared to us telling my family,' Beth then said, dreading the weekend ahead when they were planning on making the trip back up north to announce the news. It would also be her first time back home since her big move.

'I'm sure it will be fine. I've told you, I'll have a word with Paul to see how I can try and calm down my chilliness a bit. I'll be on my best behaviour, I promise.'

'You're not the one I'm worried about! You're the best thing to ever happen to me, they'll just have to love you. It's not that, it's the fact that my mum's going to kill me when she finds out that I got married without telling her. And to a Mr Bird as well! I'm Mrs Bethany Bird. How silly does that sound!' Beth gibed.

'Thank you very much! I think Beth Bird sounds charming,' Simon chuckled.

'You would!' Beth smirked, then she looked to the clock. It was only half past eight and she knew the office would be quiet now. If they moved fast she could avoid the gossip for a little longer. 'Come on, the work day awaits!' she ordered, opening the car door and stepping out. Simon quickly joined her, looking unusually bright in a purple tie, picked out especially by Beth that morning.

As they entered the reception, Beth waved to Margaret as normal, who half waved back, a little stunned by Simon's presence. Beth prayed that she'd assume their arrival time was merely coincidental. Margaret wasn't a major gossip, but Beth wanted to keep the news under control.

They made their way straight to the lifts and waited patiently.

'I forgot to say, Paul's waiting for us in my office, we need to go and see him first,' Simon stated.

'Now? But I've got work to do.'

Simon laughed at this. 'Do you now? It's very noble that you're so dedicated to your role, Mrs Bird-'

'Shh!' Beth interrupted, so worried that someone would hear. All her other worries aside, Beth knew that she had to tell Gayle, Diane and Michelle before any gossip was allowed to reach them. The walls around the office were very thin and news travelled fast. She felt she owed them the courtesy of hearing it from her lips first; she was their direct colleague after all. And she'd become a friend.

'The owner of the company requires a meeting with you. What shall I say you're caught up with?' Simon teased.

'Okay, to your office it is,' Beth capitulated with a reluctant grin, knowing she couldn't really argue.

They got in the lift and headed for the tenth floor. Stepping out, Beth walked coyly behind Simon as they made their way to his office, past the disinterested glances of the now six directors.

Paul was sitting relaxed on the sofa drinking coffee and reading through some paperwork. 'Morning lovebirds,' he greeted as they walked in. 'How was your weekend?'

'Lovely!' Beth smirked.

'The usual, you know,' Simon shrugged, flashing Beth a lascivious look.

'Glad to hear it!' Paul smiled, pretending to ignore the energy between the pair. 'Anyway, take a seat, we need to talk.'

Beth sat down next to Paul on the sofa, suddenly a little worried. 'Not more problems?'

'Nothing of the sort, don't worry,' Paul assured her. Simon sat down at his desk and waited for Paul to start.

'You're family now, Beth,' Paul began, sitting forward. 'And we want you to feel properly part of our family unit.'

'That's so sweet,' Beth responded, although she didn't really have a clue where this was heading.

'You may or may not know, but I was chatting with Simon first thing this morning and we both came to the same conclusion.' Beth looked to Simon, confused, wondering at which point that morning he'd had this elusive chat.

'So,' Paul continued, catching Beth's attention again. 'Simon and I would very much like you to join us here on the board of directors of the firm.'

'What!' Beth shrieked, shocked by the offer.

'It's a family company, Beth,' Simon explained. 'You're a Bird now too. It's only right you become part of it.'

'That's incredible! Are you sure?'

'It would be wrong of us not to bring you in,' Paul clarified.

'I can't believe it, that's so amazing. How will it work?'

'That was Simon's idea,' Paul explained, turning to Simon to elaborate.

'We've been a little snowed under here of late, and a gap has arisen for an Administration Director. If you're up for it?'

'What? I don't know if I can do that. That's a big job,' Beth replied, a little overwhelmed by the enormous proposal.

'I know it's a big step for you, Beth, but I know you can do it. I've heard nothing but great things about you. It seems you're quite a star in the making,' Simon assured her.

'What?' Beth asked, taken aback by his admission. 'Who said that?'

'I'm more in touch than you think,' Simon smiled.

'That's so nice. I have tried my best.'

'We've no doubt you're going to be fantastic,' Paul declared. 'I've only known you a few days but I've seen nothing but good things. You're going to be great for us Birds.'

'Administration Director!' she chuckled. Then she looked back at Simon more seriously. 'Doesn't someone already do that job? Will I be treading on anyone's toes?'

'Far from it!' Simon stated, standing up and walking round to her. 'Eric's been doing the job to date along with about fifty other things and he's been begging me for help. We're yet to tell him, but don't worry about that, he'll be relieved. He hates that part of the job anyway, he much prefers dealing with the contracts. And I know he'll be a great mentor for you to begin with, while you find your feet.'

'This is so amazing. I can't thank you enough. When does it all start?' Beth asked.

'At nine am this morning,' Paul grinned, looking to the clock on the wall that showed it to already be ten past nine.

'Oh wow!'

'Don't worry about the package either, we'll look after you,' Paul added, but Beth hadn't even considered remuneration yet. 'You'll get your own shares, of course. We'll also get you a company car, and Simon's got some ideas on the salary I'm sure you won't be disappointed with. But I'll let you work all that out with him, he is your new boss.'

'Oh God! Is that going to be an issue?' Beth asked, looking to Simon with concern.

'I don't think so, do you?' Simon uttered.

Beth thought for a second. 'I suppose not.' Then she thought again. 'With my company car, does that mean we have to drive to work separately?' She was surprisingly upset by this.

'No, don't be silly! Although I am relieved to hear that's an issue. If I'm in the office, I really hope we'll still come in together. The company car is just so you'll have your own independence. And who knows where the role might take you.'

'It all sounds so good,' Beth nodded, still trying to process yet another massive surprise that Simon had gifted her way. 'Do I still sit downstairs? I suppose I'll have to be with the admin team.'

'Absolutely not!' Simon exclaimed. 'All the directors sit up here. You won't be treated any differently.'

Beth looked out across the floor beyond Simon's office. There was just one desk free, and it was Damien's old one. She didn't like the thought of sitting there.

'Although, I was going to suggest that you join me in here,' Simon added. 'It does seem so wrong to make my wife sit outside my office like a secretary or something. I was thinking you could have one end and I'll have the other. What do you say?'

'Really?' Beth beamed. 'I'd love that! I promise I won't mess it up!' She ran over and hugged Simon tightly, her happiness reaching new levels of excitement, a welcome change after the madness of the past few days.

'Great, I'll get a desk moved in here straight away,' Paul announced, standing up and stretching. 'Right then, let's get you down to business,' he said turning to Beth. 'Are you ready for you first task as Administration Director?'

'Absolutely!' Beth grinned, rearing to go.

'It seems on Friday the Administration Manager quit.'

'Trisha?' Beth queried, stunned.

'Yes, apparently something to do with the new electronic filing system not being quite as she'd expected. It was very strange. She just left, asked to go straight away.'

Simon and Beth glanced at each other happily. 'Why do I get the feeling you know something about this already?' Paul asked, curiously.

'I'll tell you all about it another time,' Simon replied.

'So your first task, Mrs Bird, is to find a new Admin Manager. Is that okay?'

'Okay? That's brilliant! I know just the right person for the job.' Beth kissed Simon firmly on the lips. 'I'll see you later. I have quite a lot of news to deliver downstairs.'

She walked proudly out of the office and through the floor, passing her, now fellow directors. As she waited for the lifts she realised that she was about to tell her colleagues everything. But it didn't worry her anymore. What could they say that would disrupt her happiness now? She was a Bird, and she was so happy to be part of the family. This family made her dreams come true and it felt wonderful.

She proudly headed to her old desk, but was suddenly aware of the platinum ring on her finger. She hid her hand behind her back, not wanting them to guess too soon. This would take some explaining.

'You're back!' Gayle cheered as Beth approached them. 'Where have you been?'

'It's a very long story,' Beth replied, standing behind her old chair. 'Can I talk to you all for a second?'

Beth led Gayle, Diane and Michelle into Trisha's old office. She shut the door behind them and then rested against Trisha's old desk before meeting their expectant gazes, keeping her hand still awkwardly behind her back. The three of them stood together utterly confused.

'Things have changed a little for me over the past few days,' Beth started.

'Since your mugging?' Diane asked, trying to be sympathetic. 'It changed my husband, I remember that. It's a terrible thing to have to go through. But your face has healed quite quickly so at least that's something.'

'No, this is nothing to do with that. Not exactly. Not that you need to worry about. I mean...' Beth paused for breath. She not only needed to tell them that after being in the company for just a few weeks, and as a junior in the department, she'd now suddenly been promoted to their overall boss, but also, in the same short time period, she'd married the CEO of the company, the man that everyone was scared of, the person they all happened to believe drank blood. It sounded ludicrous to her and she'd lived through it. She couldn't predict for a second how they were going to react.

'Last week I got married,' she began, flicking her left hand out as if the ring fully proved what she was saying.

'Oh my God, that's fantastic news!' Michelle congratulated, patting Beth gently on the arm.

'I didn't even know you had a boyfriend,' Diane stated.

'We haven't been together very long, it's sort of been a whirlwind romance.' Beth smiled to herself as she thought back to how it had actually been more like a tornado.

'Who is he then?' Gayle probed, a giant grin on her face.

'You know him,' Beth hesitated.

'That's so exciting!' Michelle squealed. 'Who is he?'

'I don't want you to freak out when I tell you.'

'Why would we freak out?' Diane asked.

'Oh God, it's Mr Bird isn't it?' Gayle guessed with clear joy.

'What?' Beth replied, shocked by Gayle's keen judgement. And even more shocked by her seeming approval.

'Mr Bird? Why on earth would she marry that creep?' Diane chirped back to Gayle.

'Not Mr Bird,' Gayle corrected, pointing to the ceiling suggesting an office upstairs. 'Mr Bird! As in Paul Bird! That's why he took you away isn't it? You've had a mad affair with him and then he swept you off your feet. How romantic! He's a lovely man!'

'That can't be true, can it?' Michelle queried. 'He's so old!' All three woman were now staring hard at Beth, impatiently.

Beth felt suddenly sick. She had indeed married 'the creep'. Now she had to tell them.

'Not Paul Bird. No.'

'Oh. Well that would have been exciting,' Gayle giggled.

'Why did you say it like that?' Diane asked sharply.

'Like what?' Gayle quickly added.

'Not Paul Bird,' Diane mimicked, really stressing the Paul part.

'Because I haven't married Paul,' Beth said slowly. Then she finished it off even more slowly. 'But I am now a Mrs Bird.'

All three women gasped.

'For the love of God, please tell me there's another Mr Bird around here!' Diane exclaimed.

'I'm Mrs Simon Bird. I've married our very own CEO.'

'Bloody hell!' Michelle chimed.

'How could you, Beth?' Diane almost hissed.

'Are you okay?' Gayle muttered, reaching out for Beth's hand.

'I'm the happiest I've ever been in my whole life. You don't know him like I do. He's the most amazing man and we're wonderful together,' Beth beamed. She knew she had to make them see. 'I know he feels a little weird to be around, but it's not really him. If you could just see past that then you'd see the best man ever. If you got to know him I'm sure you'd love him just as much as I do. Well maybe not quite that much!' Beth giggled, now starting to sweat at their gapes.

'We'll have to take your word for that,' Diane stated.

'You've been so wrong about him. He's never killed anyone. And he's never sacked anyone either, well without very good reason, believe me. And as for drinking blood, that's crazy! He's just a normal bloke.' The three ladies looked at her bemused. 'Okay, so he's not your average, every day bloke, no. He's far more than that. He's very special and kind and loving, and he cares so much about this company and all of us here.'

'If you say so,' Diane muttered.

'If you're happy, Beth, then we're happy for you,' Gayle stated, squeezing Beth's hand reassuringly. 'I'm sure he's just as great as you say he is.'

'So you're now mingling with the big boys?' Diane then

added in.

Beth opened her mouth to answer and then she realised it was time to bring up her second lot of enormous news. 'That brings me very nicely on to something else,' she said.

Again, the three ladies waited eagerly for her to continue.

'Now I'm part of the family - the Bird family, that is – I've been offered shares in the business.'

'Of course you have, that's only right,' Gayle agreed.

'The shares, though, come with a little extra,' Beth said, trying to impart the news softly. She felt so guilty for her rapid succession after they'd all done the same job as her for so much longer. Still, Beth conceded to herself, much to her own surprise, if there was one thing that her move to the city had taught her, it was that life was seldom fair. She looked to her colleagues with strength. 'I've been offered a seat on the board of directors.'

'What!' all three of them exclaimed.

'You're looking at the new Administration Director,' she stated, humbly.

Her announcement was met with a short, awkward silence, before Gayle chirped up with seeming happiness for her. 'That's great news, Beth. I'm happy for you. You've done so well.'

'You really have landed on your feet haven't you,' Diane dryly stated.

'I know it's a shock, but it's not been easy for me. And I promise I'll do my best in the role, I'm not going to take this opportunity for granted.'

'Shush, Beth, you don't have to justify anything to us,' Gayle assured her.

'I feel I do,' Beth replied honestly. 'Anyway, I've already been given my first task, and that's to find you a new Administration Manager. Do you know about Trisha?'

'I know, it's great isn't it!' Gayle sneered. 'About time she left. I can't see the department missing her.'

'So are you in charge now?' Diane asked Beth.

'No. I mean I'll be overseeing things, for sure, but we need a new day to day manager to take care of things down here.' The three ladies nodded, expecting no more from Beth. Then Beth looked to Gayle. 'Gayle, I'd like to offer you the job.'

'What?' Gayle replied, shocked.

'No offence ladies, but Gayle you've been here for so long and you've been virtually doing the job anyway. How about we make it official?'

'Beth, are you sure?'

'There's no other option for me.'

Gayle hugged Beth tightly. 'Thank you,' she whispered. 'This means the world to me.'

'You deserve it,' Beth said, hugging Gayle back. 'I know there's lots of official stuff to sort out, I just have to find out what I need to do. But I promise, I'll get it all sorted as soon as possible. And in the meantime, don't hesitate to start moving in to your new office. I won't mess you around.'

'I don't think for a second you will, lovey.'

'We better get back to it,' Diane announced.

'Thank you,' Gayle whispered again. 'And congratulations.'

They left Trisha's old office and Beth waited for them to go so she could catch her breath. She hadn't enjoyed that at all. But in some ways, it could have gone a lot worse.

She headed back up towards Simon's office - or her new office as she'd have to get to know it - feeling a mixture of relief and discomfort. She opened the door to find Simon, now alone, typing away on his laptop. Then, just as promised, she saw a brand new desk for her. She felt so welcome, and the difficulty of her exchange downstairs seemed to dissolve away to the back of her mind.

'Your computer's on its way, don't worry,' Simon

explained, popping his head up momentarily from his huge backlog of emails.

Beth sat down and scanned her nearly empty desk. All that existed on it was a Bird Consultants notepad and a small pot of Bird Consultants pens. They seemed so lonely against the vastness of the wood.

'How did it go?' Simon asked, mid-typing.

'Very well. Gayle's our new manager.'

'I'm sure she'll do a great job,' Simon nodded, although Beth did question to herself whether Simon even knew who Gayle was.

Beth looked around the room, not sure really what to do with herself now. She twisted back and forth in her chair feeling a bit lost.

'I think I should head back to my flat at lunch, check up on it,' she announced, remembering her residence just a short walk away.

'Of course. Do you want me to join you?' Simon asked, not even taking his eyes off the screen.

'That would be lovely. I've got some bread in the freezer,' she started muttering. 'I could probably whisk us up a sandwich. But no, do you know what I really fancy? Have you been to that lovely tea shop down the road, they do the nicest...' Beth stopped herself as a thought dawned on her. 'Simon,' she said, slowly.

'Yes, my darling wife,' he answered, giving her just seconds of attention.

'You know how I just crazily and magically won that one thousand pounds a few weeks ago?'

'Vaguely,' Simon replied with exaggerated nonchalance, now looking fully at her.

'Was that you?'

'I don't know what you mean,' he declared, trying to hide his smirk.

'You fixed that all up didn't you? I knew it was too good to be true. What did you do, bribe the lady or something?

'Beth, really?' Simon laughed, sitting back. 'I'm a Malant, we don't have to bribe people. I just made it happen.'

'You little...' Beth stood up to have a playful rant but she was stopped in her tracks. A pen flew straight out of her pot, up in the air, across the room and smack into the closed door ahead of her. Then it fell straight down to the floor quickly with a crack.

'What did you do that for?' she asked, a little taken aback by the impossible acrobats of the biro.

'I didn't,' Simon said, standing up, now quite pale.

'Don't be silly. Pens don't just fly out of pots randomly. Were you trying to make a point?'

'You don't understand, Beth, I didn't do anything. It wasn't me,' Simon uttered, now eerily pale.

'Well, who did it then?' she asked accusatorially.

'You did,' he replied.

They both stared at the pen lying idly on the floor, then they looked to each other with astonishment. Things were about to get weird again.

Coming Soon

Simon and Beth's adventures continue in
"The Birds"
by Lindsay Woodward

16140070R00194

Printed in Poland
by Amazon Fulfillment
Poland Sp. z o.o., Wrocław